SIX DAYS

Brendan DuBois

SPHERE

First published in Great Britain in 2001 by
Little, Brown and Company

This edition published by Time Warner Paperbacks in 2002
Reprinted 2002
Reprinted by Time Warner Books in 2005
Reprinted by Sphere in 2007, 2008

Copyright © 2001 by Brendan DuBois

The moral right of the author has been asserted.

All rights reserved.
No part of this publication may be reproduced, stored in a
retrieval system, or transmitted, in any form or by any means,
without the prior permission in writing of the publisher, nor
be otherwise circulated in any form of binding or cover other
than that in which it is published and without a similar
condition including this condition being imposed on the
subsequent purchaser.

*All characters in this publication are fictitious and any resemblance
to real persons, living or dead, is purely coincidental.*

A CIP catalogue record for this book
is available from the British Library.

ISBN 978-0-7515-3076-6

Typeset in Goudy by M Rules
Printed and bound in Great Britain by Clays Ltd, St Ives plc

Sphere
An imprint of
Little, Brown Book Group
100 Victoria Embankment
London EC4Y 0DY

An Hachette Livre UK Company
www.hachettelivre.co.uk

www.littlebrown.co.uk

This book is for Don Murray:
veteran, teacher and writer.

The author wishes to express his appreciation and thanks to Ron Thurlow, for his expert review of the manuscript, and to Craig MacPherson, for his technical assistance. The staff at Exeter Public Library, Exeter, N.H., were their usual helpful selves. Thanks, also, go to Hilary Hale and everyone else at Little, Brown; to my American agents, Jed Mattes and Fred Morris; my British agent, Antony Topping; and to members of my family, especially my wife, Mona.

There is a religious war going on in our country for the soul of America. It is a cultural war, as critical to the kind of nation we will one day be as was the Cold War itself.

Presidential candidate Pat Buchanan,
Republican National Convention, August 17, 1992

PROLOGUE

SIX MONTHS EARLIER

Twelve hours, he thought. In twelve hours he'd be home and away from these madmen.

Walt Phinney of the US Department of Energy tightened his seatbelt as the Air Force C-141 Starlifter transport rumbled down the bumpy runway and took off, climbing into the frigid Russian air. Below were the drafty and cold buildings of a Russian Air Force installation, and when this was done, if he never went further east in his life than Cape May, New Jersey, he'd be a happy man indeed. He was sitting uncomfortably on a row of seating made from red webbing that ran for most of the fuselage's length. He sat alone, with a clump of Air Force personnel up forward, holding their own private court. No matter if they wanted to sit apart. Damn it, he'd gladly ride on top of the cockpit if it meant going home today.

Home. He unzipped his Air-Force-issue parka and reached into the inside pocket, pulled out a creased photo of his wife Kelli and their two-year-old daughter, Sherri. He smiled and rubbed his thumb across the portrait. Little Sherri looked so much like her mother, from the blonde hair to that dimpled smile. Soon, loved ones, I'll be home soon, he thought. Three weeks on this miserable mission that shouldn't have taken more than three days, except for the damnable bureaucrats from the DoE, the Air Force, and the Russian government.

He looked to the rear of the jet, where a pallet was secured in the middle with tie-down straps and ropes. The pallet was a framework of wood and foam rubber, and centered in the middle of the pallet were twenty little bullet-shaped gifts, twenty green and yellow presents less than a yard tall that were coming home to America. Of course, these little gifts had been designed to visit American troops and American equipment much, much earlier, on the invasion battlefield of West Germany, in the Fulda Gap, where the Soviets and their Warsaw Pact allies planned to pour into the West. He put the photo in an outside pocket and folded his arms. Now, of course, the Fulda Gap still existed but there was one Germany, no more Warsaw Pact and one poor Russia that was gladly giving up these twenty ten-kiloton tactical nuclear warheads in exchange for grain and technology credits. Other C-141s in other parts of the old Soviet empire were doing their part as well this early spring, gladly disarming the pieces of that old terror in exchange for feeding civilians. Not a bad deal.

The jet bumped a bit and he stretched out his legs, the better to hold himself in the web seating. Seeing these babies home was Walt's job. He had come along with this Air Force unit to ensure all twenty warheads were ready for travel, that they were in fact what the Russians claimed they were – further back was the pallet of his own detecting equipment, which had proven just that – and he was to be with these twenty warheads all the way to Ramstein Air Base in Germany, to a refueling stop in Gander, Newfoundland, and then all the way home to the Pantex facility near Amarillo, Texas, where he had been stationed these past four years.

There, the warheads would be disassembled. And then, after a while home, it'd be time to put in his resignation and get the hell out of government service. He was tired of working so closely with such deadly materials, materials that sometimes gave him dreams so dark that he would wake up in the middle of a night with a shout. It was time to move back east, where the land wasn't so dry and where green things grew even in the absence of sprinkler systems. Time, maybe, to move into one of those gated communities, drop out and just work on raising a family and to hell with everybody else.

He folded his arms, tried to warm himself. Damn past three weeks, he hadn't been warm once. The heating system in the old Soviet Air Force barracks creaked and groaned but didn't produce much warmth. There were no showers, just baths, and every bath was missing a stopper. He had to steal a raw potato from the base commissary and use that as a plug, though the food was so awful he probably should have just eaten it instead. And there had been other things he had noticed as well. The crumbling concrete, the exposed and rusting rebar in the buildings. The grass growing in cracks along the runway. The old MiG fighters, motionless in their concrete revetments, their tires flat. The shabby uniforms of the Russian technicians. This, this had been the enemy that his father and grandfather had been so concerned about? This had been the enemy that had been the focus of so much energy, so much hate, so many dollars in defense systems over the decades? It had seemed ridiculous.

Walt looked up forward, where the knot of Air Force personnel was still clustered. They sure didn't think it had been ridiculous. They had seemed to take a perverse joy in disarming such a stubborn and old enemy. The group had been led by a Captain Raynor and they mostly had been tolerant of his presence. That had been it. No late-night drinks. No small talk. No glad handing. Just the logistics of their mission and nothing else. And not to be paranoid, but Walt always had the feeling that whenever he entered a meeting room or jet hangar the small group of Air Force people stopped talking for a second and then quickly changed the subject. Nothing he could prove, but there had been something there. A presence, a scent, like something had been changed, and just for his benefit.

Madmen. He wasn't sure who was more mad. The old Russian military personnel down there, cheerfully giving up weapons of mass destruction for bread, or these American military personnel up here, still thinking they mattered. Walt wasn't sure what mattered nowadays. The current Washington scandal involved the President's bladder habits, for God's sake, and defense budgets were being cut left and right, as the powerful aging baby-boomer generation demanded more and more Social Security and Medicare benefits. Once upon a time the economy had been so hot that the Air Force couldn't hold on to trained personnel, but such a hot economy was a fading memory in the third year of the current recession. He could see the difference, in the tired eyes of the pilots, the carefully mended jump suits, and the old equipment that still bore stenciling from the First Gulf War. They were still number one, but were fading and, worse of all, they knew it. Walt wondered if the Russian military had been so damn friendly because they knew their old rival would soon join them in disarray and disrepair.

There was another jolt, sharper than before, and a loud snap that made him clench the webbing tight with his hands. Walt looked to the rear of the jet. Damn it all to hell, talk about disrepair and old equipment. The last jolt of turbulence had snapped a couple of the tie-down straps, and one of the warheads was leaning away from its protective berth. Not that it was much of a problem: the C-141 could suddenly plow into the steppes – not a very pleasant thought of course – and not a single warhead would detonate. The triggering devices would simply be crushed. But it wasn't good to have the damn thing hanging like that for the rest of the trip. Suppose there was more turbulence? Goddamn thing could fall out and roll around the metal flooring, crush a few toes in the process.

He looked forward. No one up there had noticed. Walt unbuckled his seatbelt and got up, a bit unsteady as the jet still climbed to its cruising altitude. Let's take a look and then get back up to Captain Raynor. Get a couple of the more muscular sergeants back here and put things right. He walked the dozen feet aft, holding on to wall straps and webbing to keep his balance. There. The little bastard was leaning out. Maybe we could push it back in place. He reached out and touched it and—

Something was wrong.

He stepped back. Why? Why was something wrong?

Walt wasn't sure, but there was a sour taste in his mouth. His gut was telling him something was wrong, and after five years at Pantex, assembling and disassembling nuclear warheads, he always listened to his gut. Always.

What was it?

It was a warhead, like any other, with serial numbers and Cyrillic lettering, and openings for probes and connections to mate it with an artillery shell or a rocket body.

So what was wrong?

Touch. He knew there was a problem when he touched it.

Walt touched it again. The casing was smooth. He rubbed at it.

Too smooth, idiot.

True. He touched the other warheads, noticed the bumps and rough patches where the old Soviet technicians had done a good job, but not a great job, in putting it together. The joys of a command economy. You got the job done and that was that.

He touched the leaning warhead again. It didn't match. It didn't belong. It was too well polished.

The sour taste grew stronger in his mouth. Somebody had just pulled a fast one.

And he had caught it just in time.

Walt made his way quickly up forward, passing his seat and the mid-aft doorways on each side, and then to the seats that the Air Force guys were occupying. Again, that damn feeling he was being watched in a critical fashion. One of the tech sergeants, however, did smile up at him. Ramez, who was originally from Miami, just like Walt, and the only guy who treated him as more than just a government weasel. They had spent at least a few minutes during the past few weeks discussing yet again another disappointing Florida Marlins season. Walt passed through and Captain Raynor glanced up from a military-issue lapbot that he had been typing on. He had a large nose and his skin was slightly pockmarked, and with his large brown eyes he looked like a hawk, always on the hunt.

He leaned down, yelled above the engine noise in Captain Raynor's ear. 'Captain, we've got a problem!'

'What is it?' the captain asked, closing the gray lapbot cover.

'A couple of tie-down straps on the pallet just let loose, and that's not all,' Walt said, trying to choose his words carefully. 'One of the warheads doesn't match. It looks like a fake.'

The captain's eyes seemed to bulge out. 'What? A fake?'

Walt nodded. 'Yeah, a dummy warhead. All of the warheads checked out yesterday. I think someone scammed us, just before takeoff. Captain, we've got to turn around and go back. Once we're on the ground, I can prove it's a fake. Then we can take it from there.'

The captain shook his head, almost in disgust, and said something to a lieutenant sitting near him. The lieutenant got up and went toward the cockpit. The captain stood up and said, 'You better show me, Mr Phinney.'

Walt turned and started back to the rear of the jet, and he stumbled again as the jet made another turn and he could feel it suddenly start to descend. Good. The pilot was heading back to the Russian Air Force base. Once on the ground and once he got his detecting equipment unpacked, he could prove that the warhead was a dummy. Nicely made, but a dummy nonetheless, and it'd be for the guys upstairs to figure what to do next, how to untangle this crisis, and—

He gasped as something struck him from behind. Walt fell to the floor, jamming his fingers. He yelped in pain and gurgled as something hit him again, stunning him. He fell flat on his face, crushing his nose. The plane rolled and bucked. Light suddenly flared at him and there was the rush of wind. He moved his head, blinked at the fierce breeze blowing past him.

One of the side doors was open. He was looking down at the brown surface of the earth, thousands of feet below.

He started to slide.

Sweet Mother of God, no!

He moved over on his back, tried to grab something, anything.

His stomach rolled in terror as he felt his feet go through the door.

Something, something, we've got to grab something!

He flailed out with his hands, felt a sharpness and then—

A flapping tie-down strap, firm in his right hand, the uninjured one.

The jet tilted again and now his knees and lower thighs were hanging outside over the void. The wind tore at his feet, flattening them against the side of the fuselage. The strapping cut into his hand. He dimly realized his crotch was soaking wet, for he had just soiled himself.

He looked up, not able to say anything, only screaming in loud, repeating grunts.

There! Coming forward was that Tech Sergeant, Ramez. He had a safety harness on, and a long belt, fastened to the nearest bulkhead. Ramez inched forward, closer and closer, his face knotted in concern and concentration.

The wind seemed more fierce. Now his upper thighs were at the door's edge.

Closer, damn it, get closer! He tried to form the words but he couldn't. All he could do was yell in terror.

Kelli, Sherri, I swear I'll get off this jet once it lands and I'll never fly again.

Ramez came closer, grabbed a free hand. He clenched it tight in joyous terror. Close, we're gonna make it, we're gonna make it. Ramez motioned with his head, to the other hand that was tangled up in the strapping.

Of course. He couldn't be dragged in if that mess was still tangled around his hand. He moved quickly, as quickly as he could, and the strap came free and Ramez nodded, grabbed the other hand.

There! Oh, sweet Jesus, we're gonna make it, we're gonna get back in—

And the last thing Walt Phinney saw was Ramez letting go.

Captain Raynor was in the cockpit, talking to the pilot, as the C-141 resumed its heading towards Germany. His hands were slightly sore from holding the fire extinguisher that he had slammed into that DoE clown just a few minutes ago. A hard thing to do, hitting him like that and opening the door, but it had to be done.

He put a hand on the shoulder of the pilot, leaned forward. 'Will we lose much time to Germany?'

The captain felt the shrug of the pilot. 'Ten, fifteen minutes, not much. We'll probably make it up as we get along.'

'Good.'

'It's going to be hard to explain what happened back there to that Energy guy.'

'How long to Germany?'

'Four hours.'

The captain said, 'I'll think of something by then.'

The pilot turned his head, looked up with a smile on his face. 'God bless.'

He smiled back. 'God bless.'

Captain Raynor went aft, looked at his carefully chosen crew in their seats. He felt a flush of pride in what they had just done, in flying thousands of miles in and out of enemy territory, doing what had to be done to make things right. He grinned at them and gave them a thumbs up, and they all smiled back, especially Ramez, who had done a very tricky job indeed. Would have to write up a commendation – carefully crafted, of course – for the sergeant when he got home.

He sat down in his seat, pulled the seatbelt taut and picked up his lapbot. Before opening the cover, though, he saw something on the metal flooring. A little square of paper. He reached down and picked it up.

It was a photo, of a woman and a child. Both with blonde hair. He turned it over and saw a woman's handwriting, and it was hard to make out the words. But the first two did say, 'Dear Walt.'

Well, the captain thought. There you go.

He crumpled up the photo and shoved the waste piece of paper in his parka, and then went back to work.

ONE

Buried deep inside a Virginia mountain, a vast, top-secret installation – one of the great artifacts of the cold war – remains at the ready. Known as Mount Weather, it is a Strangelovian relic of yesteryear intended to shelter the President and other top US officials in case of nuclear war . . . Mount Weather is operated by the Federal Emergency Management Agency, which for years has fended off inquiries about the installation with a firm 'No comment'. Jokes Bob Blair, a FEMA spokesman: 'I'll be glad to tell you all about it, but I'd have to kill you afterward.'

Time, December 9, 1991

It was a cool September morning, and Drew Connor surveyed their campsite with a pleased and practiced eye. It looked pristine, like no one had ever stayed here before, and he was glad of that. They were high up in the White Mountains, in the western part of New Hampshire, less than twenty miles from the Vermont border, probably another sixty miles from Quebec. Their campsite was a half-hour bushwhack from one of the maintained trails in these parts of the mountains, and had offered both privacy and a central spot to do some other hiking during their stay. He had broke camp about an hour ago and Sheila was down by a small stream, washing her hands. Sheila was . . . well, what could he call her? 'Girlfriend' sounded like they were back in high school. 'Companion' sounded like they were in a retirement home, sharing their last meals together. And 'significant other' sounded like someone from the US Census Bureau, trying to fit them onto a computer form.

Well, there was one way to fix that quandary, and he had planned to do it, earlier in the week, when he and his Miss Sheila Cass had started their four-day hiking and camping trip into the Monroe Range of the White Mountains. He reached into a side pocket of his backpack, where the small ring case was hidden. Drew sighed. He hadn't taken it out, not once, during their four days together. He had thought about it, lots of times, wondering what she would say and do once she saw the case. But every time he had touched its hard surface, he had hesitated. Let's see, he thought with disgust. For a number of years, I've been in service to my nation. I've parachuted out of planes and helicopters. Several times in my life, I've been fired upon and have returned fire. I've been alone in hostile territory, everywhere from Serbia to Bolivia. And yet this one thing, this one question he was prepared to ask of her, frightened him like nothing else.

He took his hand out of the pack pocket. Later, he thought. Later I'll pop that question, and looking at the form of Sheila down by the streambed, he knew why he was fretful. Sheila had been married before, an eleven-month disaster a number of years ago that she claimed had forever soured her on the idea of marriage. Living together, well, that was all right, and the two of them had shared a home these past two years. But marriage? 'No way,' she had said. 'No offense, Drew, but I like what we have. It's comfortable, it's relaxed, and that little wedding ring and wedding license would weigh everything down.'

Drew zipped the pocket shut, looked around the campsite. It was on a small bluff of land that had good views of the surrounding peaks, but was also protected enough that the night winds didn't disturb them. He had set up their tent beyond a clump of boulders, offering them privacy from not only other hikers but also peering eyes from overhead. The Forest Service now had surveillance drones checking out the surroundings for timber thieves and wildfires, and Drew liked to keep out of their view. The drones recorded everything that they saw, and while he and Sheila were doing nothing illegal, nothing out of the ordinary, he didn't like the idea of being permanently recorded in some government computer somewhere, forever accessible to some nosy bureaucrat. He'd had run-ins with bureaucrats before, and had always vowed to stay away from them for the rest of his life.

'Hey, you!' came a voice, and he turned. Sheila was standing up, wiping her hands on her T-shirt bottom. 'Ready to head home?'

'You got it,' he yelled back, and he stood up, pulling up his dark green backpack. He put it on and felt his back wince, and it was like his poor spine had its own memories, for little thoughts flashed through him of all the times he had put on a backpack: as a Boy Scout back home in Nebraska; the first weeks of Basic Training; the first weeks at Special Forces school in Fort Benning, and the many other times saddling up for a mission, feeling that strange buzz of nervousness and excitement all at once. But this time, cinching the straps tight, this time it was for fun and relaxation. Nothing else. We be heading home, and it's time.

As he waited for Sheila to amble her way back up, he looked again at their campsite. He had wetted down their campfire ashes enough so that they were as cold as the surrounding ground. He then placed pine needles and old leaves over the small firepit, and had also done the same for where their tent had been. A random hiker going through here in a half-hour would never know that he and Sheila had been here, and in a week, even the best investigators – from the FBI to the DoD – would be hard-pressed to find a trace of their presence.

Paranoid? Who, me? Just heightened awareness, that's all, he thought. In his new life, retired from everything that he had done before, he was proud of maintaining a low profile. Once he had done many things at the command of others, but that time was in the past. He now worried about himself and Sheila and no one else.

He turned as Sheila came up, and he helped her on with her own light red backpack, and got a kiss as a reward. Her face was a bit shiny from being freshly washed and her brown eyes looked like they were laughing at him. She grabbed a free hand and said, 'Okay, sport, listen up.'

He squeezed her hand. 'All right, what's that?'

She leaned up and gave him another kiss. 'That's my way of thanking you for a wonderful trip up here in the woods.'

And before he could say anything, she grabbed the back of his head and gave him a deeper kiss, running her tongue around his lips, slightly moaning for effect. 'And that's my way of thanking you for not taking me on another trip like this for a few months.'

He laughed. 'We live on a lake, we go canoeing almost every day and stargazing every night. Are you telling me you don't like the great outdoors?'

She stepped back, smiling, a wisp of blonde hair falling free from her ponytail. 'I love the great outdoors, but only in small pieces. I also love electricity and indoor plumbing, and right now I'm looking forward to our hike out and the drive home. I want to make sure we hear the loons one more time before they leave.'

'Sure,' he said, heading out to the trail, and she laughed again and smacked his butt with her hand as she strolled by. 'Don't be so quick to be in front, Drew. You move so slow that we won't get to the car until dark. Let me set the pace.'

For a moment he thought about grabbing her shoulder and saying wait a minute, and then having her reach in and pull out the small black box with the engagement ring. But he couldn't do it. He thought about what she might say, how words and expressions might be exchanged, how this perfect trip up in the mountains would be ruined. Later, he thought, after a shower and good meal and out on the dock, listening to the loons, as they called to each other before their winter migration out to the Atlantic. I'll pop the question tonight, at home, at that safe sanctuary that with her help had healed him these past months.

'All right,' he said. 'You lead on.'

Another laugh. 'Don't I always?'

A couple of hours later, Drew shifted the pack against his back, tightened the straps some, peered down the steep trail at the tiny red dot that marked Sheila's pack, perched on an outcropping of rock. He didn't like it when she went ahead, he never did, but she never listened. She teasingly said that when she got moving she hated to wait for anyone, even him, her sweetheart. How true. He looked up at the darkening sky. They were on the Monroe Trail and about ninety minutes from their parked car at trailhead, and – if he guessed right – about five minutes away from being seriously rained on.

As much as he wanted to get closer to her, he had to rest for a moment. His forty-year-old knees were screaming at him from the hike down. Hard to believe, but hiking down a mountain – for him, at least! – was worse than going up. That constant *thump-thump* jarring his knees, stretching the cartilage and tendons, making everything ache, was the price he paid for mountain climbing. Yet he had no regrets. He looked about him, enjoying the view despite the thick and black line of clouds that were rumbling in towards this tiny valley. The trail was steep and rocky, and the trees and shrubbery were thin at this point. Fall had come early this September, and some of the hardwood leaves had already drifted down. The nearest range – Mounts Ida and Lovell – were to his right. Even though he had grown up on the plains of Nebraska, he had always loved mountains. Mountains were beautiful, they were majestic, and they offered so many wonderful places to hide out. Not like the flat plains where he had grown up, where you can be spotted, miles away, and definitely not like the hot, flat plains in Asia where everything had gotten bloodily screwed up, eventually sending him to exile in this northern state.

Now, it was going home time, though of course, he thought, by the time we do get home, we're going to be soaking wet. He gave the straps another tug and started down the trail. His pack was lighter since the day they had begun, most of the food and water having long since been consumed, but as well as his smelly and unwashed clothes he still carried his sleeping bag, mattress pad, a small gas stove and two-person tent. He had on his leather hiking boots, thick cotton pants, and a pullover shirt, and, if he was smart, he'd stop and take out his rain gear. But he didn't want to stop, not until he reached Sheila's pack. He always told her that it was bad business hiking alone, even if the backwoods were reasonably safe, because you never knew if you'd run into a militia group or body smugglers or dropouts. Even here. But did she ever listen?

There. He stopped again, breathing hard. Damn, old man, you are getting old, despite what you think. Around the straps of Sheila's backpack was a small notepad. This had been a running joke in their hikes. Sometimes the note she left would be something like, 'Gone to the streambed to the right for more water.' Or teasingly, 'Hey, hiker-stud. If you can find me, you can have me.' He smiled at the memory. That had been nice, two days ago.

This afternoon it said in her clear writing, 'Hon, have to pee, and it looks like there's a shelter or a building off to the left. Come up and join me! S.'

A rumble of thunder, coming closer. He looked up to the left, saw a faint, overgrown trail, heading up. The trails all through these mountains were maintained by volunteers from the Appalachian Mountain Club, and some were decades old. Sometimes, though, because of misuse or overuse, old trails were abandoned, and nature soon reclaimed them in a growing season or two. He peered through the overhanging trees, saw a faint shape, up there in the distance. Looked like the tip of a roof. Damn, that woman had good eyes.

The wind stirred the trees, causing some of the orange and red leaves to tumble free. A storm was coming, and it might not be a bad idea to go up there. He picked up her pack, swayed for a moment from the extra weight. Jesus, it was still damn heavy, and he knew why. Sheila had insisted on carrying her lapbot throughout the hike, and after he had said it made no sense to haul it on the trip she had said, 'What do you care? It's my pack and I can carry it. I don't complain about the weird things you pack, do I?'

He started up the abandoned trail, her pack awkwardly shouldered on one side. She had a point. She wanted her lapbot with her, and that was fine.

He hiked with a 9 mm Beretta stored in another one of the side pockets, and as far as he was concerned, that was even better. He smiled at the thought. Engagement ring in one pocket, pistol in the other. Love and death, all together.

Sheila Cass paused in front of the tiny building, slightly out of breath and with her bladder, screaming at her for release, feeling like an overinflated tennis ball in her gut. Behind her was the rumble of thunder. 'Oh, this is just great,' she said aloud. 'First we're gonna wet ourselves, and then Mother Nature is gonna take care of the rest.'

She ran a hand across her face, feeling the sweat and grease. A shower would be wonderful. In fact, a shower right now would even be better than sex, and sorry Drew, right now if I had a choice between you and a hot shower, soap and water would come first. She touched her shoulder-length brown hair, pulled back in a ponytail, and grimaced at the feel. Sorry, hon, right now, even a warm shower with no soap would come before you.

But right now, first things first. Like a toilet. She knew Drew loved these excursions into the woods, knew they calmed him down and made him a joy to live with, but after the first day, she started missing things. Like a refrigerator. Like plumbing. Guys have it easy, standing up and watering trees and shrubbery whenever they had the urge. Even Drew, as smart as he was, could never get the point of how uncomfortable it got, squatting and hoping you didn't hit your boots or your socks. And even when you were finished, you didn't feel particularly clean, having done the deed outside.

Which is why she was here, in front of this tiny building. She had caught a glimpse of it a while ago and thought it was an overnight hiking shelter. And even if the shelter just had a two-hole outhouse, that would be fine. Beats squatting and hoping you're not over a clump of poison ivy. The building was in a flat area of land, surrounded by low shrubbery and trees. She was sure that if it hadn't been for the dropped foliage, she would have missed it.

She got closer, saw what was there, and said, 'Shit,' in a loud voice. It wasn't a shelter, not at all.

The building was small, about the size of a large garden shed. It was made of brick and cement, and had a steeply pitched roof. Two small satellite dishes were on the roof, along with a couple of tall antennas, and there was one metal door. On the door was a sign:

> PSNH RELAY STATION TWELVE.
> KEEP OUT. NO TRESPASSING.

Sheila had no idea what a relay station was, but knew PSNH stood for the state's largest utility, Public Service of New Hampshire. The door handle had one of those electronic locks with punch-in numerals. She halfheartedly tried the door. Locked solid. Wouldn't budge.

'Shit again,' she said. Time to look for a log or something to sit on, to do our business.

Then everything lit up, like a floodlight had clicked on and off, and she instinctively ducked. There was a sharp *crack-boom!* and she yelped in surprise at the nearby lightning strike. The wind came up, gusting, and she felt drops of water on her bare arms. Damn, that was close, and without thinking, she tried the doorknob again.

This time it clicked open.

She grinned. She was a PSNH ratepayer and if they didn't like her trespassing, too bad. She was just going to get out of the rain, and if she was lucky, maybe there was a bucket or something in here she could use.

Sheila opened the door and could not believe what she saw.

Drew reached a place where the land leveled out and saw the small brick building a couple of minutes after a nearby thunder strike had made him wince. The noise was too close for comfort, eh? The door was ajar and he was sure Sheila was inside, hunting for a toilet or something. Odd place for a building like that. Took a lot of work and effort, hauling up all those bricks. Most structures in these woods were made from the local timber, not bricks. He walked closer and stopped, feeling out of place. Something wasn't right, and he sniffed the air. That was the problem. He smelled something that didn't belong here, something . . .

The Crescent. Now, why in hell had he remembered the Crescent? Jesus, that was a place he never wanted to think about, ever again.

He sniffed the air again. That's why. Aviation fuel. Somewhere around here, aviation fuel had been used. Or spilled. He got closer to the building, dumped the packs. A quick look-see and then I'll find Sheila, he thought.

Drew walked to the center of the small clearing, which was flat scrub and rocks. He knelt down and touched the gravelly soil. There . . . and there. Stains. Aviation fuel had been leaked here, and not too long ago. He stood up, looked again at the flat area, and then squeezed his eyes some, trying to put everything out of focus, just for a moment. Sometimes a trick that worked. Sometimes it didn't.

This time it did.

He noticed six rocks, placed in a wide circle, each with a small piece of low shrubbery growing nearby. He went to the nearest one, ran his hands across it. Nice piece of work. It looked like it belonged. He knelt down and examined it further, saw the little overhang and then reached in. His hand encountered smooth glass. He rubbed at the glass and then stood up. Sure. Made sense. Hidden landing lights, set in a circular pattern, for a helicopter landing pad next to a building that looked like it could hold a John Deere tractor and not much else.

A lot of work and effort had gone into this place, this very strange place.

Where Sheila had now gone inside.

He walked quickly back to the dumped backpacks, unzippered a side pocket and took out his 9 mm. Fine, everything's just fine, he thought. We're just taking precautions. That's all.

He put the pistol in the rear of his waistband, knowing how Sheila felt about weapons. She put up with him having them, but she never liked it when he brought one out in the open. He looked at the nameplate on the door, saying it was a relay station for PSNH. Yeah, right.

Then he grabbed both backpacks and went through the open door, just as the rain started falling.

There was so much to see, so much to look at, but first things first. When she descended the steep staircase, past the tiny glass-enclosed booth, she went along the dimly lit corridors, past cubicles, until she found a women's room. After the long days and nights up in the mountains, it felt wonderfully decadent to actually sit upon a real porcelain goddess, and to use toilet paper that wasn't soggy and spotted with pine needles. When she was done she came out and went to the nearby sink. A tiny little sign over the sink said CONSERVE WATER. 'Sure,' she said. 'Maybe tomorrow.' She turned on the faucet and used the soap dispenser, and washed and rewashed her hands, and then did her face and arms. Jesus, that felt good, she thought. The water was hot and though it smelled heavily chlorinated it felt delightful on her skin. She dried off using some paper towels and saw in the far corner two shower stalls. Tempting . . . but if she knew Drew, he was probably wondering where in hell she was, and what she was doing.

Drew. He had tried to be so casual and relaxed these past four days, and she had seen right through him, like he had been trying to hide a tattoo on his butt. An innocent phone call from a jewelry store in Laconia, inquiring as to whether Drew was satisfied with the setting of the diamonds, had told her everything she needed to know. And a quick sneaking look into his backpack while he was showering before they had left had confirmed it. Her Big Lug was going to ask the Big Question during the hike, and she was wondering when he was going to do it, selfishly enjoying the far-off look in his face over the past few days that no doubt meant he was trying to screw up his courage.

Poor man. If he didn't say anything about the ring by the time they got home she would wrestle it out of him, and she smiled at what she had planned. She didn't plan to say yes but she also didn't plan to say no, either. She planned to offer him a strong maybe, with just a request for a little more time. After that disaster with Tom, she never thought she would ever consider marriage, ever again, but Drew was different. Drew was worth waiting for, and she hoped he felt the same way about her.

Sheila opened the ladies' room door and went back to the main area, and there she saw Drew coming towards her, his face ashen, moving quickly, a pistol in his hand.

He stopped as he reached the entranceway of the tiny building. Recessed lights in the cement ceiling were on. A stairway led down and to the right. Before him was a glass-enclosed booth, with a speaker's grill in the center, and two metal slots built in. It looked like a teller's cage for a driveup, but he didn't like the two metal slots. They looked like gunports.

Drew peered in through the glass, seeing a couple of chairs, a closed door, some empty clipboards hanging on the far wall and not much else. He tapped on the glass. Thick. Bulletproof. He stepped back and looked at the setup again. A checkpoint. A nice little checkpoint.

Guarding what?

He went downstairs, his feet echoing in the tiny space. The entranceway opened up to a flat cement floor with a chained-in enclosure off to the right. A sign overhead said DECONTAMINATION AREA. Before him was a twin to the checkpoint booth upstairs, except this one was larger, with four gunports instead of two. Drew went past the checkpoint, into a large open area. It was dimly lit and he found a set of light controls on the near wall and flipped up a palmful of switches. The large room came into focus, and he tried to take it all in at once. The waist-high set of cubicles in all directions. The long tables with chairs and phones. The maps and whiteboards and graphboards hanging on the far walls. The glass-enclosed offices out in the distance. Hanging from the ceiling a post with directional signs and little arrows pointing down the corridors. He stepped closer, looking up at the signs. INFIRMARY. CAFETERIA. CONF. ROOM A. CONF. ROOM B. DORMITORY.

On the nearest table he could make out the rows of telephones, each with a little nameplate attached to the handset. NAWACS. NORAD. FERA REGION 1. FERA HQ. NRC. DOD DUTY OFFICER. The words seemed to sink right into his chest. Jesus, what have we found here . . .

And with the lights on, he could also see the maps clearer. There was a national map, and another depicting northern New England. Beside the maps were a whiteboard with magnetized signs and shapes. One sign said NUDET, another PLUME DIRECTION, yet another TRAFFIC CONTROL. Beside the whiteboard was a lined graph whiteboard. The sign above it said INTERNMENT CENTERS. The rest of the graph was empty. The whiteboard to the right of that was completely blank, except where someone had left a handwritten message. It was large and to the point: *Case Shiloh: On September 19 we take her back!*

'Sheila?' he called out, disgusted at how weak his voice sounded. 'Sheila, where are you?'

Even with the added lights, he felt claustrophobic and slightly nauseous. Everything was wrong here, quite wrong. This place didn't belong here. The whole damn top of this mountain had been hollowed out, and he and Sheila shouldn't have gotten in so easily.

'Sheila?'

He looked around at the cubicles, at the long rows of desks, and then froze as he spotted what was in the far corner, up near the ceiling.

A surveillance camera.

With a tiny red light at its base illuminated, meaning it was on.

From behind him came the sound of a toilet flushing.

He turned and ran towards the noise, pulling his 9 mm free.

Drew was right to the point. 'Sheila, we've got to get out of here! We've got to get out of here right now!'

She started to say something snappy in return, like, don't you want to use a real bathroom before we leave? But everything about his look – the red face, visible behind the four-day-old growth of beard, his constantly shifting eyes, the way he was holding his pistol out like that – made her stop.

'Drew, what's wrong? What's going on?'

He reached over and grabbed her wrist, hard. She winced and started moving with him as he raced back up the corridor. 'Not here, I'll explain it when we get out.'

'Drew, wait, I can't move—'

'Damn it, woman, there's no time to explain! You've got to trust me, right now! Move it!'

She did as he asked, moving along with him as they ran back through the facility – only now, having finished her business in the bathroom, could she appreciate how large this place was – and then went back up the stairs that had led in. Along the way she started feeling frightened, wondering what had gone wrong. Drew's face said it all. It was a look that he sometimes got when he had a particularly bad dream, one that would wake him up at night. He never woke up screaming or shouting from his nightmares. She only knew that the night demons were within him when he started breathing heavily, like he had just finished a long road race, and his arms started twitching. When that happened she had learned to wake him up slowly, whispering into his ear that everything was all right. Then he would come to with a gaunt look, of fear and terror, and he would gently kiss her and then go out onto the front porch that overlooked the lake, not saying anything, just sitting on the couch with a thick blanket about him. And he would never tell her what the dream had been about, and too frightened herself, she had never pressed him.

But there was no front porch here, no blanket, nothing comforting to calm him down. She ran to keep up with him, holding on to his hand, and then they were outside. The air was damp and the sun was out. Rainwater glistened on the rocks and scrub grass, and she didn't even have time to enjoy the view before Drew was beside her, practically throwing the backpack onto her, after he had slammed the door shut. She was still frightened but she didn't like how he had dragged her up here, and she said sarcastically, 'Oh, thank you, Mr Scoutmaster. I guess I just plumb forgot how to put on my little ol' pack.'

If Drew noted her sarcasm, he sure as hell didn't show it. He just put on his pack without a word and started down toward the trail, still holding that damn pistol in his hand.

When they were back on the Monroe Trail, heading down to the trailhead, Drew knew he had some explaining to do. From the pursed look on her face he knew that she was about one minute away from losing her temper and he wanted to head her off. But he wasn't sure how much she'd understand, how much she would realize. Sheila was a Web designer and computer graphics consultant, and she had made a great business and name for herself, working out of their home on Lake Montcalm. He doubted she could see, as quick as he did, what had been back there. So he owed her plenty of explanations.

But he didn't want to waste time. He couldn't, feeling the fear starting to churn around in his gut.

'Sheila,' he said, looking down the trail, glad to see it was empty. 'Can you hear me?'

'Yeah, I can hear you.'

'Good. First things first. My apologies. I should have explained more back there, but I couldn't.' He checked his watch. Five minutes since they left. Still have at least ninety minutes to get to the car. And how long for a response from whoever was on the other end of that surveillance camera? And damn it, am I overreacting?

'And why the hell not?' she demanded. 'Damn it, hon, you were acting like a crazy man. Running around with that pistol, grabbing my wrist. What's going on?'

Of course, the car might be gone, alarm system or no alarm system. Car thefts were up this year in the entire state. Then what?

'Drew?'

'Yes?'

He felt himself jerked to a halt as she grabbed a strap from his pack. 'I asked you a question! Why the big production back there? Why were you in such a hurry?'

Drew turned and looked at Sheila, the woman he had been with these past two years, the damn best years of his life. He thought about the ring in his backpack and instantly dismissed it. Some other time. Not today. He looked at that pretty face, the bright and angry brown eyes, her bare legs in the shorts, strong and streaked with dirt and sweat, the backpack nearly overpowering her small back.

'Dear, I was scared to death, that's why.'

Now she was frightened as he resumed his fast pace down the trail. Drew had burst into her life a little over two years ago, when she had been sailing by herself on Lake Montcalm one hot summer afternoon. She had a small twelve-foot sailboat and was doing well, making long tacks, back and forth near the north end of the lake, when a sudden squall came up from the west. She had been soaked in the rain and the winds had torn away both the mainsail and tiny jib, leaving her with a tiny oar to paddle her way back home. About an hour into this backbreaking task – the sailboat wasn't designed to be powered by a single oar – a man a few years older than her passed by, paddling a canoe.

He was muscular, dark-skinned and wearing a pair of khaki shorts, a khaki cap and sunglasses. He had a nice wide smile as he called out to her, 'Feel like a tow?'

'Unless you're hiding a couple of sails in there, mister, yeah, I'd love a tow,' she had said.

He had expertly tied off a rope to the bow of her sailboat, and then after getting directions from Sheila he had dug in with his paddle and taken her home. All the way across the lake she admired the muscles in his arms and back, and she was intrigued by the pink scars in his brown skin. She never thought she'd be one to be attracted to musclemen – even after that disastrous marriage to Tom, with the poet's body and sharp eyes that gnawed at you – but she found it hard to take her eyes off that body. That night she had dinner with him, finally learned his name, and found out that he was originally from Nebraska and was retired from something he only called government service. Military, probably, but she didn't press him. A month later he had moved in with her to the house on the lake that she had been left by her parents. Two years later, she still found him strong and mysterious and a joy to be with most days. But even with the occasional nightmares he had, she had never seen him frightened. Not once.

Until today.

She looked ahead to him, the way he was pushing himself down the trail, like he was in some great hurry. He stopped for a moment at a point where the trail went over a small wood-plank bridge that spanned a fast-moving stream.

'Why, Drew? Why are you so scared?'

He looked up the trail and, damn it, he was spooking her so much that she turned as well. The trail was still empty.

'It was that place,' he said. 'It didn't belong there, and we didn't belong inside.'

'I don't understand what you're saying.'

He motioned back up at the trail. 'Did you see the sign on the outside door? Did that look like a relay station for the local utility?'

'No, it didn't. It . . .'

She stopped, not wanting to see the fear in those eyes. It made everything in her world wrong, as if the ground was slowly tipping beneath her. She took a deep breath. 'Drew, I don't know what it was. Do you?'

He nodded. 'Yeah, I do.'

Drew saw the concern in her eyes, was running through the options of what to tell her. She deserved the truth – and what about Pakistan, an accusing voice reminded him – but he didn't want to scare her. But he also didn't want her to think that he had gone nutso on her.

He realized he was still holding on to the pistol. Drew shrugged off his pack and as he returned the 9 mm to an outside pocket started talking.

'For lack of a better word, that was a bomb shelter back up there,' he said. 'Or a retreat, or a hideaway. Call it what you will. What's up there is a place for government officials to go during times of disorder. Like a biowarfare attack. Or a nuclear strike. Or something else. It had secure phones to other government agencies, meeting rooms, an infirmary, a cafeteria. All the comforts of a government-issued home.'

'How would they get up there? Hike up this trail? Bureaucrats?'

'Nope. Remember that cleared spot, to the east of the building? A landing pad for helicopters. I saw some hidden landing lights, found a place where aviation fuel had been spilled. A lot of military air traffic use these mountains for training. What's a few more helicopters in the area? Who'd notice?'

Now her eyes were quite wide, watching him as he zipped up the pocket. 'Then how were we able to get in? The door was locked, first time I tried it. Only when I tried a second time did it open.'

He shrugged. 'Don't know. Right now that's not important. What's important is that I'm pretty sure we were spotted when we were inside. There was a surveillance camera, up in a corner in the large room. It looked like it was operating.'

Drew picked up his backpack, swung it back over his tired shoulders. Man, this had been one long day already, and he could feel himself start to tire, start to crash while the adrenaline rush slowly dissipated in his bloodstream. It was going to be a grueling hike over the next hour.

'Drew, are we in trouble? Is that why you got us out of there so quick?'

Those eyes of hers seemed to grab hold of him. He reached out and squeezed a hand. 'Hon, if we're lucky, all that camera did was record to a self-contained unit that gets changed out once a week. Or maybe it is transmitted somewhere. And some tech sees a couple of worn-out hikers come in and one of them use a bathroom. No big deal. All right?'

He walked across the wooden bridge, his hiking boots making the timbers rattle. Sheila followed close behind. 'Then why are you in such a hurry now?'

Drew stopped on the other side of the streambed, trying hard not to snap at her. Damn it, didn't she understand? Didn't she know what was going on?

'Sheila, there was something else up there, written on one of the whiteboards. It said, *Case Shiloh: On September 19 we take her back!* That's just six days away.'

'What does "case" mean?'

'Military term, for an operational plan. An air strike, an invasion, any kind of plan is called "case". What it probably means is that they just had a drill up there, a practice drill, and someone forgot to erase the board when they were done.'

'But suppose it wasn't a drill? Suppose it's for real? And what could it mean, "taking her back"?'

He tried to keep his voice even, tried to focus on keeping an eye on the trail. It would be awkward if he stumbled now and sprained an ankle, an hour away from their vehicle. 'That's why I want to get off this trail and into our car,' he said. 'Get the hell out of here before something happens.'

Sheila's voice was now trembling a bit. 'Drew, do you mean we might get arrested?'

Only if we're very lucky, he thought. Very lucky indeed. INTERNMENT CENTERS, one of the graphboards had read. People who usually go into internment centers don't come out. Aloud he said, 'Sheila, let's just keep on making tracks, all right?'

As they descended, there was another rumble of thunder as another band of storms approached them.

TWO

A feeble executive implies a feeble execution of government. A feeble execution is but another phrase for a bad execution: And a government ill executed, whatever it may be in theory, must be in practice a bad government.

Alexander Hamilton, Federalist Paper No. 70

Three hundred and fifty miles southwest of the Monroe Trail in the White Mountains, Ira Woodman, administrator for Region One of the Federal Emergency Response Agency, sat in a conference room in the Reagan Office Building in Washington, DC, idly toying with a pen and his personal notepad, thinking wonderful thoughts about murder. It was one of those identical rooms cookie-cutted out for use in the Federal government from coast to coast in this troubled country: comfortable leather-bound chairs, wide and polished conference table, recessed lighting in the ceiling, and a little place set up in the corner with snacks, soft drinks and iced water.

How pleasant. A wonderful place to hold a meeting, and an equally wonderful place to waste six hours from one's life to take part in yet another sensitivity training session. And the older he got – Ira was only a few months away from the half-century mark – the more he begrudged those lost hours wasted in budget meetings, planning conferences, and idiotic training sessions like this one.

Especially now, oh God, especially now. Things were moving quickly, like a long freight train slowly moving down a mountain track, gaining speed with every passing minute, and he shouldn't be in here, wasting his time, wasting his energy. But the word from his boss, right from the very start, more than three years ago, had been clear enough: keep to your regular work schedule, your regular habits, always. There was no chance for errors, no chance for screw-ups. There was just one chance, presented to them on a silver platter the size of an aircraft carrier, and they couldn't afford to lose it.

Before him was a glass of water, and he took a sip, grimaced when his stomach started burning. Even water was now hurting him. All that work, all that stress, all that juggling, had started to eat at him from the inside out, and he was sure that his stomach was beginning to resemble a bubbling toxic-waste dump site. He sighed, opened up his notepad, looked at the list of names there. It was a worn list, more than twenty years old and begun when he was a sergeant in the Kentucky State Police. As he looked over it he thought again of his favorite Gilbert and Sullivan operetta, *The Mikado*, and he began humming his favorite tune: *I am the Grand High Executioner . . .*

Up forward was the likely occupant for the next name on his list, one Grace Mueller, from the Training Section of FERA. She was in her early fifties, and to Ira's practiced eyes she looked like the kind of woman who always regretted never having gone to Woodstock in '69. She wore a wraparound tan skirt, some type of multi-colored blouse, sandals, jangling jewelry on both tanned wrists, and long earrings that reached down to her shoulders. Her dark black hair had a racing stripe of white that ran through the middle that made her look like a plump skunk. She was bubbly, infectious, and treated everyone in the room like they had just graduated from potty training, and Ira couldn't wait to get out.

'Now, let's move on to our next subject,' Grace said, returning to an easel where a thick flowchart pad had been propped up. Sheets that had earlier been written on and torn off from the pad hung on the walls of the conference room by masking tape. Different-colored marker pens had been used for different topics, such as Assumptions, Fears, Responsibilities, and so forth.

Grace said, 'Let's examine different ways that having an asexual employee working for you will challenge you to use your full capabilities as a manager or a supervisor. For example, if an asexual employee comes to you and says that he or she feels threatened by a co-worker's display of a family picture on the desk, what should you say?'

Piss off and die, Ira thought, and caught the eye of a fellow member of FERA's Region One, Henry Harrison, who sat three places away. Henry was ten years younger, with a thick black moustache and black hair that he shaved almost to a stubble over his head. Henry looked over and rolled his eyes, and Ira nodded in exasperation. Henry was ex-Navy SEAL and was officially listed as Ira's administrative assistant, but unofficially he was Ira's bodyguard and the first person he went to for unique and unusual assignments. Henry's suit hardly fit him well around his thick shoulders and muscular neck, and throughout the past few hours, he had not said one word during the training session.

Grace kept on. 'Somebody, anybody? You have this situation, where an employee who has no sexual desires or wants sees a public display on a co-worker's desk that reaffirms that co-worker's sexual being. That flaunts to any visitor that he or she has sexual desires and needs. What should be done?'

A hesitant hand was raised, halfway down the conference table. A man's meek voice: 'You'd ask the co-worker to remove the family picture from the desk?'

'Exactly!' Grace said, making a note on the paper that said REMOVE PHOTO and adding a smiley face for emphasis. 'And what would you use as a reason?'

'To maintain the diverse and cooperative attitude in the workplace,' the voice said.

'Very good,' Grace said, almost clapping her chubby hands in glee.

My God, Ira thought in disgust, rubbing at his face. For this the Founders pledged their lives, their fortunes and their sacred honor when they signed the Declaration of Independence? He shifted in his seat, folded his arms, and almost grinned in relief when the pager at his side started vibrating. Saved by a vibration. He unsnapped the pager and punched in the code letters that brought the message up, and then sat up straight. He needed to see the FERA Director immediately. Now he didn't feel so relieved. Jesus, only days away. What the hell could be going on?

Henry was looking over at him, an eyebrow arched questioningly. Ira nodded and stood up, shoving his notepad into his suitcoat, grabbing his briefcase from the floor. He and Henry made their way to the conference room door, and despite his anxiety at seeing the Director, he enjoyed seeing the jealous looks from the other government managers and supervisors, stuck in here for another couple of hours. Grace, however, looked irritated.

'Excuse me?' she asked.

Ira moved past the chairs.

'Excuse me, sir?'

He reached the door, grabbed the door handle.

'Sir, would you please tell me where you're going?'

Henry joined him. Ira said, 'I'm sorry, I'm off to see the Director. It seems I have real work to do.'

Grace frowned. 'You just can't leave in the middle of this training.'

'Watch me,' Ira said, as he opened the door.

Grace called out. 'You'll have to repeat the whole session, from the beginning!'

'Oh, I don't think so,' he said, finally walking out.

The last thing she said, before the door closed, was, 'We'll see about that!'

He and Henry strolled quickly down the tiled corridor, heading for the bank of elevators. Other offices and conference rooms were on this floor, reserved for FERA and its employees. Ira said, 'You know, Henry, I do believe that woman threatened us back there.'

'I think you're right, Mr Woodman.'

As they waited for an elevator to arrive, Ira put his briefcase down for a moment and took out his notepad, flipping to a fresh page. With pen in hand, he carefully wrote down *Grace Mueller*. Henry saw him at work and quietly smiled, and when the elevator opened up, Ira resumed whistling.

I am the Grand High Executioner . . .

On the top floor of the Reagan Office Building Ira and Henry exited the elevator, walked over the FERA insignia on the shiny floor as they headed to the Director's office. The agency had been in this building for just over three years, and the agency itself wasn't much older. It had been put together four years earlier, after a disastrous hurricane season that roared endlessly through the Gulf of Mexico and the Atlantic Coast, causing billions in damage and hundreds of deaths. The old Federal Emergency Management Agency hadn't been up to the task in responding to the storms – sometimes not getting assistance to a devastated area for weeks – and during Congressional hearings to design its successor, one senator had said, 'Damn it, we need somebody to *respond* to emergencies, not to *manage* them!'

Thus was born his new home, Ira thought, as he went through the outer offices, past the reception area and public affairs rooms, and slipped his ID through a scanner that let him into the inner office. Unknown to most was some backroom trading that occurred when FERA came into being. It was also a time of some serious budget cuts, and in order to preserve pet weapons projects in certain Congressional districts, some Department of Defense responsibilities had been spun away to join the new Federal Emergency Response Agency.

Ira remembered those Congressional hearings, when he was the number two man in the Kentucky State Police, wondering about his future and that of a man he had worked for for many months during that primary season, trying to elect him President, only to see him fail during the convention. Other backroom dealing had also led to this man being named FERA's first Director, and as Ira nodded to the executive secretary staff just outside the Director's office, he smiled at remembering all those backroom negotiations. Be careful for what you deal for, he thought. Be very careful.

Henry took Ira's briefcase and sat down in one of the black leather couches, underneath a large color photo that showed a FERA team at work in some Midwestern city after a tornado strike. The day's *Washington Post* and *Washington Times* were on a coffee table, and Henry snorted and picked up a copy of the *Times*. The Director's executive secretary – Gayle Sellers, retired warrant officer from the Air Force, with white hair and sharp blue eyes and a fierce loyalty to her boss – nodded at Ira as he approached.

'He's on the phone,' she said, 'but he's expecting you. Go right in.'

Ira gave a courtesy knock on the thick oak door, which had a simple FERA DIRECTOR sign outside, and walked in. The man behind the large desk was on the phone and nodded, and waved him over. Ira once again marveled at the sense of power, the sense of electricity he got from being in the same room as Michaelson Lurry, Director of the Federal Emergency Response Agency. Lurry was fifty-five but looked several years younger. He stood an inch over six feet, and his dark blue suit, plain white shirt and red tie were flawlessly tailored. His dark brown hair was trimmed short, and there were speckles of gray about both temples. His pale blue eyes had the unerring tendency of seeming to look right through you, and when he was serious – as he was now, on the phone – his jaw clenched and he looked like a man who could (and did!) fly an F-16 Falcon jet right into Baghdad airspace without a moment's hesitation. Lurry had done that during the last Gulf War, and his bitter commentary on that conflict's murky end had cashiered him out of the Air Force.

A term in Congress from a district in Virginia had followed, and then he had left Washington for a lucrative career writing political essays, and then doing television and NewsNet commentary that put his face and opinions before millions. Less government. Lower taxes. Restricted immigration. Higher trade barriers. Right to life. No special programs for special interests. Prayer back in the schools. Morality back in the media. Twice he had run for President, both times against the former Texas governor who now sat in the Oval Office. The first time he had been in a field of candidates, and had done reasonably well before running out of money before the California primary. The second time, though, Lurry had run against the now-incumbent President from his own party, disgusted at his flip-flopping policies and programs, and though he had won a few primaries, most times he had lost against the power of the incumbent.

As he came into the office, Ira remembered the first time he had visited this place, and how everything had changed with that one meeting.

It had been the first time he had really spent time with Michaelson Lurry. Oh, he had met the commentator and presidential candidate a handful of times as he toured Kentucky during campaign appearances, but those were formal 'Hi-how-are-you, what's-on-the-schedule?' type meetings with about a dozen other aides, advisers and the usual hangers-on.

No, the first time he had talked to Lurry one on one was after the man had taken the Director's job, and Ira – much to his surprise – had been asked to become Region One administrator. That had been an odd time in Ira's life, trying to get back to the daily grind of the State Police, when for a brief few shining months he had seen himself in the White House as part of the Lurry administration. He hadn't expected anything grand at the White House – perhaps something to do with vetting and investigating potential Lurry administration members – but that dream had evaporated at the convention, when the pro-Lurry delegates had been outgunned and trampled. Then it had been a long flight back to Louisville, drunk from too much bourbon and not enough sleep.

As he told one of his staff members, 'It's like dating a Hollywood actress for a half-year, foolin' around and getting your hands on her titties, knowing that in just a little bit you'll be banging her in the sack, and then boom! Back to the trailer park you go with your fat wife and six screaming kids.'

But he had gone up to Boston without hesitation to take the Region One job and then a couple of months later came down to Washington to meet with the man himself. It had been a rainy day, the ride in from the airport a long one. He had looked at all the government buildings, the Lincoln Memorial, the Capitol Building and, from a distance, the big house itself. He saw all the bustling bureaucrats and office-holders, smug and arrogant drones who had had their feet upon the necks of their countrymen for so long, and he felt a slow burning anger, that it should have been different, all quite different, if only . . . If only what?

If only the special interests, from the Jews to the blacks to the gays, hadn't told so many lies about his man.

If only the media elite hadn't broadcast so many hours of nonsense about his man, calling him everything from a homophobe to a Nazi in a three-piece suit.

If only . . .

Up in Lurry's office, most of the lights were off, and Lurry had been standing near one of the rainswept windows, look-ing out to the lights of the other buildings in DC, as if he were a sailor in a stormy sea, catching the first glimpse of the reassuring beam from a lighthouse. Ira had sat down while Lurry stood there, hands clasped behind him, occasionally turning his head to pose a question.

'Do you believe in God's will, Ira?'

He sat there, hands together in his lap. He was confused, thinking that he was down here on some orientation session with the other regional administrators. He hadn't expected a meeting like this.

'I surely do, sir,' Ira said.

'So do I,' Lurry said, returning his look outside. 'So do I. When I was out campaigning, meeting the voters, sensing their hunger for a change, their demand for a new beginning, I felt their power and their love. It was intoxicating, Ira. I truly believed that this time, this time, I would not fail them, and that God would not fail us.'

Lurry half-turned again, slightly smiling. 'Arrogant, wasn't I, to presuppose that God was going to grant me the nomination.'

'I'm not sure what you mean, sir,' Ira said.

'Arrogance,' Lurry said. 'The good Lord will always punish arrogance, but in punishing you sometimes he shows you a different path.'

'Yes, sir.'

'Which brings me back to my original question. God's will. When I got here, I thought that this was going to be my exile, a quiet place where I would do some good work for the nation, but nothing like I had planned had I become president. I know that's what my political enemies had planned for me. A quiet exile.' Lurry then stepped away from the window and sat behind his desk. He picked up a thick black binder and began slowly leafing through the pages.

'Then I started reading what was expected of me in these briefing materials, and what was expected of this agency. I was quite surprised, Ira, quite surprised with what I found out. About 80 percent of this agency's budget and tasks are dedicated to the public duties that people associate with FERA. Flood relief. Response to hurricanes and earthquakes and other disasters. But the other 20 percent . . .'

Lurry slowly slid the briefing book across to Ira. 'There are some other duties in that 20 percent that are classified, that are unique, and present us with a challenge, Ira. I'm going to leave my office for a few minutes. I want you to read Appendix B, and I mean really read it. There's something there we're responsible for, called the National Program Office. Then we'll come back and discuss what you've read. And then I'll have an important question for you.'

Ira picked up the thick binder. 'And what's that, sir?'

'I'm going to ask you to join me in another campaign for the White House.'

'So soon?' Ira asked, the briefing book in his lap. 'You mean, in three years, when the primary season starts again?'

Lurry gently tapped his shoulder with a hand as he headed to the office door. 'No, Ira, I mean now.'

In the quiet of the office, as more rain streaked down the windows, he read and reread Appendix B, feeling at first horrified in learning what the Feds had planned and prepared for all these years, and then quietly triumphant, in realizing that these plans and procedures were now under the leadership of one Michaelson Lurry. He remembered seeing those smug and arrogant faces of the Washingtonians as he came in from the airport, and when Lurry returned to the office Ira stood up and handed the briefing book over.

'Yes,' he said simply.

Now, more than three years later, Ira looked again around the office, noting again the few decorations on the walls.

Photos of Lurry when he was in the Air Force. A photo of him with his wife, Sondra, on their wedding day some years back. And a signed photo, showing an uncomfortable Lurry being sworn in as FERA Director by the man he had tried to unseat as President, and in seeing that photo Ira again remembered the flash of anger and betrayal from that noisy convention in San Diego. Lurry had threatened to go to the convention, to raise a fight for the delegates in a last attempt to wrestle the nomination away from a man he detested, but the President and the party's leaders had offered him a deal: a high-visibility Cabinet post in exchange for shutting up and supporting the ticket.

As a good soldier, Lurry had done just that. And they had paid him back with an agency directorship that nominally had Cabinet status, but which everyone inside the Beltway knew was just one step above a joke. At the cocktail parties in Alexandria and Georgetown, people had laughed about the ineptitude and naivete of Michaelson Lurry. Ira had heard the jokes as well, including, 'What's the difference between a nine-year-old kid and Michaelson Lurry? Lurry still believes in Santa Claus!'

Still on the phone, Lurry said, 'Yes, Senator, I hear you. I understand fully.' Ira came forward as Lurry motioned him closer to his desk. The desk was fairly clean of papers and folders and had a computer terminal on one corner. On the near wall was a bank of four television sets, and Ira watched for a moment as Lurry kept talking. The televisions automatically changed channels among all of the major networks, and in between the game shows and the soap operas Ira caught flashes of news programs:

Click: A continuing prayer service outside of Lafayette Park, to help the President regain his skills as a leader, and to fight the renewed budget deficit and continuing recession. A hand-held sign said WE BELIEVE IN YOU.

Click: Another disappointing day in a long string of disappointing days on Wall Street.

Click: A rubble-strewn street in what was identified as Tel Aviv, as a wounded soldier in fatigues was carried by his comrades to an armored car. The scene shifted to the Orthodox unit that had ambushed the Army patrol, intense-looking young men with long beards, forelocks, yarmulkes and Uzi submachine guns.

Click: A tent city with huddled refugees in central Asia, people who had fled the remains of their nations, years after what was known as the Crescent War had escalated into a brief nuclear conflict, killing hundreds of thousands.

Click: An outdoor Muslim prayer service, outside a quiet and still oil refinery in Saudi Arabia, as the fundamentalist embargo continued for another month.

Click: Somewhere in one of the African Relief Mandates, showing soldiers with the tri-colored flag of France on their shoulders, setting up feeding stations for long lines of refugees. A little lettercrawl on the bottom of the screen said CLEARED BY FRENCH MILITARY CENSORS.

Click: A chattering head news show on one of the cable news programs. The little logo on the bottom left said WHITE HOUSE IN CRISIS. Thankfully the sound was turned down, and then, of course, the news show cut to the famous Rose Garden footage, twelve seconds of tape that had been broadcast about twelve million times during the past couple of months. There is the President, wrapping up some Rose Garden ceremony behind his podium. Behind him are aides and staffers. He waves to the camera, and gives one of those famous crooked grins that twice had endeared him to a majority of Americans. He walks away from the podium, but instead of heading back into the White House he moves to the left. You can see confusion in the eyes of his aides. He starts to move out of camera range, going behind some hedgework, and then he pauses, his back half turned. His hands are before him. There's a pause. And then an arc of something reaches out, splashes against a rose bush. The camera jiggles as aides desperately get in front of the pool camera to block the view of the President. Cut to black.

Ira turned away and looked out the windows, at the afternoon light of downtown Washington. My father's generation viewed and re-viewed the famed Zapruder film to try to determine the awful truth behind what had happened to their hero president, he thought. And my generation, a nation tied up in scandal, spin, polls and controversy, on whether or not in full view of the nation this particular president had pissed in public.

'Right you are, sir,' Lurry said, and then gently put down the phone. His face was red, jaw still clenched, and then he picked up the phone receiver again and slammed it down. 'There, you miserable son of a bitch, see what you get next week,' he said.

'Sir,' Ira said.

Lurry looked up and locked those eyes on Ira. Ira didn't like this look, not at all. Something was wrong, seriously wrong, and he literally had to replay the next words in his mind twice before he could comprehend what the Director was saying.

Lurry's voice was flat and to the point. 'Ira, a few minutes ago there was a serious breach at the Northern New England Recovery Center. Two hikers gained access. A male and a female. They didn't stay long, but we sure don't know what they learned while they were there. We also don't know how in hell they got into the facility.'

Ira now found himself sitting in a chair, hands on his knees, trying to stop the trembling. 'Entry . . . they gained entry?'

'Yes,' Lurry said, his voice tight. 'I don't have to remind you, Ira, that the recovery facility is in your Region One. And is your responsibility.'

'Understood, sir.'

Lurry nodded. 'Good. You know what kind of timetable we're on, what's scheduled. There's a car downstairs to take you to the airport. From there you'll jet back to Boston.'

'Framingham,' Ira said, running through options, choices, decisions, wondering how in God's name this foul-up of all foul-ups happened. Jesus! 'That's where our primary command and control facility is located. I just want people I can trust. I'll see that they are there when I arrive.'

'All right,' Lurry said. 'Framingham it is. Ira . . .'

He stood up, eager to get going, to show Lurry that he could handle this, get a handle on this problem, make it disappear so nothing would impact on what was going on, nothing.

'Sir, I'll take care of it. You can rely on me.'

'I know I can. I just want to make sure everything is clear. You have full authority and discretion to nip this in the bud. Full authority. Understood? Find these hikers, debrief them, arrest them, whatever. Just be sure that they're in our custody soonest. We don't want wild stories being spread around about that recovery facility. Hell of a thing, wouldn't it, to have a news helicopter up there tomorrow?'

Ira started for the door. 'It won't happen, sir. I guarantee it.'

As he reached the door, Lurry called out. 'And Ira?'

'Sir?'

'God bless.'

A firm nod. 'Yes, sir, God bless.'

He closed the door behind him and Henry was on his feet, seeing his expression. They strode out to the elevator banks and Ira said, 'Got your cellphone?'

'Right here,' he said, unclipping it from his pants belt.

'Good. Get a message up to Boston. Unannounced drill now commencing. Personnel on Able list to report to Framingham. No one else. And make sure Quentin is there, Mark Quentin. He's head of Facilities. He's got some explaining to do when we get there.'

They entered the elevator when it opened, and Ira nearly sprained his finger punching the button for the ground floor. He saw himself in the reflection of the polished metal and, as always, didn't like what he saw. His black hair was thinning and turning gray, his eyes were pudgy from not much sleep these past months, and just this year he had to buy another closetful of clothes because his waistline had expanded. He sure as hell didn't look like the Kentucky state trooper whose clothes had fit him, had made him The Man To Be Feared on the highways and backroads of Pendleton County. Even when he moved up the ranks, he had managed to keep in shape, in good enough shape to eventually marry a first runner-up in the Miss Kentucky USA contest, one Miss Glenda Sue Morris.

God damn it all to hell. Henry started to make the call and Ira leaned against the wall of the elevator, tried to relax, tried to unwind the tension that had now seized his chest. Everything he and so many others had worked for, all these long and lonely years, was threatened. Jeopardized by a couple of tree-huggers getting into a secure facility, damn it, a secure facility that ultimately belonged to him, Ira Woodman.

He opened up his coat, found his notebook, turned over a blank page.

Ira had a hunch that a few more names would be added to his list before the day was through.

Drew recognized the last bend in the trail. Just a few more minutes, that's all. He wasn't sure if he was in range or not, but he'd give it a try. He pulled his keyring from out of his pants pocket, flipped on the toggle that started up his Chevrolet Fortress. By the time he and Sheila got to the trailhead, their four-by-four would be warmed up and ready to roll. The closer they came to the end of the Monroe Trail, the easier their path became as it leveled off, and he tried to keep up a steady pace.

Sheila was behind him, and even with his back to her he could sense her mood. She was probably building herself up to one serious blow-out here shortly, and Drew hoped she would at least wait until they got into the Chevy Fortress. She could argue with him and say anything she wanted as long as they were moving. He had been razor-sharp as they came down the trail, looking for any movement coming up the trail, listening overhead to the sounds of aircraft or helicopters. All, however, had been quiet, except for the occasional grumble of thunderstorms to the south of them. A few times she had tried to ask him questions, and each time he had given her a one- or two-word response. It's all the time he could afford.

The trail flattened out and he picked up the pace. He even saw some candy wrappers and an empty beer can.

Close, very close, and at another bend, the trees thinned out and he saw the boxy shapes of other vehicles belonging to other hikers, and heard the reassuring low grumble of their own four-by-four, parked between two pickup trucks.

The trailhead was a wide, gravel-packed parking lot, bordered by pines, and Drew pushed another toggle on the keychain that opened up all four doors and the rear hatch. He shrugged his pack off and tossed it in the rear of the Chevy, and then helped Sheila with her own. She glared at him but he pretended not to notice. Get in, get in, he thought. We've got to get moving.

But she seemed to take her sweet time getting in, taking long swigs of her water bottle, wiping down her face and arms with a bright red bandana, until she finally clambered in the front seat. Before she had even closed the door he had shifted the Chevy into drive and started down the access road. About a couple of miles, he thought. Then we hook up to Route 302.

And then what? It was another hour's drive home, but did that make sense?

Easy, son, he thought. You're letting your paranoia take the best of you. There's probably nothing to worry about, and you know it.

Yeah. Probably. Just like your last mission was 'probably' going to be an easy one all those years ago.

Sheila sat back, folded her arms. 'We need to talk, Drew. I need to know why you're driving like we're heading to a fire, and why you pushed us down off that damn mountain. The worse thing we did back there, if anything, is a little trespass. So what?'

Bit by bit the pressure that was squeezing against the base of his skull while they were on foot was easing up. Now they were mobile they had options. The Chevy Fortress was a rugged four-by-four with seats that pulled out to sleeping bunks, a mini-fridge and microwave, and its own potable water supply, plus a dashmap system that boasted it covered every freeway and cattle path in North America. It had a combination power system – both internal combustion and electric – which was important in these days of spotty gas and oil shortages.

What it didn't have was one of the new autopilot systems, which Drew thought was just fine. He couldn't get comfortable over the idea of getting on to one of the highways set up for autopilot and then taking a nap while computers drove you from Point A to Point B, and recorded where you had been. No, he preferred to be in control. Like right now.

He cleared his throat. 'What's going on is that I'm trying to put as much distance as possible between us and that bomb shelter we were in. There's a chance, a very small chance, that there may be some kind of response. If so, it was better that we be out here on the road than still up there on a trail.'

She turned to him. 'Are you saying we could still be in trouble?'

'I don't know,' he said. 'All I do know is that getting out of here as fast as possible means the chances of anything happening lessens. So that's why I pushed us off that mountain. Sorry, but I thought that was the best thing to do.'

'You could have told me up on the trail.'

'Then we would have lost ten minutes or so, talking. I didn't want to chance it.'

Sheila said something under her breath, looked out the tinted window. 'All right, that makes sense, but it doesn't mean I have to like it. Jesus, Drew, my feet feel like they're going to swell up and fall off.'

He checked the odometer readout on the heads-up display on the windshield. Another mile to go. Good thing this access road was in fair shape.

Drew tried to keep his voice light. 'What do you think about another trip? Say, a drive up to Canada?'

'When?'

'Now.'

She slowly moved her head from gazing out the window. 'Are you out of your mind?'

'I don't think so.'

'Well, I'm beginning to think so. Christ, Drew, I stink. You stink. We haven't had a shower in almost a week. All of our clothes are a mess, and . . . No. I want to go home. I want to check our mail, spend a good chunk of time on the Web, and get back to work. I don't want to go to Canada. I want to go home. Besides, we don't have our passports.'

'I wasn't thinking about Quebec. I was thinking about Federal Canada, maybe Ontario or New Brunswick. We wouldn't need passports then.'

She folded her arms, stared straight ahead. 'Absolutely not. Drew, please, take me home. If you feel the need to go out in the north woods some more, be my guest. But only after you drop me off. I want to get back to the lake.'

Drew said nothing, just felt the pressure return back to his skull. He braked hard as they reached the paved road. Route 302. He looked both ways, saw no traffic. In his mind's eye he knew that turning right would eventually lead them to Interstate 93. From there, Federal Canada was about two hours away. That meant in one hundred and twenty minutes they would be safely across the border, and away from whatever was being planned for back in that bunker.

To turn left would eventually bring them to the small village of Corinth, and from there, south to Lake Montcalm and home.

Drew sighed, turned left. Home it was.

The road was near empty as they sped towards Corinth, and from the heads-up display he saw that he'd have to fuel up when they reached the town. As he drove he snuck a glance over at Sheila, remembering the first time he had met her. He had just been pensioned off from his government, and he had settled on a routine of sorts, going up and down the Northeast corridor, sticking close to the Appalachian range. He had fallen in love with mountains the first time he had seen them, right after joining the Army. Mountains were huge, powerful, and offered lots of hiding places. Even having grown up in Nebraska, he never liked flat land. You were vulnerable out there on the flats. There were lots of times, as a teenager, he'd be running a tractor out on the fields, and he'd see Dad – usually drunk, more often than not – stalk across the field, demanding to talk to him, chastise him, punish him for some wrong, usually imaginary. It took long minutes for Dad to stride across, long minutes where as a young boy he'd sit there on the tractor's seat, waiting, wondering what was about to happen.

Exposed. He hated being vulnerable and exposed, which was why he so loved mountains.

On the day he met Sheila he was passing a week or so near Lake Montcalm near the center of New Hampshire. He had spent some days just climbing up and down the trails in the nearby hills, and most times, if he heard approaching hikers, he would fade into the underbrush or trees, letting them go by without talking to them. Other times, he'd take a canoe out by himself and hug the shoreline, exploring rocky coves, narrow streams and small islands. One day he had been caught in a rain squall, and had taken shelter under a large pine tree, overhanging a tiny cove. When he had paddled out after the storm had passed he had spotted the tiny sailboat with the shredded sails. A woman in light blue shorts and a white bathing suit top that was filled out nicely was trying to paddle her way back home.

He could have done the traditional thing by ducking back into the cove and letting her struggle by, but this time . . . well, he couldn't. Something about the way she was working, the spirit of not giving up, of not sitting there dejected and waiting for help. He had approached her and asked if she needed some help, and after some pleasant bantering had paddled her boat back to her home. All along the way back to her shorefront house he had the feeling that he was being watched, that he was being evaluated by the cool young woman behind him, and to his surprise he rather enjoyed the feeling.

He enjoyed it more, too, when she had invited him in for a cold beer, and then, later, a simple barbecue eaten on a deck overlooking the lake. The conversation had been relaxed, comfortable, as if they had known each other for ten years rather than just ten minutes. He had spent that first night on the couch, and the second as well, and he would have spent the third night on the couch except for that delightful interlude on the secluded dock involving suntan lotion, glasses of wine for both of them, and some strawberries.

Their time together seemed to drift along, and among the many things he noticed was that the old dreams and memories were beginning to fade the more time he spent with her, the more time he spent on that dock, just looking at the lake water. That dock now belonged to the both of them, unofficially, and would officially if he could ever convince her to marry him. But Sheila had gone through a bad marriage, with some dreamy poet who—

'Drew!' Sheila called out.

He snapped out of the memories, saw what was happening, and started braking.

He swore. They should have turned right, to the interstate.

Because before them, blocking the road, was a line of fatigue-clad men carrying weapons.

THREE

I want you to just let a wave of intolerance wash over
you. I want you to let a wave of hatred wash over you.
Yes, hate is good . . . Our goal is a Christian nation.
We have a biblical duty, we are called on by God to
conquer this country. We don't want equal time. We
don't want pluralism.

Randall Terry, Operation Rescue, *The News Sentinel*
(Fort Wayne, Indiana), August 16, 1993

This conference room was different from the one back in
DC, and was one that made Ira Woodman feel more comfortable. A few whiteboards, a telephone, old table and
chairs, plus a TV and VCR unit set up in one corner.
Cinderblock walls painted light green. Plain and to the
point. Just the way things should be. He and other select
members of FERA's Region One office were at the not-so-
secret hideaway bunker in Framingham, which shared
quarters and facilities with the Massachusetts Emergency
Management Agency. In times of usual crisis – tornadoes,
hurricanes and winter storms – the access doors between
both agencies were wide open, and information, supplies and
personnel were willingly exchanged.

Today the access door was sealed, with armed Federal
police standing on the FERA side. Today wasn't a usual

crisis. Earlier, as he went down the cement corridors, he remembered another structure, three years ago, a structure made of cement. And the quiet order from Michaelson Lurry to do something about that structure. His first mission, his first success, in doing what had to be done to make this country great again.

Some months after that first meeting in DC, where he had first learned about Appendix B and the National Program Office, there had been other meetings as well, as the brief outlines of what they were planning began to be filled in with small details and actions. In one session between the two of them, Lurry said, 'Over the next year or so, I'm going to need to have some tasks of a delicate nature taken care of. Can I depend on you?'

'Certainly.'

'Even if these tasks are of a violent nature?'

Ira shrugged. He knew how to handle himself and others. You have to, if you want to work your way up among the other troopers in what they called the Thin Gray Line back home in Kentucky. Whether it was taking down some drunk father assaulting his daughter or teaching a couple of snotty teenagers all about justice in the rear seat of a cruiser with a police baton, violence had never bothered him.

'Not a problem, sir,' he said.

Which is why he had found himself on a hillside at night in Alabama, climbing a rough trail, his companions a number of individuals who were among the most sought-after fugitives in America. His old cop mind had been bothered about what had been going on – consorting with criminals, for God's sake – but the part of him that was now enjoying every minute with Lurry, planning and working, saw it for what it was: a part of doing a necessary business.

That night he had gone to meet the fugitives with a man named Henry Harrison, who was later to become his administrative assistant. Henry had been dressed in an old fatigue jumpsuit and carrying a large zippered black duffel bag over a bulky shoulder. In a dimly lit parking lot Henry had said, 'Don't you worry, I'll know exactly where you'll be, and I'll be ready when the time comes.'

'How are you going to do that?'

Henry laughed. 'That's what I do,' he said, as he slipped into the parking lot's shadows.

An hour later Ira continued walking up the hillside trail, following the bulk of a large man ahead of him, a man who with his comrades made up the Regiment of God, or as the news media and NewsNet channels liked to say, 'the shadowy Regiment of God'. Ira wasn't impressed by the so-called Regiment – they looked like the typical weekend county militia types, with surplus fatigues, a gaunt look about the eyes and lots of bad teeth. But Ira had been impressed by his contact with the group. The FBI supposedly had been tracking the Regiment of God for years; Michaelson Lurry had set up the meet within the space of a week, no doubt through the aid of some of his more militant campaign contributors. That had been one hell of an advantage from the very beginning: lists of campaign contributors meant a list of people all across the country, in different fields of business, government and military, who had already become the nucleus of a new movement. They had proven their worth through their money; soon, many of them would be asked to prove their worth through actions, and most would not hesitate in doing just that.

The trail leveled out at the crest of a hill, at a small clearing. Ira sensed more well-armed bodies out there in the woods, keeping an eye on him. He was relatively defenseless, except for a computer diskette and a cigarette lighter in his coat pocket, for when he had met his contact at a nearby WalMart parking lot he had been politely and expertly disarmed of his 9 mm pistol. They had traveled in the back of an unmarked van for some long minutes before the start of this hike.

Now a couple of figures came towards him, and a small lantern with a covered shade was lit. Two men were before him and they looked like brothers: tall and gangly, wearing fatigues and with weapons slung over their shoulders. The one on the left had a thick beard and the one on the right was clean-shaven, with large sideburns.

The one with the sideburns said, 'No names, if you please.'

'That's fine with me.'

The other said, 'We voted for your boy, twice, in the primaries. Even sent him some money. Too bad the fags and niggers didn't let him in.'

Ira said, 'Some things back then you couldn't control. But we're learning.'

The bearded one said, 'Enough chatting. Let's show you our problem.'

They led him through the clearing, near a dropoff that fell to a ravine and a mass of brambles and saplings. The whirr-whirr of the cicadas was a constant sound, like an army of watchers, keeping an eye on them. A pair of binoculars was handed to him and Ira lifted them up. Several hundred yards away was a roadway, brightly lit by a strip mall that had a McDonald's and a Piggly-Wiggly and a bunch of other stores

Ira couldn't make out. To the right was a large, nearly vacant lot, bordered by a barbed wire fence. Inside the lot was a two-story building, illuminated by large spotlights. It was bare and concrete and had narrow windows. He moved the binoculars and noted the parked police cruisers, lights off and engines running, just outside the fence.

One of the men leaned over and said, 'That's the sole remaining abortion mill in the northern part of the state.'

'It looks pretty well defended,' Ira said.

'That it is,' the man said in disgust. 'They've got cops all around the perimeter, TV cameras, motion detectors, and all their mail gets sent to a special Post Office facility where it's opened and screened. Some of our brothers and sisters, they were active in protesting there, day after day, until some Jew judge set up a boundary, says they can't perform their constitutional rights of protest within two hundred yards of that butcher's place. You know how many babies get murdered there, week after week? Dozens, and hundreds every month, thousands every year!'

Another, softer voice: 'Easy, brother, easy. Our visitor doesn't need to be converted.'

He kept his view of the abortion clinic steady. 'How do the doctors and nurses get in there?'

'Helicopter,' the softer voice said in disgust. 'They land on the roof and they wear masks, so we can't find out who they are.'

'Every day, a helicopter comes in?'

'Nah, do you think those feminist witches can afford that? No, they come in and drop off a shift. They stay in there a week, get food and showers and bunks, best we can figure. The women who are killing their babies, they get trucked in by armored car. They set up a rotation where they pick 'em up and drop 'em off at different places in the county. A regular fortress of Satan they have down there, mister.'

'Unh-hunh,' Ira said. 'So there might be a shift of nurses and doctors in there right now?'

'Yeah, you got a problem with that?'

'Nope.'

'Look,' the other man said, the one with the louder voice. 'We agreed to meet with you 'cause you said you might be able to help us with that butcher's mill. That was the deal. You help us, and later on we'll help you. What can you do?'

'Oh, something, I'm sure,' he said. 'Anybody got a cigarette?'

Some muttering and a pack of cigarettes was pressed in his hand. He took out the cigarette lighter, flipped it open and held it up high, like a male Statue of Liberty. He clicked open the flame and somebody said, 'Hey, what are you—'

Even though he was expecting it, he flinched at the light and noise. From further down the hill was a brilliant blossom of light and smoke, the light too intense to look at, and there was a snap-growl of something being ignited, and a loud whoosh that quickly died away.

Inside the Greater Jackson County Women's Healthcare center, Gail Murray, an RN specializing in OB/GYN work, was wrapping up some paperwork. Her desk was illuminated by a set of flickering fluorescent lights that were giving her a headache, and she looked longingly at the hallway, where the women's staff dormitory was located. Just a few more minutes and it's sleep time, and just three more days and our shift is over. Then it's back to the farm and a whole day of nothing but riding horses and trying to unwind the knot of muscles at the base of my skull.

She checked the paperwork again. Just one patient being kept overnight. One Sally Doe, age thirteen, who had come in yesterday. Poor girl could hardly read or write, and during the past three years she had been on the receiving end of some attention from her stepfather.

Well, Gail thought savagely, when we're done with you, Mr Doe, we'll make sure you don't abuse any more teenage girls. Children's services in this part of the state were woefully underfunded but Gail had a cousin in the sheriff's department who sure could make things interesting for Mr Doe in the near future. There had been a time when problems like this could be handled in the system and the courts, but that point had passed. Not enough money, not enough interest. A little rough street justice was sometimes the only choice, and Gail wasn't afraid to make that choice. It would only take a few minutes of Net work to find the real name of Mr Doe, and she intended to do that first thing tomorrow.

She heard someone approaching and looked up as Dr Ray came over, carrying a bottle of water. Like her he wore surgical greens and a bulletproof vest. Her own vest was making her lower back itch from the sweat.

'Saw you working and thought you might like a drink,' the doctor said. 'And I also figured you wouldn't need caffeine so late at night.'

Gail smiled in appreciation and rolled her chair back. 'Thanks, Ray,' she said, taking the bottle from his outstretched hand. He was about her age and looked just a few years out of residency training. She had worked with him off and on for a half year, and liked his brisk, friendly manner. She had no idea where he had gone to school or where he was accredited or even what his last name was.

Nobody in the building knew anyone's last name or

home address. Security had been beefed up since an incident – hell, she thought, let's call it by its right name, a massacre – in a clinic in Oregon last year. One of the RNs in that clinic had secretly belonged to one of the radical fringe groups and one night had given up the security codes for the clinic, one of the last ones still operating in the Northwest. In the machine-gunning that had followed even she hadn't been spared, and there were at least a dozen Websites set up in her honor, a martyr to the cause.

'Ask you a question, Gail?' the doctor asked, sitting on the edge of her desk.

'As long as it's not a dating question, go ahead.'

He smiled, though his eyes were tired and he needed a shave. 'Someone told me that you've been here the longest, almost three years. I'm just curious, that's all. I mean, coming in here for a week is almost like being in a prison. Bad food, snoring companions in the dormitory, and lousy laundry facilities. Plus, I hate flying in a helicopter and I still don't sleep well at night, knowing that somebody who thinks he's talking to God is going to shoot me while I'm mowing my lawn.'

She took a swig of the water. It was warm but she appreciated the thought. 'You know why, Ray? A woman's right to control her own body. That's all. My mother and her mother marched in the streets and pressed for votes in the state house, all for a woman's right to choose. That's what this country is about, right? Marching in the streets, not fighting in the streets. I figured two things. One, I owed them for what they did for us. Second . . . well, I always figured, if the almighty "they" take away that woman's right, that they won't stop there. They'll keep on going. So I see this as a barricade, one that has to be defended.'

'Unh-hunh,' he said. 'Sounds good.'

She gently tapped him on his leg with her foot. 'And what about you? You said you hate the surroundings, the danger, the helicopter ride in. How come you've put up with it all this time?'

He smiled again. 'Loans.'

'Excuse me?'

'Student loans,' he said. 'You wouldn't believe the loans I have to pay back.'

'Oh, come on,' Gail said, bringing the bottle back up to her mouth. 'The money's not that great, believe me, I know. What's the real reason.'

'Okay, the real reason is – shit, what's that?'

She sat up, hearing a dim roar and seeing the barred windows with bulletproof glass light up, and dropped the bottle of water, wanting just to hold Ray's hand in that last second.

She didn't make it as the concrete ceiling fell upon her.

'Holy Christ,' came another voice up on the hill. Below them the abortion clinic lit up as every window in the building blew out, each flying chunk of shattered glass followed by a tongue of smoke and flame, and in one heartbeat from another the building collapsed upon itself as the shuddering boom of the detonation reached the small group up on the hill.

Ira blinked his eyes from the glare and the light and the noise. Behind him he saw that two of the Regiment of God members had fallen to their knees in prayer. He looked back at the dust rising up from the ruins of the building and that brief pang of regret came up, from that young man who had joined the Kentucky State Police to serve his commonwealth and make sure its laws were obeyed. Where had that young man gone to? What had happened?

Sacrifices, he remembered his daddy saying, in telling one of his stories from his service in the Second World War. Sometimes you had to make sacrifices for the greater good, and sometimes people get killed in those sacrifices.

The man with the beard grasped Ira's arm and said, 'How did that happen?'

'That happened because we wanted it to happen,' Ira said, pushing away the thoughts of that young state trooper. 'I had an associate with me, an associate with a laser-guided US Army Viper anti-tank weapon, complete with a depleted uranium warhead and two-second fuse delay. You saw what happened. It punched right through one of those bulletproof windows like it was made of tissue paper. You satisfied?'

'Praise the Lord, yes,' he said, squeezing Ira's arm. 'We did God's work tonight.'

Ira gently pulled away, shrugging off the grip of the bearded man, wondering what Lurry had planned for these folks. 'No, it was our work tonight, and I'll remind you of our agreement. Our services in exchange for your cooperation.'

'What kind of cooperation?' the man with the sideburns demanded, stepping up to him.

'Whatever cooperation we decide, that's what. That's the deal.'

'Brother,' the man with the sideburns said, speaking to his companion. 'I don't like this deal. We've done our work by ourselves, answerable to no one. This . . . this government official, I don't like the idea of following his orders, even if he does work for Lurry. I think there should be another way.'

'Such as?'

'Such as leaving him here and getting on with other work. We might have needed his help here with that abortion mill. Who says we'll need his help again? Let's leave it right here.'

Ira felt the atmosphere change as other members of the group listened to the man with the sideburns. He felt exposed, knowing what was going on in their minds, knowing that it made sense. Just climb back down this hill and leave Ira up here with a bullet to the head or a knife to the throat. No witnesses, no outsiders knowing about the Regiment of God. He felt like he was a rookie, making his first traffic stop at night in the backwoods of Pendleton County, bladder suddenly feeling full, knees beginning to shake.

He reached into his coat pocket and pulled out the computer diskette. 'If I can say something for just a moment, this is for you.'

Ira tossed the diskette and the bearded man caught it. 'What's that?'

'It's something my superior gave to me before I came here tonight. It has information you might find useful. That is, if your name is Mr Jackson, and your companion there is Mr Tollins, which I believe is true.'

There were a few mutters and an intake of breath. Jackson, the one with the beard, stepped closer. 'What do you mean by this?'

'Ever hear of the Colombian option?'

'You're not making sense,' Jackson said.

'Just give me a second.' From a distance there came the sounds of sirens, and out of the corner of his eye Ira could make out the flickering flames of the crumbled building. 'Back during the cocaine wars of the 1980s, when the Colombian drug cartels were fighting for control, if you double-crossed someone or upset someone in the cartel, not only did they kill you, they killed your wife, your children, your parents, your cousins, your maid and your first-grade teacher. They killed everyone associated with you.'

Some more muttering. There was a clicking sound as safeties on weapons were being switched off.

'Go on,' came a voice. Ira couldn't tell if it was Jackson or Tollins, not that it made any difference.

'We had a deal here tonight. We came through on our end. If you decide to back out on your end – whether it's by leaving me up here on the hill or trying to blackmail me or just saying no when the time comes – then everyone on that diskette is dead, no matter their age or sex. And at the top of the list are your names, Mr Jackson and Mr Tollins, followed by other members of your group and members of your families.'

Silence, save for the sound of the cicadas and the sirens out by the highway. Ira wondered if Henry Harrison was watching this, out in the brush, and what he would say to Michaelson Lurry if things went to the shits. *Sorry, Mr Lurry,* Henry might say. *It went well and then they shot him up there. I couldn't do a thing to help.* And Lurry might say in reply, *Oh well, he tried. Let's try someone else.*

Sure as hell is different from working a primary campaign, lining up deputy sheriffs and precinct workers to support your man, he thought.

'One question,' Jackson said.

'Yeah?'

Jackson looked around at his group of men, and then looked back at Ira. 'Two counties over. There's a nightclub and dancehall where sodomites attend. Males upstairs and females downstairs. It's almost as well guarded as that place had been. Do you think you could help us there too?'

Ira let out a breath. So he would live tonight. 'Sure,' he said.

Someone said, 'God bless.'

Ira nodded, put his hands in his coat pockets, suddenly exhausted. 'Yes, God bless.'

Below them, the clinic still burned.

Now Ira's admin aide, Henry Harrison, was sitting by him in the FERA Region One bunker. Sitting in a circle around the table was what would probably seem to an outsider to be an odd collection of FERA personnel: Clem Badger, an obese man with a carefully trimmed goatee who was a computer systems engineer with FERA and who secretly frightened Ira with his depth of computer skills; Tanya Selenekov, a thin, intense woman with blonde-white hair whose parents had emigrated from Russia during one of the many financial crises that had led to tanks in its streets and who was a spokeswoman for Region One; and Mark Quentin, tall and thin, whose shirt cuffs always rode up on his wrists, responsible for all of FERA's facilities in New England. He blinked his eyes a lot in nervousness as he probably counted down the seconds to what was going to happen next.

An odd collection, true, but all chosen and groomed over the past few years as Ira slowly put together a group to implement Lurry's instructions.

Mark and Clem wore suits and ties, and Tanya had a blue dress that, while modest, did show a bit of her legs. Ira ran a tight shop and there were no casual Fridays, casual Mondays or casual anything at FERA Region One. Ira also didn't waste time. Unlike the session down in Washington, this was his meeting, and none of that touchy-feely New Age crap was allowed.

'Mark, facilities are your responsibility. How in hell were they breached today by those two hikers?'

The facilities man nodded and audibly swallowed, leafing through a black loose-leaf binder notebook. 'Electrical storm, that's how.'

'Explain.'

Ira noted the serious looks on the other people in this room. Everyone knew what was riding on the next several days, hell, what was riding on the outcome of this meeting. Another quick nod from Mark. Ira was reminded of a toy from his youth, a bobbing crane that dipped its beak into a glass of water over and over again. A mindless toy, that's all. Mindless.

'Electrical storm,' he repeated. 'There was a lightning strike on a transformer unit about ten miles away. There's an underground cable that services the recovery facility. Because of the strike, power to the cable was lost. Without power, the electrical locks on the access door were disabled.'

Clem Badger spoke up. 'Aren't there back-up batteries for the vital systems? Like air handling, priority computer networks, access locks . . .'

Good for you, Ira thought. Clem most times was a royal pain, gluttonous and sometimes blasphemous, but not only did he know his own areas of responsibilities, he knew others as well. He was a good resource, both for FERA and for the upcoming operation.

A fretful nod this time from Mark. 'Yes. Back-up batteries for those systems and more. What we've been able to determine is . . . well, the batteries assigned to that locking system were dead.'

Ira thought of reaching for his notebook, decided it would be a waste of time. *I am the Grand High Executioner . . .* His stomach lurched with dismay at what he had just heard. Dead batteries. That's all. A nation lost because of a handful of dead batteries. Jesus.

'You had a facilities drill up there last week, correct?' Ira asked.

'Yes, we did.'

'Wasn't all of the equipment to be checked and tested, in preparation for next week?'

'Yes, it was.'

'What happened to that battery system?'

Mark looked down at the briefing book. 'It . . . it was missed. The surveillance on that system was missed.'

Tanya spoke up, in her slight Russian accent. 'So these two hikers, they gained access for a few minutes earlier today. What possible consequences can there be? What is our vulnerability?'

Ira glowered at Mark as the man quickly became interested in his briefing book. This, this was what had set off Ira, about one minute after landing in Framingham, when Clem had briefed him on the scale of the security breach. Ira spoke up, his voice low. 'Clem, run that videotape segment, will you?'

Clem picked up a remote control unit, aimed it at the television. Lights in the conference room dimmed automatically when the set was turned on and the tape began to play. It was in color but the contrast was muddy as a result of the room being photographed under low lights. A man rushed by, moving from left to right. The room was empty, showing the display and whiteboards on the wall. Then the camera zoomed onto one of them. When the words written on it came into focus, someone in the conference murmured, 'Oh, for God's sake.' *Case Shiloh: On September 19 we take her back!*

Ira turned and stared at Mark, almost demanding him to look back at him, but Mark kept his head lowered, looking down at his papers. Ira forced himself to keep his voice soft, though he so wanted to break into his state police mode, with booming voice and sharp curses and maybe even a slap to the face. But that wouldn't work here, no, not at all.

'Mark, what was the meaning of this?'

The man's voice was barely audible. 'We . . . we were excited, that's all. That it was all coming together. We had worked hard that day, getting everything ready . . . One of my guys, he was feeling exuberant, that's all. He wrote something up there and . . . Well, we felt good, that's all . . .'

Clem spoke up, his voice sharp. 'Better you had followed your equipment surveillance procedures than play games up there.'

Henry remained silent and Tanya made to speak but Ira held up his hand. 'Mark, there's a phrase German philosophers used, back in the 1920s and 1930s when their country was in torment. Somewhat like today. There was a depression, whores and decadents and homosexuals were taking over the cities, and political parties were arguing and scrambling for control. The phrase those philosophers used was *ernste Menschen*. That means "serious men". They felt it would take serious men to set things straight.'

Ira nodded and managed a slight smile for Tanya's benefit. 'With apologies to our female colleague in the room, we are all serious men here. Many of us have sacrificed families, careers and even our health for what we have planned. *Ernste Menschen*. Serious men. Mark, you have proven to us today that you are not serious. I'm not sure what you are, but I know you're not serious in implementing and protecting this operation.'

Mark started talking and Ira spoke over him. 'Clem, I'll meet you in a few minutes in the Op Center, to see where we can go with this. Tanya, I'm going to need some press releases prewritten, everything from explaining to new-shounds what the Northern New England Recovery Center is all about if the word does get out, up to and including a press release explaining why these two hikers have been arrested.'

'If we can find them,' Henry said, speaking up for the first time.

Clem moved his large bulk from his chair. 'Don't worry, SEAL man. We'll find them.'

After Clem and Tanya left the conference room and shut the door behind them, Mark started talking again, his words tumbling over one another. 'Mr Woodman, look, I know I've made a mistake, I know this is a screw-up, but I'll help out, honest to God I will. I'll call my wife, tell her I won't be home tonight, won't be home for a couple of days. I'll camp out here and help in tracking down those two people, what-ever it takes, honest, whatever it takes.'

Mark kept on talking and Ira nodded in all the right places. He picked up his briefcase, which had been resting on the floor beside him, set it on his lap, and nodded again as Mark leaned over the table, making promises, issuing excuses. Ira felt the fury building inside of him, remembering all of the things he had done these past years, all of the people he had met, the dark places visited, the late-night air-line flights and bad food, all working to one goal, one achievement. All those months of work and sweat and heartache, threatened by this creature before him.

Ira unsnapped the briefcase top, reached in past his cell-phone and lapbot, and took out his 9 mm Smith & Wesson pistol, with silencer attachment, and, just as Mark said he would give up a vacation this winter with his wife and two sons to make it right, Ira shot him twice in the chest.

The man's eyes widened, and both hands grasped at his chest. He gurgled and then slumped back in his chair, an arm quivering. Blood seeped through his fingers. There was another gurgle and he started a slow slide down until his arms got hung up on the sides of the chair. His head drooped forward in one last nod. There were droplets of blood on the open briefing book on the conference table before him.

Henry spoke up. 'Somehow I don't think our training instructor this morning would have approved.'

'A week from now, if all goes right, she'll have more important things to worry about.' Ira put the pistol back in his briefcase, looked around the floor and picked up the two empty shell casings. Those went into the briefcase as well and he shut the lid down with a satisfied slam. If only all problems could be solved so easily, he thought, but then the sense of satisfaction just dribbled away. More blood spilled. The story of his past three years. He wondered if it would ever stop, even after Case Shiloh.

Henry said, 'We'll have family issues in a day or two, if he doesn't get home.'

'Make a call to his wife,' Ira said, now feeling exhausted. 'Tell her there's been an emergency. He'll be out of contact for a few days. In a couple of weeks we'll let her know that he died gloriously in the service of his country, sacrificing his life for his children's future, blah blah blah. My guess is that in a year or so his hometown will erect a statue of him.'

Ira grabbed his briefcase, stood up. 'In the meantime, I've got to keep on cleaning up after the idiot.'

'Which raises a point,' Henry said. 'I'll need some help in here, getting this place sanitized.'

'Pull Tanya off that press release assignment,' he said. 'Besides, it's what she's suited for. Women's work, cleaning up.'

Henry smiled as he stood up as well. 'But just a few minutes ago you apologized to her for using a non-PC phrase like "serious men".'

Ira said, 'I lied.'

When the Chevy Fortress got closer to the line of armed men, Sheila couldn't help herself. She started giggling and would have continued laughing until she got that sharp look from Drew. At first glance she thought there had been a line of soldiers blocking their way, soldiers brought down upon them because of their trespassing in that bomb shelter. Jesus, she had thought. Drew had been right, damn it . . .

But then she had a closer look, and saw that first set of smiles. They weren't soldiers, not at all. The youngest looked to be about sixteen or seventeen, and the oldest close to sixty or seventy. Their military clothes were a mish-mash of different types of camouflage, and though she hated the sight of so many weapons at least they were slung over their backs. A couple of the men – could she call them 'good ol' boys'? – held open cans of beer as they stood on the side of the road.

Drew lowered the window and one of the larger men, with a beard that came down to mid-chest, nodded and passed over a sheet of paper. 'Afternoon, citizens,' he said.

'Afternoon,' Drew said.

The man nodded to the sheet of paper. 'We're members of the Grafton County Free Militia, and this here is a voluntary, informational checkpoint. You didn't have to stop for us, not at all, and you can leave at any time.'

Sheila covered the smile with her hand. That's how the militia units operated nowadays, by pretending to perform public services, like picking up trash along the side of the road, delivering meals to elderly shut-ins, and holding Christmas parties for the new state orphanages. Of course, at each charitable event they were armed and dressed for combat and would pass out their leaflets about the Jews and the New World Order and White House conspiracies.

Drew looked at the sheet of paper, and carefully placed it on the seat between them. 'I appreciate that.'

The man leaned towards the open window. 'You look to be a reasonable man. You see anything up there in the woods that might interest us? Smugglers, refugees, dropouts? Anything at all?'

Sheila noted Drew's wide smile but also noticed the quiet quivering of his leg holding down the brake pedal. 'Nope, not a thing. Just me and the missus and God's great outdoors.'

'Well, ain't that the truth. You both have a good day, now, all right?'

He stepped back and the line of men moved onto the side of the road, and Drew waved and accelerated. Sheila noticed a younger man, about seventeen, and she winked at him, and even through the glass of their four-by-four she thought he blushed.

Drew let out a sigh and Sheila picked up the sheet of paper, smiling again. At the top it said GRAFTON COUNTY FREE MILITIA and there were rows of dense text, with an old woodcut illustration showing a happy settler family in front of a log cabin. The paper had been poorly photocopied and she scanned it and said, 'Did you know they can't spell Freemasonry? And they mix their plural possessives. Like when they write "Black Helicopters' conspiracy" they don't put in an apostrophe where they should.'

'Thanks for not pointing that out back there,' he said, eyes on the road.

'And why not?' She laughed. 'They must be bored, standing in the road, drinking beer and harassing tourists. A little humor could have done them some good.'

'And not done us some good,' he said quietly. 'Sheila, uniformed guys with guns, even jokers like that crowd back there, don't have much in the way of a sense of humor. They might have gotten pissed at us, and then they could have held us up. I don't want to lose any travel time.'

'Still worrying about our little trespass back there?'

He was quiet for a moment, and Sheila wondered if she had pressed too hard. But then he turned and spared a glance, smiling. 'Just want to get us both home before sunset, that's all.'

But the smile didn't reassure her. It was the same fake kind of smile he had been using just a few minutes before when talking to the militia leader.

The lights in the Op Center were kept low, the better to see what was on the screens, and Ira stiffened with distaste when he saw what was on Clem Badger's computer. It was a screensaver for the latest and most popular cable television cartoon series, featuring two characters, Deffy and Kate. They were animated human excrement, who invariably, during their adventures in the depths of the New York City sewer system, would swarm over their foes and cry out, 'It's poop power!'

Ira said, 'Get that off your screen, and get rid of that file. I don't want it on the organization's computer system.'

Clem just laughed and punched in a few keys. 'Whatever you say, Mr Woodman. Whatever you say.'

Ira closed his eyes for just the briefest moment, again feeling that awful weight on his shoulders of what was happening, what was set to happen. All this planning for Case Shiloh finally coming together. Less than one week left to change a nation. Six days. And at the end of those six days there would be a lot of changes, hundreds of changes. And one of those changes would ensure that nothing like that horrid cartoon show would ever be considered, produced or aired ever again.

Clem's voice brought him back. 'Here's what I've been able to capture from the recovery center's video feed.'

Ira looked past the large man's shoulder at the computer screen. It was split in two, showing two figures, a man and a woman. There you are, he thought, the couple who have tossed everything up in the air and who just ten minutes ago made a widow of Mrs Mark Quentin. They didn't look particularly distinguishable. The woman was reasonably good-looking, though she could have used a shower, and it was apparent that she wasn't wearing much of a bra. The man had a recent growth of beard, and there was something about those eyes. Alert, they did look alert, but they also looked exhausted, he thought, like he had been up for days.

'What now?' Ira said, feeling again that tinge of jealousy and fear over what Clem and his computer skills could achieve. Ira didn't completely trust computer wizards at all, but in this age of chips and automation there was no other choice. That was another place where this country had made the wrong choices. Instead of making cars and steel and airplanes and farm equipment, hands-on work that made something at the end of the day, too much of his nation's time had been wasted by fat men and quiet women in windowless offices, clicking away on keyboards. He didn't understand, could never understand it, and that would change too when the time came.

'Well, let's tighten things up, shall we . . .' Clem leaned his large bulk in and started making motions with the computer's mouse. Boxes made up of moving lines were suddenly placed around the heads of the man and woman. There was a couple of clicks on the mouse and then the two torsos disappeared, just leaving the heads on the screen. A few more clicks and they were brought into focus and seemed sharper.

'All right . . .' Clem typed in a few more commands. 'Let's start with the New Hampshire Department of Motor Vehicles. Get into their license photo database, do a cross-comparison, and if that doesn't work we'll just widen it to Vermont, Maine, Massachusetts . . .'

A sharp beep from the computer, and Clem looked up at Ira, grinning. 'Spoke too soon. Must be your lucky day, Mr Woodman. We've got two good hits. Let's see what we've got.'

In another few seconds two overlapping computer screens appeared, showing more formal pictures of the two hikers. Ira leaned forward, trying to ignore the smell of sweat and old food coming from Clem. 'Drew Connor,' Ira said, reading the photo captions. 'And Sheila Cass. What else?'

'He's forty and she's thirty-five,' Clem announced as he navigated through a series of computer screens. 'No criminal record for either of them. Not married. They live on Lakeshore Drive in Montcalm, New Hampshire. He's on some sort of disability pension from the Department of

Agriculture. She owns her own business, looks like a Web business. Something called Hand-Held Solutions. Um . . . okay, here we go. They own a late-model, Chevrolet Fortress. We activate their Stolen Vehicle Transponder and in ninety seconds, Mr Woodman, you'll know exactly where they are.'

'Do it,' Ira said.

Sheila sniffed again, noting the gamey smell inside the four-by-four. Lord, could she use a shower. And that's not all. She was feeling the faint grumbling of hunger. 'Drew?'

'Hmmm?'

'When we get gas, can we get something to eat? I'm starving.'

'Sure,' he said, looking straight ahead as he drove. 'Not a problem.'

'Well, well, well,' Clem observed. 'Aren't we being a bit tricky. Their SVT is disabled.'

'Meaning what?'

'SVT could be disabled because of any one of a number of things. Might have burned out. Might have been hit by a stray rock through the undercarriage. But I doubt it.'

'And why's that?' Ira asked.

'Because if it's disabled a little light appears in your dashboard saying it's not working. For most people that would be enough to get their car into a shop.'

'But not these people.'

'Nope,' Clem said, again typing on the keyboard, making clicking motions with his mouse. 'Some people, well, the privacy types, they disable their SVT. They don't like knowing that any police agency can determine their vehicle's location by activating the SVT without their knowledge or say-so.'

'Or the criminal types,' Ira said, gently grasping the rear of Clem's seat. 'What can you do next?'

Clem's voice was quiet. 'Well, that's up to you, Mr Woodman. I can initiate a "sniff and pounce" program in about thirty seconds. That means if they use a credit card, cash a check, visit an ATM, pass through a tollbooth, get a parking ticket, purchase ammunition or a firearm or send an e-mail, we'll get them. Their names will be on the whole law enforcement net. But that's taking it to a whole different level, Mr Woodman. You've got to Federalize those two, give us the authority to track 'em down.'

He paused, if only for a second. He had hoped against hope that this would be a quick matter, a quick matter indeed to round up these two. Perhaps get a good hit on their vehicle, send a helicopter up there and scoop them up within the hour. That would have been perfect. No fuss, no muss. But Clem was right. If he was going to do this, he'd have to kick it up a notch. No other option. He remembered when he was a child, growing up in Kentucky. Back then a man could keep quiet, keep his head down and nobody would know a thing. His own business and affairs would belong to him and no other. But now . . . hell, you could hardly take a piss without your photo being taken and your DNA being tested and your credit record being checked. He remembered those simple times with a quick sense of nostalgia, of hunger for what had once been right in this country. All that information, everything about you, available to some fat glutton like Clem Badger and a computer. How wrong could that be?

But he also remembered his meeting with Michaelson Lurry. He remembered a dead man back in the conference room. He remembered there were only six days left. He squeezed the back of Clem's chair again.

'Go ahead,' Ira said.

'I'll need an authorization code.'

'Use my name and department. Authorization code is JERICHO.'

'Understood, sir,' Clem said, hands moving.

'And another thing.'

'Sir?'

Ira looked about the empty Op Center, the cubicles and computer screens, all holding enormous power, enormous knowledge, but only if you had the skills and commitment to use it. *Ernste Menschen.*

'I need to know what assets we have up there in that part of the state. Those two might still be on a mountain trail. They might not be mobile for a while. If so, I want some of our local people to be in a position to detain those two when the time comes. And while you're at it, make sure there's a helicopter waiting for me up top.'

Clem pulled up additional computer screens. 'What kind of assets are you looking for?'

'Law enforcement or military. Someone who'll be serious about what has to be done.'

'I'll see what we've got.'

Corinth was small, with a population of only a few hundred people, and Drew pulled the Fortress into a small service station in the center of town. He grimaced when he saw the price of gasoline. Up twenty cents per gallon since their hiking trip had started less than a week ago. The street was narrow, and part of the Fortress's bulk jutted out onto the pavement. The roadway was wet, probably from the same storm system that had almost caught them back up in the mountains. There were some small shops, two-story wooden buildings on either side, and all painted white with black shutters. Drew knew these kinds of stores, these kinds of towns. They scratched a living just outside of national forests, catching whatever cash they could from hikers and other tourists.

Across the narrow street was the Corinth general store. Sheila stepped out with her cellphone in hand. She stretched and said, 'I'm going across the way, hon. Check messages at home, and get some munchies and something to drink. Need anything?'

Yeah, he thought. Us going north. 'A Coke would be great,' he said as he headed to the pumps.

She came over to him, gave him a quick peck on the cheek. 'A Coke it is, my smelly knight.'

He watched her walk across the road, admiring yet again the way her shorts hugged her curves. Damn it, man, you've got a lot of good things going with her. Why are you trying to screw it up with this paranoia crap? Back there, with the militia checkpoint, you were about ten seconds away from running them down before recognizing who they were, a bunch of unemployed or underemployed locals, full of fear, wanting to find some reassurance with their neighbors. Fear of the battered economy, grinding along in one of the longest recessions ever. Fear that the cheap oil of the previous decade would never come back because of the fundamentalists taking over the oil fields. Fear that their jobs would be taken over by smart machinery with even smarter computer chips. Fear that in Washington their Congress was squabbling in factions and their president was strangely silent, not respond-ing to the latest crisis about his leadership, not responding to the demands of the media to hold a news conference, not responding to the rumors about his ill health.

Lots of fear out there, he thought. Lots.

'So let's keep ours under control,' he whispered as he watched the numbers roll by on the gasoline pumps.

But in any event he was going to pay in cash. No use in leaving a record.

Clem spoke up. 'Got someone. Fits the bill as best as I can figure. One Roland Gray, a deputy sheriff with the Coos County Sheriff's Department. He's within easy driving distance for any of the trailheads to the north. I'm still working on the southern and western part of the national forest.'

Ira said, 'Give him a call. Secure comm link only. Tell him to start heading to the nearest trailhead from the Recovery Center.'

'You've got it.'

When Sheila got across the street she saw a number of people sitting quietly on a long wooden bench on the front porch of the general store near a small metal sign that announced it was a Greyhound bus stop. It looked like a family, complete with Mom and Dad, Grandpa and Grandma and four kids – three sons and a daughter. They were reasonably well dressed and each had a small suitcase by their feet. As Sheila went up the steps, she overheard Mom saying to the daughter, 'I tell you, dear, we don't have money for any candy, so stop making a fuss about it.'

Sheila ran the sentence through her mind again, hearing the word 'about' pronounced 'aboot'. Canadian, that's what they must be. Poor folks, probably refugees from Quebec. Kicked out across the border with most of their possessions and land confiscated. She shuddered, wondering where they would end up. There was something called the Maple Leaf Railroad, helping the refugees out of Quebec and back into

Federal Canada, but most times the poor folks made do in the States on the kindness of churches and local charities. But with the local economy the way it was, sometimes that kindness was a little stretched.

The store was dark inside, and the crowded shelves had everything from motor oil to canned goods to fishing gear. She put her cellphone in her shorts pocket to free up her hands, picking up two cold Cokes for herself and Drew and a large bag of popcorn for herself. That should last her until she got home. At the cash register a large, older woman who had on a dungaree smock and who peered over half-glasses, counted everything up.

'That'll be four fifty, dear,' she said.

Sheila reached into her shorts pocket, pulled out a crumpled five-dollar bill. Her only cash, except for what might be back in her backpack. She passed the bill over and then noticed the racks of candy.

'Hold on, will you?'

She smiled at what she was going to do. She reached over and grabbed a handful of candy bars and other sweets, and when the store clerk tallied up the cost – it was now fifteen dollars and twelve cents – she passed over a SmartCard from the Bank of New Hampshire, which was drawn through a card reader at the side of the register.

Wait 'til those kids see this, she thought.

Ira was coming back from the men's room when Clem shouted out, his voice gleeful, 'We've got a hit! A real-time hit, about thirty seconds ago!'

Ira sprinted over to Clem and leaned over his shoulder, not making any sense out of the jumble of letters and numbers on the screen. 'What is it, what do you have?'

'SmartCard used at the Corinth general store, in Corinth, New Hampshire. On Route 302, which is west of the Recovery Center. Belonged to the woman, Sheila Cass. Total purchase was—'

'I don't give a shit what she bought,' Ira said, his chest pounding with the joy that this was almost wrapped up. 'Get that deputy sheriff on the line and get him out there. Use any means necessary to secure those two, and I mean what I say: any means necessary.'

Clem picked up the secure comm phone. 'You've got it, sir. Hey, won't Mark Quentin be happy when he hears that we've gotten these two?'

Ira nodded, tired no longer. 'I'm sure he'd be thrilled to know.'

FOUR

With the end of the Cold War, America's Army has been tested across the entire continuum of military operations . . . Closer to home, and with much less fanfare and public attention, the US Army has participated in an arguably unprecedented number and type of domestic employments. These include disaster relief operations, military support to law enforcement in the war against drugs, and discrete cases of military support to federal law enforcement agencies.

Colonel Thomas R. Lujan, *Parameters*,
Autumn 1997

Deputy Sheriff Roland Gray sped west on Route 302, his cruiser's strobe lights flashing, gripping the steering wheel so hard in excitement that he was sure there'd be imprints left from his fingers when he was done. He had been a deputy sheriff for just two years, and a member of the organization for three, and at last it had asked him to do something important.

Other work he had done over the past three years had been relatively simple stuff. Serving as a courier between households, between men he had only met once, dropping off and picking up small packages. Providing surveillance on a writer from New York City who had rented a cabin deep in the woods one winter, seeing who had come by to visit. And in one memorable instance disabling the brakes on the car of some activist woman who had been bitching in the news about the goodness of allowing homosexual teachers in the local school systems. One car accident and one obscene pay-phone call to her hospital room later, she had shut her mouth and moved to Vermont.

But today something important was going down, something important indeed. His pager had chimed about fifteen minutes ago with the message – GABRIEL TWELVE – and after a quick phone call he had been going south to the head of the Monroe Trail. And just as he had reached the trail-head there was another phone call of intense conversation – with someone who identified himself as the cell leader for all of New England – and now he was going west to Corinth, way out of his jurisdiction, but on an important mission.

He glanced down at the photo-fax that came through about two minutes ago, showing pictures of the man and woman he was to detain. Pretty straightforward business. He grinned as he looked about the interior of his cruiser. It was a new model, only a couple of months old, and had stuff that would have seemed like a dream when he first joined the Coos County Sheriff's Department. There was the com-puter console and keyboard, of course, but there was also the fax machine and the radio communication gear that could connect him to cops in San Diego, if need be. Hell, the cruiser even had one of those new autopilot systems, and he had tried it a couple of times, racing up the interstate with his arms folded, watching how the computer sensors in the car navigated him safely for miles, the tiny radar sys-tems built all around the frame detecting the road surface and any nearby traffic.

But not today. No sir. He wasn't going to rely on any hi-tech equipment to take care of today's business. It was going to be straight up and narrow, and if either of those two gave him any shit there would be serious problems. For them. The message from his cell leader – a man who only identified himself as Jericho – had given him his directions. Any means necessary to detain those two. He had been with the organization long enough to know what that meant.

Up ahead there was a line of guys in camo gear, most likely this county's militia, and he popped his siren a couple of times as he raced by. A couple of the guys waved at him, and he waved back. He knew militia members back in his own county, and rather liked them. They were guys, and some gals as well, who didn't like the way the country was heading, didn't like the way the special-interest groups were making rules and getting people fired, and didn't like the way the government was being run.

Deputy Gray agreed with them on almost every point, which is why – when asked by his uncle, a retired Army sergeant – he had enthusiastically joined the organization. He shook his head at the memory. Hell, the organization was just a name he gave it, that's all. He had no idea what it was called or how many members belonged to it or how long it had been in existence. All he knew was that he was asked to join some fellow patriots in doing what had to be done to make this country great again, and he had gladly signed up. With the news media and NewsNet channels all being controlled by the big corporations, and the lobby groups donating millions to political campaigns, what was the point in voting? Nope, it was time for something more direct than voting.

Deputy Gray's uncle was his group's cell leader, and he only knew two other members: an attorney from Concord and a lumberyard salesman from Colebrook. There were never any meetings or such – as his uncle had said, being part of the group meant that you had gone beyond meetings and into action – but he had a sense that they were part of something bigger, something huge. He grinned again, wondering if he should tell his uncle what had happened tonight. Security was important and talking out of school could get you punished, but hell, how often did you get to talk to the cell leader for all of New England?

He reached down, switched off the strobe lights, and eased up on the gas as he went through the outskirts of Corinth. Up ahead was the general store . . . and sure enough, there was the Chevrolet Fortress with the right license plate number.

Deputy Gray parked a few yards behind it and stepped out of the cruiser, the engine still running. He unsnapped the holster at his side and waited.

Yep, he had gladly signed up to make a difference, and he was damn sure he was going to make a difference in the next few minutes.

Sheila was warmed at the response of the kids when the candy was passed out, and though the parents had protested some the grandparents had intervened on the kids' behalf. The kids each grasped a piece of candy in their pudgy little hands, eyes bright with excitement, and Sheila felt good, if only for a moment. She couldn't imagine what lay ahead for this family.

She started back across the street to the Chevy Fortress. She could make out Drew inside the tiny gas station, standing in line to pay up, and she smiled at the sight. At least we're safe, she thought. We both have large chunks of money here and overseas, the house on the lake is paid for, we have six months of food stored up in the cellar. Plus Drew was on some sort of government pension and she did well with her freelance computer work, so she'd never be laid off in one of those corporate sell-offs and lay-offs that so dominated the business news nowadays. The recession was affecting a lot of people, but so far they had been lucky.

Yep, they were as safe as one could be in this decade, and while she felt bad for those poor Canadians back at the store, she knew that at least her and her man, they would do all right.

She saw some sort of police cruiser parked some yards behind the Fortress but then realized she hadn't made that phone call to check on home messages. She shifted the small bag of groceries to her other hand, and reached into her shorts back pocket for the cellphone.

When Sheila pulled the phone out, somebody started screaming at her.

Drew counted out the money again as he stood behind a stooped old man, paying for his gasoline with a fistful of quarters, nickels and dimes, which he laboriously slid across the dirty countertop. The service station was crowded with drinks coolers and racks of snacks and cigarettes, and a teenage girl was idly chewing gum as the change was placed before her. Drew took a deep breath. Relax, just relax. The Fortress is fully gassed up, the electric motor has a full charge, and we could be in a foreign country in just a few hours if need be. So relax. So what if this fueling takes care of most of our cash? There's plenty of money back home at the lake. He was looking forward to returning, to resting by the lakewaters, to feel the knots of tension in his neck and back finally drift away. Probably by tomorrow at this time he'd be laughing at himself, at how overwrought he had become.

Through the dirty windows he thought he saw Sheila walking across the street to the Fortress, and when the old man finally stepped away Drew went forward, holding out the money to the girl, who had a tattoo of a penis on her wrist, and—

A man started shouting.

The sharp, flat sounds of gunfire.

Sheila falling down.

Drew ran out of the store, the money still in his hand.

Deputy Gray hated to admit it, but when he saw the target woman walking just a few yards ahead of him he suddenly grew nervous. This wasn't escorting prisoners from the local lock-ups to the county jail. This wasn't serving subpoenas or eviction notices to people living in the homes and trailer parks of the county. This wasn't providing back-up to the State Police or the local police. Nope, this was it, this was some serious shit about ready to happen, and as he reached down for his service pistol he remembered a night in a hunting cabin up past Berlin, a gas stove hissing its light against the darkness and his uncle speaking quietly as he was recruited: 'We have a window of opportunity over the next few years to take this country back, to do what has to be done to set things right, but only if we have the right, strong, God-fearing men and women who have the guts to see it through.'

He pulled his pistol out, yelled, 'Down! Down on the ground! Right now!'

But the woman pulled something black and angular out of

her pocket, was turning to him, was holding it in her hand, was pointing it at him—

Gun!

He opened fire.

With the first gunshot Sheila dropped the groceries and fell to the ground, skinning her knees, feeling the pavement's wetness, and the gunfire went on and on, and she quickly crawled in front of the Chevy Fortress, screaming at the man to stop shooting, screaming for Drew, just screaming. The gunfire would not stop, would not end, as the rounds started hitting the Fortress, the sound of the bullets as they passed through the metal turning her insides to water, and she felt herself shriek as the bullets screamed overhead.

Drew was outside of the service station, the sound of the gunfire bringing it all back, all he had tried to hide and put away since being pensioned off, but too late to worry about that now, because that son-of-a-bitch was out on the street, firing at his woman. He felt everything slow down and compress as he took in the scene, took in the surroundings. A light brown sheriff's cruiser from Coos County was parked near him, the engine running. The deputy sheriff, in a tan and light brown uniform, was in the middle of the street, exposed, shooting at the Fortress. Where was Sheila? The deputy kept on firing and didn't even pause when the clip was exhausted, popping out the empty and replacing it. Where was Sheila?

People on the porch of the general store were bailing out, were running inside, running to hide behind other parked cars. He heard her screams. By the entrance to the gas station were some tools for sale, rakes and shovels and axe handles. He picked up an axe handle and trotted to the street, moving in an arc so the cop's peripheral vision couldn't spot him. Damn it, why was the cop firing at Sheila, firing at his woman?

Focus, pay attention. Plenty of time for that later.

He moved as quickly and quietly as possible, right up the middle of the fucking road, axe handle in his hand, holding it like a baseball bat, when one of the citizens cowering by the sidewalk yelled out a warning. The cop – whose reddish hair was cut in a crewcut – started to turn, started to bring his weapon to bear upon Drew, Drew recognizing it as a 10 mm Glock semi-automatic pistol, a hell of a reliable gun, and Drew was recalling how many rounds each clip took as he buried the end of the axe handle into the cop's face.

The gunfire stopped but Sheila couldn't move. She was hunkered up in a ball, the cellphone in her hand, and a small part of her mind, the very small part that was remaining rational in all this craziness, said, well, we've got the phone. Why don't we call the cops?

Because that was a cop shooting at us, that's why, stupid!

The cop fell down like a sack of cement, the rear of his head striking the pavement, mouth opened up in pain. Drew saw the weapon clatter to the ground, and he kicked it away. He rapped the axe handle against the deputy's forehead and enjoyed the sensation of the wood vibrating in his hand as the wood struck bone. The cop was gurgling through a broken nose and Drew took the handle back and swung with all his might, like those softball games back at Fort Bragg during those alerts, passing the time, and blasted the handle into the cop's crotch. He howled and hunched over in a ball.

Drew looked up. 'Sheila!'

Her head, shaking, peered out from the edge of the Fortress's front fender.

He dropped the axe handle and raced over to her, and she was crying, running to him, hands held open for a hug—

Drew held her at arm's length. 'Are you all right?'

She was weeping, chin quivering, 'Why? Why was he shooting at me? Why, oh shit . . . I was so scared . . . I was so fucking scared . . .'

He looked at her critically, started patting down her arms, her torso, moving her around, looking for rips in the clothing, looking for wetness, looking for blood. Her hands were scraped, but that's all right. He ran a hand across the back of her head, feeling her hair, not feeling blood, not feeling anything matted, not feeling the sharpness of bone. Good. A glance back. The deputy sheriff was rolling back and forth, keening in pain. People were beginning to stand up from their hiding places, pointing and talking and looking in their direction. He saw a teenage boy run to a phone at the corner of the general store, pick up the receiver and start dialing.

He tried to keep his voice level. 'Sheila, we have got to get the hell out of here, right now. Do you understand? Right now.'

She could only nod. He went around to the driver's side of the Fortress and then stopped.

Three out of the four tires were shot through and flattened.

She moved in a daze, that little rational voice saying, girl, when this is over you are going to have one long drunken collapse, and a well-deserved one. Drew was talking, his voice louder than before, and she put her cellphone back in her shorts – what in hell was that out for anyway? – and helped him empty the Chevy Fortress of their gear, which was dumped in the back of the police cruiser. The same cruiser with the cop that had slowly rolled onto this street not five minutes ago and had torn everything up, torn everything asunder, and if she hadn't been so scared she would have run over to those Canadian refugees and begged and pleaded to go along with them.

Drew bundled her into the front of the police cruiser and jumped in next to her. He backed up the cruiser and swerved around, and she thought to point out something to Drew, that they were stealing a police cruiser and that was definitely not a good thing, but she found her mouth was so dry that her tongue couldn't move.

Ira couldn't hear much but he didn't like what he was hearing. Clem's face looked even more pale in the subdued lighting in the Op Center, and he murmured, 'Yeah, yeah,' a few times, and then said at the end, 'Keep cool and keep your phone next to you. We'll be in touch.'

He sighed as he put the phone down and Ira took a deep breath, stomach now doing dips and dives, knowing that in a day or two he might be meeting Mark Quentin in the Great Beyond because of what was going to happen in the next hour or so.

'Failure?' Ira asked.

'Failure? Mr Woodman, that word doesn't even begin to enter the arena of the foul-up that just took place up there.'

Ira snapped, 'Spare me the dark words, just tell me what happened.'

Clem spoke quickly as his fingers flew across the keyboard. 'It seems our hero cop up north came across the vehicle and the female subject, the woman named Sheila, right in downtown Corinth, however big a downtown such a shitty little place has. Instead of quietly detaining her, he tried to shoot her in front of about a dozen witnesses.'

'He tried to do what?' Ira yelled.

'Shoot her, that's what. He thought she had a weapon and was threatening him so he opened fire.'

'Is she wounded? Dead?'

'Nope, but the deputy's one hurting fellow. It seems that while he was popping off the rounds, Sheila's boyfriend, that Drew character, attacked him with a baseball bat or something. End result, you've got a deputy with a broken nose and other injuries, and a stolen police cruiser. You see, the deputy also disabled their vehicle.'

'Mother of . . .'

'Yep, and the two subjects, probably now aware that something is amiss, are heading out of town in the deputy's cruiser.'

Ira pulled an empty chair over and sat down. Shoot-out. With witnesses. And a stolen police cruiser. And just a few days left, just a handful of days left and all of the years of prep work and sacrifice, now converging on this little hole in the ground and the actions of some nitwit deputy a couple of hundred miles north. He felt like dropping his head in his hands.

Clem looked over and laughed. Ira snapped his head up. 'What the hell is so goddamn funny?'

'Just your look, Mr Woodman, just your look. Hey, they stole a police cruiser. I've activated the cruiser's transponder. I know exactly where they are, and where they're headed.

Plus we have another asset up there, one I've just put a call into. A military asset. One that I guarantee won't screw up like that deputy.'

Ira stood up, his anger gone. 'I thought you said there were no military assets available up there.'

Clem pointed to his computer screen. 'This one just arrived.'

Army Chief Warrant Officer Eugene Parker keyed his microphone again and said, 'Control, please repeat last, over.'

The static-underlined female voice of the military air traffic control for northern New England said, 'Raptor Nine, Raptor Nine, prepare to receive KEYSTONE message. Prepare to receive KEYSTONE message. Over.'

'Control, Raptor Nine, understood.'

He moved his head some and stretched off to the left in the deepening twilight saw the running lights from the flight of Apache AH-64 attack helicopters that were heading back to their base at Plattsburgh in New York following a training mission in a stretch of Federal lands in Maine. The last couple of hours had been spent running missions, shooting up and destroying old Soviet-style armor that were lined up in a mock village set among the Maine hills. It had been a blast but he sure wished that he'd get deployed for something real, something where he could show off his skills. Last year he had spent six months in the American Relief Mandate in Nigeria, protecting the oil facilities there, but nothing had happened, except for the daily grind of patrols up and down the Biafran coast.

Today's drill had been a bit sour, too. One of the Apaches was scrubbed back at base when its engine wouldn't start, and another had to turn back on the way to Maine because of low oil pressure. Same old story. Too few maintenance personnel and maintenance dollars. Now they were over the White Mountains of New Hampshire, less than an hour or so from landing and having a couple of cold ones. Below him the peaks of the mountains fell away as they headed west.

Another voice came into his headphones. 'Gene, what do you think?'

'Trying not to think,' he replied, speaking to his weapons officer, Sergeant Tony Demko, sitting before him, three feet ahead. 'Can't recall anyone in the squadron ever receiving a KEYSTONE message.'

'Must be serious shit then, to call us in. What do you think? Terrorists? Hit squads from Quebec?'

The female voice returned. 'Raptor Nine, KEYSTONE message follows. A deputy sheriff was attacked less than fifteen minutes ago and his cruiser stolen. Cruiser heading to Interstate 93, north of the Piscassic River. Cruiser transponder code is CSSD Twelve. Cruiser containing two fugitives. Fugitives have been Federalized. You are authorized to terminate. Repeat, you are authorized to terminate. Authorization code is JERICHO. Repeat, authorization code is JERICHO.'

Parker pressed the transmit switch. 'Understood. Cruiser transponder code is CSSD Twelve. Fugitives have been Federalized. Authorization code is JERICHO. Raptor Nine, out.'

He moved the control stick gently to the right, depressing the cyclic pedals as well, and he noted the running lights of his flight falling away to the left. This will be a hell of a story to tell them later, except of course, it was a KEYSTONE mission, and those were never discussed after completion. Never.

Demko came back on the helicopter's intercom. 'A KEY-STONE message, and a JERICHO authorization . . . Do you think this is it?'

'I don't know,' Parker said. 'I'm just doing my part. Same as you.'

'Roger that,' Demko said. 'And God bless.'

'God bless,' Parker said, increasing the Apache's speed, eager to complete his mission this evening. Up north were two enemies, two enemies of this great nation that needed help to regain its greatness, and Chief Warrant Officer Parker was going to ensure that these two enemies did not live through the night.

Drew drove fast, using the cruiser's strobe lights to get traffic out of the way, and he noted with small – very small! – amusement the line of militia men, some of whom waved as he sped by. He spotted the gear along the dashboard and between the driver and passenger seats of the Ford Crown Victoria. Pretty elaborate set up for a county sheriff. Full computerized autopilot. Computer screen and keyboard. Printer and fax. He glanced down and saw a sheet of paper, picked it up and glanced at it. So that's what happened. He looked over at Sheila. She was curled up against the passenger door, hugging herself. Drew handed it over.

'Take a look.'

Her voice was quiet. 'I don't want to.'

'But there's the reason,' he said. 'The reason you were attacked. Right there.'

Sheila took the paper from Drew's hand and then sat up and looked over, face troubled. Her eyes were red-rimmed from crying but there were no tears now. 'Those are pictures, of the two of us. Our driver's licenses and . . .'

'Surveillance photos, taken when we were in that bomb shelter earlier today.'

She looked down and shook her head. 'All of this . . . for trespassing?'

A pickup truck and then another pulled to the side as Drew sounded the siren for a moment and he had to raise his voice over the noise. 'No, not trespassing. Not at all. This cruiser and that deputy back there, they were from Coos County. Honey, we're in Grafton County. This guy wouldn't have come after the two of us for simple trespassing, no sir.'

'Then what happened?'

Lots of things had happened, lots, he thought. And nothing good was on the horizon, no sir. He slowed down as the exit sign for the interstate came up and reached down and switched off the overhead strobe lights. On both sides of the road were some pine and oak trees, the oak trees' leaves quite colorful, orange and yellow. It was getting towards dusk. Damn this day. If he had been more direct, more forceful, he could have convinced her and they would be well along this interstate, heading up to Federal Canada and safety. But now . . . The bad guys, whoever they are, were now after them in full flight, in full terror, and he knew he and Sheila were running out of time. He checked the fuel gauge. Almost full. Plenty of distance that could be covered if he planned it right.

'What happened is that someone got pissed at us, severely pissed. Someone connected to that bomb shelter, someone who has friends around here. A message probably was sent out. Either capture or kill us.'

'Kill us! For trespassing?'

There, look at that. Up ahead, just past the exit. A country store, just around the bend. Lights were on. Good. Time to stock up on some supplies.

'No, not trespassing. We found something out, something that has to be kept secret, that's what I'm figuring.'

Sheila said, 'That Shiloh thing. With the date that's coming up. Do you think that's it?'

He sped past the exit and pulled in near the store, close enough to walk over to it but far enough away that the clerk couldn't see what they were driving. He braked and put the cruiser into park and said, 'What I'm thinking is that we've got to get some supplies, and fast. Come along.'

And as he stepped out, he heard the sound of thunder again in the distance.

Several minutes later the helicopter's intercom came to life. 'Got 'em, Gene. About two miles up, northbound lane of the interstate. Transponder code matches, got two heat sources in the front seat. Man, they are moving. About ninety miles an hour.'

Parker said, 'Roger that. Arming weapons system.'

'Confirm, weapons system armed.'

Before Parker the universe was now a light green, and he felt a sense of wonder and fulfillment, speeding ahead at such a rate of speed, seeing the hills and the roadway and the moving vehicles in a light, ghostly green. At times like this, he knew what it felt like to be a hawk, lord and master of the terrain, on the hunt, fearing nothing and knowing that you had the power over life and death over the creatures below you. Everything seen through his faceplate was the same nightscope tinge, except for that moving vehicle in the left-hand lane of the interstate, the one with the target reticle lit up over it in a deadly red.

'Target acquired,' Parker said. 'One burst should do it.'

'Roger, sir, one burst. Don't want to frighten any of the other commuters tonight.'

'That's for sure. All right, here we go.'

It was fifteen minutes after they left the country store when Sheila said, 'Drew, I think I hear a helicopter.'

'I do, too.'

'Drew, I'm scared.'

He reached over, took her hand. 'I know.'

It was just like a practice session, that's all, as the target closed in and he held the firing switch down for a full second, and he could actually see the tracers interspersed with the .30 caliber armor-piercing rounds that squirted ahead of the attack helicopter. The roof of the stolen police cruiser seemed to disintegrate in a flower of flame and debris, and in another second it swerved off to the left, pitched over a guardrail, and tumbled into a ravine. He barely noted the other traffic braking to a halt, and imagined for a moment the dinnertime conversations that would be taking place later tonight. Honey, I was coming home and missed being turned into bloody hamburger because of one lane change . . .

He put the Apache into a tight turn and came back and hovered for another moment, then, just for good measure, sent another burst of rounds into the overturned wreckage. As he pulled up and left the area, he switched on the radio.

'Control, control, control, this is Raptor Nine. Over.'

'Raptor Nine, control. Go head. Over.'

'Control, Raptor Nine. KEYSTONE mission accomplished. Repeat, KEYSTONE mission accomplished.'

'Roger that, Raptor Nine. Come on back home now, why don't you?'

He double-clicked the key mike twice for an answer and then headed the Apache northwest, back to Plattsburgh. All in all they'd be about twenty minutes late getting back to base, which was pretty fine considering what they had just accomplished.

Demko came back on the line. 'Good job, sir. Right down the middle.'

'Thanks.'

'But Gene . . .'

'Yeah?'

A sigh. 'Don't you think that second pass was too much? A bit overkill?'

'Why, are you going soft on me?'

A laugh. 'No, I just want to make sure we left enough to identify.'

Parker laughed in return. 'Aren't we being considerate tonight?'

'It was a thought. Man, I took a look back and that fucker is still burning.'

'Good,' he said, as he looked ahead and saw everything in front of him turn back to that God-loving light green, no enemies or red targets in sight. It had been a good day.

FIVE

The Constitution of the United States, for instance, is a marvelous document for self-government by Christian people. But the minute you turn the document into the hands of non-Christian and atheistic people they can use it to destroy the very foundation of our society.

Pat Robertson, televangelist and presidential candidate, December 30, 1981

Ira Woodman felt his stomach do a little queasy flip-flop as the FERA helicopter flared down into a landing on a blocked-off stretch of interstate in upstate New Hampshire. He wasn't too sure what was causing that reaction: the way the pilot had brought the helicopter down onto the pavement in such a quick movement, or the sight of all those lights, up and down the highway. My God, will you look at that circus? In all directions police cruisers were pulled over to the side, there were at least three fire trucks, and the bright camera lights of a news van were spotlighting the overturned police cruiser halfway down a wooded ravine off to the left.

He stepped out in a blur of lights and noise, briefcase in hand, as the FERA pilot throttled back the engine. Henry Harrison followed, as well as Clem Badger and Tanya

Selenekov from the rear seats. It was now dark and the different-colored strobe lights illuminating the scene gave him a headache. What a mess. If he didn't pull something good out of this he was sure he was going on Director Lurry's list, and that list tonight ain't a Christmas list. At least there was an evidence tape cordoning off part of the mess, and as he walked to a crumpled section of guardrail he caught the scent of burned rubber, gasoline and smoke. A couple of firefighters were trudging up the side of the ravine, rolling up a length of firehose. Flares had been set out on the middle of the roadway, and traffic, as best as he could make out, was backed up for miles.

'Henry, go down to that cruiser and see what we've got,' Ira said, raising his voice over the sound of the engines. 'Clem, find out who in hell is in charge of this mess. Tanya, I'm going to need some wordsmithing to get us out of this one tonight. Be creative.'

Ira rested the briefcase on the ground and put both of his hands in his coat pockets. It was pretty damn cold up here in these mountains, and he wished again that he could have stayed back home in Kentucky. By now he would have been the head of the State Police, running his own show, with the perks and budget and responsibilities that were rightfully his. But no, duty called, duty in the name of one Michaelson Lurry, and he had gladly followed the man and gone where he had been needed, which was the cold Northeast and the six New England states. FERA had nine regions of responsibility in the United States, and this one belonged to him. Still, sometimes he missed those hills and bluegrass fields and small towns back home so much that it made part of him ache.

He looked over at the wreckage of the cruiser and felt a brief pang of regret. He wished it could have been different, for he would have loved to have had these two in custody, to debrief them and find out just how much they had learned while they had been inside the Recovery Center. Sure, it did look like a case of mistaken entry, a foul-up that had allowed them to gain access, but Ira would have liked to have been certain. With Case Shiloh coming due next week he wanted all loose ends tidied up. Which was why that helicopter crew had received the orders they had, under the KEYSTONE program, where US military forces could be called upon to be temporarily assigned to other Federal agencies, such as FERA, the Justice Department, CIA, Interior Department, whatever. Ira had given that clown deputy sheriff a chance to clean it up, and he had failed. No more second chances.

'Mr Woodman!' came a voice. He turned and saw the bulk of Clem Badger approaching, a tan coat tangled about his pudgy legs. A uniformed New Hampshire State Police officer was with him, wearing a dark green coat, a wide-brimmed 'Smokey' hat and one pissed-off expression on his reddened and clean-shaven face.

Clem made the introductions, puffing from exertion. 'Mr Woodman, this is Captain Moorland, of the State Police. He's in charge of the scene.'

Captain Moorland didn't offer a hand and Ira didn't mind. He knew from experience what was going on in this officer's mind, and he hated what he was going to do next. After all, in another time, they would have been brother officers. But duty was duty. Ira reached into his inside coat pocket, pulled out a thin leather wallet, flipped it open.

'Captain Moorland, Ira Woodman, Federal Emergency Response Agency.'

The state police officer barely glanced down at the identification and said, 'So?'

Ira sighed, put the wallet back into his coat. 'Captain, under the Domestic Terrorism and Tranquility Act of 2001, I'm assuming command of this crime scene. We have reason to believe that the individuals in that police cruiser are members of a terrorist organization. Those two individuals were Federalized not more than an hour ago. I appreciate your assistance and cooperation, and I will ensure that you will receive a full report from my office when our investigation is completed.'

'What kind of terrorists are you talking about?' Captain Moorland demanded.

Another shout, and Ira looked over and saw Henry Harrison, waving at him. Ira went on. 'You'll be informed at the proper time, when our investigation is complete.'

'Hey, wait a minute—'

'Captain,' Ira said. 'You're wasting my time and wasting yours. Check with your department's standing orders. You'll see all is in order, under that 2001 Act of Congress. Now, if you'll excuse me, I've got important work to do.'

And damn it, the State Police officer actually grinned. 'Sure, go ahead. Goddamn Feds, think you know every-thing . . .'

Ira stepped over the guardrail, being careful not to lose his balance while carrying the briefcase. He stepped down the side of the embankment, remembering all of those traf-fic accidents he had investigated back home, how after a while there was a certain sameness to them all. The same smells of oil and gasoline, the sights of broken glass and crumpled metal, and the sounds, the same sounds. The engines of the rescue apparatus, the whine of power tools, and more often than not, the screams or sobs of the victims or the survivors.

He looked at the burned-out wreckage of the cruiser on its roof, the insignia of the county sheriff's department charred away on the side, the wheels shredded with hanging flaps of rubber from the helicopter's cannon rounds. No sounds coming from this mess, no sir. Squatting next to the wreckage was Henry Harrison, who was wearing a knee-length fur coat to ward off the chilly air. Ira wasn't sure, but he thought Henry was a fur-buster, a guy who liked to dress up in fur and go out in public in order to receive taunts and insults from the animal rights kooks and then have a perfect excuse to break someone's face. It seemed to fit Henry's character.

Henry looked tired, a large flashlight in his beefy hands. As Ira got closer, there was another scent, an odd, charred odor. What could that be?

His admin aide spoke up. 'Well, we've got something here, but you're not going to like it.'

Ira put his briefcase down. 'Show me.'

He knelt down next to Henry, who shone his light into the interior of the cruiser. The roof was crumpled in and there wasn't much room to see, but he could make out wisps of smoke, twisted pieces of radio and computer gear, burned papers, and two forms, still buckled in. They were charred black and something odd was tumbling out of them, as if their skin had burst and their organs, round and bulbous, had oozed out, the two of them losing legs and arms in the process. And that smell reminded him of cooking, but why in hell—

Ira sat back up, looked at Henry. 'Those aren't bodies in there, right?'

Henry nodded. 'Best I can tell, we're looking at fifty-pound sacks of potatoes.'

'Potatoes?' Now the smell was explained. Burned potatoes.

Henry sat back, the flashlight dangling between his legs.

'Little piece of tradecraft that not many people know about. You take a late model cruiser like this, the one with the autopilot system so you can sit back and get a BJ from your girlfriend while cruising the highway? Well, there's a couple of sensors installed so that someone has to be in the front seat before it's activated. You don't want some kids stealing a car and sending it empty to New York City for the hell of it. No, there's both a weight and thermal sensor up forward to indicate that a body of a certain mass is in charge. Fine. But if you pop a couple of circuit breakers, then that system isn't so hot. You can fool it. Fool it with a hundred pounds of potatoes and' – Henry got up, poked around in the debris and pulled out a crumpled can – 'a couple of cans of lit Sterno. Just like this guy did to us.'

Now he knew why that State Police captain had been grinning at him back up on the highway. 'Department of Agriculture.'

'What?'

Ira said, 'Department of Agriculture. We did a trace on this guy, this Drew Connor. Records indicated that he was retired Department of Agriculture.'

Henry laughed. 'Shit, sir, this wasn't no Aggie guy. Hell, you pull up my record without too much digging, and you know what you find out about me when I was in the Navy? That I was a cook, that's what. No, Mr Woodman, this guy is more than you think he is. You better get that tubbo Clem working on really digging for his record, and I mean serious digging. We've got to know what we're up against and so far . . .' Henry looked around him, at all the lights and the vehicles and the destroyed cruiser. 'So far, he's winning.'

Ira nodded and stood up. 'So far, you're right. Come along, Henry, we'll let the locals clean this mess up. We've got a long night ahead of us.'

They both started going back up to the highway, and Ira kept up a narrative as they made their way up the embankment. 'First up, we'll need Clem to do a full dig on these two. I want to know anything and everything about this man and woman. Hell, if they bought a newspaper last week, I want to know which one. Second, we've got to work with Tanya to get a story out, something about these two so that we can get the local law enforcement involved. Something serious, something that will make every cop, every sheriff, every game officer within a hundred miles eager to track them down and then turn them over to us. We don't have the resources for such a search.'

Ira stopped, a bit out of breath. Damn all this desk work. He couldn't remember ever being so much out of shape. Henry said, 'That might be a problem. So far there's nothing that serious. Just a stolen cruiser, that's all. That might not be enough to get the right people that spun up.'

There was a voice from down in the ravine. A man emerged from the underbrush and woods, walking unsteadily. He came towards them, talking with every step, but Ira couldn't make out what he was saying until he came within a few feet of them.

'Did you get 'im? Did you get 'im? Oh, Christ, my nose 'urts, it 'urts so fuckin' much.'

Now Ira saw that the man was a police officer of some sort holding a bloody handkerchief to his face, walking awkwardly, and Henry stepped up. 'Who the hell are you?'

He took his handkerchief away, showing a swollen and bloody nose, a split lip and a forehead that had a lump the size of a hen's egg in the center. He coughed up some blood and said, 'Deputy Sheriff Gray. I'm the one who got ambushed by that fucker. I commandeered a civilian car from Corinth and got here as fast as I could. Is he in there? Is he dead? Is he?'

Ira looked at the miserable bloody man in front of him and took a deep breath, ready to chew him out at least two new body orifices, when Henry calmly said, 'Sir, remember that problem we were just discussing.'

'What problem?'

'You know, the one about impact. I think Deputy Gray here might be in a position to help us out. Deputy Gray, did anyone see you come to the scene?'

The man shook his head and winced as he dabbed at his lip with the handkerchief. 'No. Traffic was so backed up I dumped the car and walked over here on the southbound lane. Spent the past half hour thrashing around the fuckin' ravine, tryin' to get up here.'

Ira calmed down. Of course. What an opportunity, and it was times like these that he was certain that all would be right, all would come together. It had to be Divine Intervention that brought this little failure of a man to him at just the right time.

'Deputy Gray, do you know who I am?'

'Uh, no sir.'

'We contacted you earlier. Your codename is Gabriel Twelve. And mine is Jericho.'

The handkerchief came down from his face and he blinked twice. 'Jericho? Sir?'

Ira put his arm on the man's shoulder. 'How long have you been with us?'

'About three years, sir.'

'And am I right in assuming that you are completely and utterly devoted to our cause? And that you would do anything, anything at all to further our goals?'

An enthusiastic nod. 'That's right, sir. Without a doubt.'

Ira gently slapped him on the shoulder. 'Very good. That's exactly what I expected, and I know we're going to ultimately succeed with your kind of man within our organization. Mr Harrison.'

'Sir,' Henry said, stepping closer.

'Deputy Gray has agreed to assist us in a delicate manner. Could you please brief him down by the cruiser, perhaps behind that area of brush?'

'Absolutely, sir.'

Ira hefted up his briefcase. 'Will you be needing this?'

Henry smiled. 'No, not tonight, sir. Deputy Gray, if you will.'

As the two of them descended back to the cruiser, Ira waited and said a little prayer. The good Lord was certainly testing him tonight, and he had tried to do his best, every waking second, minute and hour, to do what was right. Lord, he thought, I know you're testing me, and that is good. But please let us succeed, oh, please let us succeed in doing what must be done. *I am the Grand High Executioner* . . .

Down below, from an area of brush and sapling, there was a small yelp, and then a snap, as if a twig had been broken. In another moment Henry reappeared, wiping his hands on a handkerchief. Returning to Ira he said, 'Sure is nice to get some hands-on work every now and then.'

Ira resumed walking, the briefcase thumping against his legs. 'I have a feeling you'll be doing a lot more before this is over.'

'Hey, thanks.'

Sheila was breathing heavy, the backpack on her back seemingly gaining an extra pound of weight with each step taken.

Before her in the darkness was Drew, who hadn't said more than a dribble of words over the past half-hour. When it was getting past dusk she had gone to dig out her flashlight, but he said, 'No,' in a quiet, curt voice that she had never heard before. He had hauled out a small length of rope and tied it off to his belt, handing the free end to her. 'Can't risk having a light out for any length of time. Use this to follow me.'

She had no idea where they were. Again, Drew hadn't been much for saying a damn word. After setting the police cruiser north on the interstate, Drew had taken out his pistol and holster and was now wearing it at his side. Any other time the sight would have frightened her. She didn't like his collection of guns and had only reluctantly learned how to use them, though she still hated them. Now, she was disgusted to admit, the sight of Drew's pistol was comforting. They had bushwhacked away from the interstate, following a power line that had a cleared right-of-way underneath it. It was almost like being on a regular trail and they had made good time, but after hearing the helicopter roar past them, heading to the interstate, he had veered off to the west. And she only knew that because of the setting sun, up there past the mountains. Now they were in deep woods, so dark that she couldn't even identify the trees they were passing except for an occasional birch, the stark whiteness of the trunk suddenly looming out at her as she went by.

But Drew seemed to know where he was going, or at least was making his own trail. In his hands Drew had a folded-over topo map and a small flashlight, which he lit up for a second or two every few minutes or so to see his way. Sheila again was disgusted at how she felt. I am a grown woman, she thought. I have my own business. I make enough money each year to set me up in the top 10 percent income bracket,

I threw out my first husband when I realized what a jerk he was, and I managed to get through Stanford even when I lost all financial aid and scholarships. After Stanford I even left California in under a day when I thought things were getting too hairy with my new line of work. So I should be demanding to know where we are going. I should be in control here, in equal partnership with my lover, determining what to do next.

Oh, shut up, she thought, as she stumbled over a tree root for a moment, not letting go of the rope leading to Drew. Next thing you know, we'll be singing a chorus of 'I Am Woman, Hear Me Roar'. Let's face facts, shall we? The fact is we are scared out of our wits. The fact is we were never so happy as when we saw Drew back in that town beating in the head of the deputy who had been shooting at me.

The fact is – and as much as you'd hated to admit it – while it's nice to be a woman of the new millennium, confident in who she is and what she can do, it's even better to have a strong man on your side, a strong man like Drew, when the bullets start flying in your direction.

Even if the lovely son-of-a-bitch wasn't saying a word.

I do love you, she thought, feeling the backpack gain another pound on her tired shoulders, but I also love a hot shower, clean sheets and a hot meal, and I would love so very much not to be scared any more.

Scared. She remembered being back in Stanford as a student, how scared one could be, and it was all because of lack of money. One day in her apartment she sat on her bed, back up against the wall, looking at the pile of bills before her, plus a snotty handwritten note from Margaret, who subleased the apartment to Sheila and their other roommate, a girl named Terry. Margaret was oh-so-politely telling Sheila that if she didn't pay her share of the phone and the rent within one week the locks would be changed and her stuff dumped on the sidewalk. Have a nice frigging day.

She had crumpled up the note and looked across the tiny room. I will not cry, she said to herself as the tears started trickling down her cheeks. I will not cry. I will think of something, something right away, because I have just one semester left, just one blasted semester, and all I need is to get over this hump. Just this little hump, which has grown to the size of Mount Everest.

Money problems. Quite a simple phrase, with plenty of blame to go around. She could blame herself, for not saving more during the summers, for not getting better jobs than freelance tech assistance at the Silicon Valley companies that flourished around Stanford. Maybe blame Mom and Dad, for running a gift shop in Portland, which meant she was ineligible for most student aid and loans. And maybe blame those damn baby boomers, the most spoiled generation ever on this planet, who were so frightened that their Social Security and Medicare and Medicaid were going to be altered, and who badgered those weak-knees in Congress to take funds from Pile A (student assistance) and transfer it to Pile B (greedy baby boomers who think the universe revolves around their needs).

There had been a knock on the door. Probably Margaret, wanting to know what Sheila had planned. Beats the shit out of me, dearie, since my checking account currently has a balance of eighteen dollars and fifteen cents.

'Yeah, who is it?'

'It's Donna, Sheila. Do you know where Terry is?'

'No, I . . . uh, I uh . . .' Shit, the tears were flowing now.

Donna came in, Terry's good friend. She was athletic, with long red hair and a bright smile, a sports marketing major, and when she saw Sheila's tears she sat down next to her and said, 'What's wrong?' Sheila let it all out, in one ten-minute sobfest and gabfest. Donna nodded and crossed her legs. She had on white shorts and a bright pink polo shirt and said, 'I take it all of the customary and usual avenues have been exhausted.'

'Oh, Christ, yes,' Sheila said. 'There's not a waitressing job or tech assistance job to be found in the Valley. About several thousand other students and me were given the old heave-ho this past month alone.'

Donna nodded. 'I know the drill, hon. Same thing happened to me last year. Look . . . can I make a suggestion, if you promise not to get mad?'

She looked over at Donna, hands still holding her bills. 'Sure. Why not?'

'Kid, for the past year I've been a CyberGal, and you would not believe the money I'm making,' she said. 'And it's so easy, you can practically do it in your sleep.'

It had taken a week of convincing, but in the end she had gone with Donna to her contact. He was in a rundown section of East Palo Alto – a place Sheila never knew even existed! – and had his business set up in a basement of a three-story apartment building. He was tall and gaunt, and his skin was the color of old paper. No names were exchanged and Donna had agreed to front the money for Sheila, which made her even more uncomfortable. Donna had noticed this and said, 'Relax, kid. In a month you'll be making more money than you can imagine.'

She rubbed at her arms. The basement was cool and damp. 'I've got a hell of an imagination, but I don't need that

much money. Just enough to pay the rent and get through
school and get out.'

Donna said, 'Well, you'll see. Once you've got money
coming in . . . Oh, and one more thing.'

'Yes?'

She touched her arm, just briefly. 'When he's photo-
graphing you, pretend you're on your back, in the OB/GYN
office. It's the best way to get through it. Trust me, I know.'

Then she left, and for the next several hours Sheila did
just that, staring at a far point on the wall as the photographer did his work with an extensive network of digital
motion and still cameras. She disrobed and shivered in the
damp air and walked and moved and jumped and sat and
smiled and frowned and bent over and did everything she
was told. She tried not to see the dead eyes of the photographer or the flashes of the cameras. All she saw in her mind's
eye was the stack of bills back home.

Later, she went home and threw up and stayed in bed for
a full day.

And later, too, she thought she could never be frightened
as much ever again.

Until today, she thought, stumbling again, following
Drew into the dark woods. Until today.

About a half-hour after Deputy Gray volunteered his last
service to the cause, a mobile support van belonging to
FERA Region One had arrived. Ira was in a small conference
room at the rear, as Tanya Selenekov finished writing up a
statement that was going to be released to the ever demanding news media outside. There were at least two television
stations from New Hampshire, one from Vermont, three
from Massachusetts and a handful of writers for the local

newspapers, NewsNet and wire services. Tanya was a strong-willed woman, with a loud voice and white-blonde hair that almost hurt one's eyes to look at. She smoked the occasional cigarette, and, to Ira's dismay, also favored wearing short skirts. He admitted that she did have a nice pair of legs, but there was a vocal contingent in the Shiloh task force that wanted to get skirts that short banned once things were underway.

That was another problem, for another day, probably another year. There were more important things to worry about, and Tanya seemed to sense that when Ira came in through the rear door. She was at a small round conference table, working on a lapbot. Behind her was a low shelf filled with communications equipment, television screens, and a computer printer, and there was the low murmur of a power generator coming from the rear.

'Just a few more moments, and I'll have a draft for you to look at,' she said, her voice still betraying the ten years as a youth growing up in Moscow.

'Fine,' he said. 'I'll be curious to see what you've come up with.'

She smiled and swiveled in her chair as the printer came to life. Three sheets of paper came out, each with the logo of FERA and *Official News Release* emblazoned across the top. Ira started reading, and about halfway down the first page looked up.

'That's a hell of a gamble, saying those two might be linked to the Church of the Final Apocalypse.'

She shrugged, started going through a pack of cigarettes. The ration and tax sticker on the side of the package was a bright orange. 'If we want the police agencies to be serious in looking for them, I thought it might work. Don't you agree?'

Ira hated to admit it, but she was right. Late last year, an outbreak of anthrax had killed hundreds in Detroit. Later it turned out that one of the many apocalyptic sects that had sprouted up at the start of the new century had been responsible for spreading the disease. This particular church – which boasted a few hundred members, mostly linked on the Net – had been disappointed that the world hadn't ended on a certain December 31 and were determined to help things along on their own. Its members were still hunted, city by city, state by state. Saying that the man and woman responsible for killing a sheriff's deputy and stealing his cruiser were linked to this group would even get local citizens – militia or not – out in the countryside looking for them.

He said, 'Someone starts digging, they might find out that we were stretching the truth.'

'Which is why in the second paragraph, I said "believed to be linked". That gives us an out, am I right?' She lit up her cigarette. 'Besides, in about a week it won't make much difference, will it?'

Again, she was right. He kept silent as he read through the last of the pages, then took a pen and signed each sheet, okaying it for distribution. Tanya took a deep puff and said, 'I wish I was trusted enough so that I would know what is to happen on the nineteenth.'

'Not a matter of trust, you know that, Tanya,' he said, passing the news release back over to her. 'It's a matter of security. The smaller the number of people, the smaller the chances of a leak. No one doubts your commitment and dedication. Of that I'm certain.'

She slowly nodded as she took the papers from his hand. 'I remember many things as a young girl growing up in

Moscow. I remember the long winters, when sometimes we lived on potato soup, day after day. I remember the street demonstrations, the people waving banners, demanding jobs, demanding bread, before the police came in and attacked them. I even remember seeing the fat politicians on the television. The communists, the capitalists, the anarchists, the fascists, all of them promising to make things right, all of them lying, as things got worse, month after month, year after year. One had the feeling that everything was in a slow spiral, spiraling to some awful chaos. I was never so happy as when my family came to the United States.'

Tanya picked up her cigarette, took another deep puff and then stubbed it out. 'Then, I see it all begin again. I see the elderly and the poor, trying to live on oatmeal and cheese handouts from the government. I see the people in the streets again, demanding jobs, demanding food. And I see the same fat politicians again on the television. Except this time they are not Democrats or Republicans. No, they are the gun lobby, the welfare lobby, the insurance lobby, the software lobby, the energy lobby, the old people lobby. But they make the same promises, the same lies. And all the while, our president hides in his Oval Office, afraid to say anything, afraid to do anything. All that anyone cares about is whether or not he pissed like a peasant in the Rose Garden. I saw this happening, and I said to myself, no. I shall not let this happen in this country, my new home. Which is why I am with you, Mr Woodman. You and everyone else. No matter what you do, no matter what happens. Even if that does mean . . . Mark Quentin being let go.'

He stood up, knowing he had to get back home, and soon. It had been a very long day. He had an urge to touch her on the shoulder but no, that wouldn't be right. Instead, he said,

'Tanya, you have nothing to fear. In one week's time, we're taking her back. And things will be right again.'

She smiled, nodding. 'That will be a good day indeed. Tell me, do you know what is to happen on the nineteenth?'

'Not at all,' he said, lying with ease.

It was now pouring rain, and as Drew worked Sheila sat under a small overhang of rock, not saying a word. He felt guilty at what must be going through her mind and how short he had been with her, but there was no time. Later they could talk and discuss and maybe even cry a bit together, but not now. There was no time. He had pushed the both of them as far as possible, and had only stopped when the rains had begun. Drew also hated to admit it, but he wished he was alone. By himself, he could live for a year or two up here in the woods, without anyone even knowing that he was there. All those years of service had given him many bad memories but lots of survival experience. But with Sheila, as much as he loved her, that wasn't possible. So. To make do with what was available. One of the many lessons he had learned years ago, in the service of this poor country.

A few minutes earlier she had asked for a fire, and he had said, 'No, I'm sorry. We can't.'

'Why?'

'Thermal emissions. Aircraft overhead see a fire and two bodies resting nearby, then we might be caught. If they just see our two shapes . . . well, we could be a couple of deer, resting for the night. But a fire would tip them off.'

'And who's them?'

'I wish I knew. God, I wish I knew.'

With that she had moved under the rock overhang and had not said another word, huddled up in her raingear, head slumped forward, her now wet backpack on the ground before them. There was another grumble of thunder as their landscape was illuminated for a brief second by a distant lightning flash. They were in a hollow of rocks and boulders, a place that was wide enough to set up the tent and deep enough to provide some cover. He rolled out the ground-cloth and then the tent, and hammered in the stakes and then inserted the poles. His hands were cold in the rainwater, and he was soaked through. It would be a difficult night, but maybe they could sleep. And then, well, let tomorrow come. *We'll decide what's what in the morning.*

Case Shiloh: On September 19 we take her back! Six days away and obviously – now there's a bit of humor! – the people planning Case Shiloh were serious about keeping it a secret. So what? He unzipped the tent – which had a storage vestibule – and dragged his backpack and Sheila's inside. If they want to keep their secret so bad, then fine. Maybe the smart thing would be to keep hidden for a week, let Case Shiloh come forward, and when it didn't matter anymore if it was a secret or not, then maybe they could come out.

He looked over at the drenched shape of his woman. But probably never to go back home, back to Lake Montcalm. Maybe to Federal Canada, maybe Alaska, maybe to some-place rural where you could drop out and carve out a comfortable life. But that lake would be too dangerous. Right now there were probably serious young men in ill-fitting suits going through their possessions, trying to find out what they could about the two of them. The same young men who had put up a graphboard called INTERNMENT CEN-TERS back at that bomb shelter.

Drew zipped the tent shut, slogged over to Sheila and held out his hand. She took it without a word and he led her back to the tent. In a few minutes they had squirmed their way into the confines of the tent, stripping off their wet clothes and boots in the vestibule. Drew switched on a tiny electric lantern and undid the mattress pads and rolled them out, followed by their sleeping bags as well. The smell inside the tent was thick, of dirty clothes, wet socks and sweaty bodies that hadn't had a decent shower in nearly a week. He found a dry but smelly towel in his pack and handed it over to Sheila, and she wiped her hair and skin without saying anything. He stripped himself down and crawled into the open sleeping bag, and he watched Sheila. Even with her greasy hair and frowning face, even with the goosebumps and shivering skin, even with her dirty fingernails and feet that were wrinkled and stained from sweaty socks, he found her the most desirable woman he had ever met.

She pulled out a crumpled dark green flannel nightgown and shrugged it over her shoulders and then crawled into her own sleeping bag. She zipped up the bag up to her shoulders and shivered some more, and looked up.

'Drew, I'm hungry. I need to get something to eat.'

The thunder came closer, the lightning flash making the walls of the tent translucent for just a moment. 'You know I can't light a stove.'

She let out a heavy breath. 'Hon, please don't lecture, all right? All I said is, I'm hungry. Please.'

He felt a flush of anger at himself for having snapped at her like that, and he went back to his backpack in the tent's vestibule and rummaged through a couple of the outside pockets. At that country store, just before sending away the deputy sheriff's cruiser, he had bought a few supplies, but not much. They had very little money and after the fiasco in downtown Corinth he knew that SmartCards or ATM cards or credit cards or even checks were out of the question.

Back inside the tent he laid out a metal dinner plate and said, 'Best I can do tonight, Sheila. I'm sorry. I'll do better in the morning. Promise.'

She just nodded and they ate quickly, drinking warm water from one of their water bottles. Dinner was two sets of cheese and crackers, and one can of corn beef hash, eaten cold. When they were done eating Drew took their trash and the plate back to the vestibule and Sheila said, 'A favor, Drew? Will you do me a favor?'

'What's that?'

'Get me my lapbot, will you?'

He paused for a moment, wondering how he could say what he had to say, when she anticipated him and said, 'Drew, it'll be safe. Honest. You know I know computers. I've got a couple of accounts through a server in the Cayman Islands, through a cut-out corporation. When I set it up I didn't use my real name or any of my real accounts. The access is through the Skybolt satellite system. It can't be traced. Honest.'

But how can you be sure, he thought. These people out there . . .

'Drew, please. I need my lapbot tonight. More than you know.'

Another second, then he went to her backpack and zipped it open. He reached in, felt the familiar black cushioned case, and hauled it out. He crawled back to Sheila, nude and shivering himself, and gave it to her. She smiled when she opened up the case and looked up at him. 'Give me a kiss, will you? Bad breath and all.'

'Of course, bad breath and all.'

He kissed her, gently holding her head with one of his hands. He started to talk and she put a finger to his lips. 'No. Don't say anything. We have a lot to discuss but I'm scared and I'm tired and I don't want to think anymore. I want to log on and go Webbing and try to forget, just for a while, that this day ever happened.'

'Sheila, it won't go away, we've got to—'

Another gentle pressure on his lips from her finger. 'I know it won't go away. But I need this, Drew. I need some time where I don't have to think about what happened. Please. Let me have that, so at least I can sleep.'

He nodded and kissed her again. 'All right, but one thing, just one thing.'

'Which is?'

'I won't let anything bad happen to you. I promise.'

She smiled, but it was a tired smile. 'I'm not sure you'll be able to do that, but thanks for the promise anyway. Now, let me get on-line, all right?'

He laid down in his sleeping bag, watched as Sheila unzipped the storage bag and took out the lapbot. She rubbed the slick black plastic finish, festooned with cartoon stickers from Bugs Bunny to Daffy Duck, and he said, 'Lights out, okay?'

'Sure.' She switched off the electric lantern and he watched her for a while. She rolled on her side and opened up the lapbot cover, and her fingers started tapping the keys. She put in a set of tiny earphones and in the darkness of the night, he could make out colored shapes on the walls of the tent fabric as she entered the world of the Net. Her face seemed more relaxed, or it might be a trick of the moving light, but he could sense some of the tension ease from her.

Drew rolled over on his side, eyes open. He envied Sheila for her lapbot, for having something that would temporarily halt the screaming voices in her head. All he had was his 9 mm pistol, and as he grasped that and tried to get to sleep the metal and plastic form in his hand was not comforting, not at all.

He remembered the last time a weapon in his hand had proven comforting, back during his last real job, going in covertly in a Stealth helicopter one horrible day a few years back. It was Master Sergeant Coughlin (Ret.) who had spotted them first, and he did so by breaking procedures. Then-Lieutenant Drew Connor (Ret., Special Group, Detached/Defense Research Agency) watched as Coughlin had undone the anti-flash shield at one of the side portholes in the chopper, and even over the noise of the engines Drew could make out the whistle of amazement. 'Bleedin' Christ, loo,' Coughlin said. 'The goddamn water's full of boats. Take a look.'

Drew knew that by the book Coughlin should be reprimanded for doing what he had just done, for endangering the mission, but the book hadn't been written for an op like this one, one so tense guys were stumbling to the rear of the chopper to vomit into buckets or empty bags. Coughlin's face wore anti-flash goggles – like everyone else – and was blackened with crystal camouflage, and his look had a mocking gaze, like he was testing Drew. Drew stared right back and then handed his M-16 over to his seatmate – Grayson – and unbuckled his harness and then stood up, leaning over the aisle to look through the open porthole.

His chest had tightened as he saw what was beneath them as they flew closer to the coast. Watercraft of all types, from rowboats to dhows to ferrycraft, were streaming away in the

Arabian Sea, heading away from the smoke and the fire on the horizon. The area from Yemen to Sri Lanka, once known as the Crescent of Crisis, had become the Crescent War, as certain countries and tribes and cities had turned on each other, trying to settle centuries-old feuds. And just two days ago, some had used nuclear weapons in a final spasm of madness. The Stealth chopper was flying only about fifty feet above wavetops, and Drew knew that the pilot and co-pilot were flying through video screens, not daring to expose their eyes to the sudden flash of a NUDET. Drew looked for another moment, seeing a mother hold up her child in her arms as they flew overhead, as if praying or hoping that they would be picked up, and then he closed the screen and got back to his seat. It seemed like all of the faces of the twenty-man squad were looking at him, and he looked over at Coughlin and had said, 'You're right, sarge. Boats everywhere.'

Coughlin shook his head. 'Damn brave, to be heading out in the ocean like that. None of those things looked like it was designed for the open ocean.'

'They don't have a choice,' Drew said. 'They're trying to escape hell. That can be difficult sometimes.'

At his side, Grayson spoke up. 'You think they're going to make it, loo?'

Drew retrieved his M-16. 'Not a chance. Every port is sealed off, and every navy of every little country in the Arabian Sea and the Bay of Bengal is sinking anything coming from this part of the world. Trying to stop the contamination.'

A voice from someone in the squad: 'Hell of a thing, to be flying into someplace that everybody's trying to get out of.'

'God bless the Department of Defense,' came another voice, and someone laughed, and then the whole squad began laughing, and Drew had to join them, for there was nothing else to do.

A voice came into his right ear, from the chopper pilot. 'We're feet dry, Lieutenant. We'll be reaching the air base in ten minutes.'

Drew clicked on the mike switch at his side. 'Copy that.' He looked at Coughlin. 'Ten minutes, Sergeant. Ensure the men are ready.'

Coughlin nodded and got up and began walking to the rear of the chopper, bellowing, 'Ten minutes! We're landing in ten minutes! Make sure your gear's functional! We're depressurizing in ten minutes, so your suits will have to be working, and if they're not, there's gonna be an ugly corpse to send home to your momma and poppa when the rest of us are done!'

Drew checked the digital read-out on the cuff of his NBC suit. Everything was nominal. He tightened his helmet strap and pulled down the anti-flash goggles. Two places down on the opposite side of the chopper's bench was the Doc, and his gear would tell the squad if they could breathe the air or not. Doc was the second-most important man on the chopper, and in a moment or so Drew would give orders regarding the most important man.

Coughlin came back and sat down and said, 'Squad's all set, Lieutenant.'

'Very good.' He motioned with his hand and Coughlin drew nearer as Drew bent forward. 'After we land, detach two men – make it Stokes and Harrison – and assign them to the Rad Officer. They are to protect the Rad Officer to the highest degree, even if it means letting the rest of the squad go. Do you understand?'

Drew could tell from the way the Master Sergeant was

tightening his lips that he didn't like the order, but he was still professional in many ways and said, 'Yes, sir. Understood.'

The chopper pilot spoke again. 'Five minutes to air base, sir. AWACS reports the base has been neutralized. Repeat, neutralized.'

'Copy that.'

Then the speed of the engine shifted and Drew felt his stomach tightening up, knowing what they were getting into, knowing the horrors that they were about to see, and he tried not to think of that, tried very hard, and then they were on the ground and an alarm started hooting and yellow lights mounted on the bulkhead began flashing, and it seemed that in one motion the entire squad put on their clear facial air masks. There was a tightening sensation against his face and then the feeling of cool air, and then the rear hatchway swiveled open and Coughlin was screaming, 'Move, move, move!'

Drew went out with the squad and into instant chaos and confusion. He tried not to grasp it all at once but instead took little snapshots with his mind. It was the only way he could cope. He was standing on the runway of the destroyed air base of what was left of this nation's air force. There. Rows of old-style MiGs in their concrete revetments, burning and smoldering. Over there. Control tower, shattered like a glass bottle. Runway dented and pockmarked. Hangars at the far end, burning. Corpses scattered along near some of the buildings. There. Low-built wide hangar, just before the slowly rotating blades of the black Stealth transport chopper. Glow in the sky, off to the east. A city burning? Maybe. A fence, way off there, and what was a highway, and it looked jammed with vehicles, all heading west, all heading to the ocean. Lemmings, he thought, lemmings looking for some safety in the sea. He looked up to the sky. It was a swirling horror of gray and black and white, and the clouds up there weren't formed by nature. White stuff that looked like snowflakes were drifting down, and these flakes were spawned by hell itself.

Coughlin came over and Drew said, 'Standard procedure, sarge. Set up a defense perimeter, and put two observers up in the tower. I want a report on how the runway looks. We've got less than a half-hour before the C-5X shows up. Fire only if fired upon. We're not here to fight. We're just here to steal.'

The Master Sergeant nodded and Drew went over to Doc, who was on the concrete surface of the runway, his black boxes and gear spread across a plastic poncho. Doc looked up, his eyes wide with fear, and said, 'The air's breathable and I'm not picking up any airborne toxins, Lieutenant, but we're getting a healthy dose of radiation. About 500 millirem per hour. We must be right near the plume from the second nuclear strike.'

Drew nodded and said, 'Doc, you get anything, anything at all, you sound the alert.'

Now he breathed deeply, noticing the stench of soot and fuel oil and other indescribable burned offerings. He clicked on the mike switch and spoke to the pilot. 'Advise you shut down and move the chopper into the near hangar.'

'Sir, orders are to stand ready to extricate you and the squad.'

'Pal, we're not moving unless we get the job done, and that's gonna take a while. You want to sit outside and play at being an exposed target, go ahead. All it takes is one bomber or missile to get through the air CAP and get even a near

miss, and you're just a burned shadow in concrete. Now.
Move it.'

The engine pitch changed and the chopper moved ahead
into the open maw of the concrete hangar. He followed
them in, looking with a practiced eye at how the squad was
setting up its weapons, the rocket launchers, the mortars
and the SAW machine guns. The air base had been hit just
a few minutes ago by a B-2 flying a special anti-personnel
mission, and it looked like it had been successful. No resistance upon landing, nor any sign of anybody left alive. The
United States wasn't officially at war with anyone, but Drew
and his squad weren't officially here, and nor were similar
squads coming in up and down this tortured coastline to certain military bases. Every single squad belonged to the
Defense Research Agency. They were a contract force, not
officially part of the government, in case things went to the
shits. But, Drew thought, they were the best damn contract
force in the DoD.

Inside the hangar some of the soldiers were dragging air
force personnel to the far wall. Each of the dead men had a
scorch mark around the heart. Anti-personnel gear works
again. If you didn't wear a special chip in your dogtags then
a little heatseeking missile about the size of your thumb came
at your heart. And it never missed. The hangar was empty of
aircraft save for the Stealth chopper, which he noticed the
crew had turned around, ready for quick escape. He knew the
fear, the tremblings, felt them himself. Nobody wanted to
spend an extra second on the ground here, not when they
could become part of Ground Zero so quickly.

Walking further into the hangar, past ordnance gear,
empty bomb racks and electric tractors, he found Stokes and
Harrison at the far concrete wall, doing a heel-to-toe

protection of Rudman, the Rad Officer. Rudman was looking at a vault door and was attaching clear putty around the lock area. The door looked like it belonged to a bank, and there were black boxes, warning lights and red-lettered signs written around the wall. Three other corpses were against the far wall, and they were dressed differently – in black berets – and carried Swedish NPK-90s. Special Forces, guarding the caged beast behind the vault door.

'How does it look?' Drew asked.

'Shit-ass stuff,' Rudman said, his face red and sweaty. 'Looks Russian, or even late Soviet. Hard to tell. But this stuff should do the trick.'

'You sure we got the prize back there?'

Rudman nodded to his own black boxes of equipment, lying by his feet. 'That stuff don't lie, loo. Either it's in there or all these boys were guarding an X-ray unit. All right, clear.'

Everyone took several steps back and Rudman squeezed a triggering unit in his hand, and the clear putty smoldered and then smoked fiercely. After a minute or so Rudman came forward and started tugging at the handle. The door moved out about two inches and then halted.

'Guys?' Rudman asked. 'Want to give me a hand here?'

The two soldiers slung their M-16s over their shoulders but even with three of them tugging the door would not move. Drew felt like yelling in frustration. Each second of every minute that ticked away was more time spent in a target area, more time to be struck by the horrible lightnings that were raining down on this part of Asia.

'Damn thing's stuck, loo,' Rudman said. 'Some of the bombing must have knocked it out of alignment.'

Drew tried to keep his voice even. 'See if you can get one

of those electric carts running. Get a length of chain and try to pull the goddamn thing out.'

'Yes, sir.'

He went back to the entrance of the hangar, and then he went blind.

Drew blinked his eyes hard a few times and yelled, 'On the floor, on the floor! Get shelter, get shelter!'

He flung himself to the concrete and then the ground moved, like an ocean swell, and the roaring of the biggest freight train in the world seemed to burst into his head. It seemed as if a lot of men were yelling and screaming, and he tried blinking his eyes a few times, and nothing was working, he was still blind. As the noise started grumbling away, he began to hear other things, of objects falling and striking the concrete around him, and as he thought to cover his head with his arms, something whacked him at the base of the neck and the blackness in his eyes got deeper.

Blackness. Sleep, blessed sleep. Drew sighed. He sure could use some sleep now, here beside Sheila with lots of bad people chasing them.

Outside, the rain hammered the side of the tent, and the thunder still grumbled on the other side of the ridge.

SIDEBAR I

Rose O'Toole sat in one of those damn uncomfortable metal folding chairs that was set up in a basketball gym at Brewer Air Force Base in Collins, Montana. She was the head of the local Red Cross chapter, and sitting with her in the cold auditorium were representatives from the air base, the state highway patrol, the local county sheriff, the Montana Emergency Management Agency, volunteer firefighters and some sharp-tongued young woman from Region Nine of the Federal Emergency Response Agency. Eight hours earlier they had assembled in the gym to take part in a practice response drill, sponsored by FERA, simulating an evacuation of Billings following a chemical accident.

Everyone had pads of paper in their laps as the FERA woman – Beth Goodwin – went down the checklist, recording their post-drill comments. Rose sighed and rolled a pen around in her chubby fingers. About every six months or so she suffered through a similar drill. There was a simulated disaster and simulated victims, along with simulated press conferences with simulated reporters. About the only thing that wasn't simulated was the same lunch food, cold sandwiches. The joke among the participants was that the state bought the sandwiches in bulk, once a decade, and doled them out during the drills.

During previous occasions, Rose had done her job – and done it well, thank you very much – but something about this one had pissed her off. It had happened when she was supervising the setting up of a tent city on the grounds of the air base's athletic fields, and she could hardly wait to bring it up.

'Well,' the FERA woman said in her chirpy voice. 'Are there any other comments before we wrap this up?'

'Yeah, I've got a comment,' Rose said, raising her hand. 'There's something that went on during today's drill that I found very upsetting, and I'd like to talk about it.'

There were some murmurs and a couple of the men made a point of checking their watch, but Rose pressed on. She knew that they all liked to poke fun at her, the two-hundred-and-fifty-pound woman sitting on a tiny metal chair, but damn it, she was good at what she did, and her job was protecting her fellow citizens in Montana. She had done it before, being woken at 2 a.m. to help house families after an apartment building fire, coordinating the monthly blood drives, or helping some of the same Air Force people stationed at this base who needed a warm voice to talk to during a family crisis. She pressed on.

'I was out in the athletic fields, watching as the tents were going up, and I saw supplies there as well, a kind I've never seen before. You know what I saw? Wire fencing, complete with razor wire. One of the airmen told me it'd take only an hour to fence in the entire yard. What's going on? Are we going to force any evacuees who come here to sit behind a barbed-wire compound?'

There was some shuffling of feet and a loud cough. Beth Goodwin smiled and just nodded. 'It's just a precaution, Mrs—'

'Miss.'

'Miss O'Toole, it's just a precaution. For security purposes.'

'What security purposes?' she demanded. 'I've been coming here for drills like this for seven years, and this is the first time I've ever heard of fences being put up around the tent city. It'll be like a goddamn concentration camp out there. Who decided this anyway?'

That same smug smile on that damn woman, probably a size three. The FERA woman said, 'Policy, that's all Miss O'Toole. Just policy.'

'Well, that's just fine. And by this time tomorrow my regional chief is going to know, as well as the Governor's office and the news media. If we're going to put up refugees from Billings, I'll be damned if we're going to crowd them into a compound like animals or war criminals.'

The FERA woman nodded. 'I'll make a note of your complaints, Miss O'Toole. And trust me, you don't have to make a big stink about it. It will be looked into.'

'And you can trust me, Miss Goodwin, that I don't trust the Federal government. No offense, I intend to make a stink of it, no matter what you promise.'

Beth slowly nodded, wrote something down. 'That's entirely within your rights, Miss O'Toole.'

She nodded sweetly back at the well-dressed bitch. 'You bet it is.'

An hour later, as the sun was going down behind the Snaptooth Mountains, Rose drove back into Billings, composing a list of who she would call tomorrow to complain about the wire fences and barbed wire. Policy, she snorted, switching on her headlights. Damn Feds, that's all they cared about. Policy! She switched on the radio, got an afternoon drive-in sports show from KDKA-AM out of Billings – she loved following the Green Bay Packers, though their home turf was hundreds of miles away – and when she looked up into her rearview mirror, she saw the headlights behind her. Somebody in a hurry, she thought. Well, pass away, there's nothing in front of us for miles and miles.

Which is just what the vehicle did. It came up behind her and switched on its turn indicator, and as it began passing a spotlight came from the passenger's side, illuminating the inside of the car.

'What the—' she started. She didn't finish her sentence, as her side window blew in from the force of the shotgun blast, killing her instantly. Her car went over the side of the road, flipped over twice, and the wreckage was still smoldering when a highway patrolman – someone who had been at her side hours earlier during the drill – pulled up.

In Galveston, Texas, Luis Raminez was working under the sink in the kitchen when his wife Maria came in. From the sound of the bags thumping on the kitchen table he imagined that she had just come in from the local Safeway store. Luis eased his way out from under the sink and wiped his hands on a rag. Maria looked down at him, her brown eyes glaring. He knew the signal and said, 'What's wrong?'

'What's wrong?' she said, as she moved around, the bags of groceries not quite hiding the six-month swell of her belly. 'What's wrong is that we have new neighbors, and I don't like the look of them, that's what's wrong.'

He slowly stood up, winced as his back ached. The sink had been leaking the past few days and he was damned if he was going to pay some plumber to come in and fix it.

'What kind of neighbors, baby?' he said, walking past her to look out the kitchen window. There was a small driveway and a chain-link fence, and he could barely make out the flat roof of the house next door.

'Anglos,' she said, spitting out the word. 'That's what. White trash. Is that the kind of neighbors we're going to have to put up with? Is it, Luis?'

He felt his heart grow heavy at what she had said. He wasn't prejudiced but this was a nice quiet place, one they had chosen to raise a family. They had scrimped and counted out every penny, and they barely kept ahead on this little home, but damn it, it belonged to them. Now . . . well, he imagined what kind of Anglo would be moving into this neighborhood. White trash, just like Maria said. Loud Aryan music, maybe skinheads, maybe some toughs from the city, trying to lie low.

And they had to move in here, in their neighborhood!

Maria was angrily unpacking the grocery sacks and he went behind her, nuzzled her sweet brown neck, placed his rough and worn hands over her swollen belly. 'Not to worry, baby, we can manage. I know we can.'

'We had better,' she said in reply. 'Because I want a safe neighborhood for our children. Nothing else matters. Do you hear me? Nothing else matters.'

In a range of hills near Los Gatos, California, the sniper settled in for a long stay. His Remington 270 was still in its zippered black case and would stay there until shooting day. In a little washout he had made his shelter, with an overhead tarpaulin, sleeping bag and small knapsack. He had enough food and water for the duration of his mission, and there were plenty of trees around for urination and little plastic bags for his other waste. A quick ten-minute walk from here led to a motel parking lot, where there was a rented car that could get him to the San Jose airport within thirty minutes.

Below him and almost a half-mile away was a high school. He shifted his position and looked through his Bushnell spotting scope. The playing fields near the school were filled with football players, out doing their September practice drills. He watched them for a while, and when he got bored turned his attention to the cheerleaders.

It was a beautiful day, and he thanked God that he loved his life and his job.

SIX

Don't be misled by politicians who say that everything is great, that we are on the verge of this
wonderful, new era thanks to technology or the stock
market or whatever. These are lies. We are not in the
dawn of a new civilization, but the twilight of an old
one. We will be lucky if we escape with any remnants
of the great Judeo-Christian civilization that we have
known down through the ages.

Paul Weyrich, Moral Majority co-founder,
February 16, 1999

Early morning, out on the high Nevada desert, reminded
Cyrus Montgomery of his tours during the Gulf Wars: the
sound of the crunching sand underfoot, the cold air that
seemed to hold your face in its grip, and the clear desert
night that showed every star so bright it almost hurt your
eyes. He moved his feet, exhaling a bit and seeing his breath
form little clouds. It was cold. Damn cold. Even though he
had been retired for nearly two years, he was wearing full
battlefield gear, including a helmet and NBC (Nuclear,
Biological, Chemical) ArmourSuit, and the heater was on –
about mid-level – but even then the damn thing didn't
work. Something else to bitch about, he thought, the next
time there's a hearing up on Capitol Hill about failed

weapons systems. But at least this time, he thought with bitter satisfaction, it won't be my black ass sitting in the chair, getting grilled by rich morons who wouldn't know which end of a cartridge was the pointy one without an instruction booklet.

A voice from a speaker near the test trailer: 'Fifteen minutes.'

Then again things were different back when he was a scared trooper from MoTown, trying to act tough and swaggering. Now that he was a Retired Chairman of the Joint Chiefs of Staff – and my, how proud Momma had been when he had been named to that post! – he didn't have to swagger as much. But there were still the tough days as Chairman – before being eventually forced out over that Crescent disaster – days when he wished he was back on the outskirts of Baghdad, M-16 in hand, listening to his Master Sergeant, Kilmer, piss and moan as the rounds were falling in about them. 'Colonel, let this here be a lesson to you of finishing a job right from the start. If we'd done that back in '91, your ass and mine wouldn't be here.'

Good lesson. He wished other people he dealt with had Kilmer's wisdom. He looked around at the people standing with him on this ridgeline, feeling a sense of pride. Good people, most of them. Should be, since he picked them, during his years in the field and in the Pentagon. The test personnel were near the trailer and a couple of officers from the Public Information Office were by their side, ready to give a briefing later in the morning to all the newsies from Las Vegas and beyond. General Jay Keegan, head of the *Excalibur* project, was standing next to his Air Force liaison, General Karl Summers. They actually became friends during the development and testing phase, which Montgomery always thought was amazing. He remembered early on, when he was a green lieutenant, fresh from ROTC at Norwich, being told by a captain that, 'Montgomery, the Soviets are our adversary. The Air Force and the Navy are our enemies.' So true then, and much more now, as fewer defense dollars flowed into the Pentagon each budget cycle.

Standing next to Montgomery was his personal adjutant, bodyguard and Scribe, Captain Maurice Blakely, who was still on active duty. After Montgomery's forced retirement Captain Blakely had volunteered to come along to help him in the transition to his civilian career and to also help him in researching the book he had promised to a New York publisher. The man stood only feet away but seemed to be by himself, a half-smile on his face.

'Ten minutes,' came the speaker's voice. Blakely's job made him like the fact he stood alone. He was also wearing his NBC gear, but he had a small frame about his waist, where his own military-issue lapbot sat. He wore glasses that allowed him to see data in 3-D, and small earplugs attached to the side of the glasses allowed him to hear information from his lapbot as well. Being military issue, the lapbot contained an encrypted data link that could connect Blakely to almost any data and computer system in the world that the US Army could enter, and they could enter a lot. With all of the information out there, and with information management being the key to winning battles nowadays, the smart general learned to depend on his Scribe. And even though Montgomery was now battling over words and sentences in his book, he still depended on Blakely's research skills.

Montgomery looked up at the sky and saw a fast-moving dot of light. Knowing it wasn't *Excalibur*, he asked, 'Blakely, what's that we have up there? Space debris?'

The man's head swiveled and his eyes blinked a few times as he processed data seen on his glasses, and he said, his voice calm and rational as always, 'Upper-stage booster, General. From the Japanese satellite launch last week. Their surveillance series, Yamamoto 3. Do you desire more information?'

'No, that's fine, Blakely. Just testing you, son.'

That same half-smile. 'As you wish, sir.'

The wind shifted some and Montgomery made out the faint engine noises. He brought up his hand scopes and looked down at the desert floor. There were nearly thirty tanks down there – all obsolete and unmanned – playing pretend, and the game they were playing was a major tank battle. Blue Force against Red Force, and the Blue Force was friendly. Each tank – an old M1A – was identical, save that the fifteen tanks within Blue Force had a little chip in their turret, squawking them as friendly. Inside the scope he could faintly make out their shapes, until he flipped the scope's setting to nightview. In the green glow the tanks were a clear shape, the dust clouds only barely obscuring them.

'Seven minutes.'

Standing by themselves on the ridge were two men whose names Montgomery had easily forgotten. The far man wore jeans and a thick parka, and was a representative from the Governor of Nevada. Politics being politics nowadays, everyone knew that the man was also a stooge for the Governor of California, and he was given wide berth. The Governor of California was a bitter enemy of the man in the White House, and he was taking full advantage of that occupant's current crisis to forge his own path. That included instructing state agencies to ignore Federal regulations he opposed and allocating Federal funds earmarked to certain public works programs to his own pet projects. He had even set up embassies among the richer Pacific Rim countries, though he had innocently called them trade missions.

Given equally charming treatment was the other man, who wore the blue beret and uniform of the United Nations. His shoulder patch said WALES. Montgomery had yet to meet a man in the Army who had anything good to say about the UN, whether it be about their peacekeeping forces on the Mexican border or their relief efforts this past summer in Detroit, during the anthrax epidemic. Maybe they had come in on purely humanitarian grounds, or maybe they were testing to see just how far they could get away with by coming in from only the invitation of the very frightened and very ill Mayor of Detroit.

Whatever. Both men were observers, and he could tell from the looks of his own people that they were suspicious that the two spent so much time talking together.

'Five minutes. Break, break. Unauthorized helicopter, registered to KQUV-TV of Las Vegas, has entered the test range.'

There was a stirring in the crowd and General Keegan of the Army and General Summers of the Air Force both started cursing, loudly and fluently. Montgomery turned to his Scribe and said, 'What's going on Blakely?'

'Sir, the helicopter entered the test airspace approximately ninety seconds ago. Two Army Comanches from the 7th AirCav have intercepted but the helicopter refuses to leave. The TV pilot is mentioning something about freedom of the press.'

'Don't they always,' Montgomery muttered. 'General Keegan!'

'Sir!' From the voice tone Montgomery knew that Keegan was equal parts furious and equal parts scared shitless that things were going so bad so fast. 'I've got Air Control on the horn,' Keegan said. 'In a minute or two I'm sure we'll be able to force down the—'

Montgomery rubbed at his scopes and said, 'If I can make a suggestion, Jay. No.'

'Sir?' came Keegan's incredulous voice. The faces in the crowd turned to look at him, and the UN representative and the man from the Governor's office stepped over a few paces, intent on finding out what was going to happen next.

'Give word to the Comanches,' Montgomery said. 'Order them to break away.'

'General, I don't see—'

'Then contact the TV crew. Ask them their type of helicopter, speed, weight and number of souls on board. Then thank them very much for adding another dimension to the *Excalibur* test, and then ask them for names of next of kin. Just a suggestion.'

It was done and there was some muttering and Blakely said quietly, 'The two Comanches have broken away, sir. And the helicopter is following them.'

'Very good.'

He lifted up the scopes and the speaker voice said, 'One minute,' and Blakely said, 'Sir, Space Command is reporting successful deployment of *Excalibur* test round. Sir, test round is visual.'

'There it is!' someone yelled, and everyone on the ridge line craned their necks and looked up. Montgomery did as everyone else, except he left his scopes resting on his chest. He wanted to see this one bare eye visual. There. Fast-moving dot of light among the stationary stars, getting brighter and brighter as it re-entered the earth's atmosphere, moving at an incredible rate of speed. Then the bright dot suddenly expanded, and within a matter of one heartbeat to another it seemed like a fine network of lines flew out of the dot of light and touched the desert floor beneath them.

Out on the flat sands of the desert more than a dozen blossoms of light flew up and there was a grumbling of explosions, echoing and re-echoing among the sands. Cheering and applause broke out from most of the people – save for the two men standing by themselves – and Keegan was yelling, 'One hundred percent! God damn it to hell, we got a one hundred percent kill rate! Un-fucking-believable!'

'Blakely?'

His Scribe nodded. 'All of the tanks associated with the Red Force have been destroyed. There was no damage, collateral or otherwise, to the Blue Force.'

Montgomery nodded. It had worked. The United States had just demonstrated that it had an operational space-based kinetic energy weapon capable of destroying entire tank regiments within seconds using a network of surveillance and spy satellites that could narrow down a battlefield to within inches. Up in orbit *Excalibur* was now racing away, one of its kill-rounds – a bundle of titanium rods with minimal guidance systems – having been used. There were thirty-five left, and they could be used to destroy targets ranging from the tanks they had just annihilated to a hidden command-and-control bunker, and if things ever got too hairy, one of the old shuttles or the WASP could go up and rearm *Excalibur*.

Blakely said, 'Congratulations, sir. The test was a success.'

Montgomery grunted. 'So it was, Blakely, so it was. And tell me,' he said, turning to his Scribe with a wry smile on his face, 'just how effective will *Excalibur* be against inner-city gangs next summer, when the wars restart? Or when the Nigerians start bombing the oil platforms in our relief mandate? Or if the Israelis ask us to intervene in their civil war?'

'Sir?'

'Bah,' he said, rubbing his hands together. Damn, it was still cold. 'All we proved tonight is that we still have some serviceable technology, a Defense Department with a few deep pockets and contractors who are still willing to pick those pockets with great glee. You tell me when we'll be fighting the next tank battle with a major land power, and I'll tell you how much of a success *Excalibur* was.'

Blakely didn't reply and Montgomery looked at Keegan and Summers, still talking like high school boys, excited over their first football win. He still felt sour about the matter, but he would keep his silence for now. Let Keegan and Summers have their victory. God knew there weren't many victories nowadays.

Montgomery said, 'Blakely, we're done for the evening. You take the rest of the morning off, and I don't want to see you back at the Test Center until tomorrow afternoon.'

'Yes, sir. And may I ask where the General will be?'

He stamped his feet. 'This Retired General is going for a walk, if he doesn't freeze first. And then he intends to go back to quarters.' Blakely nodded, and then Montgomery slipped away from the crowd at the ridgeline and started descending a trail on the other side of the ridge, away from the carnage of the burning tanks.

Captain Maurice Blakely watched the General walk by himself off the ridgeline, saw how he dodged the group of handshaking and backslapping officers who had just witnessed the *Excalibur* test. It was a sight to see one of the most famous black men in the country, wooed by politicians and the news media alike, walking by himself, hands in his pockets. He felt a sudden flash of anger at what had happened to the man more than two years ago because of that clown in the White House. A clown who wasn't fit to shine the General's shoes.

He shivered as a breeze came up over the ridge. Damn, wasn't it ever warm in this goddamn desert? The cold made him think of a duty station where temperatures had been higher, down in Colombia, where he had been helping the government forces against the insurgents. The memory of that tour made him smile and actually warmed him up some.

The General then disappeared from view. Blakely remembered what he had said. That they were both done for the evening. The General and his obedient Scribe.

Yeah, right, he thought, putting his fingers back to his lapbot's keys.

The walk was a short one, and he came upon a cleared area, near a dirt road. There were sentries about but Montgomery knew the chips in his dogtags – retired or not – would let him enter the perimeter with no problem, without challenges. At the center of the cleared area was a large tent and parked near it were two third-generation HUMVEEs. Further down the slope a Stealth chopper rested, its blades bowing down like willow-tree branches. He took a deep breath and undid the tent flap and walked in. A woman's face looked up at him, and Montgomery had a gleeful thought that the TV crew in that helicopter would probably be a hell of a lot more interested in what was happening inside this tent than what had just happened out on the test range.

Air Force General Leslie Coombs nodded as he entered. She had on an NBC suit just like Montgomery, the camouflage dialed to WESTERN DESERT (US). The rest of the tent was empty and he took a folding camp stool and sat down. There was a small wooden table and in the middle was General Coombs's own lapbot. He said, 'I would've imagined you'd have a bigger smile on your face.'

'Because the test was a success?' she said. 'So what.'

'It wouldn't do for the rest of your folks at Cheyenne Mountain to hear that.'

She nodded and rubbed her face in exhaustion. Just over fifty, she was the commanding general of the US Space Command – formerly known as NORAD (North American Air Defense Command) – and by all rights she should have been in Colorado at her headquarters this evening, instead of Nevada. But she had sent him a message through very unofficial channels last week, asking him if he would meet with her at the *Excalibur* test site. He had said yes without hesitation.

'You know what I was thinking, Cyrus?' she asked, her voice tired. 'I was thinking of what I could do for my troops with all the money that gets spent for *Excalibur*. Some of my younger troops, they have to make do on food stamps and county assistance. Can you believe that? Troops who volunteer to serve their country – volunteer! – can only survive if they go on welfare. What that does to morale . . .'

'I know, Leslie, I know,' he said, suddenly feeling tired himself, remembering all those budget battles up on the Hill, fought and lost, over and over again. Most of those Congresscritters didn't seem to care about the young men and women in uniform and what they had to put up with, day to day, sometimes on overseas duty that lasted years.

Nope. They only cared that this particular base in their district remained open, or that their favorite corporation got a weapon-systems contract that kept their bottom line healthy and their campaign contributions regular.

She rubbed at her eyes again. 'Shit, I know you know. Sorry. I just feel like pissing and moaning, and you were an available target. That's not what I asked to see you for.'

'Then what was?'

Her hand moved over to her lapbot, nervously began rubbing at the keyboard. 'A couple of odd things are going on. Quite odd. And I wanted to talk to you, face to face. I didn't trust phones, didn't trust e-mail or even the courier we've been using. Just face to face. I felt you needed to know.'

Montgomery clasped his hands together, under the table. So. Another piece of the puzzle was about to come to him. 'Go ahead.'

'It's just that I've noticed, the past six or seven months, I've been losing some of my personnel. Transfers coming in and sending them elsewhere. It's like my command is being raided, and I don't know why.'

'Where are they going?'

Coombs shrugged. 'Here and there. No particular rhyme or reason. Except for a couple being sent to liaison duties with FERA. But not in DC. No, they were sent to their regional offices. Strange.'

'Are these good people?'

'Yeah, some of my best. But there's no thread to who they are. I mean, it's all different ranks, different specialities. About the only thing they have in common is . . .'

His hands were getting colder, and he slowly rubbed them. 'And what's that?'

She laughed for a moment, like everything had suddenly become quite ridiculous. 'They're all straight-shooters, every one of them. Perfect records. Quiet, church-going types. Not a lick of trouble or checkmarks on their personnel files. Nothing. It's like . . . it's like someone upstairs has gone raiding for Boy Scouts and Girl Scouts.'

'And have you tried to find out who's been pulling the strings to get these people out?'

'I have. And I've come up with nothing. So. I know you're retired, Cyrus, but you've got your fingers in some things. I know you're doing more than just some lecturing at Norwich and book-writing. What have you heard?'

Outside a breeze had come up, making the sides of the tent flap some, the sudden noise irritating. He leaned forward in his chair, hands still clasped together. 'Nothing firm. Just . . . odd, like you say. Unexpected transfers, here and there. Some redeployment of rapid-response units. Some good people being passed over for promotion. Rumors that something big is coming down within the next month or so. But nothing I could figure out.'

She kept her voice level. 'Could the White House be up to something?'

'Like what?'

'Like something to get people's attention away from the latest crisis, the presidential urination in the Rose Garden. Maybe a raid on the UN peacekeepers on the Mexican border, an intervention in Israel or Saudi, something like that. Wouldn't be the first time the White House bombed some innocent peasants to change the topic on the evening news.'

'I don't think this particular White House can be that imaginative.'

Leslie again touched her keyboard. 'If that's the case, what do you hear from this particular White House?'

Montgomery said, 'Officially, the President is so busy with his duties that he doesn't have the time to make public appearances or to hold a news conference, though there's a tale he might be considering a special address to Congress one of these days. Unofficially there are wild rumors and not-so-wild rumors. The not-so-wild rumor is that he's suffered a small stroke, and, as with Woodrow Wilson last century, his wife and Cabinet are keeping it a secret, taking care of the day-to-day business. The wild rumor is that he's lost his mind, and that he's being kept in a wing all to himself at St Elizabeth's.'

'And what do you think?'

'I think it's trouble, no matter how you spell it.'

Another gust of wind, and the Air Force General looked up at the moving walls. 'When I was in War College back in the late '80's, one of my history professors said he was envious of us. He said that we were now entering an era of a sole-superpower world, where the United States could set the pace and agenda. He said it would be challenging, but it would be nothing like the old world, with two alliances armed to the teeth and staring each other down. Envious . . . I guess it seemed right, back then. But I don't think he ever imagined the chaos, if there was only one superpower left, and no one was there to run it. Which brings me to another point . . .'

'No,' Montgomery quietly said. 'Don't even think about it.'

Her face looked bleak. 'The presidential primary season begins next spring, Cyrus. You know that.'

'And you know why I'm not going to budge. I've already given enough to this country.'

A sad nod. 'I know. I'm still sorry about what happened to Grace.'

He sighed, not wanting to bring back those memories, not tonight, but knowing he had no say in the matter. 'Thanks. I appreciated the card and the letter.'

'How're your boys?'

Then it came to him, with a brutal sense of urgency that almost made him gasp. He and Grace had been at a literacy conference last year in Buffalo. An enthusiastic crowd was in a crowded ballroom at the Hyatt Hotel. He and Grace were up on stage with the literacy committee, and he had made his stump speech, about how getting back to the basics was the only way to set things straight. You had to do it, one child, one classroom, one school at a time. Open their eyes and minds to what they could do, and they would join this wonderful American experience, would become productive citizens. Just like he had done growing up in Detroit, setting his sights high. He had been lucky, quite lucky, and other children in this nation should have the same luck. An old speech but the cheers came nonetheless. He had stepped away from the podium as the cheering went on and on, lifting his heart, making him grin. Grace was there, radiant, smiling, knowing the little secret they shared, the little fantasy that ended in a certain house on a certain avenue in a certain district. Among the cheers, then, the chants: 'Run, Cyrus, run! Run, Cyrus, run!' Then that harsh noise, the pop-pop-pop that he recognized instantly, the screams, and Grace, now looking puzzled, slumping down against a set of chairs. And then those harsh words, screamed over and over as the man was led out by Buffalo cops and hotel security: 'That's what uppity niggers get! That's what they get!'

Grace. Oh, how I miss you.

He spoke mechanically. 'They're both well. Raymond's on the SecDef staff at the Pentagon. Paul's doing his postgraduate work, excavating old slave quarters at a couple of plantation sites in Georgia. Raymond still talks to me. Paul doesn't, and I guess he never will.'

Then, a surprise. Leslie reached over and grasped his hand. 'General, you know we need you. We in the military and the civilians in this country. We need what you have to offer.'

He tried not to make his voice sound bitter. 'Leslie, I've already done my part. I just want to stay at my place in Vermont, learn to be a gentleman farmer, talk to some students at Norwich, and work on my book. That's all.'

Leslie stood up, reached for her helmet and lapbot. 'The nation and the people might leave you with no choice.'

'Then I'll have to disappoint them.'

She gave a wan smile and held out her hand. 'Thanks for coming, you civvie you. Even though you were a ground-pounder, I always enjoyed working with you, Cyrus. You don't mind if I keep in touch?'

He took her hand in both of his. 'I'd be disappointed otherwise.'

'Then you can count on it.'

George Clemson was a fifteen-year veteran of the Baltimore Police Department, active in the community and the local Abyssinian AME Church, and in the middle of his midnight shift on this drizzly night he was facing two equally important but separate problems. The first was trying to keep that black Dodge Orca in sight as he chased it through the north-west section of the city, his own city-issue cruiser wheezing and rattling as he drove, sirens and horns blaring, lights flashing, with the pedal to the metal. The Orca had been involved in a hit-and-run a few minutes earlier, popping out a streetgirl working in the Harbor District of the city, and George had been on his tail for the last two miles. That was problem number one.

Problem number two was his partner for the past six months, one Nancy Thon Quong, a tiny Vietnamese girl who'd been on the force less than a year, and who barely made the minimal height and weight requirements. Her uniform looked like it could fit his fourteen-year-old boy Clarence, but on her it was sleek and tight, especially around that delectable young and firm bottom. Which was the problem.

George was falling in love with his partner.

She picked up the radio microphone, her fine black hair falling about her face. 'Central, Central, this is Able-Twelve. Now eastbound on Fourteenth Street. Eastbound on Fourteenth.'

'Roger, Able-Twelve,' came the dispatcher's voice. 'Still trying to get back-up for you. Hold tight.'

'Able-Twelve,' Nancy said, slamming the microphone back into its cradle with disgust. 'Goddamn city can't keep enough cops out here at night even to give directions to tourists.'

'Ain't that the truth, rook,' he said.

Up ahead the Orca made a tight corner, skidding on two tires, and George eased up on the accelerator for just a moment, feeling the cruiser's balding tires barely hold on to the slick pavement. A few minutes ago they had been in a run-down section of Baltimore, where city and Federal redevelopment dollars had passed by another generation of Baltimore's poorest citizens. But here the buildings were getting better repaired, the homes were more upscale, and the lawns were getting wider and greener. The Orca was pulling away and George wished again that his department could have afforded a better computer terminal for his cruiser, one that had a ferret trace. With one all he would have to do was grab a pic of the car and its license plate and he could keep on following, no matter if it was out of sight. The computer and the traffic surveillance cameras throughout the city would do the rest, feeding him info, block by block.

But on this late night they were doing cop work the old-fashioned way, by keeping things in sight, even as the Orca sped up. He tunneled his view right down the middle of the road, staring right at the raised bumper and trunk of the other car, letting his partner warn him about jaywalkers, traffic on the cross streets, and anything else that could get in the way. At each intersection she'd lean forward, do a quick scan and yell out, 'Clear!'

He did a quick in-and-out with two cars that had stopped in the middle of the road, freezing with indecision as he roared up behind them, and then Nancy yelled, 'He's broke right! He's broke right!'

'Got it!' George pumped his brakes, felt the squishy response as the cruiser slowed down, and now they were in an even better neighborhood, and he saw where the Orca had turned in. There was a six-foot-high brick wall expanding outward from both sides of a guardpost. On top it had what looked to be razor-wire as well as lights every few feet or so. The guardpost had gates for both the outbound and inbound traffic, and George saw the inbound one come down just as he also saw tail-lights race up the drive and bear off to the right. An illuminated sign near the guardpost said FRANCIS SCOTT KEY ESTATES – A PRIVATE COMMUNITY.

He turned right, raced right up to the gatehouse and pounded on the horn. A man came out, mid-forties, beefy white and wearing a light green uniform. He grimaced and moved a finger about his ear, and George flipped off the siren and rolled down the window. 'Hurry up!' he yelled. 'Get that gate up! We're in pursuit!'

The damn security guy sure was taking his time, and even Nancy whispered something harsh he couldn't make out. The guard came over, clipboard in hand, and said, 'What seems to be the problem, chief?'

George scowled. 'What the problem is, asshole, is that I'm in pursuit of a late-model Orca that just turned in here, and you're preventing me from going after him. Lift the fucking gate!'

The guard smiled, looked down at the clipboard. 'Yeah, I did see a car come through here, but I couldn't tell if it was an Orca or something else. You see, chief, that car had a chip in it that let that gate up, which means he lives here. The type of people who live here, I don't think they'd be chased in here by one of Baltimore's . . . finest.'

George threw the cruiser in park and stepped out, swearing again. The lights from the overhead strobes made everything stand out, from the brickwork to the surveillance cameras to the shiny green fabric of the security guard's uniform. 'Look, asshole, you're about ten seconds away from getting your ass arrested for impeding a police pursuit. For the last fucking time, open that goddamn gate!'

The guard kept the smile on his face. 'Thing is, chief, you're about five seconds away from having the Francis Scott Key Corporation file a complaint against you and the department. You know the rules, just as well as I do. Private communities like this, people pay for everything in here, from cops to fire protection to their own little form of government. They want safety and peace, and what they don't want is poorly paid civil servants in here, racing around, disturbing their sleep. I only let you in if there's evidence of a crime in my purview, or if there was hot pursuit. I didn't see anything criminal go on all night long, and you came in a while after that car. That don't qualify as hot pursuit. You come back here tomorrow with a city attorney, we'll see what we can do. Until then, get that ugly piece of shit off our property. Understood?'

George was trying to keep a hold of his temper and blood pressure at the same time, and it was a losing battle. 'The kids in that Orca, they ran down someone a while ago, just for the fun of it. You understand? Just for the fun of it.'

'Where?'

'What the hell does it matter, where it happened?'

The guard motioned back to his shack. 'I've got a police scanner in there. Heard about a hit-and-run, down by the Harbor. Some cranked-out hooker ran down. Boo-fucking-hoo. I'm not letting you in here because of some hooker. Now, get in your crap cruiser and get out.'

From inside the cruiser Nancy was saying something but he ignored her. He was staring at that fleshy, smug face. George said, 'How is it, anyway, working for corporate assholes like these guys?'

He leaned forward, close enough so George could smell tobacco on his breath. 'Truth is, I love it. You know why? Years ago, I was just like you. On the job and working for the city, each year seeing perps and terrs get arrested and then let loose, each year seeing benefits getting cut back, each year seeing fewer and fewer cruisers out there, fewer and fewer fellow cops to back you up. So I pulled the pin and went private. Got good hours, decent pay, pension plan and dental. You guys on the force got dental, hunh?'

Nancy leaned over to his side of the cruiser. 'George, we've got to get going. MV accident, six blocks away, people hurt. We're the closest unit.'

The guard started back to the shack. 'Listen to your banana partner, chief. Get the hell out of here, will you?'

George let his hand rest on his service pistol, just for a moment, and then got back in. Nancy started telling him where the accident was and he said, 'Rook, just shut up for a sec, all right? Just shut up and don't say a word.'

He threw the cruiser into reverse, backed up with a squeal of brakes onto the street, and then gunned the pedal as he shifted again. From the left he caught a quick view of the guard waving and yelling something, something that was overpowered by the tremendous *bang!* that occurred when he plowed the cruiser through the gate. Pieces of black-and-white painted wood skittered up over the hood and the windshield, and Nancy started swearing in a sing-song dialect he couldn't understand. Probably her native Vietnamese. Why not? Wonder if she talks like that in the sack, when she's feeling particularly frisky . . .

George raced about fifty feet up the wide drive and made a tight, spinning turn and then sped back to the guard shack. Nancy said, 'Oh shit, not again,' as he barreled through the other barrier. Another explosion of wood and splinters, and again, out of the corner of his eye, that guard yelling and holding up a cellphone to his face. He made a screeching turn to the right, and flipped on the siren again. He was looking at the rain-slick road, at the traffic bearing off as he headed to the accident scene, and all he could really see was the smug face of that guard back there.

Nancy spoke up, over the siren's sound. 'So let me get this straight. We got the call for the motor vehicle accident. You found that the cruiser couldn't use its reverse gear. You did the only thing possible in order to respond in time to help these people. You had to break those two barriers. Am I right?'

Now he was smiling. Damn, she was something else. He glanced over, seeing her own smile, those exotic-looking eyes, that light brown and smooth skin. 'Hey, rook, you're learning fast.'

She laughed. 'I've got a hell of a teacher.'

'Tell me, what did he mean back there, by calling you a banana?'

Nancy made a dismissive gesture with her hand. 'Oh, he was trying to insult me, and it didn't work. The jerk. A banana means I'm yellow on the outside, white on the inside. Like I'm giving up my Asian heritage and background to work for the city. Fool thing is, though, that's usually an insult the Chinese use with their own. Not the Vietnamese.'

'And what kind of insults do Vietnamese use?'

Nancy laughed. 'You keep on teaching me like tonight, maybe I'll teach you back.'

Oh my. He looked one more time at her and then went back to the driving at hand. He wondered what she looked like out of uniform. He also wondered what she wore under her uniform. He wasn't that stupid, or that horny, 'cause he knew most woman cops wore just basic cotton stuff under there, stuff that could take the day-to-day exertion and sweating. Nothing fancy. But still . . . he had heard whispered stories, in the men's locker room, about what some of the woman cops wore, the ones who felt like being a little dangerous, a little out there. Some lacy stuff, both top and bottom, and he wondered what Nancy would look good in. Damn, that woman would look good in anything, even burlap, but maybe something red, something to offset that skin of hers, something lacy and red that he could practically tear off her with his teeth if the moment was right . . .

Nancy said, 'Didn't you hear me?'

'Uh, no, I'm sorry. What did you say?'

'I said, you'll have a hell of a story to tell Carol when your shift is over. About what just happened back there.'

'Oh. Yeah, right. Carol.'

Oh, yes, George thought, as he drove to the accident scene. That was problem number three facing him tonight, after problem number two, which was his increasing affection for his partner.

For problem number three was that George was married.

SEVEN

You have zero privacy anyway. Get over it.
        Scott McNeally, Sun Computer Systems CEO,
                                January 25, 1999

Drew woke up with a start, his pistol in his hand. He blinked and rubbed at his face with his free hand, and then gently rolled over in his sleeping bag, which was cool and clammy against his skin. Sheila was still sleeping, her eyes closed, one arm protectively cuddling her lapbot. The power was off, which was good, because Drew wasn't sure how many powerpacks she had for the machine, and he knew they were in no position to buy any for a while.

He got out of the sleeping bag as quietly as possible, then went out to the vestibule, which he unzipped. In a minute or two he was outside, wearing socks and nothing else. He yawned again. Didn't get too much sleep last night, did we, he thought. Too much racing through one's mind, but right now let's concentrate on our stomach, shall we? He got dressed in the cold morning air, finding the least dirty pair of cotton slacks and pullover sweater. All of his clothes were damp and had a thick, musty odor. If the deadly Them ever decided to try to track by smell alone, he and Sheila would be in custody within the hour.

The clouds of the previous night were gone, probably now

making life miserable for whatever fishermen were at work this morning in the Gulf of Maine. It was sunny and looked like it might warm up later. The hollow they were in was a pretty good hide-out spot, but only for the night. Saplings and alders grew up among the rocks, but their tent was a bright blue and stuck out like a pig at a goat convention. He brought his backpack over to the rock overhang, and in a few minutes he had a gas stove running. He figured that underneath the rock, no thermal detectors would probably detect them, and he got to work.

But even as he made breakfast he was running and rerunning yesterday's events through his mind, beginning with that disastrous entry into that damn bomb shelter, the entry that had set everything off. All right, he thought, as he put a cooking skillet over the gas flame and melted the last of their butter, kept in a KoolPak along with a couple of leftover sausages and three eggs. That bomb shelter back there is active, no doubt about it. That fresh smell of aviation fuel and the markings on the whiteboard. *Case Shiloh: On September 19 we take her back!* – which was now only five days away. All right. Then, less than two hours later, we're ambushed by a deputy sheriff from the next county over, right after Sheila used her SmartCard.

Conclusion? He broke open the eggs, started scrambling them. Conclusion is, the particular Them who are running the show are organized, are quick to respond, and are deadly serious. They knew within minutes we had got into that bomb shelter, were able to ID us off the surveillance system, and had tracked everything we owned so that using a SmartCard would bring in the artillery. Maybe that deputy sheriff panicked back there. Maybe not. Maybe the orders were to eliminate two witnesses, on the spot, with no chance of questions, no chance of anything more leaking out. INTERNMENT CENTERS. Why not? Japanese-Americans of a certain age certainly knew what that had all been about.

The eggs were done and he shoved them over to a cooler side of the skillet as he started warming up the sausage. And after breakfast, what then? He looked up at the sky. We take stock, that's what. Clean up where we can, and then stay in the woods. There are lots of trails through here. We stay in the woods, maybe visit a farmhouse or small store to buy a few supplies – like soap! – and we stay put. Then, on September 20, after Case Shiloh does whatever it is, we slide on out into public for a few hours, get a vehicle, and then head north. A few years ago he had spent a training session up in the Canadian Rockies. Impressive mountains and beautiful country that a man and woman could hide out in for decades.

Nice plan. And he was sure it would fail. It took convincing Sheila, and while she was one smart woman – the smartest woman he had ever met – she was naive when it came to people like the almighty Them. He had once worked for people like Them, people who would cheerfully send in their fellow Americans to get slaughtered for a five-point opinion poll boost.

As the sausages started sizzling in the pan, a little voice spoke up. Is that it? Hide in the woods like a scared little rabbit? Man, they tried to gun down your woman, and for payback you're going to stay in the trees and maybe beg the local farmers for some food and handsoap? My, how brave and noble you are, Drew Connor, retired field agent for the Defense Research Agency, previously assigned to Gamma Force, the darkest, spookiest and best warriors ever made, sent in to do the dirty work, the black tasks. Your fellow troopers would wet themselves laughing at seeing what you had planned. Play bunny in the woods. How sweet.

Yeah, well fuck you, he told the insistent voice. The Crescent took care of that business, and we are done. Finished. Never to raise a weapon in anger, ever again. Especially after the Crescent, after he went blind during that last mission.

He remembered waking up, sitting against the hangar wall at the target air force base. He had blinked his eyes a few times. Damn, he could see again. Those anti-flash goggles really do work, and he had almost giggled in relief at having not been blinded. He rubbed at his neck and looked over to where Master Sergeant Coughlin was kneeling before him.

'You okay, loo?'

'Yeah, except it feels like somebody used my head for kicking practice.' Drew saw that part of the hangar had collapsed, and also that the vault door had been opened. About a dozen tubular metal objects – their prize for the day – had been loaded on wheeled carts. The rest of the hangar looked strangely empty. He couldn't figure out why. He was going to say something about the scene when gunfire erupted, rounds chipping at the concrete floor and the side of the hangar walls. He ducked and so did Coughlin, and there were some shouts and return fire from a squad sandbagged out front at the hangar entrance.

'Coughlin,' Drew said, his mouth feeling like it was filled with dust. 'Report. How long have I been out?'

'A couple of hours, loo, and a lot of things have gone to the shits.' Coughlin motioned outside. 'We had a NUDET about thirty klicks away. About the only damn good thing is that the wind is blowing away from us. Damn thing is, we took some fucking bad hits from that NUDET.'

'The chopper,' Drew finally realized. 'Where in hell is it?'

'Gone and flown away,' Coughlin said bitterly. 'After the NUDET, those flyboys decided they had enough and they scampered, loo, they fucking scampered us without even looking back.'

Something cold started to gnaw deep inside him. 'Casualties?'

'The guys we had as spotters on the control tower . . . they're gone, loo. That blast just blew them off like they was made of paper. We've also got two KIA from gunfire—'

'Who?'

'Burns and Moore. We've also got a handful of wounded. Loo, it's easier to count up who's not hurt, you know what I mean?'

More gunfire from outside, but none of the rounds seemed to make it into the hangar. Drew struggled to his feet, felt the floor spin beneath him. Coughlin held him up and said, 'Easy, loo, easy . . .'

'Who's doing the shooting?'

'Best we can figure is some of the personnel from some of the outlying buildings. Maybe the B-2 didn't do a good enough job with its antipersonnel rounds. All I know is that they're out there, mightily pissed, and they've been chipping at us for a couple of hours.'

Drew glanced at his watch. Four p.m. local time. That wasn't right. That couldn't be right. Coughlin noticed his expression, nodded. 'Yep. You got it. The pickup from the C5X was supposed to come two hours ago. It never showed up. Loo, we are some seriously stuck.'

Drew had spent the next half hour going around the hangar, not liking what he was seeing, not at all. The hangar was about the best place to be in this madness, but all it would take would be a couple of RPG rounds through the open doorway to make things interesting. The roof was thick and could take hits from whatever the locals had, but it still wasn't good. In one corner of the hangar the first aid station had been set up, and guys were in there – good guys, guys he had trained with for years and years – moaning and crying out, and there was blood and soiled bandages and wrappings underfoot. One of his crew was sitting against a metal desk, legs splayed out, hands folded quietly in his lap. Rooney, that was his name. Ex-Green Beret, ex-Delta Force (D-boy), now a contractor like all of them.

He looked up. Something was odd about his face. 'Who's there?'

'It's me, Connor,' Drew said.

The man smiled. 'Hey, loo, if you get back, can you do me a favor?'

'Go on.'

The smile was still there, but he was staring right through Drew. 'Make sure that field training really, and I emphasize the word really, points out the importance of wearing your anti-flash goggles in a hostile environment with the threats of nukes.'

Oh, Jesus . . . 'Rooney, I . . . I . . .'

He motioned with a hand. 'Go on, loo, it really doesn't hurt that much. Thing is, I can still see the flash. I sure as hell hope it goes away. I don't want to see that image the rest of my life. You got work to do, loo. Go to it.'

He went away, ashamed at doing what the young soldier told him.

But a few minutes later the shame had turned into anger.

The comm officer, Powalski, was almost crying with frustration as he looked up from the office he had commandeered, his communications gear around him. 'Loo, I tell you, I'm not getting a thing. Not a fucking thing!'

Coughlin was with him as well. 'Could the atmospherics be screwed up, all that radiation being spewed out?'

Powalski shook his head. 'Not a chance, sarge. Not a chance. This is hardened gear, designed to handle this stuff. It's working well. I'm picking up all kinds of traffic, everything from airliners over the Persian Gulf to military stuff on Diego Garcia. Thing is, nobody's responding to our call sign. Not a damn thing.'

Coughlin looked over and Drew noticed a couple of other soldiers had drifted into earshot as well. Coughlin said, 'Loo? What do you think?'

That worry gnawing at him had grown colder. Drew looked at the faces of the men, knew they were only a few seconds away from turning into a mob. He could bullshit his way through a quick story but knew that in this fear that was going through them that it would just feed the terror. Some of the things they never taught you at OCS.

Drew nodded and said, 'Guys, we're a contract force. We've always known that, ever since signing up. This is just a job, no matter what's going on with DC or the UN or whatever. And our job was to come in here and take these nukes away, before Libya or Iraq or the Russian mafia got here first.' He looked down at the comm gear. 'I'd say with the C5X not showing up and nobody replying to our messages, our contract just got canceled.'

'The fucks,' a low voice said.

Drew spoke up. 'All right, here's the drill. We can't stay here, not with the locals shooting at us and this place still a prime target for an Indian warhead. Sarge, how are we set for transport?'

Coughlin shouldered his M-16. 'We've got that one truck, and it must have been hardened, too. That last NUDET didn't short out its electronics. It can start up all right. Thing is, loo . . .'

'Yeah?'

Coughlin stared right at him. 'We can fit the squad on the truck, or the warheads and a few guys. We can't do both.'

Drew nodded. 'All right, let's see if we can't scrounge another truck or two. But let's get ready to clear out of this hole.'

An hour later Coughlin was stretched out on a work-bench, as one of the medics – Carlisle – worked on a bullet wound in his upper thigh. It was getting darker and the locals outside were getting bolder. The pace of the gunfire had increased. Drew said, 'Sarge, I don't like it, not at all.'

'Fuck, that hurts! Sorry, sir, not at you. Loo, look, it makes sense. You know it does. There ain't another working truck around. And a couple of us just got hit, and Robby got him-self killed, looking for another one. Time's up and you know it. And you can't leave those warheads behind.' Coughlin coughed and said, 'Hey, Carlisle, any chance for another morphine hit?'

'In a while, sarge, in a while,' the medic said. 'There's a couple of guys ahead of you that are worse off. Be patient.'

Drew rubbed at his face, hearing the groans of the wounded on the other side of the building, the sharp crack of gunfire. 'Those fucking civilians . . .'

'Well, that's what civilians do,' Coughlin said. 'Think up intricate ways of advancing their careers while sending us into harm's way.'

'No, I was thinking of those fucking civilians, years ago, who didn't do anything while countries who hated each other with a passion developed nuclear weapons. Who let these countries just blunder along while they worried about who was up and who was down within the Beltway, who was scoring points on what talkshow, all the while this shit was going on.'

Coughlin gritted his teeth. 'That's what we get paid for, to clean up other people's messes. Loo, contract being canceled or not, you can't leave these warheads behind. So you go ahead like you planned. Head for the coast, broadcast in the clear, and hope somebody comes and picks you up. I'll stay here with the wounded and the dead. Leave us the heavy weapons and we can stay here for a while. Just don't forget us. Make sure you come back.'

Drew knew what the Master Sergeant was saying was right. He was trying to think of something noble to say, something that would make everything come out fine, but his mind was tired. All he could think of is what he saw out there, the burning cities on the horizon, knowing what might happen if one of the weapons here was dropped on Manhattan or Los Angeles.

He held out his hand. Master Sergeant Coughlin shook it firmly. Drew said, 'Sergeant, we're heading out. And we'll be back. I promise.'

Coughlin nodded. 'Of course you will, Lieutenant. Now, get going.'

And that had been the last time he had ever spoken to Coughlin, and the real last time he had ever raised his weapon in anger.

Except for yesterday, right? The voice from before returned: Sure was nice beating the hell out of that deputy sheriff, though. Wasn't it?

Because he deserved it. As he started putting the breakfast

out on two small metal plates, the zipper opened up on the tent. He turned and Sheila was there, hair a tangled mess, wearing wool socks and her dark green nightgown. Her lapbot was under her arm.

'Give me another minute,' he called out. 'I'll have some coffee for the two of us.'

She shook her head, and he saw that her chin was trembling. 'You've got to see this, and right now.'

When Sheila woke up she saw the empty sleeping bag next to her and, in spite of the terrible dreams she had encountered during the night, smiled. She and Drew were on two different clocks, which was just fine. He was an early-to-bed and early-to-rise kind of guy, and she was exactly the opposite, yet from the very start they had adjusted within a day or two of him having moved in. Give and take. What made relationships work, and over the past two years this had been a special one indeed, as she had learned more and more about this man. More good things than whatever had happened with that dreary Tom, whom she had married shortly after moving back from California, when she had been one scared and lonely woman.

All right, then, what was the deal with that cop and what Drew did yesterday? She closed her eyes, shivered. Drew had gone right up to the cop, the cop with the gun, and Drew had dropped him and then had struck him while he was down. That was the first time she had ever seen Drew do anything violent. Hell, the man had never raised his voice, not once in all the times she had known him. So what had happened yesterday? Who was the man back there with that deadly look on his face, the way he moved, the way he swung that axe handle? Where in hell had that Drew come from?

Plus he knew exactly what to do with that sheriff's cruiser, to make the computer think that two people were sitting in the front seat so it would automatically go up that interstate. Who was that Drew?

Sure, he had his guns, his one vice. And she knew he had served for a while in the government, something hush-hush. But she had never . . . well, there had been that one time, last summer. She hugged herself, remembering. July, right? Yeah, the beginning of July. In their rural neighborhood, up on the north end of Lake Montcalm, a bunch of kids had got into mailbox baseball. It sounded so innocent, like little pranksters. They would get in their cars and travel the country roads, drunk or cranked up, leaning out of the windows with baseball bats, destroying mailboxes. Lots of yucks, except when it was your mailbox you saw laying on the ground, broken in two, and when you replaced it a week later it would be broken again, your magazines and letters and bills soaking in rainwater in a drainage ditch by the side of the road. The local cops just shrugged their shoulders. Minor vandalism. Sorry. Can't do much about it. One day she and Drew had been coming back from the store, and she counted twenty-one mailboxes destroyed or damaged on the way back home. Then she saw a dark look cross Drew's face when he spotted an older woman, standing on the side of the road, shaking her head in dismay at the mailbox at her feet. It had been painted to look like a little red schoolhouse, and now it was crumpled, like it had been driven over by a truck, and as they got closer they could see the woman was weeping.

That night Drew had gone outside, carrying a sleeping bag and satchel. Going out to stargaze, he had said. Won't be back for a couple of hours. That had happened every night for the rest of the week, until early one morning he had come back. Well, got my fill in of stargazing, he had said, and she had noted how sweaty he looked, like he had just run a marathon. She also observed that he had a self-satisfied grin on his face as he climbed into bed.

Well. Two days later, the Montcalm Gazette had a story about a car that had gone off the road the other night in an apparent traffic accident when one of its tires suddenly went flat. When police arrived they found the four young male passengers sitting on the side of the road, moaning with pain. Inside the car were two dented baseball bats and a couple of six-packs of beer. And, in an amazing coincidence, all four youths had suffered the same injury as a result of the apparent accident: a broken right arm. The youths had also been silent about everything else, like something terrifying had scared them deep inside the woods.

All right, she thought. Drew can be violent when he wants to. Let it be. Yesterday he saved your little butt, and you should be thankful. She yawned, heard something outside that made it sound like Drew was fixing breakfast. Her stomach grumbled. Good. Let's hope it's hot and better than last night's dinner.

She flipped open the lid to her lapbot. Just a few minutes of surfing before we get out, before we have to face the rest of the day. She gently rubbed the plastic surface of her lapbot as it powered up, looked at her little Warner Brothers cartoon characters. These powerful little machines used to be called laptops, but as more and more computer power was shoved into their tiny gizzards and as more and more tasks could be done by them – lots of homes had docking ports where an installed lapbot could order groceries, mail out customized Christmas cards and adjust the heating and lighting – their name changed. Laptops with the power of robots. Lapbots. And she loved hers dearly, though she would never admit that to Drew. He thought computers were idiot machines, very powerful indeed but often so stupid that they could kill people in an instant.

Funny boy, she said. Computers don't kill people. People kill people.

Then why did you leave Stanford so quickly, girlie? What do you think Drew will think about you if he ever found out what you did as a CyberGal?

Shut up, she thought. That was a while ago and Drew won't find out, so leave it be. The earplugs went in as the screen came into focus, and she quickly flipped through the opening menu, past some of the paid banners that were the equivalent of commercials in cyberspace:

THE NECROPAGE
Tonight it's a special treat, 8 p.m. EST, 7 p.m. CST.
Death in the Evening: See camera footage of
convenience store clerks facing their final checkout!
Plus as an added feature *Cheerleader Slaughter*. Actual
amateur footage of the Morton High School pep
rally, when sixteen-year-old Glen Curran last year
brought more than his homework from home!
Click **[HERE]** for pricing and AdultBarrier
information.

CONSPIRACY UPDATE
Continuous. The latest government report on the
JFK assassination has been released. What do you
think of the new theory? Oswald as a brainwashed
sleeper agent? True or does the coverup continue?

Other areas as well on TWA Flight 800, Pearl
Harbor, Detroit Anthrax.
Click **[HERE]** for pricing.

GOD HATES JEWS. GOD HATES FAGS. DOES GOD HATE YOU?

The US Family Defense Council needs *your* support
to save the True American Way Of Life. The
Council also offers its prayerful support for you if
you'd like to convert away from your sinful excesses.
Click **[HERE]** to learn how you can support the US
Family Defense Council.
Click **[HERE]** for information on how you can
change your sinful lifestyle.

Ah, sweet cyberspace, she thought, scrolling down the
other banner ads, looking for a NewsNet link to catch the
morning news. Home of the free, brave, nutso and bigoted,
and anyone else with a grudge and a modem. Plus
CyberGals, right?

Right. She remembered how a couple of weeks after her
visit with the East Palo Alto photographer her own
CyberGal page was up and running. She had picked the
name Sally from Seattle, and, again with Donna's help, she
had made up a bio page. Sally was a student at a college in
Seattle. She was doing this to make money. Please, mister,
won't you click onto my home page and help me?

With several sets of powerful software powering her
CyberGal page, Sheila's digital and still photographs would
place her into a dormitory room. Men – well, maybe a few
women, who knew – could enter her 'room' and through a
set of mouseclicks and commands make her do anything

they wanted. Walk around the dorm room. Take a shower. Eat a meal. Disrobe and masturbate. And so forth and so on . . .

But after a week she had only four visitors, none of which had given her enough money to even begin paying back Donna. And there were only two messages on her message board: one said, *Nice tits*, and the other said, *Sally, nice bod but too vanilla*.

She wondered about that. Too vanilla? That meant too bland. One night, while ignoring the knocks on her bedroom door from Margaret, who was still demanding her rent money, she had one deeper look into the CyberGal universe and saw which sites were most popular, what was selling, what was making the real money. It was sickening, but she stiffened up as the knocks on her door continued. What sold was definitely not vanilla. What sold was abuse, pure and simple, and, for those with rougher tastes, snuff fantasies. Sneaking into the dorm room and murdering the CyberGal through a variety of means, and then coming back for more.

'Hey you in there!' Margaret yelled, pounding at the door one night. 'One more week, I swear, one more week and your stuff's on the sidewalk!'

Sheila's head ached. She bent down to the minifridge in her room and popped open a Coke, and went to work. It was going to be a long night.

The first week after her page was redone, Sheila had four visitors. The second, nine, and in the third week, twenty-three. By the end of the month her page had cracked the Filthy Fifty of CyberGals, and in another month had reached the Twisted Twenty.

It was simple, really. Sheila had trolled through the other CyberGals – from Alice from Albany to Zelda from Zanzibar –

and found that even the most popular pages were missing something. They were too fake, too unreal. Those CyberGals just existed in the here and now. No depth at all. So Sheila focused on making her page as real as possible. She had a diary where Sally from Seattle wrote hesitantly about her sexual fantasies, which involved abuse and death at the hands of a powerful man. She scanned some of her own pictures from her childhood – changing the hairstyles some – and posted those as well, as well as old high school report cards, supposed love letters from old boyfriends, and about a dozen other pages of information that made Sally from Seattle more real. Favorite recipes, pictures of pets, anything and everything.

And in those other CyberGals, the successful ones who were murder victims, over and over again, they were always unwilling victims. Sheila decided to make Sally from Seattle a babe who was intrigued by death, who would always be a victim, but maybe one who didn't mind being attacked and killed. Sick, of course (hell, the whole damn thing was one big sickness from sign-on page to message board) but it boosted her visitorship by 30 percent.

The message board was overflowing:

Sally, you're the best.

Sally, can we meet for an F2F?

We luv you Sally! We want to love you and kill you!

Sally, Sally, deadly Sally, we want you so bad!

In a month she had paid up her rent and moved out. Tuition was no longer a problem, and she had graduated, not bothering going to the ceremonies, just content in knowing that she had done it and was making lots of money. Job hunting could wait. CyberGals was going well. So well, in fact, that she was socking away a healthy amount of money and was even considering a stint in grad school the following year.

Things were good. About the only thing that bothered her was . . . well, the fact that it wasn't bothering her. She was a strong woman, a feminist with a firm sense of self who was content about her skills and abilities, and she knew that helping sickos with their fantasies of abusing and killing women was wrong. For one thing, it certainly wouldn't help with the Sisterhood to know what she had been doing.

But in fact it was fun. Twisted fun, of course, but fun nonetheless. It was powerful knowing that she attracted all these men, all these losers, all these emotional and mental midgets, and that she was adept in taking money away from them. Day after day, week after week. All that money, and all they really had to play with was a fake, an avatar, someone who didn't even exist.

It was going great, her bank account in Calgary was increasing every day, she was planning an overseas trip to Hong Kong with a couple of friends, and it would have been going great even to this day except for that phone call one night.

She shivered now in the tent, remembering that call. Please, let's just get on with things, all right? Sheila got onto the NewsNet but double-clicked by accident on a national newsfeed, not a local one. She saw two talking heads in a news studio, or chattering skulls, depending on your point of view. Since Sheila never voted and was proud of it – why encourage the morons? – she thought the news media and politics were so intermixed so as to be the same thing. The graphic behind the two men showed a broken Presidential Seal with the overlay WHITE HOUSE IN CRISIS. Probably had that graphic in storage for the past ten years. Through her earphones she could hear their debate, as they yelled and tried to talk over each other.

Administration Supporter: . . . can't believe that a special prosecutor is needed to look into a matter such as this . . .

Administration Opponent: . . . but if the President forced his aides to say no, that he did not sully the memory of previous presidents by blatantly and obscenely urinating onto that sacred soil, then he's guilty of obstructing justice . . .

Administration Supporter: . . . all his opponents are interested in is obstructing the administration's programs and policies . . .

Administration Opponent: . . . what programs and policies? Most of us in the Congress would be pleased just to see a public appearance, a photo opportunity, a news conference . . .

Administration Supporter: . . . his time is too valuable to waste . . .

Administration Opponent: . . . but he hasn't been seen in public since that urination incident last month, why is that? Will you explain . . .

Administration Supporter: . . . with the Israeli civil war, the continued oil embargo against non-Muslim states and domestic unrest, the President has obviously decided to use his limited time to deal with those issues instead of this alleged event . . .

Administration Opponent: . . . alleged? Alleged? Look
at the tape . . .

Administration Supporter: . . . the President's
spokesman said it didn't happen. That's good enough
for me . . .

Sheila double-clicked her way out of that mess and went
back to local newsfeed and found the Web connection for
'Channel 21/The One For NH!' When she saw the top story
for the morning, she grew sick to her stomach and fought her
way out of the tent, the lapbot under her arm.

Drew went up to Sheila, who held her lapbot up and
adjusted the screen so he could see it in daylight. 'Don't ask
anything, all right?' she said, sitting down on a boulder. 'Just
sit with me and watch.' She worked the keyboard and from
the lapbot's speakers he listened to a news channel jingle,
and watched the screen as the logo for Channel 21 snapped
up.

Visual	*Audio*
[Young news man, belted trenchcoat, microphone with station logo in hand, standing on stretch of highway. Lots of parked police cruisers behind him.]	Good morning, Tom. The scourge of domestic terrorism struck home in New Hampshire last night, as two suspected members of the Church of the Final Apocalypse murdered a Coos County deputy sheriff after stealing his cruiser.

[Static shot, formal portrait of a Coos County deputy sheriff. Reporter does V/O.]

Dead is twenty-seven-year-old Deputy Sheriff Roland Gray, a two-year veteran of the department.

[Footage showing the downtown of a small community, with a general store and nearby gas station. V/O continues.]

Authorities said the incident began late yesterday afternoon, when a shoot-out erupted between Deputy Gray and the two suspected terrorists.

[Old man near general store, gray stubble beard, wearing a US OUT OF UN sweatshirt.]

'First there was a Christly amount of shootin', and then I saw this fella beatin' the deputy out in the middle of the street.'

[Back to reporter, now standing next to destroyed police cruiser on its roof.]

The brave deputy, injured though he was, commandeered a private vehicle and followed the cruiser to this vantage point on I-89, where another fight ensued. It was during this fight that Deputy Gray's life was tragically lost.

[Static shot, showing two photos from NH state driver's licenses. Man and woman, side by side. Reporter continues V/O.]

Local, county, state and now Federal officials are looking for these two. Drew Connor, age forty, and his companion, Sheila Cass, age thirty-five. Both are from Montcalm, NH, and both are, according to authorities, members of the super-secret and super-dangerous religious cult, the Church of the Final Apocalypse.

[Footage of interview with NH State Police Captain, ID'd as *Captain Wayne Moorland*. There is a line of police officers standing behind him, except for a woman with blonde hair and a balding man wearing a trenchcoat.]

We've just been informed by Federal authorities that the individuals involved in this incident are believed to be members of the group responsible for the Detroit anthrax epidemic. These two should be considered armed and dangerous. A thorough, statewide search is now underway. Anyone who spots either of these individuals should contact their local police. Do not attempt to

confront or detain these
people on your own.

[Camera now returns to reporter doing stand-up on the interstate, in front of line of police vehicles.]

There you have it, Tom. The deadly threat of domestic terrorism, striking at the heart of rural New Hampshire. Reporting live for Channel 21, this is Clay Coyne.

Drew rubbed at his face, the rough stubble almost comforting. At least that was something he could touch and feel. Next to him Sheila breathed in and said, 'You want to see that again?'

'No, I don't.'

He could feel her trembling at his side as she closed the lid of her lapbot. 'Drew . . .'

'Yeah?'

'What . . . what can we do? They said we murdered that man!'

For just a moment, he felt anger. Damn it, Sheila, if you hadn't wandered off that trail, hadn't gone poking where you didn't belong, where you had no right to be . . . He grabbed her hand, clenched it hard. No, no anger. That wasn't right.

'Not a hell of a lot, except to keep hiding out until the search dies down. Things like this, they start out fast and furious, with lots of news coverage and volunteers in the woods. A couple of days later most of it dies down. The news guys go somewhere else, and the volunteers decide it's too much effort to keep on tramping through the woods. We could probably keep our heads down and miss being found.'

'But we're innocent! We didn't do anything wrong!'

He squeezed her hand again. 'That doesn't matter. Hundreds, hell, thousands of people this morning now know a lot about us. They know we're killers, that we're terrorists, that we're cultists. And any of these local people will be thrilled to find us. The City of Detroit still has a hefty bounty out on any surviving members of that church.'

'We could call a lawyer, a newspaper . . .'

'We could. And who are they going to believe? The authorities, or two nutty religious cultists? Even if we do tell the truth, that this all started because we went into a government-built bomb shelter, they'd think we were raving. By the time someone listened to us, September 19 will have come and gone and . . . well, we'll be two extraneous witnesses. Whatever's planned for Case Shiloh will have occurred. It has to be something extraordinary for all of this attention, all of this lying that we're seeing.'

'So we do nothing? We just hide and run away?'

All of these safe mountains around us, he thought. Lots of hiding places. 'Yeah, that's what I think we should do. Hide and wait for this to blow over, and then think of something else. Do you have another idea?'

'Yes,' she said, snapping the lid of her lapbot closed. 'I think we should fight.'

Sheila saw the shocked expression on her man's face and pressed forward, not wanting to give up so easily. 'Those assholes out there have just ruined us, do you realize? Do you think your government pension is going to continue after you've been identified as a cultist? How many more days do you think my business is going to last when my customers realize who I am? Or who they think I am?'

Drew folded his arms and stared out, a look she had rarely seen before and one that always concerned her. It usually happened after one of his trembling dreams, and it made him seem ten years older. 'And our bank accounts, our savings. We can't reach them, we can't get any more money, because they've probably been frozen, right? So what do you suggest, Drew? Are you going to take up hunting out here? Are we going to root for nuts and berries? Break into people's homes and local stores? And it's going to get colder and colder over the next few weeks up here in the mountains, my friend. And I'm a modern girl; I like roughing it for a few days, but not for a few weeks.'

Drew said quietly, 'Go on.'

'Hold it, you'll see.' She put the lapbot down, went to her backpack in the tent and poked through a side pocket. She came back with a sheet of paper that she handed over to Drew. He looked at it and said, 'The photo-fax we found in the deputy sheriff's cruiser.'

'Right. And look at the top up there. A phone number, right? A phone number from the machine that issued the fax. I find out who sent the fax, then I'm halfway there to finding out who's chasing us, and why. And from there I find out about Case Shiloh. And then we fight. We go public. We spoil their plans. We make them stop chasing us, telling lies about us.'

'Sheila, these are organized people. They know computer security. They know how to keep things secret. You—'

'You'll be surprised what I can do,' she said. 'And these people may be organized, they may know computer security, and they may know how to keep things secret, but they should have known better than to fuck with me. Because I'm not going to let them get away with ruining our lives. We'll find out who they are and blast that info all over the Net.'

She was surprised at how shrill her voice had become, but damn it all to hell, it was true. Why couldn't Drew see that? What was going on in his mind?

'Are you sure?'

'Hell yes, I'm sure.'

He gently held on to her hand again. 'Are you really ready to do what you just said? We push these people, they're going to push us back, ten times as hard. Understand?'

'I understand. Drew, it's important for the both of us. We can't let them take away our livelihood, our lives, through all these lies.'

'All right.'

Then he sat there in silence for another minute.

Her hand was comforting to hold but that was the only comfortable thing going on. Those words of hers were making sense, were waking up part of him that he thought he had closed down and packed away ever since the Crescent. My God, what a horror show that had been, he and his crew in the middle of a conflict designed and committed by madmen, not knowing from one second to the next if you were going to live or if you were going to be flashed out of existence.

The Crescent. One screwed-up mission and he had sworn never to have anything to do with the suits who had sent them there, who had abandoned them. When he had left his job he had squeezed that disability pension out of the higher-ups, and they had agreed and he had sworn never to go back to that world, never to fight a big fight, and for God's sake never to be caught out in the open again. Just me and my woman and to hell with everybody else.

Sheila gently squeezed his hand. He looked at her, looked at that face gazing up at him with love and concern, and he remembered the terror in the face, the terror that had been placed there yesterday when men with guns came after her and him, and all because of a simple trespass.

Sheila.

He touched her face.

'All right,' he said. 'We fight.'

EIGHT

Republicans would like to see Medicare just die and go away – that's probably what they'd like to see happen to seniors, too, if you think about it.

White House spokesman Mike McCurry,
March 12, 1995

By the next morning a temporary command post had been set up in the parking lot of the country store where the two fugitives had purchased supplies before sending that deputy sheriff's cruiser up the highway. There were now two of the FERA mobile units in the parking lot, and Ira had assigned Clem Badger to one of them, to continue his top-to-bottom data search on the two fugitives. 'I know you haven't come up with much yet, but keep at it. Pay close attention to the male subject, the guy called Drew. He's supposedly on disability from the Department of Agriculture. It's obvious he's more than just that. So get to it.'

'Dark and deep,' Clem had said, munching on his third doughnut of the morning. 'Just the way I like it. No wonder I haven't found anything yet.'

'And don't forget the woman as well. I want to know everything about both of them, and soonest.'

With Clem at work Ira was in the other mobile unit, talking to a special agent from the FBI's office in Concord, the state capital. The agent's name was Tulley and he had long legs, which he stretched out almost across the entire width of the support van. He had on a two-piece dark blue suit and tan raincoat, and his face was flushed as he talked loudly.

'So far all we've been doing is following your lead, and the Bureau doesn't like it,' he complained. 'The only thing we've done since this baby came up is to search the house they live in. That's not very much. There's nothing there, except a lot of books, a few firearms, and a computer system belonging to the woman, which our tech crew is taking apart. There's no documentation, no lab equipment, nothing to indicate these people were part of the Church of the Final Apocalypse. I think we're getting the runaround from you folks.'

'Too bad,' Ira said. 'I've got the local and state police out there, keeping the crowds and news media away from this command post, and they don't like it either. This is our jurisdiction, our matter, under the—'

'Yeah, yeah, I know, the Domestic Terrorism and Tranquility Act of 2001. Jesus. Look, why are you guys so quick to jump on this? I thought you only handled disasters like hurricanes or tornadoes or earthquakes.'

Ira looked down at his lapbot, typed a quick e-mail to his wife. He hated having spent last night away from her and their two children – Aaron and Elizabeth – but things had got away from him when they had set up the initial search. All that coordination between state, county and about a half-dozen local agencies took hours. By the time everything was in place it had been 2 a.m. He and the rest of the crew had bunked out in a local motel, and after a quick breakfast from the country store they had gone right to work. He hoped she would get the e-mail but he wasn't sure. Glenda Sue was wonderful in many ways, including maintaining a safe and religious home for their children, but she often used the home lapbot for nothing more than ordering groceries and researching recipes.

Without looking up Ira said, 'We also respond to man-made disasters as well, and serve as the coordinating agency, even in matters of law enforcement. You know that, Agent Tulley.'

'Yeah, well, we don't have to like it.' He folded his arms in disgust.

Ira rested his fingers for a moment. 'Look, Agent Tulley, let me tell you something. I didn't want to respond like this, not at all. But I got pressure from DC. You know the feeling, right? They wanted us to jump on this first, show every-body – especially the appropriations committees – that we're up to the job. That's the way of the world. Achievements for appropriations. But to tell you the truth, we're not up to the job. You're right. We're designed to respond to storms and disasters. Set up shelters, field kitchens, field hospitals. This is way out of our field, no matter what the 2001 Act of Congress states. Open to a suggestion?'

'Sure.'

'Give us enough rope to hang ourselves. Don't get caught up in this mess, or when this blows up – and it will! – you'll find yourself somewhere else. Like the regional office in Butte, Montana. Or working for a special prosecutor, being sent into the Rose Garden with a garden trowel and a plas-tic bag, to see if you can collect soil samples containing traces of the President's urine.'

'You don't seem too concerned. Hell, why are you trying to help me out?'

Ira forced a smile. 'Just following orders. This blows up, the higher-ups get chopped, room for advancement.'

For the first time, the FBI agent smiled. 'Man, you're a cold one.'

'So I've been told.'

Tulley got up and made for the door, started buttoning his coat. 'All right, I'll follow your lead. Just make sure we get copied on all your reports.'

'Guaranteed,' Ira said, and when the door closed behind the FBI agent, he added, 'you asshole.'

Back to the lapbot he went. The door opened up again and he said, 'Good Lord, can't anybody out there read? The sign outside says *Do not disturb*.'

'I didn't think you'd mind,' came the voice, and Ira looked up into the face of his boss, FERA Director Michaelson Lurry.

Clem Badger looked at the chocolate doughnut on the side table and let it rest. It was going to be a reward for working non-stop for the next hour, looking into information about those two hikers, and it helped him remain focused.

He shifted his bulk as he got into the Net, thinking again that the idiots up high should have paid more for better seats in these mobile units if they expected quality work to be done. And speaking of quality work, he decided to spend a few minutes on one of the NewsNet channels before getting too deep into the day's tasks.

He clicked on and a couple of stories popped up:

WHITE HOUSE ANNOUNCES NEW CHILD CARE INITIATIVE

The White House announced today a new initiative to help children during the cold winter months. Called 'Helping Hands Helping Others', the new program will ensure that children have an adequate supply of mittens and gloves during the winter months. In a statement the President said, 'In this fast-paced society, where one's future can be determined on how accurate one uses a keyboard, we must protect our children's most precious asset: their fingers.'

However, White House spokesman again declined to comment on the President's health or his urination habits.

HOTTEST IPO THIS QUARTER IS ETERNAL PEACE INC.

The most popular Initial Public Offering this quarter on the New York Stock Exchange has been Eternal Peace Inc. (Stock Symbol EPX), which closed the day yesterday at $24.25, well above its offering stock price of $12 per share.

Company spokesman Doris Tessler said the company, based in Atlanta, Georgia, was pleased with the first day's worth of trading.

'It's encouraging to see the marketplace respond positively to a company such as ours,' Tessler said. 'We're obviously fulfilling a need that had yet to be addressed.'

Eternal Peace Inc. maintains and supplies rapid-response teams to handle mass casualties arising from regional conflicts, natural disasters or, in the case of Africa, nation collapse. Depending on the region it responds to, Eternal Peace Inc. can supply within twenty-four hours' notice earthmoving equipment or mobile crematoria to handle up to 10,000 bodies a day.

HUNT CONTINUES FOR COP KILLERS
The Federal Emergency Response Agency is
continuing to coordinate one of the most massive
manhunts in New England history for two suspected
cop killers and alleged members of the Church of the
Final Apocalypse.

Clem rubbed at his face, looked longingly at that doughnut. This last story showed him what had to be done if he was
going to have a good snack later on. Time to get to work.

While Drew broke camp Sheila sat up on a boulder, letting
the sun warm her shoulders as she worked on her lapbot.
Drew was quiet, airing out the sleeping bags, taking down
the tentpoles, pulling up the tent stakes. She wasn't sure if he
was being quiet because he was trying to think things
through, or because he wanted to give her time to work.
Whatever.

She touched the keys with affection as she got into her
task. To Drew and others out there with a minimal knowledge of what went on along the millions of miles of cable and
wire that made up the Net, the whole place was just one big
entity. Ye Olde Omnipotent & Monolithic Internet. But
there were levels out there, hundreds of levels, and Sheila
liked to think that there were three overarching tiers of the
Net: White, Gray and Black. The White areas of the Net
were where the legitimate business and interests were available, from the homepages of governments and the
corporations, to the hundreds of NewsNet channels, to the
special-interest pages that dissected each episode of the several permutations of the *Star Trek* opus or displayed Hummel
collections or traded tips on how to view satellites at night.

The Gray level was a bit more sharp. This is where the amateur sex pages were set up by lonely couples in the suburbs, the mainstream porn was offered from off-island corporations, and, in this new wired age, where the information brokers plied their trade. Info brokers bought and sold data among corporations, government agencies and the voyeuristic and curious, and right now Sheila was looking for one broker she had used before in setting up a couple of Web pages for paying customers who were looking for a particular phone number or address.

There. The Number Hound, whose logo was a smiling bloodhound holding a paper phonebook in his droopy mouth. At a time when Web businesses came and went like the morning frost, she was pleased to see the Number Hound was still operating. She didn't know who he was or where he lived. Probably nobody knew, except for the National Security Agency, the biggest, best and oldest info broker of them all. But the Hound was as legit as one got. He always delivered. She set up an order page from the Hound's homepage, and typed in the telephone number from the photo-fax that had come from the deputy sheriff's cruiser. She shivered for a moment. The dead deputy sheriff. Can't hardly forget that now, can we? When she came to the payment option, she hesitated. All of their accounts were probably now frozen or keyed with a 'sniff & pounce' program. Transfer funds now and the all powerful Them would know that they were up to something, and that was unacceptable.

But there was another option. She had a good chunk of change, squirreled away at an account in the TransCanada Bank in Calgary under a different name. It was her savings from her CyberGal days, untouched all these years after leaving Palo Alto. Another quiet shudder. All right, fair enough.

We'll use it this time and then we'll forget it. And we won't tell Drew where the money came from. Not now, and not ever.

She made the transfer, waited. A box on the Hound's homepage started blinking. ORDER ACCEPTED.

There. Drew looked up, as if he had noted something, and she powered down her lapbot. 'All set. We should know in a few hours who sent the fax.'

'Fine,' he said. 'Tell me, how much more power do you have on your lapbot?'

'A few more hours' worth, if I'm careful,' she said. 'Shouldn't be a problem as long as I keep on shutting her down after each session.'

Drew just nodded, went back to stuffing his knapsack. For a moment she was tempted to bring him over here and tell him a story, about how a scared girl from Portland, Maine, was by herself out on the West Coast when all of the scholarships and financial aid programs began disappearing, when she needed more money than was possible from waiting on tables or cleaning apartments. That through a friend of a friend she became a CyberGal and soon was making more money than she ever thought possible. That for months she lived and worked in a part of the Net where the pedophiles, death fetishists, Net stalkers and snuff players resided, in the Black level.

And that, for a strange few months, she had even liked it.

Director Lurry took the chair recently vacated by Agent Tulley. He carried two cups of coffee, and passed one over to Ira. He gratefully accepted it and began sipping, even though he saw that it contained cream. Ira always drank his coffee with one sugar, no cream, but he wasn't stupid enough to point this out to his boss. While Ira felt like he had spent the night on a steam grate, Lurry looked rested and refreshed, wearing a long gray wool coat over black slacks and a white turtleneck.

Lurry said, 'I've read your overnight report. What's the current status?'

'We've got every law enforcement agency within a hundred miles offering their full cooperation,' Ira said. 'Full photos and bios of the two have been given to all news media, both regular and NewsNet. The Air National Guard has loaned us two of their old Huey helicopters, with thermal imaging and sound-sensing equipment. Both Federal Canada and Quebec have announced extra border patrols. Even the county militias are sending their folks into the woods. This is turning out to be one of the biggest manhunts in New England's history.'

'What's up with the FBI?'

'They're sniffing around but I've managed to delay them, for long enough I'm sure.'

'Good. Getting FBI attention at this stage is not a wise thing.' Then Lurry stared right at him. 'Truthfully, Ira, were those two really connected to the Church of the Final Apocalypse?'

Ira didn't move. 'It's a possibility. Extremely remote, but a possibility. We might have exaggerated a bit, to help us get these search resources.'

'I see,' the Director said. 'So, how soon before they're detained?'

Ira hesitated, and Lurry noticed. 'Ira, I asked you a question.'

He put the cup of coffee down on the table. 'Sir, there's a lot of woods, trails and ravines out there. The searchers could get within a yard of the fugitives and not even notice them. The thermal-imaging equipment will be helpful but, with all of the search parties and usual groups of hikers up there, it'll be a tough job separating the hunters from the hunted. We also know these two have outdoors experience, which makes it even more difficult for us. So, I'm sorry, Mr Lurry, I can't predict if and when we'll detain these two.'

'Good, I'm glad you can't make a prediction,' Lurry said. 'I have to deal with so much spin every day, it's nice to hear the truth. Even when the truth isn't what you want to hear.'

'But I don't think it will matter in the end, sir.'

'Go on.'

Ira took a sip from his coffee cup, tried not to grimace from the taste. 'In five days it won't make a lick of difference. All we have to do is to keep the pressure on, make it so those two go to ground like a couple of squirrels, and we're all set. And even if they do get free of the search and try to say they're innocent of any wrongdoing, who will believe them? Mr Lurry, believe me, it'll be fine.'

Lurry grinned and Ira wondered yet again how come this talented and gifted man had not been able to reach that goal at 1600 Pennsylvania Avenue. 'Glad to hear that, Ira. Very glad.' He turned and looked out one of the tiny, black-tinted windows to the crowded country store parking lot.

'You know,' Lurry said softly, 'I've always loved the people in this state. Despite what the media and elected elite thought and predicted, twice these people gave me primary victories, helped jump-start my campaign. These good people listened to my message, and they gave me their votes and trust.'

'I remember well, sir,' Ira said. 'I worked your campaign here during both primary seasons before working in Kentucky.'

Lurry nodded, reflective. 'They listened, and that made a difference. Lower taxes. Restricted immigration. No more special preferences for any group of people, no matter how well funded or oppressed they were. Putting prayer back in the schools, putting people back to work in the factories, putting mothers back in their homes, putting everything back to where it once was, when things were better. They listened and made a difference.'

'That they did, sir.'

Lurry turned to him, a rueful smile on his face. 'But the well-paid others listened as well, so even after my victories here they wouldn't let my message get out as the primary season went on. Nope, the message they portrayed in their evening news shows and hourly cable updates and minute-by-minute Net programs, that message was different. Lurry, the nut, homophobe and woman-hater. Which is why we lost, both times. Because the elites wouldn't let our message get out to the people. Hard to win when everything is stacked against you.'

'But you didn't let the defeats ruin you, sir, either you or your message.'

Lurry nodded and Ira waited, knowing he had a lot of work ahead of him, many phone and e-mail messages to return, but also knowing he would not disturb this moment, this special time when his boss was letting him look into his soul. Even then, he was surprised at what Lurry said next.

'You've given us years of service, Ira, right from the very first campaign,' Lurry said. 'But what made you decide to join the Shiloh task force? It was something to do with your father, am I right?'

The sudden grief surprised him, causing his throat to clench and eyes to water. He took a couple of deep breaths, blinked, and looked down at the table. 'In a way . . . Yes, I think you're right, sir. My daddy was in the infantry during the Second World War. Fought in the European Theater of Operations for six months, was wounded and sent home. Recovered and was then sent as a platoon commander in the Pacific. Won another Purple Heart and a Bronze Star. From what he told me, I guess he should have gotten the Medal of Honor for some of the things he did. A real hero, sir, a real hero. Raised me and my three sisters, worked as a trooper in the Kentucky State Police all his life. That's why I became a trooper, too. There was no other choice. Then he retired, and even then wanted to keep busy. Managed a convenience store in Louisville. He didn't have to, Lord, he didn't have to . . .'

Damn it, those damn tears were returning. Why did it strike him so hard, even years later? Lurry said, 'I'm sorry to have brought it up. The two men who murdered him, are they still in prison?'

Ira just nodded, afraid to speak, and then he cleared his throat. 'Yes, they're still serving their sentences. The trial was a joke. They both claimed that they had suffered stress as youngsters and were suffering from something called "urban post-traumatic stress disorder". They should have gotten life, but the jury didn't think so. You know, they're due to be released next year, for good behavior.'

Lurry smiled, and Ira smiled in return, recalling the first two names on his old notebook, the one he had started right after the trial was over. 'Not hardly,' his boss said.

'Yes, sir, not hardly.' *I am the Grand High Executioner . . .*

Lurry stood up, held out his hand. Ira shook it and Lurry said, 'We would have won, both times, if we could have gotten to the rest of the country like we had connected to the people of New Hampshire. It would have never come to this if the elite weren't so against us. But what else could we have done?'

'Not a thing, sir.'

As he went to the door, Lurry said, 'You look exhausted, Ira. You should get home tonight, spend some time with your family. No matter how important Case Shiloh is, we can't ignore the family. That was our country's downfall, decades ago. Ignoring the family. We won't make that mistake again. Have your man take you home. Harrison. That's an order.'

'I understand, sir.'

Lurry buttoned his coat. 'Harrison. You still think he's up to the job next week?'

'Absolutely.'

'Good. One other thing . . .'

'Sir?'

Lurry motioned to the cups of coffee on the table. 'There's just a few days left, and I want to make sure there's no misunderstanding. That coffee that we drank. I believe it was Colombian. Do I make myself clear?'

A little shiver ran through his legs. Glenda Sue. Aaron. Oh, my little Elizabeth.

'Perfectly clear.'

'Good. Take care, now, Ira, and God bless.'

'God bless, sir.'

When the door slammed shut behind his boss, Ira sipped at the coffee, now not minding its chalky taste, not even minding the hardly veiled threat. Not to worry. He had no intention of betraying Lurry or Case Shiloh. Twice before he had worked long hours and miles to make that man president, and this time – this time! – he and the others would not fail.

*

Drew stopped their hike in the late afternoon as they continued heading west. Lunch had been a clear broth from their last soup packet and a final handful of crackers, eaten quickly in a narrow part of the trail where a rock fissure had opened up. Twice during their hike Drew had held up a hand to freeze them as he heard a helicopter, out in the distance. It wouldn't have mattered much if they were using thermal devices, but if the helicopters were equipped with either motion or sound detectors he didn't want to give them any help. He knew he was being extra cautious and didn't care. It had been a while since he had used these escape and evasion skills, and he knew he was rusty. Plus he had the disadvantage – though he would never tell Sheila that – of having an untrained companion along, as much as he loved her.

Now they were on the high banks of a small stream, which was trickling its way down past a jumble of rocks and boulders. It was cool out of the direct sun, and Sheila shivered some as she took off her pack. She began undoing the black zippered bag that held her lapbot, and Drew gathered up the water bottles and headed to the stream without a word. Computers were fine and they were handy tools, but that's it. They were *tools*, and most of Drew's experiences with them had been with the utter complexity they had brought to the art of killing human beings. He couldn't quite understand the rapture that sometimes came over Sheila's face when she got to work on her lapbot and she surfed the complexities of the Net. The Net wasn't real, it was just fancy optics and a computer screen and a whole bunch of information. What was real was what you could touch – like the slick rocks around the streambed as he knelt down – and what was real was what you could taste – like the remnants of their meager lunch – and what was real was what you could smell – like one sweaty Drew Connor.

He filled up two water bottles and slipped in purifying pills, then shook the first bottle for the proscribed thirty seconds. He checked around their spot, keeping eyes open for movement, ears open as well for the sound of leather striking stone or a stick snapping. But there was nothing out of the ordinary, save for the slow trinkling of the water and the sound of the wind through the leaves, and the faint tapping as Sheila worked on her lapbot.

One bottle done. Time for a second. He remembered snippets of training, exercises that had occurred in these mountains in New England, in the deserts of Nevada, in the steppes of Siberia and once even the snows of Antarctica. It had helped him many times before but he had thought he'd never have to call on it again. Well, times sure do change, don't they, but one of the things that never changed was survival. The keys to survival, the instructors said, over and over again: good health, water, food and shelter.

Good health. Besides being dirty and smelly and maybe with sore feet and shoulders, they were in pretty good health.

Water. Not a problem. There were plenty of streams about, and in another day or two they'd be smack dab against one of the biggest rivers in the region, the Connecticut River, which came down from northern New Hampshire, divided the Granite State from its neighbor, Vermont, and then bisected both Massachusetts and Connecticut on its way to Long Island Sound.

Food. Definitely a problem, and due to get worse. By tomorrow they would be out of everything that they had packed for their hiking trip, and that would force them either to live off the land or try to scrounge from the small towns and farms that they'd be passing by. Sub-problem one: scavenging for plants, fish and maybe a small animal or two took time, and took time sitting still in a pretty narrow area. Pretty easy to get picked up by the searchers out there. Sub-problem two: scrounging from local farms or towns meant a higher risk of being spotted. And the result? See sub-problem one. Food was going to be tough.

Shelter. They had their tent, but Drew wasn't going to use it tonight. Its bright blue fabric just stood out too much. He shouldn't have used it last night, except for the rain and Sheila's exhaustion, but tonight would be different. They would hole up somewhere and make do with their sleeping bags.

The keys for survival. So far they had them and that was something in their favor, but there was one big factor against him, something he remembered from a training course he had received in the wilds of upper Scotland: *If you're in an escape and evasion scenario, wee ones,* the instructor – an ex-SAS trooper with a heavy Scottish burr – had said, *always take heart that somewhere out there rescue personnel are looking for you. It's just a matter of time before the good guys pick you up.*

Drew started heading back to Sheila. That was the ultimate problem, and it didn't matter much how many keys for survival they had. There were no good guys out there. Only lots of bad guys, and so far the only thing they had in their favor was Drew's pistol and Sheila's lapbot.

She looked up at him as he got closer, pulled a strand of hair free from her sweaty forehead. 'Got it!'

He sat down next to her. 'Got what?'

'A report back from the info broker.'

'And this info broker, you think this is good information?'

She moved her fingers across the lapbot's mousepad. 'The Number Hound is one of the best, Drew. The best. I've no doubt this is good stuff.'

He put one water bottle back into his knapsack. 'And you're sure the way you paid for it allows no chance of it being traced back to you?'

Something seemed to darken about her face. 'I told you that before, Drew. Now, do you want to keep on dancing about, or do you want to know what the broker found out?'

He knew he had pushed her too hard, and could also tell she was in no mood for apologies. 'Yes, tell me.'

'The fax machine that sent the photo-fax to that sheriff's deputy,' she said, her voice now a bit prideful, 'it was from Framingham, Massachusetts, and belonged to something called FERA Region One.'

He put the second water bottle back in her knapsack. 'FERA,' he said thoughtfully. 'Federal Emergency Response Agency. The people who respond to hurricanes, tornadoes, other emergencies. They have different regional offices, for different parts of the country. New England is Region One.'

'And what does that mean?'

Drew zipped up both knapsack pockets and leaned back, thinking hard. Good question, what does it mean? 'It means that somebody connected with FERA discovered that we were in that government shelter. Which means the shelter belongs to FERA. Which means that this person also had a contact with a deputy sheriff more than two hundred miles away from his office.'

'So what do we know about FERA? Wasn't it the Civil Defense Agency?'

'Sure, in a way,' he said. 'Used to be Civil Defense, and then became the Federal Emergency Management Agency.

Responsible for coordinating the government's response to emergencies such as hurricanes, tornadoes, flooding, stuff like that. Couple of years ago it got renamed, became the Federal Emergency Response Agency. Congress thought changing its name to a responding agency rather than a management agency would make a difference. Typical Congressional move, thinking renaming something will make a difference.'

Sheila nodded. 'Now I remember. That nut Lurry, the one who ran for president, used to be on all those cable talk-shows. Isn't he running it now?'

'Yeah, he is. And . . .'

'And what?'

'Well . . .'

She glared up at him. 'You're trying to hide something from me. You're trying to protect my precious little feelings. Forget it. Yesterday somebody tried to kill me, tried to murder me because of the great and horrible crime of trespass. So don't worry about my feelings right now, Drew. What more is there?'

'They are also connected to other functions in government as well. Department of Defense. Intelligence gathering. Contingency planning.'

'What kind of contingency planning?'

He was remembering other briefing sessions in his old job, sessions that began and ended with a signature on a non-disclosure form, promising never to reveal all. Well, fuck 'em. It was beyond that now. And he remembered rumors as well, stories and gossip passed around bars and NCO clubs and beer blasts in some guy's backyard. Stories, that's all.

Drew said, 'Preparing for national disasters. Like nuclear

war. Or biowarfare attacks, like the anthrax in Detroit. A lot of this type of work is hush-hush, black budget. You see a lot in the news media about their public roles, in setting up tent cities and interim power supplies and food hand-outs. You don't see much about their other planning.'

'And why's that? What's to be scared of?'

'Because some of the things they have planned make people nervous. Look, in Detroit plans kicked in to keep people in their homes, set up curfews and restrict traffic. Remember how the ACLU and other civil rights groups screamed about that? Now, imagine what must be locked away for contingency plans on what to do if something like Detroit happened nationally. Or if the government finally said enough was enough when it came to illegal immigrants and they had to be detained and deported. Or what kind of martial law plans and orders have already been prewritten and preapproved, just waiting for the right emergency to be placed into effect. National curfews, restrictions on travel, restrictions on the news media. That's why stuff like that is kept secret. All sorts of planning goes on, day in and day out.' Plus internment centers, he thought.

'Like Case Shiloh?' she asked.

'Like Case Shiloh. Whatever the hell that is.'

Sheila looked up from her lapbot. 'You know, you've never really said much about what you did for the government, Drew. But you know a lot about FERA. Care to tell me more?'

No, God no. He sat down next to her, finally shrugged and stared out at the trees, which were safely hiding them for now from all those prying eyes. 'When I said I had been working for government service, that was the truth. But I could have told you more.'

'Let's see, you said you were involved in some security matters, a lot of travel, and a lot of boredom. What more could you have said? You were military, weren't you? When I mentioned FERA you lit right up, like you were glad I asked a question you could answer. What was it? The Army?'

He rested the bottles of water against his shins. 'For a while, yes. Regular Army after I joined up, and then Special Forces. Stayed in there for some great years. Then . . . well, hard to believe. Budget cutbacks came and my career ended, years ahead of schedule.'

Sheila looked over at him, smiling. 'Is that when you ended up on the lake, rescuing a boating damsel in distress?'

Drew didn't smile back. He kept on looking at the trees. 'No, that was a few years in the future. No, what happened is that me and some other guys in my unit, we were offered jobs, as a freelance contract force. Good pay, same benefits, and same kind of work.'

'Sounds pretty dangerous. Why didn't you do something else?'

He listened to his own voice get sharp. 'What else could I do? Besides the Army the only thing I knew was farming, and there was no way I was going back to do that. So when the job offer came, I took it, gladly. And for the most part, I was happy, quite content . . .'

Sheila gently nudged him. 'Something happened then, am I right? Something that brought you here. What was it?'

Three words, but still, tough words to pronounce. 'The Crescent War.'

'The Crescent War? All those countries? But we weren't involved, were we?'

'Officially, the armed forces of the United States were

not involved at all with that war. But I was there, Sheila. Me and my other guys. We were there.'

Another gentle nudge. 'Do you want to talk about it?'

He rubbed the water bottles against his legs. 'No, not right now. I want to keep focused on what's ahead of us.' Then he tried to lighten up his voice. 'C'mon, what else do you have?'

She nodded for a moment and returned to her lapbot. 'Look,' she said. 'Here's the homepage of FERA Region One. Hmmm. Says here that their main office is in Boston, and that their EOC – Emergency Operations Center – is located in Framingham. But nothing about a bunker in upper New Hampshire.'

'Their EOC in Framingham would be for public consumption. This one up here . . . Hold it, what's that?' He had caught a glimpse of some headshots scrolling by as Sheila was going through the homepages.

'What's up?'

'Go back to the beginning. No, further up, to those pictures. What page is this?'

'It's the photographs of the top personnel in FERA Region One. What did you see?'

Drew leaned closer. 'There, that one. The guy with the undertaker smile and the thin hair. Can you bring it up closer?'

'Sure.' Then she started reading aloud. 'Ira Woodman. Age fifty. FERA Region One administrator. Appointed to this post nearly three years. Previously second-in-command with the Kentucky State Police. Married, two children. Pretty thin bio. What made you stop and look?'

'The piece you showed me this morning, the news channel feed on us and the dead deputy sheriff. Do you still have it?'

'Ugh, yes I do.'

'Run it again, will you?'

'Do I have to?' she said, grimacing.

'Yeah, but you don't have to play any sound.'

'Thank God for small favors.' In another minute another screen came up, and the familiar video was playing, showing the crowded interstate, the interview with the old man in downtown Corinth, the picture of their license photos, the state police captain talking, and—

'There, right there. Freeze it.'

Sheila moved her fingers. 'All right, now what?'

'The crowd of people, standing behind the police captain. The male civilian, the one with the long raincoat. Can you zoom in on his face?'

'Sure, but it'll be a bit muddy . . . Oh shit. Drew, that's him.'

He nodded, rubbed his hands together. A tiny victory but it felt good. Damn it, at least they were doing something. They were making progress, they were learning something. Leave all those Pakistan memories back there. Let's look at what we've got here.

'Yep,' he said. 'Ira Woodman, Region One administrator. He's at the scene. Remember what that police captain said, about Federal officials informing them of you and me, and that we were cultists? Care to guess which particular Federal official might have told them that?'

Sheila shut down the machine and gently closed the lid, the little stickers of Bugs Bunny and Daffy Duck smiling up at them. 'That was a good catch, hon.'

He reached over, rubbed the back of her neck, and then leaned down and kissed her. 'No, that was you, my whiz girl. If it hadn't been for you and your lapbot, we'd be still out here, going around in circles, in all senses of the word.'

'Now what?'

'Now we know who's against us,' Drew said, surprised at how good he now felt. What was a little problem about food and shelter? Now they had information, information they could use.

'And what are we going to do with that?'

'Just you wait and see,' he said, his mind racing through the possibilities, wondering just how good Sheila was with her lapbot. 'Just you wait and see.'

NINE

We should go to Washington and stone Henry Hyde to death. And then we should go to his house and kill his family.

Actor and political activist Alec Baldwin,
December 11, 1998

In the driveway of his house in Wellesley, Massachusetts, Ira rested for a moment in a government-issue Ford sedan before going in. It was almost 10 p.m. and he had taken the Director's suggestion – more like an order, let's be real – to come home. At his side was Henry Harrison, who had driven him the three hours south back to Wellesley. The house was good-sized, with four bedrooms and a large formal dining room and a pool out back, plus a restored carriage house where Henry lived. It was a bit bigger than the place they had back in Louisville and he could not believe the price when he had moved out here. Real estate was obscenely expensive. With the money spent, he had half-jokingly said to his wife, they could have moved south to Memphis and purchased Graceland.

He rubbed at his face while Henry sat next to him, impassive and forever patient. This house. It was a stretch to buy it and even more of a stretch to keep it up, but his orders had been to fit in. And Lord, how he and Glenda Sue had tried to do that from the first day they had moved in. They had both heard stories about tightwad and flinty Yankees and had thought them so many tall tales, until that moving day, when no one from the neighborhood had come over to welcome them on the first day, the second day, or even the damn first month. He would come home late from the office, his mind jumbled with the day-to-day work of learning how to run a FERA regional office, which politicians had to be kept happy and which counties could be ignored and which ones had to be taken care of, to find Glenda Sue on the couch in their living room, weeping.

It had been the same complaint, over and over. It's too cold. The people aren't friendly enough. The churches are too liberal. Why can't we go home? Why do we have to stay here?

And he had clasped her hand and told her that great plans were being made, great plans for the both of them, and that they had to see it through. Which she did, God bless her. Oh, eventually the neighbors did come around and they found a nice church in the next town over, and Glenda Sue was even active in their local school board. But the poison had been set from the first month they had moved in, when Glenda Sue had told him through her tears about the whispers in the local grocery store about the hillbillies moving into the neighborhood.

Ira said, 'I do appreciate you driving me here, Henry.'

'Part of the job, sir, just part of the job.'

'I met with the Director for a while this morning, Henry. He asked about you.'

The man's voice showed surprise. 'He did? What did he say?'

'He wanted to make sure you were up to the job next week. I told him yes.'

'Thank you, sir. I appreciate that.'

Ira looked over at the bulk of Henry, noticing how the house lights made his shaved head seem shiny. 'So tell me, Henry. Are you really ready for next week? I mean, really ready?'

Henry playfully tapped the steering wheel. 'Sir, if you excuse me for a moment, but I love history. Always have. So let me ask you a historical question. Who has killed more Americans in history, Hitler or Tojo?'

Ira thought for a moment, thinking about his father, his great daddy, who had survived both of what those two fascists had thrown at him. 'I would guess Hitler.'

Henry grinned. 'Sorry, sir. That was a trick question. The man who has killed more Americans was one Robert E. Lee. Not Hitler or Tojo. Not a foreigner. One of our own. To this day Robert E. Lee is revered and respected. Books are written about him, television and Net shows are produced about him, and he's still considered one of the greatest Americans who ever lived. The man responsible for more American deaths in history than any other. Hundreds of thousands of dead.'

'I see.'

'So here's my point, sir. We have a tradition in this country for killing each other when it comes to great issues of state and culture. I'm honored to be part of this tradition. You and the director don't have to worry. I have what it takes to accomplish the mission. Now, if you don't mind me saying, sir, you look like you're about ready to fall asleep. Why don't you get on in?'

'Thanks, Henry, I will.'

He stepped out, briefcase in hand, breathing in the cool night air. Henry started up the car and drove out to the rear, where the carriage house was located, and Ira began walking to the front door of his own home, smiling at the thought that at this very moment he looked like any one of a thousand government bureaucrats heading home after a long day.

If only they knew, he thought. If only they knew.

Henry Harrison parked the car at the rear of the carriage house and then went into his home. It was small but he didn't mind. He had slept many a night in crappy places, from crowded torpedo rooms aboard Los Angeles class subs to hot tents in Kuwait to snow shelters in Serbia. This place was snug and warm and kept out the rain, and what else did he need?

He grabbed two beers from the downstairs refrigerator and went upstairs to the bedroom. Built right against the eaves of the carriage house, it was narrow, with a tall, triangular ceiling. He flipped on the television and looked across the way. Light on downstairs. Mr Woodman. And a couple of lights upstairs. Mrs Woodman and one of the kids. He took a swallow, wondered what it must be like to have a family. He had grown up in Seattle, child of probably the dumbest set of parents in the Northwest. Everybody else in and around Seattle was hauling in millions of dollars from doing the dumbest shit on earth, and his parents were content to scrabble out a life from pizza job to gas station job to store clerk job.

When he had left home – and had never gone back – he had joined the Navy and got into the SEALs. Another swallow of his beer. That had been a family he loved being part of. That had been a great life. He knelt down and unlocked a wooden cabinet underneath the television, which held a set of VCR tapes. Blue-tabbed ones were straight porn, red-tabbed ones were something else. He sighed, tapped the end of the beer bottle against his chin. Smart thing would have been to get rid of the red-tabbed tapes – after all, that and other shit had been used against him when he had got dumped from the Navy – but a boy needs to be entertained after a long day of work.

He took out one of the red-tabbed tapes and popped it into the VCR and then stripped and laid down on his bed, drinking the beer. Up on the television screen the picture was jumpy and fuzzy, and he had to keep the sound low, but it was an okay tape. A buddy of his had sold it to him for a couple of grand. It showed a Muslim family in Kosovo – Mom, Dad, teenage son and two teenage daughters – and a Serb paramilitary group was having fun with them. And taking their time, which was a blast.

Henry leaned back against the headboard of the bed. Now, that was entertainment.

Sheila shivered with cold as Drew pulled over a large branch of maple leaves, hiding their sleeping hole. He had said earlier that there could be no tent tonight and she was going to argue the point, except for that damn moment a helicopter had flown overhead above the trees, scaring her half to death, the thrum of the helicopter blades making the tree branches above them shake and tremble. So now they were in a hollowed-out hole in the ground, knapsacks up against some boulders, their two sleeping bags zippered together as one on top of a groundcloth.

Drew stripped and bunched up his clothes, which he shoved at the bottom of the sleeping bag. He started shivering and Sheila grabbed his shoulders and said, 'C'mon, let's try to warm up,' and she hugged him against her smelly but still warm nightgown. She hugged him tight and kissed his neck, and felt the bristles of his fresh beard scrape against her skin. She didn't care. She kissed his ear and rubbed the skin against his back. Drew's own strong hands caressed her shoulders and she knew they had work to do in the morning, but right now she was still scared in this dark area and she wanted her man.

His breath was warm against her neck and she sighed, just enjoying the strong feeling of him on top of her. He moved some and she dug her fingers into the muscles of his shoulders and she kissed him again, and he returned the kiss, harder and deeper. She sensed his surprise and whispered to him, 'Now. Make love to me now.'

'Are you sure?'

She moved underneath him, brought her legs up and about his hips, squeezed. 'Yes, damn it. Now. More than ever. Please.'

He kissed her back, a soft, probing touch that made her forget the fears that were out there, beyond the darkness. She rubbed her face against the sharp bristles on his cheek, squeezed his shoulders again and gasped as one of his hands gently reached under her nightgown, stroking her thigh. Tom, she thought, embarrassed at suddenly remembering her ex-husband, but it was a good memory, a thought for Drew. The first few times she had made love to Tom he had made a grand production of it, lighting scented candles in the bedroom, some classical music on the stereo, and he would lie beside her, reading poetry, touching her here and there. The first few times she found it intoxicating, so romantic, so comforting – especially after her disastrous flight from California – but after a few months she realized that Tom was more in love with the production itself than the damn act. Soon it was becoming rote, the whole candles-music-poetry bit, and she found herself getting bored, then resentful, and then actively hating every moment of it. Right up to the time when she moved out on him.

But Drew . . . She clenched his hips again with her legs and then moved them down, helping him along as he deftly removed her panties, her plain white cotton panties that probably smelled like they hadn't seen soap or water in a decade. Drew was always a surprise, always something different, like he had ten or twenty or thirty ways of doing things, and each time he was endlessly moving the combinations back and forth, ensuring both of their pleasure, but also ensuring that she was never bored, never resentful, never—

'Oh,' she murmured, feeling the gentle probing of his fingers. 'Oh, God, I love you so much.'

'You're mine and I'm yours, always,' he whispered back. 'Always.'

She closed her eyes, no longer afraid of the dark.

Ira went into his home, checked the mail on a table just inside the foyer. Advertising flyers and not much else. Glenda Sue handled the billing, magazines and solicitations. He could hear the sounds of water running upstairs, knew it was his wife taking her nightly shower. Morning and evening, she always showered. He went through the kitchen to his downstairs office, which originally was a guest bedroom. He didn't bother turning on the lights, but instead dropped his briefcase on the floor and closed the door. There. Everything was safe. Glenda Sue and Aaron and Elizabeth all stayed away from his office, knowing it was off limits, forbidden territory.

Upstairs the water was still running. He hung up his coat and back in the spotless kitchen drew a glass of water and drank it down, then yawned. Already he felt the tension easing as he walked about the familiar rooms of his home. Oh, it wasn't a place like back home in Kentucky, but it would do, and he felt a sharp sense of unease remembering what he had done yesterday. Mark Quentin. His poor wife was probably wide awake in her home, somewhere else in the state tonight, wondering about her missing husband. He rinsed the glass out and dried it off, and returned it to the glassware cabinet. Somehow, somewhere, he would make it up to that woman. It wasn't her fault that the man she had married had been so stupid.

On his way to the stairs he looked at the dark entrance to his office, hesitated. Just for a couple of minutes, that's all. Just a couple of minutes. He went into his office and by feel turned on the desk lamp, which lit up his desk and computer and barely illuminated the bookshelves and ego wall, with pictures of him all the way through his State Police career and up to his current position with FERA. He switched on the computer and when the screen blinked into life he went to work, his thick fingers tapping hesitantly at the keyboard. The computer was fairly new, and if he had spent weeks going through the thick operating manual he knew he could practically make the damn thing sit up and sing. But he didn't have the time and the required patience, so he knew exactly how to do four things: write memos, read and write e-mail, get on the Net, and watch this attached video file.

He leaned back in his chair, double-clicked on the icon. One of his subordinates in Kentucky had given him the fif-teen-second video file, and only reluctantly. 'Major, why in hell do you want that program? I'd think you'd want the whole thing erased.'

'Because I have to pay tribute,' he had said. 'No one else will.'

Even after having seen the video clip hundreds of times, each time it began something heavy settled in his chest. The clip only took up about a quarter of his computer screen, and was in black and white. From the moment it started, one saw that it was a surveillance camera for a convenience store.

'Oh, Daddy,' he whispered.

On the little screen on his computer his daddy was alive, working at a job he didn't need to do, except he liked having the extra money and getting out of the house and meeting people. That's all. The camera was up and to the rear of the cashier's station. He could make out the back of his daddy's head and the uniform shirt he was wearing for the store. He was leafing through a magazine – later he had found out it had been the *Sports Illustrated* bathing suit issue, and my, how that had made him smile – and smoking a cigarette. His hair was thin and the camera angle showed the large bald spot, and then . . .

Two men came into view, one black and the other white. Even at night the black man was wearing sunglasses, and his companion had a thin, stringy beard. Both wore long coats and as they approached the counter, each holding a bag of chips to purchase, they dropped the bags and flipped open their coats.

The action started moving more quickly, and even with this new computer there was a jerky quality to the video.

Handguns are now in their hands. Daddy steps back, holds up his hands. He moves over to the cash register, opens the drawer. Money is handed over. The two men lean over the counter. They are yelling, waving the guns in Daddy's face. Then they turn, as if to leave, and then turn back.

The white man fires. The black man fires. Daddy falls out of view. The white man leans over the counter, fires again. They scurry down the aisle, heading to the door.

The black man picks up a large bag of pretzels on his way out.

The video flickers, stops, fades to black. Two photos fade

into view, photos that the computer tech back home had inserted at his request. The photo at left showed Daddy at home in 1946, wearing his Army uniform, complete with medals and ribbons. The photo at right was taken fifty years later, at his and Glenda's wedding, dressed in a rented tuxedo, laughing at the camera, at finally seeing his younger son get hitched.

He reached out and gently stroked the computer screen. 'I'll make it right, Daddy. We're almost there, and I'm gonna make it right.' Ira got up and switched off the computer, and then the desk lamp, and then left his office and headed through the living room. As he walked he wiped at his eyes. In less than a month he'd see those two men from the surveillance camera again, in their prison in Kentucky. And when he did that, those two would not live out the day.

Upstairs he stopped by Elizabeth's room and opened the door. There was a fresh girl scent there, of flowers and well-washed clothes and clean dolls. She was ten years old and she slumbered quietly in her bed, which was an old-fashioned poster set with a frilled canopy on top. He had thought the damn thing was too expensive and frivolous, but Glenda Sue had won out, and he had to admit Elizabeth looked beautiful there, sleeping. He quietly walked into the room and bent over, and kissed the top of her head.

As he walked out he saw that some thin books had fallen from a bookshelf near the door, and he picked them up. There was Curious George, and a couple of books about horses, and one thin paperback, with a couple of odd-looking characters on the cover—

Deffy. Kate. A flushing toilet. 'It's poop power!'

In his house! In his daughter's bedroom! He stood up quickly, furious, holding the book in his hands, and then he shook his head and stepped out into the corridor. No, not now. He didn't want to wake her up and cause a scene, no, not now. He went down the corridor into the upstairs spare bathroom, and he stared at the book, heartsick to think that his Elizabeth had actually looked at this disgusting thing. He bent it in half, broke the thin cover and spine, tore it in half and then in quarters, then tossed it away in a wicker wastebasket by the vanity, then washed his hands and splashed water on his face.

There. A tiny victory against the sewer culture that was out there. And next week, next week there would be an even greater victory.

Out in the corridor he saw a light coming from underneath Aaron's bedroom door. He tapped once and went in. His eleven-year-old son blinked up at him, sitting up against the headboard, reading a book, a tiny desk lamp illuminating his bed. His room was covered with posters of old warplanes from the Second World War and rocket ships and – he was proud to see – one that showed a group of FERA personnel piling sandbags against a rising Mississippi River. He had brought that home from work one day and was quietly pleased to see that Aaron had put it up over his bed.

'A little late tonight, sport, isn't it?' he asked, walking in and sitting down on the desk chair, right next to the bed. The bedspread was from the Kentucky Wildcats, University of Kentucky, for he didn't want his son to forget his roots.

His son yawned, his short black hair tousled. 'I know, Daddy, but I wanted to finish a chapter in this book I'm reading.'

'What is it?'

'Oh, a book I got from the school library, about Pearl Harbor. It's really interesting.'

He reached forward, took the book out of his hands and gently closed it. 'I'm sure it is, but it's way past your bedtime. Why don't you hunker in there and I'll pull up the blankets.'

' 'Kay,' Aaron said, not protesting as he stretched out. Ira pulled the blankets up to his thin shoulders and kissed the top of his head, and switched off the table lamp. The only light coming into the bedroom was from the hallway lights. As he stood up his son said, 'Daddy?'

'Yes?'

'Can I ask you a question?'

'If your mother knew what time it was . . .'

Aaron said, 'It'll only take a sec.'

He sat back down in the chair, suddenly feeling tired. What a day this had been. 'All right, sport. Go ahead.'

'It's about Grandpa. He fought in the Pacific during the Second World War, right?'

'That's right, but first he was in Europe,' he said, letting the proud words slip out. 'He landed in Normandy during D-Day and was wounded a couple of months later. When he got better the Army sent him to the Pacific, to become a platoon commander. He won a Bronze Star and another Purple Heart while he was out there.'

His son's voice, soft and innocent. 'Did he . . . did he feel guilty?'

Ira's head snapped up. He wasn't tired any more. 'What do you mean by that, guilty?'

'Well . . . when he was fighting there, on the islands. Didn't he feel bad about what he was doing, oppressing the native peoples?'

He found he had to clench his fists to prevent himself from shouting out. 'Go on.'

His son said, 'Ms Cleo, our social studies teacher, this

week she said that the war in the Pacific, it wasn't a war of liberation or defense. It was a war to punish the Japanese, who wanted to kick out the colonialists. You see, the Japanese were for the native peoples, and not the Europeans and the Americans. Ms Cleo also said it was a war for our defense industries to gain resources on the islands. She . . . well, that's what she said.'

'I see,' he said, snapping off the words. 'Look, it's late, we'll talk about it more tomorrow.'

' 'Kay, daddy.'

Out in the hallway he was trembling with anger. What is happening to us, he thought. A ten year old girl has a picture book about human excrement, and her older brother thinks his grandfather, who fought and bled for this country, was an oppressor. Like the damn Krauts and Nips! He went down the hallway and to the bedroom, where Glenda Sue was curled up on her side, reading one of her romance novels. She was wearing some light green silk-like pajamas, and her face had the ruddy glow of having just stepped out of the shower. She looked up at him, smiled. 'Well, it's about time you got home, darlin'.'

He tried to ease the tension in his gut and managed a smile as he came in, gave her a quick kiss on the cheek. 'Good to be home, hon, it truly is.'

As he changed out of his clothes and into his pajamas, he found himself looking back at Glenda Sue, and for some reason remembering the surveillance photo of that fugitive. Sheila, right? Yeah. Sheila looked to be a trim, muscular and fine-looking woman once you got past the grimy look of her clothes and the shameless way she dressed. Not like Glenda Sue . . . who, well, who still dressed like she did fifteen years ago, when he had first met her, as part of the security detail to the Miss Kentucky USA pageant. Even now, she still had that same wavy blonde hair – though he secretly knew that some of those blonde hairs were now coming out of a bottle – and she struggled to fit herself into those tight slacks and jeans and those dresses with the sequins on the front and back that she loved so much. He once took her to a Christmas party at the Region One offices in Boston and saw with dismay how some of the other wives whispered and smiled behind their hands at the way she was dressed.

He also knew that she spent a good amount of time on her morning makeup, and he remembered a few months ago, just commenting, really, on how he was getting older – with his hair loss and weight gain – and even she looked like she had a couple of wrinkles about her eyes. My, what a disaster that had been. She had locked herself away in the bedroom all day, weeping, and the next day, still furious, she had made appointments to a couple of local plastic surgeons. Nothing much more had come out of that, but she still had the brochures from the surgeons in the top drawer of her makeup desk.

As he slipped into his light blue cotton pajamas and crawled into bed, she reached over and flipped off the light then snuggled up to him, kissing him on the cheek. Her scent was overpowering – he could never tell what kind of perfume or bath oil she used, week to week – and he had to turn his head for a moment, to be able to breathe.

'Carla Martini, from up the street, she said she thought she saw you on the television yesterday, standing with some police officers on some important case. Is that true?'

'Unh-hunh. Something going on with a couple of fugitives.'

'Dangerous?'

'Oh, it could be, but it's nothing to be worried about.' He

squeezed her shoulders and said quietly, 'I need to tell you something. I found something disgusting in Elizabeth's bedroom, just a few minutes ago. It was a cartoon book, from that obscene cartoon series. The one with the two pieces of sh . . . excrement.'

'Really?'

'Yes, really. Glenda Sue, how did she get a book like that?'

He felt her shrug against him. 'Oh, I don't know.'

'You don't sound too concerned. Glenda Sue, that book is filthy!'

'Well, maybe one of her little girlfriends brought it over. Honestly, Ira, I'll go through her books and things tomorrow. All right?'

'Fine. And another thing . . . I don't like what Aaron is learning in school. Do you know that not more than five minutes ago he said something outrageous about Daddy Woodman. He said that he was an oppressor! That he fought in the war for big business! And do you know where he learned this? From school! What are they teaching him there?'

She remained quiet, and after a moment he said, 'Well?'

'Hon, what do you want me to do about it? We can't afford to put him in a private school, and some of the private schools around here, they aren't Christian at all. They're all that fuzzy get-in-touch-with-your-feelings nonsense. He'd get a worse education there than he would from the public school. And you've always told me that we had to fit in, be good neighbors, not make a fuss. I can't do that and go down and complain to the principal, now can I?'

'There's got to be something—'

'Of course there is something we can do, that you can do. You know he looks up to you, worships the job you're doing. But how much spare time have you had for the boy this past year? I swear, with all the night work and weekend duty and drills that you've been going through, it's a wonder both Elizabeth and Aaron still know who you are.'

He closed his eyes, feeling himself about ready to blow up in a major set-to, but he hated to admit she was right, she was so right. Here he was, working to finally set things right, and what's the end result? Filth in his daughter's bedroom and a son who's been brainwashed. If there was a better definition of the word irony, he couldn't think of it.

Ira squeezed his wife's shoulders. 'You're right, darlin'. I should be home more, and I will. I promise you, by next month, it will all be different. There'll be a big change.'

She nuzzled again, kissing his jaw. 'Good, that's what I like to hear . . .'

He kissed her forehead, again and then again. With his right hand he stroked the fabric against her shoulder, and then lowered his hand to the swell of her breast, snug up against his chest. He stroked again, more forcefully, and Glenda Sue giggled. 'What do you think you're doin' there, trooper?'

'Just showing my affection, hon, that's all.'

She rolled up and pushed his hand away. 'It's Thursday night, Ira. You know it is.'

'But I wasn't home last night.'

'And who's fault is that? You know the arrangement. Every other Wednesday. It just makes sense that way, not worryin' about trying to fit in our schedules or trying to juggle things. It makes sense. Besides, I took a shower and all. I don't want to get sweaty again.'

'I see.' Ah, that would never have happened the first months they had been together. It had been wonderful, days and nights in her condo or his apartment, and brief couplings even in the back of his cruiser when they were short of time.

Raw and sweaty and wonderful. Now, regimented and scheduled, just like every other damn thing in his damn life.

She kissed him again, rolled over. ' 'Night, love.'

'Good night, Glenda Sue.'

As her breathing eased he lay there, fists clenched, looking
up at the dark ceiling.

Cyrus Montgomery and Maurice Blakely, his Scribe, had prepared dinner for their special guest – a large roast beef that
the Senator complained would set his cholesterol level off the
scale – and when they had moved to the coffee and dessert
stage, Blakely had said good night and gone upstairs to one of
the two spare bedrooms that the old farmhouse contained.

Now Cyrus sat with the senior senator from Ohio on the
rear porch of his home outside of Northfield, Vermont, looking out into the darkness of a cool September night. The
Senator's cane was leaning against a wicker table and he
held a cup of coffee in both of his trembling hands. He was
the second-oldest serving Senator and had the wrinkles,
jowls and bald head to prove it. Cyrus had known the old
man for years, ever since he got into the upper-government
tract and had served for a year as an assistant with the
National Security Council, and for six months as National
Security Advisor to the current president's predecessor. He
had made friends and contacts up on the Hill, and the one
he had always valued most was this senator. Still, there was
something in the man's presence tonight that wasn't comforting, and it troubled him.

'That's a fine man you've got there, Cyrus,' the Senator
said.

'That he is,' Montgomery said, slowly rocking back in his
chair. 'He was assigned to me at the Pentagon and it was like

he knew the ins and outs of his job from day one. Any kind of information I needed, he knew how to get it downloaded within seconds. Stuck with me for months, even during some pretty shitty overseas trips and postings.'

'Including a few sessions up on the Hill, right?' the Senator asked, smiling.

'More than just a few up on the Hill,' Montgomery replied, smiling in return, remembering those long, droning sessions, being interrogated about money being spent, about training courses in sensitivity, and about weapons systems being developed. But hardly ever being asked the questions that counted – except by this Senator. Questions like, do you have the people to do the job? Are your people paid enough? Trained enough? Equipped enough?

Montgomery said, 'Blakely went to a lot of those sessions, and others as well. Then, when . . . well, when my circumstances changed, he managed to get a temporary appointment to assist me with the transition. Has also helped me with research for my book. I tell you, he's saved me probably a year's worth of research alone.'

'A fine man,' the Senator said again. 'You know what that poet Yeats wrote, about the end times? There was a line there that always struck me. "The best lack all conviction, while the worst are full of passionate intensity." We don't have many left that are that fine or are the best, Cyrus. It seems . . . hell, it seems that all we have left are those with the wrong passion, the wrong intensity.'

Montgomery watched the old man stare out into the fields. 'There's always been conflict up on the Hill and within the Beltway. As long as I could remember, as long as anyone could remember. But when I was a freshman Congressman up there, things were different. You could spend a day chewing on the

ass of someone from the opposite party during an appropriations hearing, and then later buy 'em a drink with no hard
feelings. You got to know each other, you got to respect each
other. You fought like hell over your positions and your politics, but it never got personal. Even when I went over to the
other side of the Hill, it was still civilized.'

Montgomery said, 'Things change, even when we don't
want them to.'

'True, but usually change means an improvement,
something better.' The Senator shook his head. 'After a
while – and don't ask me to say when! – it became fashion-
able to see your opponent as the enemy, as someone to be
destroyed, as someone evil. You no longer had to just win at
something, whether it was a spending bill or a crime bill or
an anti-terrorism bill. No, you had to demonize your opponent, as being unpatriotic, un-American, or un-something. If
you leaned to the left, your opponents on the right became
racists or fascists. If you leaned to the right, your opponents
became communists or reverse-racists. Then it just . . . it just
spiraled downwards, became worse.'

Montgomery had heard this message before from the
Senator, and gently led him on. 'Then good people started
dropping out.'

'How true, how true,' he said. 'As people started tuning
out politics, started losing themselves on the Net or retreat-
ing to their suburban enclaves or co-op buildings, those in
politics had to become harsher and harsher to keep the allegiance of their hardline believers. The atmosphere became
more poisoned. Special prosecutors appointed left and right
for the stupidest things. Free football tickets. Someone
spilling a drink down a woman's blouse. And now, God preserve us, the President's pissing habits. The more vicious it

became, the more decent people dropped out of the process, didn't bother voting, didn't bother running for office. And those who were left, they had to become more vicious to appeal to their core group, which meant even more decent people dropping out. And the result?'

'Gridlock,' Montgomery said.

The Senator raised the coffee cup with both hands, took a noisy slurp. 'Gridlock. A two-party system? My friend, we have five or six parties up there, representing their groups, their lobbies, their special interests. About the only thing they do – besides spending time on the House floor sniping at each other – is pass an interim spending bill every six months so at least the bills get paid. Everything else . . . left behind. And so we look to the White House . . .'

'So we do. What do you hear?'

The Senator waved a hand in disgust. 'What does it matter what I hear? You've no doubt heard the same stories. All I know is that in that one place, that White House, we need a strong voice, a strong vision, someone to lead us away from this . . . this snarling and yapping. Not to mention everything going on out there on the horizon, from China to Israel to the Middle East. And all we have from the White House is peace and quiet. Wrong? There's nothing wrong. That's all you hear from those damn spinmeisters and talking heads. We deserve better than that.'

Another slurp from the coffee cup, and his voice softened. 'Not so long ago, we had a chance, a golden opportunity, one time that comes about every century or so. Even the bitter ones, the ones with the wrong passion, were quieted for a while. We were at peace. The economy was booming. Unemployment was low, interest rates were low, the crime rates were dropping through the cellar. Hell, a barrel of designer water cost more than a barrel of oil back then! We had a chance to set the groundwork for some wonderful things, for this new century, a chance to make it right for us and the rest of the world. Instead . . .'

'Wasted,' Montgomery offered, remembering with regret those few brief years when the problems were manageable and the promises endless.

'Yes, wasted,' the Senator agreed. 'Things were so fine then, we didn't even notice. Instead, we obsessed about Hollywood, obsessed about an intern in the White House, obsessed who was up and who was down in this spinmeister world. And when we woke up, things had changed for the worse. The passionate haters were back at it, and look where we are now.'

'Yes,' Montgomery said. 'Where we are now.'

In his bedroom, Captain Maurice Blakely was idly surfing the Net at a small desk while half listening to the conversation taking place below him in the rear porch. A small speaker set up next to his computer brought in the words of the General and the Senator with no difficulty, and he smiled with slight embarrassment at the General's kind words about himself. He doubted the General would be so kind if he knew that Blakely – during the times when the General was at Norwich or the town – had wired this house top to bottom.

He tapped on the keyboard, looking at the NewsNet channels flicker by him. Though the General shouldn't be upset at what his Scribe had done. It wasn't personal. It was just information. As a Scribe, Blakely thirsted for information, loved to wallow in it and see where it took him. Blakely also liked being in the General's household, and knowing things that he wasn't supposed to know.

Like this supposedly friendly and informal dinner with the Senator. Sure. Very informal. That was why he came here in a small car with New York license plates, driving it himself. He listened to their words as a few NewsNet headlines popped up on the screen:

JAPANESE PRIME MINISTER GREETS DELEGATION FROM CALIFORNIA

A five-member trade delegation from the State of California – which included the Mayor of Los Angeles – met today with the Prime Minister of Japan in a series of talks that some observers see as the most direct challenge yet to the Administration's Pacific trade policies by the Governor of California.

The White House had no comment.

Click [HERE] for more information.

UN PEACEKEEPERS ON MEXICO–TEXAS BORDER COME UNDER FIRE

A detachment of Russian soldiers serving as UN peacekeepers along the Mexican side of the Rio Grande River reported yesterday that they had come under attack.

Three Russian soldiers were wounded, one seriously, according to a spokesman at UN headquarters in New York City.

No group announced responsibility for the gunfire, though sources claimed that one of a half-dozen Texas militia units working in the area could have staged the attack.

Colonel Yuri Talenkov, Commander of UN forces in the region, warned that he was prepared to conduct cross-border raids into Texas to attack these militia units if further incidents occurred.

The White House had no comment.
Click **[HERE]** for more information.

CREATIONIST VIEWS ON GENETICS SEEN AS NEXT EDUCATION FIGHT

Following their success in ensuring that at least thirty states now require the teaching of creationism along with evolution in high school science courses, foundations representing creationist supporters have announced plans to require that creationist views of genetics be taught as well.

Among the tenets of creationists' views is that the study of genetics is 'only a theory', and that a supreme being has a hand in determining that certain races – such as Caucasians – do better in intelligence tests.

The White House had no comment.
Click **[HERE]** for more information.

EU NAVAL FORCES CLASH WITH EGYPTIAN REFUGEE FLOTILLAS

European Union naval forces based in the French port of Toulon engaged in a gun battle yesterday afternoon with a refugee flotilla reportedly outbound from the Egyptian port city of Alexandria. Military sources at EU military headquarters in Brussels said the flotilla was seeking to approach the southern coastline of Crete.

The latest group of refugees were believed to be escaping the latest rounds of new laws implemented by the Egyptian Parliament. Based on Islamic law, or sharia, the new measures are being resisted by many in Egypt who do not want to reside under such strict restrictions. Many escaping refugees from Egypt have fled into several nations adjacent to the Mediterranean Sea.

The White House had no comment.

Click [HERE] for more information.

Blakely didn't bother to click on any of the 'more information' boxes. It wasn't news that the White House had no comment; that had been their daily saying since the famous urination incident.

What was news was what was going on below him. He decided to click on a little icon on his computer that began recording the conversation.

Information. Ah, how he loved it so.

Montgomery looked over at the Senator, thought for a moment, and said, 'I've heard something is going on.'

The Senator didn't move his head. 'So have I.'

'Do you have any idea what it is?'

'Whispers, here and there. Nothing solid. All I can put together is that somehow, somewhere, there is going to be a rupture of some sorts. Something out of the blue, extraordinary. The most likely explanation I've heard is that some on the Hill are working with a few Cabinet members to implement the Twenty-Fifth Amendment.'

'The succession of powers?'

The Senator put his coffee cup down, reached into his suitcoat pocket and pulled out a piece of paper. He unfolded it and started reading, holding the paper close to his face:

' "Section 4. Whenever the Vice President and a majority of either the principal officers of the executive departments or of such other body as the Congress may by law provide transmit to the President pro tempore of the Senate and the Speaker of the House of Representatives their written declaration that the President is unable to discharge the powers and duties of his office, the Vice President shall immediately assume the powers and the duties of the office as Acting President." '

'And what do you think?' Montgomery asked.

The Senator shrugged, put the piece of paper back into his pocket. 'If it happens, just more of the same. Gridlock, special reports on the news channels, chatting away on the Net. A Constitutional crisis, no doubt, but at least this particular Vice President knows how to spell potato. But still, I get the feeling . . . well, there's a certain few up on the Hill who are the most rabid of the lot, and lately they've been quiet. And that's plenty disturbing. You expect them to howl, expect them to raise a ruckus, but when they're quiet I expect trouble. It's like they already know something is going to happen, and they don't see the point of raising hell. And that's what scares me. I think the Twenty-Fifth Amendment is too soft for them. I think they want something harder, with more impact. God forbid, I do think they pray each day for Air Force One to crash, that's how hardcore they are.'

'I see,' Montgomery said, wanting to wrap this up before another topic was raised. 'Well, Senator, it is getting late, and you—'

'I'm not ready for my bedpan and bed, if that's what you mean.' The Senator took his cane and grasped it in both of his hands, as if gaining some strength from holding such a familiar object. 'I had another purpose, coming up here today to meet with you.'

'Besides the roast beef and conversation,' Montgomery said, knowing he had failed.

'Yes, as agreeable as both of those items were.' The Senator raised his cane up and rapped it on the wooden floor. 'Cyrus, the primary season starts next February. You give me the word now and by the time you go over next door to New Hampshire and start shaking hands, you'll have twenty million in the bank. But I do need that word, and soon.'

Montgomery felt like the wood flooring of the porch was starting to sag about him. Why couldn't these people just leave him alone? He tried not to make his voice sound sharp to his old friend, but he couldn't help it. 'Damn it to hell, Colin didn't want that fucking job. Why should I?'

'Because your country needs you.'

Montgomery motioned to the fields. 'A couple of miles over there is Norwich, where I earned my commission through the ROTC. Some of my happiest days were out there, in the classrooms and training fields, a kid from Detroit learning more in four years than the previous eighteen. Don't tell me that my country needs me. I've already given years of work, of sweat, of treasure to this nation. I have two sons whom I hardly see – one of them won't even talk to me. When I lost Grace, this was the only place left that I could go to. A safe haven. The only place where I could find some peace. Please don't ask me to leave here. I won't.'

The Senator looked over at him. 'You might not have a choice.'

TEN

You don't dare say America or Christianity is a better way of living. When I said during my presidential bid that I would only bring Christians and Jews into the government, I hit a firestorm. 'What do you mean?' the media challenged me. 'You're not going to bring atheists into the government? How dare you maintain that those who believe the Judeo-Christian values are better qualified to govern America than Hindus and Muslims?' My simple answer is, 'Yes, they are.'

Pat Robertson, *The New World Order*, 1991

It was the laughter and the music that woke him up, and George Clemson ran a hand across his face and blinked his eyes open. Now he remembered. It was Friday. His first day off, and Carol must be getting the kids ready for school. He opened his eyes, looked up at the familiar white ceiling with the brown stain in the far corner, where the upstairs neighbors last year had let their bathtub overflow. What a mess that had been. Jesus. Even then he had promised his wife that they would boost up their savings so they could make good progress towards a down payment on their own place, get out from apartment living. But then their five-year-old Ford needed an engine overhaul, the kids needed summer clothes, and by the time school started and the bills for books and Net access started coming in, they were back to where they had started. Stuck in the same old neighborhood, same old dump.

He swung out of bed, yawned, scratched his chest. The door opened and Carol came in, carrying a cup of coffee. She had on her nurse's uniform and she sat down on the bed next to him, gave him a quick kiss. Except for the extra poundage around her legs and middle, she still looked the same as she did when he had first met her, with the smooth dark skin and wide brown eyes and that funny laugh that made him smile.

'Guess we woke you up, dear heart,' she said, passing over the cup. 'Sorry 'bout that.'

'That's okay,' he said, yawning. 'Think of all the nice sleep I'll get next week, when you're all down in DC visiting your folks.'

She laughed and gently jabbed an elbow in his ribs, and again that laugh made him smile. Then he took a taste of her coffee, tried to hide a grimace. His woman had never once made a good cup of coffee, and except for a mistaken comment in the first months of their marriage, years ago, he had never said another word about it. Carol was a good mother, a good wife and a good provider, and if she couldn't make a decent cup of coffee, well, so what. He had met her in the ER at Baltimore General, and, like most cops and firefighters, he found that an ER nurse could understand a lot about the job. The jangled sense when you worked different shifts. Dealing with bureaucrats and paper-pushers. And, of course, meeting the fine citizens of Baltimore under the most bloody and deadly of conditions. Which is why most cops and firefighters dated nurses, and later married them.

He gamely tried another sip of the coffee and Carol said, 'You need to talk to your son.'

'What did he do?' he asked, knowing it was trouble. When Clarence did good, he was 'our son'. When he got himself into trouble, he was 'your son'.

She got up and headed to the door. 'It ain't what he's done. It's what he's planning to do that has me concerned, babe. He wants to drop out of school.'

There. That little worm of fear that never came at him when he was on the job started burrowing around in his guts. From all his years on the streets, he saw the debris of families resulting from kids choosing the wrong friends or making the wrong decisions. He saw too many fourteen-year-old mothers and dead sixteen-year-old boys out there on his job, and his greatest fear was that some wrong choice, some being in the wrong place at the wrong time, would seize one of his kids.

He and Carol had been lucky, so far. Their two daughters – Clarisse and Clennie – were doing well in school, and except for some bad manners and even worse language he allowed himself to think that they would finish high school unscathed and get into college. But Clarence? Their smart boy? Dropping out?

He put the coffee cup down on the cluttered nightstand. 'What's it about? His grades going bad? Is there a girl? What is it?'

Carol shook her head. 'Nope. The boy wants to drop out, go back to Africa.'

'Oh, Jesus,' he said, feeling an urge to crawl back into bed and pull the covers over his head. 'What fool put that nonsense into his head?'

She pursed her lips, pointed a red-fingernailed finger at

him. 'I don't know. But I do know that my boy isn't going to Africa. And you're gonna make sure it doesn't happen. I don't know what fool put that thought in his head, but I know I'm looking at the man who's gonna take it out. And the sooner the better.'

His wife went back out and he could hear her talking to their daughters, and he rubbed at the bristles on his face. He supposed he could shave but he knew in a few minutes the two girls and Clarence would be heading off to school, and from Carol's tone he knew that she wanted the matter taken care of now.

He got up, put on a thick red bathrobe that the girls had gotten him for Christmas last year, and he went out to the kitchen. Carol was washing dishes and Clarisse and Clennie were sitting at the kitchen table, laughing and doing their homework. They were only a year apart but looked like twins, and sometimes – like today – they enjoyed dressing like it to mess with people's heads. They had on their school uniform of dark blue skirt – knee-length, thank you kindly – and light blue turtleneck sweaters, but their hair was done up in what was the latest fashion: corn rows beaded with the colors of different African countries. He wasn't sure which country either Clennie or Clarisse represented, and he didn't particularly care. He kissed them on top of their heads and said, 'How come you girls don't have your homework done yet?'

They laughed and Clarisse said, 'It doesn't matter when it gets done, Daddy. And besides, we do it now, we're fresh and we haven't forgotten like if we did it last night.'

He smiled and then Carol caught his eye, and he went down the short hallway on the left, past their old wedding photos and a large photo montage of their family, from the first baby pictures to a set from last year, when they were down in Florida for a long-promised trip to Disney World.

He tapped on Clarence's room door, and when the boy answered he went in. His son looked up from his desk, wearing his school uniform of black trousers, light blue shirt and black necktie. He looked serious behind his wire-rimmed glasses – he had always been a serious boy, right from the start – and he got right to it. 'I guess Mom told you, right?'

George sat down on Clarence's made bed. The young boy always made his bed, was always neat and got good grades. About the only thing that changed in his room was the wall decorations. George could always tell what was on the boy's mind by what he had up there on the wall. Early on it was the usual football and basketball players. Last year, after a visit to the Space Telescope Science Institute over at Johns Hopkins – which managed the still operating Hubble Space Telescope – there were pictures of the old space shuttle and the moon and some black astronauts. Now, though, there were some faces up there, and he guessed he should have noticed it before: Malcolm X, Marcus Garvey, Jesse Jackson, and even one of Cyrus Montgomery, wearing his full dress uniform before he was forced out by the idiot in the White House.

'Yeah, she did,' George said. 'Said you wanted to drop out of school.'

Clarence smiled. 'That's Mom. Overreacting again. I don't want to stop my studies.'

'Then you tell me what you said, smart one,' he said. 'How come your mother's so upset?'

Clarence said, 'I want to transfer out, that's all. I want to join the Africa Corps, go overseas. I can join if I get your permission. And I'll keep up with my studies with the program.

You know colleges love this kind of stuff on applications when the time comes.'

Easy, he thought, let's keep it easy. 'Why now? What's the rush?'

'There's no rush,' he said. 'I just want to do it, that's all.'

'Okay,' George said, 'let's say there's no rush. Why Africa?'

His son looked up for a moment at the wall posters. 'Because they're dying, Dad. That's why. No one cares and they're dying every day. AIDS is everywhere, there are millions of refugees, and a lot of governments have collapsed. They need our help.'

From you, my dear fourteen-year-old boy? Easy, old man, easy. 'They're getting help from the UN, other governments.'

Clarence said, 'Oh, come on, Dad. I read the papers, the NewsNet. You know what's going on. Everybody does. The Europeans and Japanese and us are carving up Africa, just like the colonialists did back in the nineteenth century. Except this time, they're calling 'em relief mandates, not colonies. Hah. That's just an excuse for the corporations to come in and steal their resources while the governments give out rice and corn meal to famine victims. That's what's going on. Uranium and oil and thorium for food and clean water. The relief mandates are just a license to steal, that's all.'

Not even fifteen yet and look how smart he is, George thought. 'Maybe that's right. Hell, let's say everything you've said is right. Let's get back to the real question. How is the young Clarence Clemson gonna help these folks by being there?'

'I know computers,' he said. 'I'm young, I'm strong. I know I can contribute, whatever it takes. The Africa Corps, it's brother helping brother, volunteers from the churches and small businesses here and from the Caribbean. No big governments, no corporations. That's why I want to go, Dad. I'll be helping my own people.'

He eyed him critically. 'No, you won't.'

'Hunh? What do you mean, I won't?'

'I mean, those people in Africa, as sad as I feel for them, they ain't your people.' He gestured to the tiny window that didn't let much light into the bedroom. 'Out there, those are your people. Your neighbors, your relatives, your friends. They are your people. Not a bunch of strangers thousands of miles away.'

'But Dad,' Clarence protested. 'They are our people. We came from there, our ancestors did. We have a duty to help them.'

'Don't be going silly on me, son.' Clarence, his boy, in the middle of that chaotic, bleeding continent. He would not allow it.

'I'm not being silly!'

'Of course you are,' he said, sitting forward, now pointing a finger at his boy. 'They ain't your people. You're an American. Be proud of it. If you think you have a duty to make things right, worry about your family and your neighbors and your city. I know some of your teachers and friends, they got this romantic vision of the mother country and all that crap, and that's what it is. It's crap. This is your country.'

'And what's the country been doing for you, Dad?' his son shot back. 'You've been a cop how long, and how come you haven't made sergeant? Hunh? You trying to tell me there's no more racists out there, no more rigged system? C'mon, Dad!'

There was a quick rap on the door and he knew that it was Carol, warning him that it was almost time for the kids to go to school. George stood up and watched the eyes of his boy, and tried to remember what it had been like to be that age, to feel your body shift, your voice deepen and your hair grow, to feel the way you think turn you almost inside out.

'Look,' he said, softening his voice. 'This ain't a perfect place. What place is? But if you stay and work, the worse that happens is you might hear a muttered phrase here or there, or some cracker might cut you off in traffic, or there might be a fight over a school loan. Over there, if they think you're from a wrong country or village or tribe, they'll hack your arms and legs off and laugh while you bleed to death. That's the truth, and you know it too.'

His son turned his head, blinking his eyes, and he knew that the boy was embarrassed at the tears coming to his eyes. George went on. 'Tell you what, we'll make a deal. I'll talk to Minister Jeffries, set you up at the church's foodbank. You can start working there weeknights when your homework is done. Then maybe you can do some other work at a home-less shelter, doing laundry or kitchen work.'

'But I want to help the people in Africa!'

Another rap on the door, more insistent. George said, 'You show me and your mother that you have what it takes to help your neighbors, right here, where it's safe and you can come home every night, and then we'll discuss it next year.'

'Next year!'

'Africa will still be there next year, next century and next millennium. It sure can wait for the likes of one Clarence Clemson. Now, get going and get on to school before your mother whacks me one.'

He walked out of Clarence's bedroom and walked quickly to his own room, stomach rolling at what had just gone on. He wasn't sure if he had done well, wasn't sure if the boy would grudgingly accept what he had just said, or if he would stew and simmer and show his displeasure by doing something else. By finding out about women, or crank, or T-bird, or any one of a dozen or so temptations that could end him and shatter this little family.

Jesus, he thought, rubbing his face and heading to the bathroom for a shave. He'd rather make a 2 a.m. traffic stop on his own in MidTown than have to go through these talk sessions with Clarence. At least Carol handled the girls, and he knew he should be grateful about that, but boys . . . Shit, there were so many creative ways that they could get into trouble.

Before he got to the bathroom Carol came into the bedroom, eyes sharp. 'Well?' she demanded.

He sighed. Would he ever get to shave this morning? 'I talked him out of it, for now. Said we'd discuss it again next year.'

'Next year? Are you out of your mind? My boy isn't going to Africa next year or the year after that!'

He smiled. 'Relax. He seems so up on volunteering, I got him agreed to do some work at the church. After a few months of sorting boxes of macaroni and cheese and being up to his elbows in sink water, I think he'll start dreaming about something else. You'll see. In another couple of months, Africa will be off the plate.'

Carol smiled in return and stepped over to the bed, and began unbuttoning her shirt, tugging it free from her slacks, revealing a white lace bra and her full breasts. George laughed and said, 'What's this all about? I thought you were set on getting to work.'

She knelt down on the bed, took off her shirt. 'I am, but I'm being covered for at least a half-hour before I have to go in. Can you think of something you'd like to do in the next thirty minutes, or will I have to do it all by myself, lover?'

He went over to the bed, dropping his bathrobe in the process, and she fell back and he clambered on top of her, feeling the comfortableness of her flesh and the familiarity of her scent and touch. Maybe it was the poor sleep or thinking about his talk with Clarence or something else, but after a minute or two something was wrong. Nothing was stirring, nothing was responding, and knowing Carol, if something didn't bestir itself shortly, she would pause and politely ask what in hell was wrong. And if that happened, then nothing would happen, because that was trying to be erect on demand, which never happened. He returned her kisses and bent his head down to kiss her breasts, and in desperation he thought about the other night. He thought about his partner.

Nancy Thon Quong, snug bottom swaying in front of him, going out to the cruiser after roll call.

Nancy Thon Quong, smiling at him over lunch at some countertop downtown, as he told her a joke about a priest and a rabbi and a minister.

Nancy, in the front seat of the cruiser, now there was a fantasy, stroking George's thigh, and then his crotch, and then deftly unzipping his trousers and lowering her head down, the hair tickling his swollen member, her lips gently—

'Oh, baby,' Carol murmured as he slid into her. 'It's been so long.'

'Oh, yeah,' he said, kissing her ear. 'Too damn long.'

Oh, Nancy.

Even though he was fifteen minutes early to work at FERA Region One's offices in Boston, Ira Woodman already felt exhaustively behind schedule as his real admin aide – to

differentiate between his other admin aide, Henry Harrison –
ambushed him outside his office door, her hand holding a
couple of message slips. Her name was Lisa McGee and she
was in the twilight zone between late thirties and early forties.
She wore pantsuits and floral blouses and light-colored
scarves, and her bright red hair seemed to fade in and out
depending on how long it had been between visits to her
beautician. She had a breathless way of talking, as if each
word had been carefully chosen after an hour's worth of
thought, and Ira couldn't stand her.

'Mr Woodman?' she asked, blocking his way to his office
door. 'Mr Woodman? Just a reminder that the three Boy
Scouts are here for their photo op, and that a . . . a Mr
Mather is here to see you. He doesn't have an appointment
but his name is on that list you gave me, of people to be let
in without appointments, which is really out of the ordinary, it really does throw the efficiency of the office out of
whack—'

'Fine,' he said, interrupting her and grabbing the message
slips from her sweaty hand, seeing that one belonged to his
computer man, Clem Badger. 'Send the Boy Scouts along in
another five minutes. Tell Mr Mather to have a seat in the
outer office.'

'Mr Mather seemed rather insistent to see you right now,
Mr Woodman—'

'Tell him I'm busy. Tell him I'll see him in ten minutes.
Give him a cup of coffee or water or arsenic, I really don't
care, but handle it. All right?'

He brushed past her and went into his office, slamming
the door shut behind him. His stomach jabbed him again
with a spurt of acid and he went past his government-issue
desk and to the three windows that looked down upon the

financial district of Boston. He was ten stories up, in a federal building that shared offices with everything from the GAO to the Social Security Administration, and he leaned forward and rested his forehead against the thick glass.

Below were the jammed lines of vehicles in the narrow lanes that the natives here laughingly called streets, and he saw other movement as well, of people surging along the sidewalks and across the crosswalks, moving as one in the early morning air. Each one of those little dots claimed they were individuals, claimed to think for themselves and were independent, but from up here they moved as one, as a mass. He wondered which ones of them cared. Which ones of them had actually voted in the last election. Which ones of them would actually put everything on the line – family, career, life – to make this country great again.

He thought about the other people who had been down there, more than two hundred years ago. For the most part they had been prosperous men, secure in their livelihoods and jobs, working as merchants or silversmiths or importers. They had everything to lose, but when the time came they had risked it all to fight against a tyranny, just like him, just like everyone else in the Shiloh Task Force. Oh, he knew what the history books had said about these men back then, but the history books had been wrong. They hadn't been fighting against a foreign tyranny overseas in England. No, the tyranny was right here, with the royal governors and royal customs duties and royal tax collectors and the thousands of citizens who had supported the overseers. Just like now. The tyranny was homegrown, the tyranny that had to be overthrown.

The door opened. 'Mr Woodman? The Boy Scouts are here to see you.'

He turned. 'Thank you, Miss McGee.'

The next few minutes were pleasurable indeed, and he tried to put Mr Mather and Case Shiloh and those two fugitives out of his mind as he met with three Boy Scouts from Maine. Last winter they had saved a family whose house had been flooded out when the Penobscot River had overflown its banks, and he presented each of the young men – decked out in their green uniforms with kerchiefs, just like he had looked almost forty years ago – with a certificate of achievement as their proud parents smiled and applauded. A photographer from the media relations office had taken their photos and Miss McGee had pointed to the watch on her wrist, and he said, 'What do you say, fellas? Would you like to see our operations center?'

With a frowning Miss McGee in tow, he shepherded them out to the outer offices, where a glaring older man in a black suit looked up from a couch. He ignored the older man – who had a paper sack with twine handles at his feet – and brought the little group to the elevators, and in five minutes they were in the basement of the Federal office building, where FERA Region One's Operations Center was located. The three Boy Scouts and their parents followed him as he pointed out the computer consoles and display screens and secure telephone system. He pointed out the links set up between this office and the emergency management agencies from each of the six New England states, as well as the links to the FERA headquarters in Washington and the National Weather Service. He also pointed out the status boards, which showed the operating levels of the nuclear power plants in the region, as well as the status of military bases. After a while he noted the drooping expressions on the Boy Scouts' faces and the fixed smiles of their parents. Oh well, he thought. Enough is enough and I can't delay this meeting any further. He brought them back up to the lobby and again shook each of the boys' hands.

'You've done your parents, your Scouts and your country proud, guys,' he said. 'Congratulations again. You've shown that all three of you can grow up and contribute a lot to this country.'

One of the mothers grasped the shoulders of her son. 'That's what I told him, Mr Woodman,' and her boy piped up, 'We're gonna see our congressman next!'

'Really?' Ira said. 'Is he here in Boston?'

The mother looked down at her son with pride. 'No, he's in Washington. He's invited us and all three of the boys to visit him next week. We're even going to get a private tour of the Capitol.'

Ira felt his eyes burn. 'When, did you say?'

'Next Tuesday. The nineteenth.'

Oh. Ira rubbed the top of the boy's head. 'Bless you all, and I'm afraid I must run.'

Standing by himself in the elevator, he dared not look at his reflection in the polished metal.

Drew shivered as he sat on top of the rock, wishing that the morning sun would rise more, so that he could warm up. Beside him Sheila was at work on her lapbot, sitting so that the screen was shielded from the sun. Both of their backpacks were at their feet, and they were along a ridge of second-growth forest, the trees a mix of pine and spruce. Somewhere a blue jay was chattering at another bird, and he wished the damn thing would just shut up.

He was hungry and wondered what he could do for lunch. Breakfast for Sheila had been a cup of just-picked blueberries, in the last of their milk and with a little sugar sprinkled over them, and a weak cup of tea, made from a once-used bag. Breakfast for Drew had been lies, he thought, watching her tapping the keys. He told her that he had eaten first, had also gobbled down some blueberries and a couple of crackers, but that hadn't been the truth. Breakfast had been cold water from the stream and that was fine. He could do all right without food for a day or two, as long as he kept himself hydrated.

But after that . . . well, things would get interesting.

And then what?

He had the cellphone in his hand, and rubbed it slowly across the bristles of his chin. Other missions he had been on there had been a sense of purpose, a plan, an exit strategy if things went to the shits and goals to achieve. Lots of goals, over the years. Get into Serbia and kidnap a warlord. Break into a bank in the Cayman Islands and steal the hard drives from its computers. Parachute into northern Quebec and help the former premier sneak across the border into Ontario.

Go covertly into the Crescent War, just after the first nukes were used, and . . .

'Drew?' she asked.

'Yeah, hon,' he said, looking up.

'Just a couple of more minutes, and then I'll be ready. The number's been predialed into the phone. All you have to do is press the send button. Got it?'

He rubbed the phone against his face again. 'Yep, got it.'

She went back to her lapbot. Missions, most of which never made the papers or NewsNet channels, but that could be marked with the word 'achieved' next to them.

And this, this thing that they were doing? What was the ultimate goal? Find out about Case Shiloh? Find out why he and Sheila have been targeted? Find out what in hell is going on here, with just a few days left to that start date?

And then what? Hold a news conference? Send a nasty letter to the editor at the *Boston Globe*?

He picked up his water bottle and took another sip. So far water hadn't been a problem. But there would be a big problem, if they kept on heading west, when they hit the Connecticut River. Then they would run into Vermont and . . .

Now, Vermont. What made him think of going into Vermont? Shouldn't they head north instead, to Federal Canada or even Quebec?

Vermont. The name gave him some sort of comfort, and he didn't know why.

'Hon?'

'Right here,' he said, putting the water bottle down.

'One more minute.'

'Okay,' he said.

A headache had made its appearance when Mr Mather finally got into Ira's office, and with each passing minute it felt like steel bands were being tightened around his forehead and temple. Each passing minute meant an additional turn, an additional squeeze, and he tried to keep focused by squeezing a brass letter-opener with both hands as his visitor blabbed on.

Mr Mather was in his early seventies and his black suit was shiny around the elbows and forearms. The edges of his shirt cuffs were yellowed and frayed, and as he talked Ira couldn't help but look at the man's discolored teeth. It looked like he had last visited a dentist during the Carter administration. With the unwashed hair and tufts of beard stubble where his razor hadn't quite made it, Mr Mather looked like one of the legion of homeless who made their home on Boston Common.

That would have been true, save for the fact that Mr Mather was one of the richest men in Massachusetts, a formidable contributor to the Lurry campaigns, and right now he had a problem to discuss. Or as Ira thought, securely squeezing the letter-opener and wondering how it would feel shoved in Mr Mather's throat, *the* problem, the only one the old man cared about. But contributors were contributors, and Lurry was clear that no matter how idiotic, how stupid, how irritating, such contributors were to be coddled at all costs. They could be counted on to make additional donations for important projects, donations that would never appear in reports to the Federal Election Commission.

'Look here,' the old man said, his thick fingers tracing columns of numbers on several much-folded pieces of paper, paper that had been stuffed in a paper sack. 'See what I mean? Britain, all by herself, owes us more than four billion dollars from the First and Second World Wars. Billions of dollars! And here's what France owes us over here . . . and look, Germany still owes us reparations from the Versailles Agreement of 1919 . . . plus Italy, let me show you . . . damn it, that piece of paper was here just a moment ago.'

Back he went into the paper bag, like some deranged squirrel, looking for nuts hidden during the winter of 1977. Ira cleared his throat. 'Mr Mather . . .'

The man's head was bowed as he burrowed through the papers. 'And Imperial Russia. Do you know how much they owe us in Imperial Bonds from 1912 and 1916? That's another few billion dollars!'

Ira raised his voice. 'Mr Mather, please, if you just give me a moment.'

'Yes?' Mr Mather asked, looking at Ira through watery eyes. 'What is it?'

Careful, he thought. Don't get the old man pissed off. 'I understand your concerns, and trust me, Mr Lurry takes this issue seriously. Quite seriously.'

Both hands were holding sheaves of paper. 'But it seems he only contacts me when there's a campaign to be run! You do know how much I've given to Lurry and his associates, and his cable program, and his educational foundation? Millions! Millions! And I have yet to hear anything about these foreign debts being settled. Not a thing!'

It felt like the letter-opener in his hands was one ounce of pressure away from breaking the skin. 'Yes, and that's for a reason,' Ira said, thinking quickly, the headache now really screaming around his forehead. 'Mr Lurry is in a sensitive position, working as he does for this administration. But he plans to make a public statement, quite soon, about the injustice of these unpaid debts. I promise you that.'

Mather's eyes suddenly got more teary. 'Are you sure?'

'Positive.'

'And when will this happen?'

'In less than a month, guaranteed,' Ira said, leaning over his desk, the letter-opener hidden in his lap. 'And I can tell you that when he makes that announcement, he'll want you at his side. To show his appreciation for all the work you've done, keeping track of the numbers, keeping this issue in the forefront.'

Mather nodded, seemingly too emotional to speak. His arms crossed his thin chest, holding the papers against him. 'Finally . . .' he whispered. 'After all these years . . .'

His phone started ringing. He looked and saw a red light illuminated, which meant that an important call was coming in, one that Miss McGee was trying to warn him about. He dropped the letter-opener on the floor and stood up, holding out his hand.

'Mr Mather, if you'll excuse me, I've got important business to attend to,' he said. 'As you can see . . .'

The old man got up and shook his hand, and Ira winced at how sweaty it felt. 'Thank you, thank you very much,' he said. 'And if Michaelson needs additional funds, please tell him to call me. At any time.'

Ira nodded and smiled in all the right places, and when the door finally closed behind Mr Mather his headache started to ease up. Jesus, what a morning. He picked up the phone and switched on the intercom and said, 'Yes?'

'Mr Woodman?'

'Yes, what is it, Miss McGee? Who's on the line?'

'I'm afraid I don't know.'

'What do you mean you don't know? And why in hell did you set off the trouble light if you don't know who the hell is calling?'

A noise on the other end of the line. Was the stupid cow sniffling? 'Miss McGee?' he asked. 'What is it?'

'He . . . he said he had to talk to you immediately. About something called Shiloh. And that word is on the list that you've given me and—'

'Shit!' he said, cutting her off and going to the blinking line. 'Ira Woodman here. Who's calling?'

An odd sound. Like the caller was outside. 'Ira Woodman?'

'Yes, this is he. Who is this?'

'Ira Woodman, Region One administrator, Federal Emergency Response Agency. Correct?'

'Look, I don't have time to screw around—'

'Case Shiloh.'

His headache was now back. 'Who is this?'

'I think you have an idea,' the man said. 'But I won't make it easy for you. In fact, to show you what I can do, check your computer files when you have a chance.'

'What do you mean?'

'Case Shiloh. Coming up on the nineteenth. You've been a bad boy, Ira, and all of your files have been erased.'

He squeezed the phone receiver so hard he thought the plastic would break. 'Who the hell is this, and what kind of joke are you playing?'

There. A sound of wind. Damn it, the man was outside. Probably on a cellphone. 'No joke,' the man said. 'Case Shiloh. All of your files. Gone. Have a nice day.'

Click. The man had hung up. Ira dropped the phone receiver and it bounced off the phoneset and by then he was in his chair, going to his computer. He logged on and then went to his personal directory, and then double-clicked on an icon marked PERSONAL, and inside was another icon, marked simply S. He double-clicked on that and was asked for another password, which he supplied. With each passing second the headache was roaring along and his legs were trembling, damn it, his legs were actually sweating, and all of that work, all of those files.

Gone? Just like that?

My God, the whole fucking thing would have to be delayed. Delayed? Jesus! Lurry would have him shot for that and—

He sagged against the chair in relief. There. Everything was there. All of the files with the little icons, all of them were there. He opened a few folders, just to make sure, and everything looked fine:

C.SHILOH/ARREST LIST, HOMOSEXUAL
   ACTIVISTS, NORTHEAST
C.SHILOH/ACTION PLAN FOR CBS, CNN,
   ABC, NBC, FOX
C.SHILOH/TEMPORARY INTERNMENT
   CENTER LOCATIONS, NORTHEAST
C.SHILOH/ARREST LIST, UNIVERSITY
   PERSONNEL, NORTHEAST
C.SHILOH/ARREST LIST, POLITICAL
   ACTIVISTS, MASSACHUSETTS

So what the hell was that call all about? He looked down at his desk, picked up the phone receiver and put it back in its place. Nearby were the pile of pink message slips, the top one coming from Clem Badger. He took a deep breath and picked up the phone.

'Clem? Ira Woodman here.'

'Mr Woodman, I've got some information here about our male fugitive, Drew Connor. Can I come up?'

'Yes, and hurry along,' he said, looking again at his undamaged files. 'I've got a few things to ask you as well.'

Drew handed the cellphone over to Sheila. 'How did it go?' she asked.

'All right, I guess,' he said, bending down to pick up his backpack. 'You were right. When I said that, it wired him right up.' He motioned to her lapbot. 'How long?'

'About a day, if we're lucky. It depends and—'

Almost from the moment the gunfire erupted he leaped on her, pulling her down to the rocky soil. The gunfire went on a long, stuttering tattoo, more than one weapon being used, and Sheila was yelling something and he covered her body with his own. Rounds whistled overhead, the sound intermixed with *pocks* and *pings* as the bullets ripped through the branches and leaves overhead or ricocheted off the boulders marking the top of the ridgeline.

With one hand Drew held Sheila down, and with the other he fumbled in a backpack pocket, getting his 9 mm, knowing he was outgunned, very seriously outgunned, and that this would not end well.

ELEVEN

The feminist agenda is not about equal rights for women. It is about a socialist, anti-family political movement that encourages women to leave their husbands, kill their children, practice witchcraft, destroy capitalism and become lesbians.

Pat Robertson, *Washington Post*, August 23, 1993

When Clem Badger came in Ira was on the carpeted floor of his office, retrieving the letter-opener that he had been fantasizing about shoving into Mr Mather's wrinkly old throat. He got up and tossed the opener on his desk as Clem took a chair across from him. The computer guy's clothes were wrinkled and there were spots on his red necktie, as if he had been eating and sleeping under his desk these past few days.

Noting the powdered sugar along the man's goatee, Ira thought that was a reasonable assumption. He sat down at his desk and said, 'What do you have?'

Clem had a set of computer printouts in his lap, and he started going through them, making underlining motions with his thick fingers. 'It took me a lot of hours, a lot of backdoors and traces, even doing some password trading with other—'

Ira said, 'Spare me the techno speak. What did you find out?'

Clem looked angered for a moment, and Ira knew why. Here was yet another chance to show his boss the scope and breadth of his computer knowledge while Ira probably still had problems programming his DVD player. The true dream of computer geeks everywhere. But Clem just nodded and said, 'It's been a cover story. The whole damn thing.'

'What whole damn thing?'

'The stuff about Drew Connor being retired Department of Agriculture. Pure crap. In less than a day I found out the real stuff, that it wasn't Agriculture. It was DoD. Department of Defense.'

The little tickle of a headache returned about his forehead. 'Go on. In what function?'

Clem laughed. 'Well, that's where it got interesting. At first I found out that he was assigned to the Assistant Secretary for Public Affairs, and everything else keyed into that, but then I remembered back up in New Hampshire, what happened to that deputy's cruiser, how he set it up to run on its own. It sure as hell didn't seem like something a Public Affairs guy could pull off. So I got really creative and started doing some random—'

Ira held up his hand. Clem nodded. 'Right, Mr Woodman. As I was saying, I found out what he really did. Mr Woodman, that guy, he was ex-Army, and was assigned to someplace called the Defense Research Agency. Mr Woodman, I've spent all morning trying to get into their systems, but even with—'

Jesus, sweet Jesus, Ira thought, as Clem continued rambling on. This whole horrid thing started with a couple of hikers getting into the Northern New England Recovery Center, and now one of them has to be a spook. And not just any kind of spook, one that worked for—

'Mr Woodman?'

'Yes, Clem, what is it?' he said, staring at the computer man.

'This Defense Research Agency, what do you know about it?'

'Enough,' he said, feeling like the walls of his office were slowly fading away from view. He remembered some of the briefing sessions earlier on, when he had taken on this job. The number of classified agencies and groups and sub-agencies had made him sick with anger. This government had so many organizations dedicated to secrecy and oppression of its citizens: CIA. NSA. NRO. DRA. The anger had lasted a long while, until Shiloh had come along, a way to do almost the impossible. To take her back. To use the oppressors' own tools against them.

Michaelson Lurry. He would have to be informed immediately about the trespasser's background. And then what? 'The Defense Research Agency . . .' Ira began, remembering. 'It started out like its name. Just a research agency for different topics that fell between the cracks at the Department of Defense. Then it began doing more than just research. It started doing direct action out in the field. It had groups of agents, groups made up of ex-military types. All for deniability purposes, in case something went wrong or someone was captured. Better to pretend that it was a couple of contractors that got caught doing something sneaky in France or Cyprus than active military duty. Most of what they've done remains classified.'

Clem said, nodding in agreement, 'Yeah, I've read some of the stories, heard some of the rumors. Supposedly there was a foul-up with a couple of groups that went in during the Crescent War.'

Ira looked over his desk, and then at the phone. 'Maybe that was him.'

'Excuse me?'

'I got a phone call a few minutes ago, from someone who knew about Case Shiloh. I'm thinking it was our fugitive, Drew Connor.'

'What did he say? Did he identify himself as Drew?'

'No, he didn't. But it did sound like he was calling on a cellphone. There was static in the background and there was the sound of a breeze, like he was outside. And he told me that I had been a bad boy, and that all of our files on Case Shiloh had been erased.'

Clem leaned forward in his chair. 'Erased? And what did you do then?'

'I logged on and checked, and they were all right. Nothing had been—'

'Jesus Christ!' Clem exploded, leaping out of the chair, moving whip-fast, even with his bulk. 'Get the hell out of the way!'

Ira fell back against his chair, his hands tingling with sur-prise as Clem moved around his desk, his hip bumping into a framed photo of his family, knocking it over and then scatter-ing papers, his knees bumping into him as Ira frantically moved his chair away. Clem started typing on the computer keyboard and then picked up a phone and dialed a number. He tucked the phone under his fat chin and in a moment he said, 'Jamie? Yeah, Clem Badger. I think we just got fucked, big time.'

Then Clem started speaking gibberish techno-speak to the man on the other end of the phone, and even though Ira recognized every tenth or twentieth word there was no hiding the fear in Clem's voice, fear that had now found a place within him as well.

Everything was wrong. Clem worked for him, Clem was subservient to him, Clem did what he was told, but now the world had been turned upside down. Clem was in charge, Clem was in front of his terminal, Clem was barking out orders. Ira should have told him to shut up, Ira should have chastised the fat man for barreling across his desk like that, Ira should have said a lot of things to Clem.

Except he was too shocked to say a word.

Sheila raised her head. It had now grown quiet. Everything was in a jumble, both of their backpacks jammed up against a fallen tree trunk. Drew was on his knees, pistol held out straight in his hands. His head was moving back and forth, in short, quick motions. She slowly got up, rubbing at her elbows. Her lapbot was still on and she closed the cover then gave it a squeeze, knowing that she was acting like a small young girl in some dark place, hugging a doll for comfort. She didn't care what she looked like. She just knew she needed to hold something and the lapbot was the closest thing.

Drew noticed her and motioned with a hand to keep down. She shook her head. 'Why did it stop—'

'Shhh!' he said, briefly bringing a finger to his lips, and his harsh look made Sheila give another squeeze to the lapbot. To hell with it, she thought, I've got to know what's going on. She awkwardly got up on her knees and slowly crawled up to the top of the ridgeline. The only thing she could hear was her breathing and the wind. It seemed like every bird in the area had gone silent, hiding and trembling from the loud sounds of death being shot out. Beyond the rocks and boulders that marked the top of the ridgeline there was a slight decline, overrun with brush and saplings and more boulders.

She moved closer, the lapbot against her chest. She looked over at Drew. Again, that movement of the head. Little, quick motions. Like he was taking pictures of the scenery. The scenery that just moments ago was filled with echoing sounds of—

Movement. Off to the right. Three men emerged from a mess of low-brush and rocks, running and laughing. They wore dark green fatigues and their hair was long, and their skin was a dark color, something and—

They all had weapons in their hands, machine-guns of some sort. Oh, God, she thought. Their laughter got louder and they started chanting something, some sort of whoop. Just as they started going past a grove of trees the one on the end looked over in their direction, and Sheila ducked just as he raised his weapon.

There was a sound like a grunt and then the shooting resumed, much louder, and she wanted to cover her ears and scream, then something struck the top of her head. Holy shit, I've been shot, oh, Drew, I've been shot, and she raised her hand to the top of her head, gingerly feeling around, feeling something metallic. She grabbed it and brought it down and just when she recognized it as an empty shell casing – stupid girl, Drew had been shooting, that's what you heard, and this casing is from his pistol – the gunfire stopped again.

Drew came down to her. 'Are you all right?' The pistol was in his hands and there was the sickly odor of burned gunpowder, and she nodded. 'Who . . . I mean, what . . .'

He looked back up beyond the ridge. 'Mohawks, I think.'

It seemed like her voice just squeaked. 'Mohawks? Indians? Are they after us?'

He moved further down to their backpacks, pulled them free and started zipping the open pockets closed. Drew worked quickly but she noted that every other second or so he raised his head to scout the terrain, the pistol still at the ready.

'No, I doubt they were after us,' he said, raising up their backpacks, checking the straps. 'Mohawks up here control the tobacco smuggling for practically the entire Northeast. They get American cigarettes cheap in their reservations, they ship it over to Federal Canada and then smuggle it back into the States, avoid the state and health taxes. Lately there's been fighting with other groups trying to horn in on their turf. County militias, Quebecois bikers, even some of the backwoods fundamentalist types. All looking for easy money, all wanting to take it away from the Mohawks.'

Drew raised his head, looked up over at the ridge again. 'That was probably a raiding party, that's all. Settle a few scores with another group. Just our luck to be in the area.'

Indians, she thought, almost giggling with terror. We have the entire government after us, from the State Police to the FBI to the Federal Emergency Response Agency, and now there's Indians. Why not? Maybe tonight we'll be abducted by aliens to round out this fucking wonderful day.

She shook her head, snapped shut the closed cover on her lapbot. Leave the hysteria be, she thought. Let's just get going and get out of here, and it was like Drew was reading her mind, for he said, 'Come on, time to make tracks, before someone comes by and checks out all this shooting. I just fired over their heads to keep 'em moving.'

Sheila just nodded, still a bit shaky after what had just

gone on, and when she put the lapbot back into her backpack and shouldered the damn weight onto her tired shoulders there came a sound. She ignored it and hoped Drew hadn't heard it, but she saw him hesitate, just for a moment.

'Hear that?' he asked, holding the pistol at his side. 'Sounds like someone.'

'No, I don't hear a thing,' she said. 'Come on, Drew, we've got to get going.'

'Just a sec,' he said, going back up again to the ridgeline, and she followed, legs trembling, wondering if that damn shooting would return. Most of her life had been quiet and peaceful and grand, and the last few days, being shot at twice . . . Jesus.

Drew stopped at the top of the ridge, and now she could no longer pretend she didn't hear the noise. It was a man's voice, a young man from the sound of it, and he was hurt.

'Is anybody out there?' came the voice. 'Please . . . somebody? I've been shot and ah, holy shit . . . it hurts . . . please, somebody?'

Drew's face seemed to set and turn gray, and she came up next to him. 'Drew, come on, you said yourself somebody will be coming along. Somebody will take care of him. We've got to get going.'

He turned and the look on his face . . . She had to step back, just for a moment. 'No,' he said, tightening the straps on his backpack. 'I'm not going to leave him. You can stay here if you like, but I'm heading over.'

'Drew . . .'

But he wouldn't listen. He headed off, just as the man started up again: 'Oh, Jesus, it hurts so much . . . so goddamn much . . . isn't there anyone out there? Please? Somebody? Oh, sweet Mother of God . . .'

He turned to her again, his voice low and deliberate, his eyes looking right through her, like she was made of tissue paper. 'Years ago I left some people behind, and I promised them I'd come back and get them. I never did. And I'm not going to leave this guy alone, whoever the hell he is.'

She took another step back. He was right, she knew he was right. Hell, just a couple of days ago, she had been giving away candy to a couple of Canadian children who looked up at her with those sad eyes. And each month she regularly sent checks to a handful of charities that she had supported over the years: Society for the Protection of New Hampshire Forests, CARE, AID/AFRICA and AID/ASIA. Not to mention the food bank drives that she helped organize back home in Montcalm, for those who still lived in the deep woods, shivering around woodstoves in poorly insulated shacks in the winter.

But now? Now she was ready to walk away from some poor shot man – hell, from his cries, he sounded like a young boy – and what had changed?

She watched the sure step of Drew before her, his hand holding his pistol as he went into the brush and among the boulders.

Everything, she thought, thinking of the past few days. Everything has changed, and it scares me so.

Sheila sighed and started walking after her man.

Ira looked over Clem's shoulder, remembering how he had been in this same spot just a few days back in the FERA Region One bunker in Framingham. He hadn't liked the feeling back then and he liked it even less now.

'Talk to me, Clem, and I mean right now,' Ira said. 'What the hell happened?'

Clem raised his shoulder a bit, as if dislodging an irritating fly. 'What happened is that we were hacked, that's what. And they did a pretty fair job of it.'

'Hacked? How? You mean . . .'

More tapping on the keyboard, and Ira could make out a distant voice on the phone, chattering into Clem's ear. Clem went on. 'It's like this, Mr Woodman . . . no, Jamie, I wasn't talking to you, just button it . . . like I said, it's like this. There are hackers and then there are hackers. Your basic hacker is a brute force kinda guy, most often a guy, a loner with few social skills . . . some funny sociological stuff I read about that once but . . . yeah, Jamie, just shut your mouth . . .'

'Clem,' Ira said, wondering how his hands could fit around this fat man's throat. 'Get to the point.'

'Yep, yep, just a sec . . .' Clem motioned the mouse around, clicked a few times. 'The thing is, for your basic hack, it's all about breaking in. Using dial-up programs that look for modem signals, encryption software to try to guess passwords, stuff like that. Basic hack doesn't much care to look for anything in particular. Just getting into a company or government computer system, that's the thrill. Exploring the system from the inside, like you're the system administrator . . . it's quite addictive. Like playing God with somebody else's world.'

Ira looked down at his computer screen, wondering what in hell Clem had done to it. The light blue screensaver and his carefully lined-up file folder screen icons were gone. In their place were rows of numbers and blinking icons, none of which he recognized.

'And then there's your specific hack,' Clem went on. 'This guy is looking to do specific things. Like letting lose a virus to shut down the climate control system in a building. Or stealing a couple of million dollars from a payroll account. Or finding out where a particular movie star or Net star lives.'

'So what kind of hack was going on here? The first kind or the second kind?'

'Neither,' Clem said, his sausagelike fingers moving quickly over the keyboard. 'It was a stealth hack. Sneakiest kind of all. Thing is, Mr Woodman, all computer systems are vulnerable. All of 'em. Just some are more vulnerable than others. The really tough ones, you get a data mole program. Real simple but deadly. Lots of programmers over the years, they've written back doors into their programs. Some of these back doors just sit still for years. Programmers then sell these back doors at a pretty price to guys who run data moles. Instead of battering at the front door, attracting attention from system security and everybody else, a data mole will slide into the back door.'

'Why is it called a mole?' Ira asked, wishing for a sudden moment that he was back at work with the State Police in Pendleton County, not having to worry about hackers and moles and systems. Just you and your cruiser and your weapon, and that was all. None of this hi-tech crap.

'Moles work underground,' Clem explained. 'They're quiet. And hackers, they find a way into a system, they'll spend days there, poking around and telling the rest of their friends. Eventually they get found out. Data moles go in quietly and quickly, usually looking for particular bits of information, for a price. A lot of the transnational corporations, they use data moles to steal information from their competitors. Most times nobody knows about it. But once I heard what happened to you this morning, well . . . Right now, we're playing catch-up, trying to find the data mole and kick it out of the system.'

'What do you mean, what happened to me this morning?' Ira demanded.

Clem swiveled his head up to Ira, looking almost apologetic. 'The second you told me about that phone call, I knew we had been hacked. I'm sorry, Mr Woodman, but it was a classic data trap. They phoned you, telling you that something bad had happened to your computer files. You responded automatically, logging on and using your passwords. They siphoned those passwords out and went to work. They set a trap for you, Mr Woodman, and you fell right into it.'

He squeezed his hands together. *I am the Grand High Executioner . . .*

'I see,' Ira said.

Drew moved closer to the sound of the voice, his head and feet feeling heavy, hearing those pitiful words being cried out. Sheila stuck close to him and said, 'What about those Mohawks? Won't they come back? I mean, you two were shooting at each other . . .'

'No, I doubt they'll come back,' he said. 'They were moving quick, just like a raiding party. They didn't want to stick around. And that guy . . . hell, I guess warrior, just shot at me 'cause he spotted me. He just popped off a couple of rounds and I returned the favor, and then they disappeared. If they were serious, they would have stuck around. Three guys with AK-47s could have taken care of us in a matter of minutes.'

The voice, a bit louder but still weak: 'Hey, who's out there? I hear voices . . . please, will you help me? Please?'

He moved around a tipped-over stump, its gnarled branches still holding clumps of dirt, and spotted the boy. A little worm of fear gnawed for a moment at the base of his skull. Let's just run out, right now, a voice told him. This shooting and running and sleeping out under the stars are bringing back lots of killer memories, and if you don't stop this, right now, you're heading back to that dark place. The place where you were kept in a quiet room for a long time, fed lots of pills and solutions, and every night the demons traipsed through your mind like they owned the place.

Turn around, right now, the voice whispered. Turn around and you might just live.

Drew shook his head, stepped over a few rocks and then knelt down. The boy – sixteen, maybe seventeen years old? – looked up at him, his face gray with shock and blood loss, his head moving back and forth, like he still could not believe what had happened to him out in these woods on this perfectly fine late-summer day. He wore jeans and heavy work boots, and an Army surplus coat that was chewed up in the front, sopping wet with blood. His blond hair was also matted with dirt and blood, and as Drew got closer the boy grimaced and tears started rolling down his cheeks.

'I . . . I'm really fucked up, I'm sorry . . .' the boy said.

'I know, I know, and it's okay, honest it is,' Drew said, gingerly raising up the jacket and then letting it gently rest down. The boy's chest was heaving up and down, like he had just finished a marathon. At his side was a rifle – a .22 for God's sake, not suited much more for shooting squirrels and rabbits – and a small green canvas knapsack that was open, spilling out its contents: packs of Marlboro cigarettes. Drew picked one up and then tossed it away. It didn't have any of the state tax or Federal ration stickers on its side. A smuggler's dream.

'What's your name, kid?' Drew asked, as Sheila came next to him, making a slight noise that sounded like a gasp and a tone of sorrow, all at once. Drew turned to her and said, 'Your water bottle, hon, right now.'

'Jeremy . . . Jeremy Knight . . . ouch, oh God, it hurts . . .'

Sheila handed him the water bottle and Drew took his handkerchief out, and then wet it down. He wiped the boy's face and he said, 'Jeremy, what happened out here? Where're your friends?'

The boy coughed, and a spittle of blood started trickling down his smooth chin. Drew wiped it clean, and wiped again, damn it. Christ, it didn't even look like the kid was old enough to shave.

'Thanks . . . thanks, that feels good . . . I'm with the Upper Valley Militia, and we was running some cigs for a guy over in St Johnsbury . . . We had done it a couple of times before, no prob . . . until today, when those Mohawks showed up . . . oh, sweet Jesus, it hurts.'

Drew wringed the handkerchief out and then rewet it with fresh water, and Sheila gently touched the back of his neck. Jeremy went on. 'They didn't even warn us . . . the bastards . . . they just started shooting . . . I . . . I didn't even manage to fire back . . . a couple of the other guys did, though . . .'

Sheila said, 'Where are they? Where's the rest of your militia?'

Jeremy grimaced, his face tightening up and tears streaming down his face. 'They ran off and left me . . . that's what they did . . . but I can't blame 'em . . . they're just kids, that's all . . . I'm the oldest . . .'

Sheila made another noise and Drew worked again with

the handkerchief, remembering those old black and white photos from the Civil War, showing teenage soldiers with rifles almost as tall as they were, serious and quiet, heading off to be slaughtered. He wiped Jeremy's face again and Sheila whispered into his ear, 'We've got to do something. We've got to get help over here, right away. Maybe I can get the State Police on my cellphone, make it a quick, anonymous call.'

Drew turned to her, saw the look on her face, the earnestness about those sweet eyes, the confident feeling that one phone call could make everything right. 'Hon, we're doing the best we can, honest. He'll be better in a few minutes.'

'But . . . oh. Oh, Drew . . .'

Drew went back to Jeremy, wiped the face again. The front of his coat looked even wetter than before. Off to the west Drew made out the sounds of one and then two helicopters. The boy raised up a hand and grabbed his wrist. 'I'm . . . I'm Jeremy Knight . . . My parents live on 112 South Street, in Colebrook . . . You'll remember that, won't you . . . won't you . . .'

Drew nodded. 'I will.' Behind him he could hear Sheila start to weep, muffling her sobs into her shirtsleeve.

Jeremy smiled up at him. 'Today was going to be a big score . . . a really big score . . . boy, I'm getting tired . . . I'm just gonna close my eyes for a sec . . .'

Drew reached down and squeezed the boy's hand. 'You close your eyes for as long as you want.'

The sounds of the helicopters grew louder and Sheila said something about moving on, and Drew just kept the boy's hand in his own and watched as the heaving of his chest slowed, stopped, started again, and then stopped for a very long time.

*

The door to Ira's office crashed open and Henry Harrison came in, a printout in his hands. 'It looks like we might have something, Mr Woodman. Looks like we caught a break.'

Ira used both hands to hold on to the rear of his chair, for it seemed like the entire room had tipped up and then tipped down again. The good Lord giveth and taketh, that was always for sure, and maybe this morning he was in a giveth mood after this hack fiasco.

'Go on,' Ira said. 'What do you have?'

Henry glanced over at Clem and spared him about a half-second of interest, and then looked down at the printout. 'About an hour ago there was a firefight up by Haverhill, near the Vermont border. Best guess was that it was a spat between a couple of smuggler groups. Two Hueys from the Air National Guard responded to the area.'

'How did they find out about the shooting?' Ira asked.

'Long-range microphones mounted on the choppers can pick up a lot if you use the right filtering equipment. They picked up the gunfire sound and zeroed right into the area. Then one of the crews spotted a man and woman in hiking gear, about the right height and mass for our fugitives. They headed southwest and managed to get under some cover. We've gotten the word out, to get some more resources up there. But it's pretty tough country, lots of mountains and ravines.'

Clem said, 'Could have been any two hikers. How did they know it was our guys?'

Henry grinned and said, 'Mr Woodman, if you'll permit me.'

'Go ahead.'

Henry picked up the phone, and Jesus, Ira thought, it was

just like before, with Clem. The same commanding voice, the same use of acronyms and buzzwords that he couldn't understand, but at least this time he was quicker than Clem. Henry adjusted the speakerphone and then put the receiver down and said, 'Go ahead, John.'

A man's voice. 'Coming right up, sir. It's from the lead helicopter. Best we could hear after the filtering process.'

Then the sound switched, and there was a low-pitched humming noise and the crackle of static. And a woman's voice, speaking with urgency: 'Drew, we've got to go, right now, or we're dead. Drew . . .'

The voice dribbled off. Ira came closer to the desk and even Clem moved his hands away from the keyboard. 'Again,' Ira said.

The woman's voice: 'Drew, we've got to go, right now, or we're dead. Drew . . .'

Ira smiled. This was the best thing that had happened to him this whole shitty day, right from when he found out those brave Boy Scouts were going to Washington next week to those long minutes with that damn rich loon Mr Mather.

'Clem, how much longer before you find out what was taken from my files?'

'Don't rightly know, Mr Woodman, but it could—'

'Shut up, Clem.' God, it felt good to say that. He spoke to Henry. 'How long before we can get a helicopter ready to bring us up there, to where those two were spotted?'

Henry smiled again, and even though it wasn't a smile designed to bring cheer to little boys or girls it was certainly making Ira happy. 'I've already made the arrangements. We're all set.'

'Good job,' Ira said. 'God bless.'

'God bless,' Henry Harrison said, saying the two words like he didn't believe in either one of them.

The hike had been a long one and they were in an old foundation from a farmhouse that had long been abandoned. The house had collapsed upon itself in a mix of boards, piping and shattered glass. The foundation was dressed stone and went into the dirt about ten feet or so, and Drew cleared out a corner and then brought in rotting planks to place overhead. It had begun to drizzle and the boards didn't keep out all of the dripping water. Drew worked as quick as he could, not saying a word. Sheila was backed up right against the far corner, like she was trying to burrow herself into the soil. She had hardly spoken to him at all since they left the ambush site, moving quickly because of those damn helicopters. He had no way of knowing but it felt like they had been spotted. Something about the tone of the helicopters' engines, the way they moved about. Nothing he could prove, but he just knew it.

When he built the overhang as best he could, he checked the time. Dusk would be along in a few minutes. He climbed back down into the dark and damp shelter and came up to Sheila. Her lapbot was open in her lap, the screen faintly illuminating her drawn face.

'I'll be back in a few minutes,' he said, gently touching the side of her face. 'How are you doing?'

She shivered for a moment from his touch. 'I didn't want to stay with that boy at first, Drew. I wanted to run. I feel like such a cowardly piece of shit. I was so scared.'

'Don't be so hard on yourself.'

She moved her face away from his touch. 'Don't patronize

me, Drew. You pulled yourself up and sucked in your gut and marched right over there. It didn't bother you for a moment, did it? So don't tell me not to be hard on myself.'

He rested back on his heels. 'It bothered me, a lot. Like you, I was scared.'

The lapbot jiggled for a second on her lap, making her face look like it was changing colors. 'I wish I could believe you. I still think you're trying to make me feel better.'

Drew got up, stroked her cheek again. 'When you hear me having a nightmare tonight, you'll see that I was telling you the truth.'

He climbed back out to the ruins of the farmhouse, pulled his rain parka tight against him. It was going to be a cold and wet night. Time to do some grocery shopping. He looked around the landscape, at the second- and third-growth trees, at the saplings and the stands of birch. He could make out the faint contours of the land, and saw an overgrown stone wall, off to the right, near some rusting farm equipment. Abandoned for years. A long time ago this country had been wild, with only the Native Americans roaming through these woods. Then the Europeans came and cut down the trees and burned the brush and killed the Indians. But farming in this thin soil had always been difficult, nothing like the deep and rich soils of his homestate of Nebraska. When those lands had been opened more than a hundred years ago, thousands of settlers abandoned their poor farms here and fled west.

Drew shook his head. Now the trees had come back, the brush had come back, and even the Indians had returned. Cycles upon cycles. Wheels upon wheels. The touch of that dying boy's hand and the look on his face. That same expression had been on the face of those wounded men in his group years ago, when he was about to leave them and said he would return. That he would not forget them. That they would not be abandoned.

Here and the Crescent. Young men dying because of decisions made by the Others: the well fed, the well educated, the well dressed, who make decisions in comfortable government conference rooms and then go out for a long, expense-account lunch. Put restrictions on tobacco so high that smuggling it becomes the trade of choice for the young poor along the Canadian border? Sure. Secretly send in troops to the Asian subcontinent, to try to correct a problem that years of fumbling diplomacy had let get worse? Works for me.

Drew rubbed at his cold, wet face and then went to work, looking along the boulders and places where it was shady among the tree trunks. Here and Asia. The young boy had told him his name: Jeremy Knight of Colebrook. He would remember, just as he had never forgotten those men left behind – to this day he could recite their names and ranks with little difficulty. In remembering he had succeeded where he had failed in everything else. He had not returned to save them. They had been abandoned. And it had been all his fault.

Sheila looked up as Drew came back into their shelter carrying something in his hands. While he was away she had focused on the screen before her, staring at the images and icons and rows of text, wanting to bury her eyes with information, not wanting to see that young boy dying, his shredded coat leaking blood. The NewsNet headlines flashed by on the screen as Drew got under the overhanging planks.

DALLAS GETS HEAVENLY

Dallas Mayor Kay Beulah Thompson has announced that all city telephones will now be answered by the phrase, 'Heaven-o,' because the phrase 'Hell-o' only gives 'aid, comfort and encouragement' to the dark forces working against America.

Click **[HERE]** for more information.

GEORGIA STATE SEN WON'T NAME NAMES

In day twelve of the special Georgia Legislature hearings on gay activists working in state government, State Senator Tara Moulange refused to answer questions as to her own sexual identity, and whether – as charged – she had let her Senate office space be used for a secret organization of homosexuals employed by the state.

Click **[HERE]** for more information.

PREZ MAY SPEAK NEXT WEEK

Administration sources said today that the President may address a special session of Congress next week to address concerns about his health and governing abilities. Majority leaders on both sides of the Hill promised a 'fair and respectful' hearing if the President does choose to speak.

Click **[HERE]** for more information.

FOREIGN HEADLINES

Jerusalem Clash Kills Four.
Oil Embargo Now In Sixth Month.
Fallout Patterns In Asia Shrinking.

'Hey,' he said. 'I'm going to get dinner going. How are you?'

Terrible, she thought. I'm cold and wet and water is dripping down the back of my neck. The brave woman who talked to you the other day about fighting these people is gone. The scared little girl in front of you has replaced her, and seeing that boy die in the woods and all that blood has changed her mind. She doesn't want to fight anymore. She wants to run away and be someplace safe with you, where it's dry and warm and I'm not hungry and I don't have to be scared anymore.

She wiped a drop of water off the tip of her nose. 'I'm okay. What do you have?'

He knelt down beside her and carefully unfolded his handkerchief. 'Some mushrooms and fiddler fern roots. With water and a bit of that leftover Tabasco sauce, I think I can make a pretty fair stew. Not a lot, but it'll be filling. Plus some McIntosh apples for dessert from an abandoned orchard.'

'Un-hunh,' she said, wiping a few errant drops of water off the lapbot screen. Then it flickered and a little box appeared in the upper right-hand corner.

[MOLE BOY WILL ARRIVE IN 23 HOURS
FIFTEEN MINUTES 12 SECONDS]

She closed down the screen and said, 'Well, I guess we'll have time for dinner after all.'

The night and the next day dragged on, with the weather still wet and drizzly. Sheila slept as well as she could in her damp sleeping bag in the basement of the farmhouse, and ate what was put before her whenever Drew came back from his foraging expeditions. She didn't talk much to Drew, and for once he respected her silence. All she could think about was that poor dead boy, and a little dark fantasy about what she and Drew might look like if they were discovered by their pursuers. Alone and bleeding to death in the wet, cold woods. Once Drew had said, 'You know, it might make sense to keep moving,' and she had answered, 'Right now, we're getting a strong satellite signal. I don't want to screw things up by moving us around, Drew. Suppose we're in a dead zone, not able to download, when the Mole Boy comes back?'

He had just nodded crisply and went back to look for more food – roots, bulbs, berries, whatever – and she had waited in the damp silence, until her lapbot screen flickered again and said:

[MOLE BOY HAS ARRIVED]

A little fuzzy sensation settled into her chest. Setting this up had cost a lot of money, almost her entire savings in the Calgary account, and she wondered what she had gotten. Damn it, it had better be worth it. It was like Drew had sensed that something had changed for he knelt down next to her, some water dripping off him onto the back of her neck, but she was too busy to complain.

'Something?' he asked.

'Yeah, let me check, hold on,' she said as she double-clicked on the message box. Then a spinning alarm clock popped up, and she said, 'Downloading now.'

'How long?'

'Not sure.'

Drew moved in closer and she could feel him hesitate, like he was trying to say something. She stared at the spinning alarm clock, knowing that was exactly how she felt. Spinning and spinning, losing time and energy with every turn.

'Drew.'

'Yeah?'

'What is it, you were going to ask me something.'

He coughed. 'Well, it's just . . . I was wondering where you were getting the money to pay for this Mole Boy. You said he was very expensive, even just searching for the two keywords, *Case Shiloh*. But if we can't get into our own accounts . . .'

Shit, she thought. One of these days she knew she would have to tell Drew the whole story from start to finish about her CyberGal career and everything that went with it . . . But here? In these damp woods? Now?

She looked at the icon of the spinning alarm clock. Damn it, why are you taking so long?

'I had some other money, set up in an account in Calgary.'

'Oh.' Damn, lots of tension in that single word. She went on.

'It's from something I did before I met you, something before I moved east. When I was in school at Stanford. It was . . . well, it was money that I always figured I could use for an emergency. Like this.'

'And what kind of work did you do at Stanford?' Again, that calm tone of his voice, barely hiding the tension beneath those syllables.

The alarm clock stopped spinning. Finally!

'Hold on, hon, let's see what we've got here.'

She double-clicked on the icon and rolls of text started appearing. Drew moved in, reading over her shoulder.

'It looks like files from that guy Woodman's e-mail account,' she said, and Drew merely grunted in reply.

FROM: WOODMANIW@FERA.ONE.GOV.PRIV
TO: KALLINTC@FERA.TWO.GOV.PRIV

Thomas –
You fool, what are you thinking??? Of course there's no Work Order Number for Case Shiloh!!!
You want the GAO crawling all over you?
Get creative and hide the expenses in training or some damn thing.
– Woodman

FROM: WOODMANIW@FERA.ONE.GOV.PRIV
TO: DISTRIBUTION LIST ONE

A reminder that the COG/National Program Office Working Group meetings for the third quarter will be supplanted by the Case Shiloh Task Force sessions. Please ensure your attendance at all sessions.

TO: WOODMANIW@FERA.ONE.GOV.PRIV
FROM: KINGSBURRYXF@DOD.GOV.PRIV

Ira –
Nice seeing you at the Case Shiloh meeting this past Thursday.
Post-Shiloh, will current plan work? Or should we go for a

General Smedley Butler-type character? Might be a few on the active list who could fit the bill. Let me know. And don't take this personally, just some constructive criticism.

Best to Glenda Sue and the kids.

– Francis

TO: WOODMANIW@FERA.ONE.GOV.PRIV
FROM: TRINGALIBT@FERA.THREE.GOV.PRIV
Message One Of Eight

Supplies for Case Shiloh Task Force have been established in following depots:

ALBANY:
    FIFTY (50) ROLLS CONCERTINA WIRE
    FIVE HUNDRED (500) CASES MRES
    FOUR (4) FIELD KITCHENS
    TWELVE (12) TRAFFIC CONTROL CHECKPOINTS
    ALL RESOURCES ASSOCIATED WITH LOCAL NATIONAL
        GUARD ARMORIES (NOTE: SEE MESSAGE OF 6/15
        FOR COMPLETE LISTING)

BALTIMORE:
    ONE HUNDRED (100) ROLLS CONCERTINA WIRE
    SW/MAGOG (NOTE: SPECIAL HANDLING IN PLACE)
    FOUR (4) FIELD KITCHENS (NOTE: NEED TWELVE [12]
        MORE TO ENSURE TOTAL COVERAGE)
    EIGHTEEN (18) MOBILE DECONTAMINATION
        SHOWERS
    SEVENTY-FIVE (75) FIELD MONITORING SYSTEMS
    SIX (6) PUBLIC ADDRESS SYSTEMS

GMC RENTAL VAN MD REG. TAA467 (NOTE: NON-
REPLACABLE BECAUSE OF SPECIAL SUSPENSION
SYSTEM FOR DELIVERY PURPOSES)
TWENTY-FOUR (24) TRAFFIC CONTROL CHECKPOINTS
EIGHTEEN-HUNDRED (1800) RUBBERIZED BODY BAGS
(NOTE: FIELD OFFICE STILL BELIEVES NUMBER IS
TOO LOW. SHOULD REVIEW AGAIN PRIOR TO CASE
SHILOH IMPLEMENTATION).
ALL RESOURCES ASSOCIATED WITH LOCAL NATIONAL
GUARD ARMORIES (NOTE: SEE MESSAGE OF 6/15
FOR COMPLETE LISTING)

BOSTON:
ONE HUNDRED (100) ROLLS CONCERTINA WIRE
SIX (6) FIELD KITCHENS
TWENTY (20) TRAFFIC CONTROL CHECKPOINTS
(NOTE: FIELD OFFICE FEELS NUMBER OF
CHECKPOINTS MAY BE TOO LOW BECAUSE OF
ROAD DESIGNS AND MOBILE COLLEGE
POPULATION)
ALL RESOURCES ASSOCIATED WITH LOCAL NATIONAL
GUARD ARMORIES (NOTE: SEE MESSAGE OF 6/15
FOR COMPLETE LISTING)

TO: WOODMANIW@FERA.ONE.GOV.PRIV
FROM: SWEENEYFX@DOD.GOV.PRIV

Woodman:
I've managed to get your personnel requests resolved. I'm not
sure if I can make another pass to satisfy the Case Shiloh Task
Force requirements, at least for six months. I already have the

Asst. SecDef for Personnel sniffing around today. It'll be hard to keep her satisfied with the usual BS about special orders.
Please advise.
Sweeney

FROM: WOODMANIW@FERA.ONE.GOV.PRIV
TO: SELENEKOVTI@FERA.ONE.GOV.PRIV

Tanya –
This draft much better than the last one. Another suggestion.
Make changes to next-to-last paragraph, last phrase.
Currently reads: '. . . gave his life in service for his country.'
Replace with '. . . was sacrificed for his country, and we will mourn his passing as we did another president, nearly a half century ago.'
Please have another draft ready for next Case Shiloh Task Force meeting.
– Woodman

The rolling of the text was complete. There were no more messages. Sheila felt water dripping on her and the coldness of the rocks through her pants, but she was focused on those flickering words on her computer screen, especially the last e-mail message.

'My God,' she whispered. 'They're going to kill the President.'

SIDEBAR II

Luis Raminez sat back in his easy chair in their tiny living room, feeling relaxed and at peace. Dinner had been a nice big bowl of chili with a side of cornbread – both recipes from Maria's mama, and my, how she could cook – and he had his second bottle of Dos Equis resting on his stomach. On the small color TV – which had a statue of the Virgin Mary and their wedding portrait on a lace doily on top – he watched the Texas Rangers as they were doing their best to crush the Cleveland Indians.

Maria came in carrying a black, leatherbound book. He looked over at the wall clock. Nine p.m. 'Maria, please, just a few minutes more, when this innings is over,' he pleaded.

She smiled and walked over and switched off the television. 'You know our agreement. Just a half-hour, that's all. And then you can have your television back.'

Well, an agreement was an agreement, and he took another sip of beer as his wife opened up the Bible and started reading from it. She had almost died at an early age from a form of childhood leukemia, and the fact she had survived and was now bearing her first child was a time to rejoice. So she promised God that each night, for a half-hour, she would read aloud from the Bible and that her husband would listen in. At first he hadn't liked the idea at all, but then he found he enjoyed listening to her voice, and even liked some of the old stories he had learned in Sunday school. Though the parts of the Good Book where somebody begat someone who begat someone could be tedious, now they were in the prophets, where the old guys really tossed around the fire and brimstone, and he liked that.

He looked around their home as she read aloud, now from the Book of Jeremiah. He had a job at Trong's Marine Supply, down on the docks. Mister Trong was Vietnamese but treated him and everybody else right, and Luis tried to keep his ears and eyes open around the store, because Mister Trong was childless and often talked about selling his store to one of his employees. And if he worked hard and kept his nose clean, why not Luis Raminez? Maria worked at a bridal boutique, further into town, helping young, giggling girls and serious-looking young boys plan their weddings. A pretty simple life, but—

Maria frowned, closed the Bible on her finger. 'Hear that, from next door? What is it, some kind of fight?'

He got up and went over to her on the couch, kneeling down and drawing the curtains open. He couldn't see much but he did hear the sounds. Low, plaintive sounds. It sounded like someone crying, but there was a bit of an accordion sound to it.

'It's music, Maria, that's all.'

She sighed. 'Anglos. Them and their loud music.'

'It's not that loud, Maria—'

'Well, it's loud enough. Go ahead, turn on your damn baseball game and watch it. I'll go to the bedroom and finish reading. Unless, of course, you want to go over and tell those Anglos to turn down their damn music.'

He shook his head, knowing a suggestion from Maria was always much more than just a suggestion. Luis got up and went into the kitchen, then outside. The music stopped. He stood out in the warm night air, seeing insects buzz around a high streetlight at the corner. Some loud voices were raised at the house and he shook his head again. Anglos. In their neighborhood. He felt a little worm of worry begin to gnaw at him, and then he went back inside, to listen to his wife read their Bible.

In the grand scheme of things, Gunnery Sergeant Chris Rockman thought the lack of news media and NewsNet attention pissed him off the most. He was in a parking lot at the Quantico base, standing near his car, an old Dodge that practically needed an oil change every week. Around him were lines of fellow Marines and their family members, standing in line for clothes hand-outs, for bags of food, and even small piles of toys. Volunteers from some of the base's service organizations would go out along the roads in the towns around Quantico on trash days, salvaging broken toys for the kids of the Marines on base. In one of those lines was his wife Amy and their twins, Jeannette and Jean, seeing what they could get on this day. But he was too ashamed to be there with them. Bad enough to be in this parking lot in the first place.

Think of that, he thought. Just think of that. Men and women who volunteered to put themselves in harm's way, to serve their country and perhaps even die for it, to go anywhere in the world to perform their duty in the face of danger. And how are they repaid? With bags of donated macaroni and cheese. With cast-off clothes from the officers. And with broken toys, repaired for the benefit of children whose parents couldn't afford anything new for them.

But that's not what really pissed him off. What really pissed him off was the lack of attention. Not so long ago this parking lot would have been filled too, with reporters and NewsNet correspondents, but now? Old news. Part of the scenery. Every year promises would be made to make things different, to improve their lives, and each year the promised funds were diverted to more health care for the boomers, or gold-plated weapon systems like that frigging *Excalibur*, out there in space. His Marines made do with cast-offs from the Army, but there was always money to be spent on hi-tech weapons. Jesus, what a country.

'Hey, gunny,' came a voice.

Rock turned, saw another Marine come over. His name was Bouchard, a sergeant in one of the supply depots. 'Yeah, right here,' he said. 'What can I do for you?'

Bouchard shook his head, handed him a white envelope. 'No, gunny, it's what I can do for you. I got something here for you. In fact, I got envelopes like these for every Marine here.'

Rock opened up the envelope, saw the thin stack of twenty-dollar bills inside. 'What the fuck is this? A bribe? A pay-off?'

The other Marine shook his head. 'Nope. A donation. Look, there's this business guy I know. Used to be active in the Lurry campaigns. Now that Lurry's not running any more, he still wants to do his part. So he's making cash donations to the local bases. He knows what's up with the DoD budgets and how we're all scraping by.'

He looked through the money, calculated which bills he could pay off this windfall. Still . . .

Rock handed the envelope over. 'I don't like it. I think it stinks.'

'Hey, gunny, I've checked with the provost office. It's all up front and legal. Check with them yourself.'

Rock thought about that and brought the envelope back. 'That true? It's all right?'

Bouchard gently slapped him on the back. 'Hell, yes. Only thing is . . .'

'Oh, okay, a catch. What is it?'

'Nope, no catch. Only thing is, if you're interested, this business guy, he'd like to talk to you and the other Marines sometimes. Just talk about current affairs. He wants to pick your brains, get your opinions on stuff. That's all. Real friendly type.'

'That's it?'

'Sure, that's it. And maybe someday, we can do a favor in return. But only if you agree.'

'What kind of favor?'

Bouchard just smiled. 'Who knows. But I'm sure it won't be something you'll feel bad about. Trust me.'

He slowly put the envelope away in a rear pocket. 'Okay. Tell your friend I'm appreciative, more than he knows. But I still don't like it.'

Then Amy came over, smiling, holding a plastic toy tricycle in her hands. 'Hon, see what we've got!' and the look on his children's faces cut through him.

'Who does, gunny,' Bouchard said. 'Who does.'

The sniper's first visitor was a yellow Labrador retriever, bounding down along the hillside, sniffing and pawing at the ground. He was laying on his side, covered with netting and tarpaulin, wearing his ghillie suit, and as the dog bounded about he slowly drew out a knife from his belt scabbard.

It was cool under the shelter he had made, but now he was concerned. People he could avoid. The place he had chosen was relatively remote and hard to get to. But a dog? A dog could cause some problems, could bring along a couple of curious owners trying to find out why Fido was digging and barking frantically. The sniper remembered a co-worker of his who had done a bit of shooting in Provence, in the south of France. Goddamn guy had a freaking pig disturb him, a pig designed to sniff out truffles, and in order not to spoil the shoot he had to slit the pig's throat and drag him under with him. For three days he shared quarters with a dead pig. Jesus.

Someone out on the hillside whistled, and the dog barked and started running up the hill, tail wagging, looking mighty pleased with himself.

The sniper smiled and put his knife away. He sure would have hated to kill that dog.

TWELVE

The strategy against the American radical left should be the same as General Douglas MacArthur employed against the Japanese in the Pacific . . . bypass their strongholds, then surround them, isolate them, bombard them, then blast the individuals out of their power bunkers with hand-to-hand combat. The battle for Iwo Jima was not pleasant, but our troops won it. The battle to regain the soul of America won't be pleasant either, but we will win it.

Pat Robertson, in *Pat Robertson's Perspective*, April–May 1992

Cyrus Montgomery was hunched over in the basement of his home in Vermont on Saturday, flashlight in hand, as he went through the dark caverns that made up the cellar. His Scribe, Maurice Blakely, was at his side, carrying his own flashlight, a toolbelt around his waist, and his lapbot under his arm. Even though Blakely was almost a half-foot shorter than Montgomery, he, too, was hunched over, to spare his head from bumping into one of the two-hundred-year-old oak beams that supported the house.

The floor of the basement was concrete, and on this fine early evening it was wet concrete, something Montgomery had noticed when he had come down to the cellar earlier to locate a cardboard box of papers from his JCS days and saw a puddle forming.

'You know, Blakely,' Montgomery said wistfully. 'There was a time not so long ago that if I saw water in the basement of the house it was an easy fix. Just call the post engineer and it'd be fixed that day.'

Blakely said, 'That's why I've got my lapbot with me, sir.'

Montgomery smiled. Christ, this cellar was huge. 'Don't take offense, Blakely, but I'm not sure how your lapbot is going to help.'

'Easy, sir,' he said. 'Every home repair and maintenance book is stored here, plus links on the Web to—'

'All right, all right,' Montgomery said. 'I should know better than not to trust my Scribe. Let's just see if we can find that leak.'

He lowered his head again. The cellar seemed to stretch on forever. There were vaults of brick and cement, bundles of wires, pipes of varying thickness and length. He could have called the local plumber but that might have taken hours, and he wanted to catch the leak before it soaked any of the boxes, filled with memories of his years of service, of the Pentagon, of dear Grace . . .

'Here we go, sir,' Blakely said. 'Right up there.'

A copper pipe was running across the bottom of a large beam, from left to right. A faucet attachment poked out halfway through, and water was leaking around its base. Blakely said, 'Looks pretty straightforward, sir. Shut off the water at the main pipe, replace and repack that faucet. Probably just too old.'

'Like almost everything else in this damn house,' Montgomery said, shining the flashlight beam to the left. There a huge oil tank squatted in one corner, holding the fuel oil for the house. More bundles of wires led out of an odd-looking box attached to the wall nearby, and some of the wires led into a unit attached to the tank. The wires were old, cloth-insulated. Montgomery said, 'Blakely, look at that rat's nest over there. What do you think it is?'

His Scribe spared it a glance as he took off his toolbelt. 'Maybe part of the old phone lines from the house. Or it could be a reorder system. Thirty, forty years ago, some of these big houses, the owners could afford to have direct phone lines linked to an oil company. Oil level gets low enough, an automatic call went out to send a fuel truck. If you want my opinion, sir . . .'

Montgomery shone the light over the cobwebs and brick-work. He wondered if some of his ancestors might have been in this house before him, centuries ago, as they took the Underground Railroad north to Canada, scared and shiver-ing as they rested here. Maybe. But then most old houses in Vermont and New Hampshire and Massachusetts tried to claim some sort of Underground Railroad history. Made it more easy during home sale time – especially during this never-ending recession – to have a bit of historical romance attached to a property listing.

'Go ahead, Blakely,' he said. 'I've always respected your opinion.'

'Sir, you might think about having all that old wiring pulled out, and the pipes rechecked. All it would take would be one spark or one more pipe leak and—'

'Yeah, I know, I know,' he said, looking at his watch. 'Blakely, if you don't mind.'

Blakely opened up his lapbot, powered it up. He smiled over at the General. 'I know, sir, it's time for your daily con-stitutional. Go right ahead. When you come back this mess will be done. And then it'll be time to start on Chapter Four, sir. No use putting it off.'

'That's right,' Montgomery said, looking at his watch again, hoping he wouldn't be late. 'No use putting it off.'

Drew hunched in closer to Sheila, understanding what she had just said, not sure if she was right, but damn it, something horrible was going on, something horrible indeed. He looked down at the flickering letters on the screen, reading through the cool words and phrases of the bureaucrat, imagining a bloodless bureaucrat gene, passed on from generation to generation, from nation to nation. Sir, sorry to tell you that the Somme battlefield requires another 10,000 coffins. Sir, pleased to report your order of Zyklon-B gas will be arriving at Auschwitz this Tuesday. Sir, the speech announcing the death of the President is ready for your review.

'Drew, if I forward this to the Treasury Department, to the Secret Service . . .' Sheila started, looking up at him, her face pale in the light from the lapbot screen.

'Then it will get dumped into another file filled with hate mail from crazies, no offense, hon,' he said. 'It'd get looked at eventually, but we don't have eventually. We've only got three more days.'

Then, a thought: Charlie Chaplin.

What the hell?

'Sheila, could you move the screen over, there's something at the beginning I want to read,' he said. 'Some of that stuff was moving by so fast I couldn't catch all of it. There's more there that I want to take a look at.'

'Sure, hold on,' Sheila said, and as Drew was thinking – Charlie Chaplin? What the hell was that all about? – he moved his head closer to her and the screen was now blank.

'Sheila, could you tilt it some more? I can't see anything.'

Her voice, as hard as steel: 'That's because there's nothing to see.'

'What do you mean?'

Then her voice changed as her fingers started tapping frantically on the lapbot keyboard. 'Oh, shit, Drew, I'm sorry, Jesus, I'm sorry. The battery just died.'

'The battery? I thought you said we had a few more hours worth of power left.'

She bent forward so he couldn't see her face. 'We did. Until that shooting yesterday . . . Damn it, Drew, I must have closed the cover without powering down the lapbot. All that hiking we did, from where that boy got shot, the lapbot must have been on. And I don't have a spare battery, just a power cord.'

Now she looked up at him, tears rolling down her cheeks. 'And I don't think there's an outlet in this fucking basement, do you?'

He touched her shoulder and she tensed up. He closed his eyes for a moment, trying to remember all the phrases and words that passed by on the screen. Planning. Meetings. Something to do with a General Butler. Body bags. Field kitchens. More meetings. And that damn speech fragment. And something else . . .

He opened his eyes, turned his head. A helicopter approaching from the west. Then another.

And then a third, approaching from the south.

Trying to box them in.

'Get your stuff together, right now,' he said, standing up awkwardly below the planks and branches, thinking again of a little man with a moustache who made millions laugh.

Face it, old boy, all this running through the woods and

gunfire has loosened you up. Best to set Sheila on her way and surrender, and pretty soon you'll be back in that comfortable room, sleeping and dreaming, muttering your way through every day.

The helicopter noise got louder, and he picked up his backpack, checked the pistol at his side.

Maybe so, but not today.

Montgomery walked along the large field behind his home, which sloped gently down to a line of trees. He turned for just a moment and looked back at the large farmhouse, Too big, of course, for a widowed man who just had a soldier staying there for a while to help him write a book and get settled in at Norwich University. But his wife had loved the place, had loved the idea of actually owning something for oneself and no longer living in a government-issued home. My word, the dumps that poor woman had to put up with in postings here and in Germany and South Korea. Places crawling with bugs, where rusty water would come out of clanking pipes, and where the heating system would wheeze and burp and fail to produce a damn bit of warmth. Only towards the end of his career did any of their homes become large enough for the two boys and nice enough to have guests over, but even then Grace hadn't been happy.

She would cuddle up with him at night and say, 'One of these days, Cyrus, one of these days we'll have our own damn place.'

And he would gently squeeze her and say, 'But suppose that house happens to be white? And is in DC?'

And then she would laugh and say, 'Oh, all right then. But at least with that posting we'll have servants. Lots of servants.'

He looked away from the house, closed his eyes at the sudden rush of memories. Oh, my dear one, how much I miss you. You have no idea. He clenched his fists at the memory of the gunshots and screams and yells, and then the noise of an airplane passing overhead made him open his eyes and keep on walking. Keep on walking, he thought. Work to do and things to achieve, so keep on walking.

After a few minutes he paused at a place where several large boulders still dominated the field and where previous generations of farmers had given up on removing them. The noise from the airplane grew louder, almost drowning out the sound of the stream running off to the east, where there was a small waterfall. Part of the old soldier in him liked being among the boulders. Walking along grass always made him nervous, and for good reason. In Bosnia and Kosovo and even along parts of the Quebec border, grass meant places where landmines could be hidden. And landmines are among the most feared weapons, not because they would kill you but because they would maim you. Better to get a bullet in your head than to have your balls blown off.

He crossed his arms, waited. Of course, when he first moved in here spreading rumors about landmines along the boundaries of the property would have helped. Reporters, autograph seekers, everyone from the curious to the crazed seemed to find their way to the driveway leading up to the farmhouse. A month after moving in he had reluctantly fenced the entire lot and installed a driveway gate, complete with camera and intercom, and Blakely had helped him install a few exotic pieces of equipment along the hundreds of yards of fencing. The price for privacy, the price for being left alone.

There. The white Cessna went overhead, waggled its wings, and then came over for another approach. The letters and numbers on the rear fuselage were different from the previous visitor, which didn't mean a damn thing. As long as the job got done. The Cessna tilted some as it roared overhead, and then something orange and fluttering came out as the airplane disappeared in the distance. There was a long, orange paper streamer that fluttered as the plastic tube thumped to the ground, just a few yards away.

He walked over, tore off the streamer and crumpled the piece of crepe paper into his pants. He popped open the plastic tube and a sheet of paper came out, which he unrolled and read, the handwriting firm and to the point:

Cyrus –
    Some more info to share. It seems like the
'something' going on has a name attached to it:
Shiloh. Don't know anything else, except that this
Shiloh is due to take place in a few days.
Coincidentally, at that time there is a low-grade alert
scheduled for this facility and others.
    I hate coincidences. I also hate the fact that you're
not back at that five-sided building, so I'd feel better
about whatever the hell is going to happen.
    More to come if I find out.
– L

L stood for Leslie, as in Air Force General Leslie Coombs, and he remembered their recent meeting in Nevada, right after the successful test of *Excalibur*. Shiloh. So now it has a name. He looked out to the treeline and knew that just a couple of miles away was the well-manicured and ordered campus of Norwich University, the 'other' West Point, proudly turning out graduates who would enter this nation's army in her service. But now what kind of service? What kind of duties? What kind of responsibilities?

He sat down on one of the larger boulders, found himself smiling. Here now was an office, not like that ornate place back at the Pentagon. Just rocks and grass and God's blue sky. Big differences, of course, except for that one similarity. Decisions. What kind of decision to be made? At least back at the Pentagon he had better information, better options, always a set number of responses to any problems that came your way. There may have been bad answers to even worse problems, but at least there were answers. Send some Apache helicopters. Raise the budget. Have lunch with a Congresswoman to soothe her battered ego. Cut the budget. Send in a Special Forces unit. Leave the budget alone.

Now? Just fog. Just questions. And something that had a name. Shiloh.

He reached into another pocket, pulled out a lighter. A long time ago he had smoked cigars, but that time had passed when he started noticing how damn short of breath he'd get from just walking out to the end of the driveway. But he still kept the lighter, a souvenir from a visit to some frontline a long time ago. From a Special Forces unit, and under the unit crest was a motto: *De Oppresso Liber*. To Free the Oppressed. Hell of a motto, but only if you knew who was oppressed and who was doing the oppressing.

Holding both the paper and the streamer in his other hand, he flicked open the lighter and burned both items, letting them drop from his fingers only when the flames came close to his fingers. With all that electronic snooping out there, from programs to intercept e-mail messages and some agencies that had the ability to read a computer's hard drive from a remote area, well, this was not a time to trust anything electronic. A handwritten message on paper, and now it was gone.

He clicked the lighter shut and put it back in his pocket, and started back to his home.

Shiloh.

To Free the Oppressed.

From the rear porch of the farmhouse, Captain Maurice Blakely saw the form of the good general walking back to the house, hands in his pockets, head looking down. Blakely wiped his hands with a rag towel, the leak downstairs having just been fixed. A while ago a single-engine airplane had buzzed the General's property, just like the week before, and also the week before that. Maybe the General thought that Blakely didn't notice, that his Scribe wasn't aware of anything that didn't appear on a computer screen.

He shook his head. He noticed everything, from the monitored conversation he noted with the Senator a few days ago and to the quiet way the General sometimes held himself as he stared out to the fields.

So. The good General was under some stress. And what had he said, just a while ago down in the basement? Something about trusting his Scribe.

Now, that was a thought. Blakely smiled again.

Ira Woodman tightened the seatbelt, more from nervousness than anything else. This was his second straight day in a helicopter and he was hating it. Yesterday, he and Henry Harrison had made a high-speed run up to New Hampshire after listening to that airborne surveillance tape, but the trail had quickly gotten cold. After a sleepless night in a cold motel room, they were back in the sky for another day of searching. Now, on this Saturday early evening, the trail had finally been picked up. He sat in a passenger compartment in the rear, headphones and microphone wrapped around his head, the comforting bulk of Henry Harrison at his side. Up forward was the pilot and co-pilot, and with Henry's help he listened in to the conversations as two other helicopters searched the area, complete with searchlights, long-range microphones and thermal imaging devices. The other two helicopters also carried six National Guardsmen apiece, all of them under FERA control because of that 2001 anti-terrorism act.

'Tango Prime, Tango Prime, this is Tango Four, I've got two targets, moving west,' came a voice in the earphones. 'Still under tree cover but thermal imaging is coming through clear.'

'Roger that, Tango Four,' came the reply, which was from the pilot up forward, Tango Prime. Henry's voice came in. 'Hear that, Mr Woodman? Looks like we're going to run them to ground.'

Ira nodded, felt his stomach heave and lurch as the pilot flew them above the darkened landscape of the New Hampshire hills and peaks. A lot of thoughts were blurring through his mind, all culminating in a sickening crash into the side of a wood-covered peak: the helicopter striking an overhead power line, the helicopter running into another chopper up here, or a goose or duck or damn eagle crashing into the plexiglass cockpit and killing the pilot.

Damn Henry for being so calm, for being so unflappable. He sat there upright and straight, smug and snug in his seatbelt, like he belonged. And, as an ex-Navy SEAL, he did belong. Ira had never quite known the whole story of how and why Henry left the service, but that was just fine. Just as long as he did his job right, both here and in DC in the next few days.

'Tango Prime, Tango Prime, this is Tango Two,' came the other voice. 'I'm over the river. Nothing yet.'

'Tango Prime, this is Tango Four. Both subjects still not visible to naked eye. Thermal imaging still clear. Both subjects still moving west.'

Ira clutched the seatbelt as the helicopter swooped and dove over a ridge. 'Any opening around, anyplace we can set these damn choppers down?'

Henry nodded and held on to an intercom switch, repeated the question to the pilot.

''Fraid not, sir,' came the reply from up forward. 'It's pretty thick woods and cover, all the way down to the river's edge.'

'Henry, how about roads? What do we have down there?'

Henry said, 'We've got a dirt access road about a half-mile from where we've got them. State and county police are moving in, along with some National Guardsmen. Don't worry, in a few minutes that place will be crawling with our guys. It ends tonight, Mr Woodman, I guarantee it.'

Ira nodded, gripped the belt again as the helicopter swooped around again. Damn it, how in hell can this idiot pilot see where he's going? Tonight, to be ended tonight. To get those two fugitives and find out why they were in the Recovery Center in the first place and why they had hacked his computer system.

'Tango Prime, this is Tango – shit, what the hell?'

Ira forgot about the pilot. 'Henry, what's wrong, what's going on?'

'Tango Prime to calling unit, what's the problem, over?'

Ira made out the roaring of the engines, the static echoing in his earphones.

'Tango Prime to calling unit, what's the problem, over?'

'Tango Prime, this is Tango Two, Tango Two calling. We've got more images, shit, we've got another dozen or say, hell, make that twenty images. There's a whole shitload of people down there. Almost making out a half-dozen or so occupied buildings. Damn it, we even got people on the river in watercraft. Tango Prime, we've lost 'em.'

Ira turned to Henry, his voice rising in fury. 'You tell him, I don't care how they do it or where they do it, I want these fucking choppers grounded, do you understand? On the ground, right now, all of 'em.'

'Sir, it's rough terrain down there—'

'On the ground, Henry. Now.'

He grasped the seatbelt again, his stomach ready to crawl out his throat, as the helicopter flew out and over a wide river and swooped down again, and another thought came to him, of crashing into the cold water and drowning, trapped with the seatbelt snug across his waist.

So what, he thought. At least then we won't have to explain to Lurry how we lost those two.

Drew paused, breathing hard. Sheila came up next to him and he held a finger to his lips. Above them was the endless roar of the helicopters, the noise rising and lowering in intensity as they kept up the chase, and my word, these three assholes were certainly on the chase. He turned and looked at his woman in the deepening twilight, and he felt a surge of pride and love at what she had been doing these past days. From the very moment back in Corinth to right now she had done as well as any recruit in this man's army, putting up with poor sleep, little food and long hike after long hike, as well as the ever present Bad Guys snipping at their heels. Not once had she said anything about giving up. Not once. He thought for a brief moment about his idea of what kind of woman she was, a woman who lived and thrived from the Net, and who probably didn't have what it took to make it outdoors.

He had been wrong, and he was glad.

Drew took her hand and followed the scent, the smell of running water, and in another minute or two of going through the thick underbrush, the branches and leaves snapping at their skin, they came to water. He looked out at the wide river, the mighty Connecticut, flowing at their feet, heading south and eventually to Long Island Sound. Across the river were the rolling hills and thick trees of Vermont, and without thinking too much about it he knew that was where they had to go. Vermont. He turned and saw a faint glow of light to the north, over a small hill. He brought Sheila to him and spoke close into her ear. 'You doing okay?'

He felt her nod against his chest. 'There are lights over there. Might be some vacation cottages or fishing camps. Let's take a look.'

She reached up and pressed her lips against her ear. 'People?'

'Lots of 'em, I hope.'

'Why?'

He hugged her again as a helicopter roared overhead, its searchlight stabbing at them in the dusk. 'Mix and mingle, and it'll take a long time for them to sort things out. Let's go.'

He took her hand again and went up the slight hill, again making out the sounds of the three helicopters moving around, snooping and poking. He felt a pang of fear that he forced himself to squash about those helicopters coming down closer with their mini-guns and cannons and cluster bomblets. Don't worry, if they wanted to shoot at us they would have done it a long time ago. They're just chasing. They think it's us but they're not too sure. They don't want to open fire and later find out they've killed Mr and Mrs Straight and Narrow Republican. Not yet, at least. Not yet.

From the top of the hill he rested for a few seconds, seeing what was below them. The river moved towards a gentle curve and along it were a half-dozen cottages, with lights on. Fishing boats and canoes and even a couple of rafts were moored in front of them. He grinned. Jackpot. He tugged at Sheila's hand and she squeezed back, and he thrashed through the small growth, saplings and some small pine trees as they went to the cluster of buildings. People were outside, shading their eyes against the glare of the searchlights, holding their hands against their ears from the engine's roar. A couple of men jumped onto motorboats and began motoring out to the middle of the river.

A man stepped out from the nearest cabin and spotted them. He leaned over a railing, a can of beer in his hand, and yelled, 'What the hell is going on out there?'

Drew yelled back, 'Looks like black helicopters to me! Maybe it's the damn UN or FBI or something!'

The man cursed and glanced up again, and Drew looked to the side of the cabin, where a dark blue canoe and two paddles rested against the building, about three yards away from the river.

The lead pilot's voice was strained and irritated, and Ira didn't give a shit. 'Tango Two is reporting a sandbar upriver, about a hundred yards. Tight quarters but they're going to give it a try.'

Ira nodded, clicked on his intercom. 'Move us up there, next in line. I want to get on the ground after Tango Two unloads. Are there still people on boats in the water?'

'Yes, about a half-dozen.'

'Anybody moving downriver?'

'No, sir,' the pilot said. 'Tango Four's got them eyeballed.'

'You tell Tango Four, if any watercraft attempts to reach the Vermont shore or go downriver they have full authority to halt them. Understood? Full authority, including deadly force. Pass it on.'

The helicopter swerved as it went in over the other chopper, making an approach to the sandbar upstream. Ira looked over at Henry, who shrugged his shoulders.

'Pilot?' Ira said, toggling the intercom switch.

A heavy sigh came through the earphones. 'Understood. I'll pass it on, sir.'

'Good. Now get us down there, as soon as you can.'

Ira sat back in the seat and looked out the near window, seeing the lights below of the cottages and other buildings, even a few lights from boats out in the river, looking up at the spectacle before them. Even though it was dusk he could easily make out the sandbar that Tango Two was heading for; his own helicopter was illuminating the way with a belly-mounted searchlight. Soon, he thought. Just a few minutes and we'll have over a dozen heavily armed men on the ground – sure, they were National Guardsmen, but they were National Guardsmen with automatic weapons – and with the helicopters still in the air with the thermal imaging devices, it wouldn't take long to sort out that mess.

Plus there was that convoy of support vehicles making their way to these campsites for additional backup. Soon, very soon. And in three short days Shiloh itself, coming due with all the mighty vengeance that Michaelson Lurry and his troops could dream up—

The pilot's voice interrupted his thoughts. 'Tango Two's making its approach.'

Ira tilted his head to get a better view. There. Typical surplus Army UH-1 Huey helicopter, maneuvering its way in. He could see the feet and legs of the soldiers dangling out of the open doorways. The helicopter inched its way down to the sandbank, moving in closer to the shore—

'Tango Two, watch yourself, you're cutting it close, Tango Two—'

Then it all went horribly wrong.

Ira couldn't move as he saw the disaster unfold, saw tree limbs and branches suddenly spurt up like a chainsaw gone amok had reached in there, and then the helicopter shuddered and started slowly rolling over, and then picked up speed as the whirring blades quickly became visible, chunks of metal flying out, and Ira's own pilot swore and pulled them up and away from the accident scene.

A man's voice – not their own pilot – strained but calm: 'Tango Two's going down.'

Sheila shivered in the water, up to her knees in the Connecticut River as she and Drew walked the canoe downstream, staying close to shore. As Drew explained it the sensing devices on the helicopter would probably think that they were two people strolling along the riverbank. Sometimes the sensing gear wasn't as sensitive as advertised. It sounded right but damn it all to hell it was cold and tough going as her feet slipped and sometimes sunk into the river muck and branches from the overhanging trees scratched at her face and arms. Plus to add to her misery, during the past hour or so she had been suffering from the occasional cramp inside, and as she counted back the days, she wondered if she was about to be gifted with another burden.

Drew was up front, pulling the canoe by a rope attached to the bow, and she still couldn't believe they had stolen it. When that man with the beer can ducked back into his cottage, Drew had marched her to the canoe and the two paddles, and in a few minutes they were on the river. She was surprised at how normal it felt to steal someone else's canoe when helicopters were buzzing overhead, looking for you and no one else.

'Drew?' she whispered.

'Yeah,' he said, not looking back.

'How much longer?'

'Want to get – Jesus, what the hell was that?'

She had turned at the sound as well. There was the sound of a helicopter engine urgently racing at a high rate of speed and then the noise of something crashing, like a car into a rock wall. They stopped for a moment, the water eddying around their legs. Sheila shivered again. 'Drew?'

He sloshed his way back to the rear. 'Into the canoe, now. Sounds like something bad just happened back there. Maybe a collision, maybe a hard landing from one of the helicopters. But it's time to get going while they're distracted.'

She rolled herself into the canoe as Drew held it steady, and she went forward, to the bow, as Drew clambered into the rear. Their backpacks were in the center and Sheila picked up her paddle and dug in, and then they were moving, and though she was cold and wet it felt good to be sitting down, to be moving, to be getting away from the noise and the lights and the men who wanted to kill them both.

The paddle in her hands was a comfortable sensation, and soon it became possible to block everything out except the feel of the paddle digging into the water, the cool breeze about her face, and the sheer pleasure of letting the canoe take them along. It was such a relief not to be walking, not to be dependent on two tired and sore feet. She remembered with a soft smile the first time she had met Drew, when he had been in a canoe and had come to rescue her after that squall on the lake. A knight in summer shorts, paddling to save one wet and tired maiden. She glanced back and said, 'How far down river should we go?'

'As far as possible before it's too dark to see what we're doing,' Drew said, also stealing a glance behind himself for a moment, like he was looking for pursuers. 'If we're lucky, we'll be able to rack up a couple of miles.'

She turned and resumed the paddling, feeling the resistance of the water as the polished wood slid into the river, hearing the tiny gasping little gurgle as the paddle moved to the rear. Stroke, stroke, and stroke some more, and let's get away from those crazy men in those helicopters. She coughed and then shivered, and thought it would be nice if they could hole up someplace where Drew could chance building a fire. That would be a thought, getting out of these wet clothes, crawling into a sleeping bag with your man, letting the heat of the flames warm everything and dry out these wet clothes. Then, in the morning, worry about food and water and about getting power to her damn lapbot, so they could find out more about what the hell was going on. Killing the President? For real?

The gurgling sound became louder, and she looked up from her thoughts. The river was curving to the right, and when they rounded a bend even in the twilight she made out the foaming whitecaps as the river roared over barely submerged rapids.

'Drew!' she called out, and he said, 'I see it, hold on,' and he expertly turned the canoe in a half-circle, placing the boat behind a larger rock in a quiet place where the river water eddied in a large pool. He kept them in one place, eyeing the rocks and the rapids, and Sheila knew he was calculating a way through, a safe passage through the rapids.

'Hon?' she asked. 'What do you think?'

He answered without looking at her, his gaze still focused on the churning water and the visible humps of the rocks and boulders along the river bottom. 'I'm sorry, dear, but I don't see another way. Hold on.'

And in another few seconds, she never thought she could have felt so cold and so wet.

THIRTEEN

I am going to say this again: I did not have sexual relations with that woman, Monica Lewinsky.
President William J. Clinton, January 26, 1998

George Clemson stood next to his Baltimore Police cruiser along with Nancy Thon Quong. It was just after sunset on Saturday and they were stationed along Lippman Street, just a block away from the city's Conference Center. The Vice President had just made a speech to some civic group, and five minutes ago the procession of limousines, police cruisers and Secret Service 'war wagons' – armored Ford Excursions containing everything from machine guns to SAM missile launchers – had driven by their spot. George had his handheld radio up to his ear and when the message came, 'Able-Twelve, you're clear,' he nodded and said, 'Able-Twelve, affirmative.'

He got into the cruiser and checked the time – about a half-hour before the shift ended. He had something planned for today and wondered if he would have the guts to follow through on it. George looked over at his partner – and my, wasn't that a word designed to stir the groin! – and said, 'What do you say, rook? Let's coop up somewhere and get some coffee, burn off the rest of the day.'

She moved some of that fine black hair around her left ear and smiled. 'Sure, George, sounds good.'

A few minutes later – after going through a Dunkin' Donuts drive-thru – he had backed the cruiser up into an alley, right off Patterson Park. If asked, George could always say that they were doing random traffic surveillance, but he wasn't worried. They were never asked. Traffic was fairly heavy as commuters made their way home to the 'burbs around Baltimore, most of them now gated and guarded so the commuters could spend a night watching television on their half-acre of paradise, surrounded by fences, motion detectors and private security and far away from the dying city that supported them during the day. The new American dream.

'So, rook, what did you think of what we did back there, providing security for the Vice President hisself,' he asked, enjoying the taste of the coffee, about ten times better than any brew his wife Carol could produce.

'Ah, if I tell you, you'll make fun of me,' she said.

'And why's that?'

'Because you will.'

On impulse, he stuck out his free hand. 'Here, shake.'

She looked over at him, that flawless skin and those exotic eyes making him feel like a rookie himself. 'Whatever for?'

'Shake my hand, and you'll get the rest of this shift laugh-free. Honest.'

She smiled and shook his hand, and he tried to hold her hand for just a second longer, just to enjoy the sensation. He was surprised at how much the simple touch stirred him.

'All right, you promised,' Nancy said. 'Truth is, I felt honored.'

'Honored? For sitting on a street corner, watching a parade of well-paid fools go by? Why should you feel honored?'

She bent forward, took a tentative sip from her coffee cup. 'Because I shouldn't be here, that's why. And to be here, and to be trusted enough to wear the uniform of the Baltimore Police Department and to help guard the Vice President of the United States, well, I found that I was honored. So there. And thank you for not laughing.'

He turned in his seat, the better to look at her. 'I don't get what you meant back there, about not being here. Why shouldn't you be here?'

She smiled but he sensed there wasn't too much humor behind the expression. 'Because I shouldn't, George. I belong somewhere else, thousands of miles away, in a little village called Han Bo, about twenty miles outside of Saigon. Even now, my family and I, we refuse to call it by its new name. Ho Chi Minh City. The hell with that. It is now and forever will be Saigon, and I was born in Han Bo in 1976, the same year as your bicentennial.'

He remembered a history class from high school. 'But a year after the North invaded South Vietnam. The war was over, right?'

'So true, so true. Many of my family members, especially the males, spent long years in re-education camps. My father should have been one of them, but for some reason he was not called in. He had been a captain in the old South Vietnamese Army, therefore an enemy of the people. But my father and mother, they were strong people, very brave, and a few years after I was born we managed to get out. First to Thailand, then to Hong Kong and then California, and a few years later here to Baltimore.'

George ignored the coffee in his hand, fascinated by the story he had just heard. 'Then what happened?'

A gentle shrug of her shoulders. 'Typical story. Father and

Mother didn't know the language that well, had no other skills, but knew how to cook and serve food. They opened up a restaurant, over on the South Side. All of us children – all five of us – worked there as soon as we could walk. Started out sweeping the floor and washing dishes, then cooking and waitressing and watching the cash register. And all of us went to college. All of us.'

'College?'

'Yes. William and Mary for me. Sociology.'

'William and – rook, why in hell are you a cop? You know there's not much future in it. More stuff to do, less money for everybody. Hell, did you hear that thing a few days ago, about that deputy sheriff getting himself killed in New Hampshire? In New Hampshire! Who ever heard of cops getting killed in New Hampshire? It's a dangerous job. So, why you?'

'Remember your promise,' she warned. 'No laughing.'

'All right, no laughing. Why?'

She sighed. 'It's going to sound like I'm just twelve, so bear with me. I don't remember much about growing up in Han Bo. I just remember it being hot, and the cooking smells. That's about it. But I do remember Father and Mother talking to us back in the restaurant late at night, after everything had been cleaned and closed up. They talked about what it had been like back home. How the communists had their hand in everything, how the communists could decide if you lived or died, if you grew rich or grew poor, even what you read or what you listened to on the radio. Then we arrived here. Not a perfect place, no, not at all. But a place unique in the world, a place where people would fight to come. And Father and Mother, they taught me that. They taught me that we should respect this place, not to dishonor it, we should pay it back. So that's why I became a cop. To pay back this country for taking my family in and giving us a chance.'

George laughed, and Nancy gave him a sharp look and he said, 'No, not laughing at you, rook. Laughing at the Vice President, a buffoon only outweighed by the buffoon above him, and how for a brief moment he was guarded today by a woman who has more horse sense than the two of them put together.'

'I know,' she said, resting her coffee cup on that taut and lovely thigh. 'The President with the urination problems, the Vice President with his own problems. How could I honor them? Because of their office, because of that. Besides' – and her tone grew sharper – 'it would have been quite different if that fool Lurry had gotten in as president. If that had happened earlier my parents might have been deported, because they couldn't speak English that well. And any relatives of mine who had the drive and determination to come here, forget it, because of his immigration freeze. Not to mention . . . well, let's just say, as poorly made as this president is, he is better than the alternative. So. I've told you my story, George. Why not tell me yours? Why did you become a cop?'

He finished his coffee, switched on the cruiser's engine. 'Why does any brother become a cop? So he can rise in the ranks and boss white folk, that's why.'

Now it was her turn to laugh, and she said, 'In some ways, we're alike. Both of us minorities. And some of us, we are minorities three times over.'

'Say again?' he asked, slightly puzzled.

'Oh, never mind. Let's get back to the station.'

He was going to ask her about that minorities crack but he knew if he didn't do what he had planned in the next minute or two, as they were heading back in, he would run out of courage, so he blurted out, 'Hey, rook. Got a nutty idea for you.'

'What's that?'

'Tomorrow morning, my family's going down to DC, visiting relatives. I got two box seat tickets to the O's at Camden Yards later in the day. You want to go?'

There. The question was put forth and he stared ahead at the street, not wanting to see what might be going across her face. God, how embarrassed he now felt. Why in hell did he even do this? What chance would he have with her, in even doing anything outside of the job with a guy like himself? Good job, Clemson, that little man between your legs has reared up and taken control and ridden you right to disaster.

'George?' she asked quietly.

'Yeah, rook,' he said, accelerating some so he could get to the station house and then home as quickly as possible.

'George, I'd love to.'

Oh my, he thought, and he eased up on the accelerator to stretch out the ride as long as possible.

The hum of the generators seemed to nestle right in the base of his skull, making everything shake around up there. Ira Woodman stood on the banks of the Connecticut River, as divers from the NH State Police – secured by ropes set out to shore – continued to work around the turned-over hulk of the National Guard helicopter. Mobile lamps from the generators illuminated the scene in a ghastly light that seemed to cast no shadows, and people from the fishing camps and cottages strained against the temporary police tape barricades to see what was going on.

Of course, what was going on was no doubt Ira Woodman's career and possibly his life, crashing into the cold waters of this blasted river, where divers still searched for two missing National Guardsmen. Ambulances were backed up as near as possible to the river bank, as if hopefully waiting for something to do. He shook his head. Pilot and co-pilot dead. Crew chief with a broken arm. Two Guardsmen missing in the river. Four other Guardsmen with assorted bruises, cuts and water in their lungs, and dark hatred in their souls for one Ira Woodman of the Federal Emergency Response Agency.

He looked back at the cottages and small homes and the people crowded about them. They had no idea, none of them, that everything that had gone on out here tonight had been for their benefit. No, not the excitement of the chase and the sound of the helicopters and the bright lights of the searchers. That wasn't it. What had been done here was part of a process that had started a couple of years ago, a process that was going to make this country right again, no matter what it took. He turned back and looked at the divers at work, the huddled group of Guardsmen being attended to by their comrades. Some time later, maybe just a couple of months or so, he would see these men again. He promised himself that he would. And he would explain to them why it had been important to be out here tonight, more important than anything else they had ever done, and he would make it right.

'Sir?'

He looked over at Henry Harrison, standing there, radio in his hand. 'Yes?'

'About four miles downstream one of the search choppers found a canoe, matching the description of the one that was stolen here earlier. It had been swamped and pretty well dinged up. It was found below a nasty set of rapids.'

Ira put his hands in his coat, watched a diver make his way ashore, walking stiffly in his wetsuit. 'Go on.'

'The thought is, maybe they got turned over in the rapids. Maybe they drowned. They're still looking, but right now they're focusing on finding any bodies.'

Ira said, 'You believe that?'

'Not for a moment. This Drew guy is good, Mr Woodman. I think he's trying to put us off the track.'

'If he is, he's doing a good job, isn't he?' Ira said, not taking his eyes off the downed helicopter. 'Some of the searchers out there, the volunteers and militia types, they'll hear rumors that these two have drowned. They'll go back home and have some beers and forget the whole thing. The regular cops and state folks, maybe they won't search as hard or as thorough, figuring they're just wasting time. Which will leave us and whatever forces we can Federalize. Plus, there's a good chance he's over the border, into Vermont. And you know what that means.'

Henry nodded. 'A Green governor. She won't feel much like cooperating with us.'

'True. All right, we continue the search, best as we can. And in two days you're heading south, correct?'

'Flying out of Boston, sir.'

'Good.'

Then Henry seemed almost embarrassed, looking down at his feet. 'There's just one more thing, sir.'

'What is it?'

'Mr Lurry, sir, he sent word that he wants to see you, tomorrow morning, in Ithaca. Message came in through Clem Badger.'

The coat seemed to get heavier with each passing second. Of course. Case Shiloh commences in three days, and it's time to tighten up any loose ends. He wondered if it would make sense to put a call into Glenda Sue. Or was it too late, and had she and Aaron and Elizabeth already been picked up?

'Understood, Henry. Thanks. And if I don't see you again, well, good luck in the next couple of days. You're doing God's work.'

Henry nodded. 'So I've been told, sir. So I've been told.'

Ira resumed watching the divers, feeling a dark urge to throw himself in the river and end it all come over him, but no, that wouldn't be right. Daddy wouldn't have approved. Daddy would have gone into it like a man, which is what he would do, tomorrow.

Damn this day, and damn this man and woman for making his life so miserable.

In a crowded bar about eight miles away from the home he shared with General Montgomery, Maurice Blakely sat against the wall, an open bottle of Heineken before him, untouched and unsipped. The bar was named The Wilde Spot – supposedly named after the English writer Oscar Wilde – and Maurice wished he was back at the house, lapbot before him, hooked into the universe of the Net. This place was too real, too smoky, too loud, but he knew he had to be here. There was no other option. He picked up his beer, took a gentle sip and looked around. Men, men, and everywhere, men. No women. There were men drinking and men playing pool and in a corner by the jukebox, men dancing, and there was a lot of laughter and good times. Why not? This was Vermont, after all, a Yankee state to be sure but also a state that had a Green governor and an abiding belief in doing any damn thing you wanted, and if the neighbors complained, tough.

A man about Blakely's age came over, wearing stonewashed jeans and a flannel shirt, carrying a mixed drink. He was balding up front but had a thick dark moustache, and he touched the rear of the empty chair next to Blakely.

'Mind if I join you?' he asked.

Blakely looked up and smiled. 'Sorry, I'm waiting for someone. A bit hitched, if you know what I mean.'

The man smiled. 'Pity.' And walked away.

He picked up his own beer and there he was. He navigated his way through the crowd and pulled out the chair and sat down. He was about ten years older than Blakely, beefier around the shoulders and waist. His blond hair was cut short and his face was tanned, and he had on khakis and a light green polo shirt. He held out his hand and Blakely shook it, gratified that he had finally arrived.

'Good to see you, Captain,' the man said.

'And good to see you, Rupert.'

Like Blakely, Rupert had been in service with the US Army but was now out doing other things. But their friendship – started back at the Pentagon – had continued, off and on, for a number of years.

Rupert looked around and said, 'Quite the place.'

'That it is. What's up?'

Rupert leaned in and lowered his voice. 'Is tomorrow okay?'

'Tomorrow's fine. The trick is, he goes out and waits for the aircraft when the phone rings twice in the morning. One ring, followed by a hang-up, and then exactly five minutes later, three rings and a hang-up. That's the signal. Two hours after the second phone call he goes for a walk. I think he doesn't believe that I even notice. Funny thing is I noticed it right from the start, three months ago.'

His visitor smiled and touched Blakely's wrist. 'The good General should know better than to try to pull something like that over you.'

'Hey!' came a voice, and Blakely looked up. Another man was standing there, wearing a black pullover and khakis, weaving slightly, smiling and holding a beer in his hand. 'You,' he said, talking to Rupert. 'I noticed you the minute you walked in. Can I get a dance?' He looked over at Blakely. 'That is, if your friend here doesn't mind.'

Rupert smiled up at him. 'Sorry, we're fairly exclusive, but thanks for the offer.'

The man smiled and walked away, stumbling some. 'Well, can't blame me for trying . . .'

Rupert turned and said, 'Okay. Two phone calls. Easy to do. Where is he then?'

'In the large field, north of his house. There's a collection of boulders there and some saplings. That's where he stands.'

'Okay. And that's where we'll go.'

Maurice nodded and picked up his beer. 'Good. What will you be using?'

'Typical weedcutter. Drops down and proximity fuse recognizes when it's six feet away from the ground. Charge erupts and shrapnel cuts everything down within twenty yards. Man, there won't be enough of your general left to ID, except through DNA analysis.'

Blakely felt good, raised his beer. 'God bless.'

Rupert returned the greeting. 'God bless. And hey, one more thing.'

'Sure.'

He leaned in again. 'A couple of weeks from now, let's say you and I come back here and take care of this place. I mean, Jesus, look at all the fags around here. Makes my goddamn skin crawl. A few hand grenades and a couple of M-16s, we could clear this place out in no time.'

The beer tasted good. Everything was going to be fine. Blakely smiled.

'Sure, why not?'

In the dim light Drew saw that Sheila's limbs were quivering from the cold. He stripped her as best he could, trying to get her out of her wet clothes as quickly as possible. He was concerned and angry and pissed at himself for not having done a better job. A while ago he knew that trying to navigate those rapids in the approaching darkness would have been too risky, and aware that the bad guys would eventually clean up their mess upriver and come after them he made a quick decision. Get ashore and then let the canoe run through the rapids, make the bad guys chase after it, maybe if exceedingly lucky make them think the two of them had overturned.

Luck. He had guided the canoe to shore and had got out up to his knees, but there was a drop-off where Sheila had climbed out and she had quickly sunk up to her neck. In the confusing next five or ten minutes practically all of their gear had been soaked through before she and the gear were on shore. Some luck, some planning on his part. Idiot. Another half-hour had gone by as he dragged the gear and an increasingly cold Sheila up the side of the steep embankments on this, the Vermont side of the Connecticut River, before he had found this hole in the ground. Cave was too grand a word to use for something that went into the embankment about eight yards and was shaped like an L. While Sheila shivered in the dirt, he had worked outside at the entrance, blocking it as best he could with branches and saplings without making everything so disturbed that a sharp eye through a NightVision scope could spot it.

Now they were in the far corner, dirt hitting his head as he worked, the only illumination coming from a flashlight that he had wedged into some roots overhead. Sheila looked up at him, her pretty lips a damnable shade of blue. 'Drew . . . I'm so cold, so very cold . . . Can you get a fire going?'

Drew unrolled both sleeping bags, found that his wasn't as wet as hers. He unzipped it and squeezed out the excess water as best he could. 'We're being searched for, hon, fast and furious. Two helicopters just raced by about ten minutes ago. I'm sorry, we can't risk it.'

She rubbed at her bare arms, shook her head, managed a weak smile. 'I suppose . . . I suppose hot tea would be out of the question . . .'

He could not look at her as he frantically went through their belongings. Wet, wet, everything wet. There. A wool sweater of his. That would work. He rolled out the ground cloth, put the open and damp sleeping bag on top of it, and he gave her the sweater.

'Here. Put this on.'

'Drew, it's soaking wet.'

'It's wool. It'll keep you warm even though it's wet.'

She pulled the dark sweater over her wet hair, the hem of the sweater reaching down past her hips. Drew stripped off his own wet clothes, stretched them out as best he could, and then switched off the light. He climbed on top of her and and then pulled the other side of the sleeping bag on top of him. He winced as the wet fabric stuck to him and he started shivering again.

Sheila whispered up to him. 'I see you're getting cold, too . . .'

'It'll pass, it'll pass,' he said. And then what? Forget that! Let's get her warmed up, and worry about everything else later.

She said, 'You know, I'm getting kinda sleepy . . .'

'No!' he said, jerking her roughly. 'It's too soon to fall asleep. You haven't warmed up enough. Sheila, you're close to getting hypothermia. You have to stay awake.'

'Awake? How?'

He rubbed at her shoulders, trying to get the circulation going, trying hard to control his own shivering. 'Tell me a story.'

'A story? Me, a story? I'm . . . I'm too cold to make something up . . .'

'Then don't make something up. Tell me something about you.'

She shivered again, bumping into his head with her own. 'Like what . . .'

He hesitated, then thought, what the hell. It'd either make her mad or make her talk, and either way, it'll warm her up. 'You can tell me how you got the money to pay for the data mole, when you were at Stanford. The money you had stashed in Calgary.'

He thought she whimpered. He wasn't sure. She clasped him tighter and said, 'Are you sure?'

'Sure I'm sure,' he said. 'Look, whatever it is you did out there, I don't care. I got you here, right now, and that's what counts.'

'Cold and smelly and wet . . .'

'No difference. Go on, tell me. What did you do back at Stanford?'

Another spasm of shivering. 'Oh, Drew . . . Lord knows I've wanted to tell you for so long . . . But I've been so embarrassed.

Listen, have you ever heard of someone called Amanda from Atlanta?'

A thought came to him. 'Some girl from the Internet who was being stalked?'

Sheila chuckled. 'No . . . not quite . . . You see, Amanda was a young lady from Atlanta . . . claimed to be a high school student . . . Beautiful, peaches and cream complexion, long blonde hair, claimed to be a cheerleader . . . She would post stories of what she did and pictures of herself on the Net . . . Amazing the response she got . . .'

'But you've shown me some of those homepages back home. Men and women who do everything imaginable for a credit card number. What was so special about this one?'

She shivered for another long few seconds, and he kept on rubbing at her back. 'Difference was, she didn't do that much . . . Just some lingerie and bathing suit shots . . . You see, she claimed to be shy, claimed to be coming out of her shell, didn't even charge for coming into her homepage . . . Guys on the Net, they ate that right up . . . One weekend she had some nude shots, her first ever . . . And a month later she said she'd lose her virginity on-line with her boyfriend . . . Pre-order of course, if you wanted to see it on your home computer . . . Probably made hundreds of thousands of dollars . . .'

Now he remembered. 'But she never showed up.'

'That's right . . . One message came from her, saying she had lost her nerve . . . But she also said she'd come back later with more nude shots . . . That was several years ago . . . She never came back on-line . . . But that wasn't the end of it . . .'

'What happened?'

'The porn freaks on the Net, they went nuts . . . They traded stories, traded pictures . . . Some went to Atlanta, looking for her . . . Others started hacking photo storage areas, everywhere from state license photos to mall surveillance cameras, looking for her picture . . . It was insane . . . Imagine this poor girl, whoever she is, being chased through the Net . . . She made lots of money but was it worth it? Jesus, I'm still cold, Drew, I'm so very cold . . .'

'Sheila.'

Just a shiver in response.

'Sheila!'

'Hmmm?'

'Tell me, were you Amanda from Atlanta?'

'No . . . no, I wasn't . . .'

'Who were you, then?'

Another shiver. 'I . . . I was Sally . . . Sally from Seattle . . .'

'Tell me about it.'

'Okay.'

So she did, from when she had signed up to when she designed her homepage, all the way to when she got that phone call that night, the phone call that would change everything. From the very beginning, Sheila had worried about security doing her CyberGal work. No names were used with the photographer from Palo Alto (she had even worn a scratchy red wig during the photo shoot) and only cash was paid. Donna knew her name but it was sort of like a MAD (mutual assured destruction) set-up: if one was betrayed, the other was betrayed as well. She had set up a fake credit card account with a Mexicali bank – easy to do and they didn't mind, so long as you paid your bills – and that account was mailed to a post office box in Los Gatos, which she visited once a month and during the busiest time of the day. Using that credit card account she had set up her homepage through CyberGals (whose real, physical location was not known; best guess was on one of the British Virgin Islands). Through a set of other dummy accounts, she was able to manage her homepage from her own home computer.

Not that she was being paranoid, but . . . well, they were still finding the remains of Betty from Boise – stupid girl had actually been from Boise – after one of her fans decided on a F2F; a face to face, with a knife of course.

A Tuesday, right? Right. Tuesday night she had come home from seeing the latest *Star Wars* movie and after settling down and checking the mail – her real mail, not the mail from Los Gatos – the phone rang.

'Hello?' she said.

Nothing, just some breathing.

'Hello, who's this?' she said again.

A man's voice, shaking from emotion: 'Is . . . is this Sally? Sally from Seattle?'

Bang. She slammed the phone down, heart racing, looked around her lovely place, the best place she had ever lived in after she had moved out on her own, and a place she knew she would never see again. In the briefest of moments she knew it was over. Others might debate and delay and think, well, just one phone call, but Sheila knew, knew better than most, what kind of dull-eyed men with moist lips were out there at the other end of the Net.

In less than a half hour she was gone. She took photos, mementos, a change of clothes, and a half-dozen computer diskettes of various projects she had worked on – none of them CyberGal-related, thank you – and walked away. She didn't take her car. Too easy to track. Nope, she walked about eighteen blocks and went to the San Jose bus terminal and paid cash for a ticket to Portland, Oregon. From there, more anonymous bus trips out across the United States, never once using her real name, never once using any of her real accounts. She stayed in quiet motels, and even though she knew she was safe she always unplugged the phone, double-locked the door and jammed a chair underneath the doorknob.

At nights, sometimes, she would wake up, breathing hard, hearing that hopeful, male voice: 'Is . . . is this Sally? Sally from Seattle?'

When she got to the East Coast, Mom and Dad had retired from their store in Portland and left the small house on Lake Montcalm to her, and she moved in and gradually started up her consulting and Web design business. It was a struggle at first, paying the bills, and it was mighty tempting at times – especially when those bills with pink invoices piled up – to go to her Calgary account and take some of the money away. But she still remembered how that one phone call had set her on this long run.

But there was that little voice. C'mon, it was more than a year ago. Just one phone call. There's been plenty of CyberGals since you. Chances are you're forgotten, last year's fashion, last year's superstar. There's probably a Sandy from Seattle who's even more popular. Relax.

One night she almost did it, a cold January night with the wind racing across the frozen surface of the lake and a letter from the oil company at her side that said they wouldn't come by to top up her oil tank until she had brought her account up to date. She was hooked into the Web and was going to make a visit to Calgary until she made a side trip to one of the Net's search engines. She typed in a phrase that

she had not done in more than a year, and her fingers felt
stiff on the keyboard.

SEARCH FOR?

SALLY FROM SEATTLE CYBERGALS.

The screen went blank, just for a second or two.

Long seconds or two.

Then—

RESULTS FOR SEARCH 'SALLY FROM SEATTLE
CYBERGALS': 114 HOMEPAGES AVAILABLE

'Holy Christ,' she whispered in the cold air of her home as
the homepages from across the world started scrolling up her
screen.

TRIBUTE TO SALLY FROM SEATTLE
SIGHTINGS OF SALLY FROM SEATTLE
LAST PAGES OF SALLY FROM SEATTLE
FAVE DEATH SCENES OF SALLY FROM
    SEATTLE
REWARD $$$ FOR INFO LEADING TO SALLY
    FROM SEATTLE
MY TRIBUTE TO SALLY FROM SEATTLE
BEST CYBERGAL EVER, SALLY FROM
    SEATTLE
TOP TEN WAYS TO KILL SALLY FROM
    SEATTLE
SALLY FROM SEATTLE, WHERE ARE YOU?
SALLY FROM SEATTLE, WHERE ARE YOU?
SALLY FROM SEATTLE, WHERE ARE YOU?

That winter she burned a lot of wood.

FOURTEEN

Mount up and ride to the sound of the guns. It is our calling to recapture the independence and lost sovereignty of our republic, to clean up all that pollutes our culture and to heal the soul of America.

Patrick Buchanan, February 20, 1999

It was dark and she was beginning to warm up some with her man cuddling her close, but she was frightened like never before. Not because of the sounds of helicopters overhead or the droning noises of motorboats on the river or even the far-off shouts of the searchers. No, what worried her in the darkness was the look upon Drew's face, and she wished for a candle or a flashlight or something to see his expression. Oh, why had she even said a word . . .

'Sheila?' came his voice, close to her ear.

'Yes?' she said, the word shivering through her lips.

A tighter squeeze. 'I'm sorry you went through that. I'm sorry that this whole mess caused you to bring back some bad memories. And . . .'

He stopped. She rubbed his back, the wet sleeping bag making his skin moist and smooth. 'Go on.'

'I . . . I just wanted to let you know something else . . .'

My God, was he crying, was her Drew actually crying here?

'Drew, go ahead, go ahead . . .'

He took a deep breath and said, 'I want you to know that you're mine, and that I'm never letting you go. I don't care about the CyberGal or anything else you've ever done. What matters is now and that's what counts. Always. I won't let you be hurt, ever, and you can count on that.'

She kissed his neck in the dark, bumping her nose on his scratchy chin, and she found that she was weeping, not sobbing, just tears streaming down her cheeks.

'Your turn,' she whispered.

'What?'

Sheila smiled and rubbed his back again. 'C'mon, fair is fair. I'm still cold and so are you. If I told you my deep dark secret, then it's your turn. And you know what I want.'

'The Crescent War.' His voice was flat.

'Yes, oh, Drew, yes, but like you said, it doesn't matter, it doesn't matter what you did back there, I love you so much . . .'

His voice was still different. 'You might not think so when I'm done telling you.'

'Hon, please . . . trust me.'

'Trust,' he repeated. 'All right, I do trust you. And that's about it.'

'Because of what you did back there?'

'Always because of what I did back there,' he said. 'Always.'

Sheila put her lips up to his ear. 'Tell me, please.'

'All right.'

So he did, from when they landed and secured the warheads and found out they had been abandoned. After Coughlin and the others had been wounded, the breakout from the hangar had gone easier than they thought, with only some wild shots blasting over their head as they sped out of the hangar, and in a half-hour they were on Highway 16, heading west to the ocean. The warheads had been strapped down in the rear, and the weight caused the gears and transmission of the vehicle to groan in protest as they joined the stream of refugees heading for whatever safety the water offered. Four of them were crowded into the cabin of the truck, and they drove with the windows down, weapons stuck outside. Three others were up on top – Lopez, Smith, Caruso – providing cover, but since they had left the air base they had only had to fire a few times over the head of the crowds, who saw a slow-moving vehicle and a chance to escape at a quicker pace. An occasional shot would come their way but they kept on going west.

Rudman was driving and cursing, looking at the odometer every few seconds, and Drew knew why. Trying to gauge how far away they were from the air base, how far away from ground zero. Beside Rudman was the comm guy, Powalski, who was chanting into the radio gear, adjusting the frequencies, saying over and over, 'Mayday, mayday, mayday. This is Quicksilver Four, Quicksilver Four, Quicksilver Four. Any American military in the vicinity, mayday, mayday, mayday. We need immediate extraction. Repeat, immediate extraction. Mayday, mayday, mayday . . .'

Beside Drew was Doc, who had his M-16 pointed out the window and had a chant of his own, though not as loud as Powalski's: 'Man, get me home, that's all I want, kill as many of these little bastards as you'd like, but get me home . . . Get me home, that's all I want . . .'

There were other noises as well. The crying and moaning of the civilians who flowed about their truck, some of them holding up children, begging to be let aboard. The chattering of the motor scooters, racing in and out of the lines of people and the few other buses and trucks on the road. The crackling sound of homes and shops in the villages along the highway burning as looters went wild in the chaos. Drew stared ahead, forcing himself to think only of what might happen if the warheads in the rear ever got loose. London, Paris, Manhattan, Tokyo . . . It was too late to help these people. There was still time to save so many millions more.

No matter what he saw, he forced himself to keep his eyes open, if only to bear witness. He saw things that made him wish he could close his eyes, but he could not do that. Duty, a dirty four-letter word, made him take in everything he saw, though he knew the nightmares would haunt him forever.

It was near midnight when they reached the coast, for he was sure that over the stench of diesel and sweat and fear and burning he could make out the smell of salt water. Rudman said over Powalski's chanting – the man's voice had shrunk to a whisper – 'Loo, we're almost out of fuel, and I don't want to run out on this road.'

'Pull out and get us somewhere flat, someplace open.'

Rudman snorted. 'Wish to hell I had a Michelin map for this fucking place.'

Somehow, and Drew was not sure how he did it, Rudman managed to force his way to the left, drove through a fence, and got on a narrow side street, empty of people. It was spooky to be in a deserted place with the diesel sound echoing along the narrow walls. 'Just a little more, that's all, just a little more,' Rudman said in a soothing voice. 'Just a little more.'

Doc spoke up. 'Looks like a clearing or something over there. To the right.'

Drew said, 'Go to it.'

After another minute of slow driving and passing through a wooden fence that splintered underneath them, they were on a wide and flat field. The wavering headlights of the truck picked out a large net at one end of the field.

'Soccer field,' Drew said. 'I don't know how you found this place, Rudman, but you just got yourself a raise.'

Rudman barked out a laugh. 'I'd be happier knowing that I'd be alive to spend it, loo.'

The truck inched its way across the field for about twenty yards, and then the engine sputtered and died. The sudden silence seemed oppressive, the only noise coming from Powalski, hoarsely whispering, 'Mayday, mayday, mayday . . .'

Doc said, 'I need to piss and stretch my legs, loo, and check out our cargo back there.'

'Sounds good,' Drew said, 'I'll join you. Powalski, keep trying. Rudman, see how the crew up top is doing.'

He climbed out and felt the bones and tendons creak, and listened to the sound of water as Doc relieved himself on the front tire of the truck. His eyes adjusted to the darkness and he could make out a low building to the east that must have been a school of some sorts. Gunfire was chattering now and again, as who knew what shot at either shadows or looters. Off towards the eastern horizon was the steady orange and red glow of cities burning. Drew wondered if this was what it looked like, decades ago, standing on the out-skirts of Hiroshima and Nagasaki. Long ago he had ceased asking Doc to check on the amount of radiation exposure they were receiving. There was not much they could do, so why worry about it?

Rudman's voice came to him from the darkness. 'Loo, you better come up here.'

'Coming,' he said. Drew walked to the truck and clambered up the side, his slung M-16 thumping against his back. In the dim light he made out Rudman, who was kneeling down, a red-lensed flashlight in his hand. There were other low voices and Rudman's voice was shaking with anger. 'It's Lopez, loo. He's bled out. Smitty and Caruso let him die up there after he got shot about an hour ago.'

Drew suddenly felt how tired he was, how tired he was of being here in this foreign land, being shot at, being abandoned, hungry and thirsty and just so damn fucking tired . . . Rudman played the dim light up past the unmoving body of Lopez to the scowling faces of Smith and Caruso. Smith spoke up, 'Not true, sir. He got hit and we bandaged him up, best we could do.'

Rudman's voice, even sharper. 'You could have told us! We could have done something better than the half-assed job you stupid fucks did.'

Caruso spoke up, eyes downcast. 'We didn't want to stop, loo. We did the best we could. We didn't want to stop. We want to get out of here, get back home . . .'

Drew wondered what to say when it felt like his back was struck by a baseball bat the size of a telephone pole.

And then darkness. Some thoughts. Some memories. Dad in the living room of the farm in Arapahoe, can of beer in hand, snarling at Mom about something, Drew wishing he was older and tougher and able to take a chunk of firewood to the bitter drunk's skull.

'Drew!'

Coming home from Basic Training, feeling good about being in uniform, about belonging, about being part of something, saying to Dad in the tiny kitchen, 'Are you nuts? There's no way I'm coming back to this farm! I don't care how long it's been in your family, it ends with you. I'll never come back here, not ever!' First time he had ever laid fists on the man, and last time he had ever seen him.

'Drew!'

Talking in his apartment, late at night, with two men in suits. The grumble of transport aircraft overhead, coming in for an approach, making them pause every now and then in the conversation, which worked well. It gave him time to think about what was being discussed. The older of the two men saying, 'Now, Lieutenant, even if you have been separated from the regular Army, we do have an attractive position available for you in a contract force associated with the Defense Research Agency. Same duties, better pay, and a chance for advancement.' And Drew just had one question: 'Would I be with my guys?' The answer, from the younger guy. 'Absolutely.' And Drew saying, 'Sign me up.'

'Drew!'

Water on his face. He blinked his eyes. Smelled smoke and wetness and fear. Rudman's face came in close to him. 'Drew, you there? Drew?'

'Yeah,' he said, his back aching something awful, as if every muscle there had been stretched and tortured.

'Loo, we are seriously fucked up,' Rudman said, his voice quiet in his ear. 'Came under fire about twenty minutes ago. You took a round to the back. Your vest took most of the impact but you're hurting. Doc's dead.'

'Shit . . . what else?'

'Me and Smitty are all that's left. Powalski's under the truck, but I think the batteries for his comm gear are about drained. Caruso ran out. We got snipers on the rooftop of that school back there. Pretty good shots. Don't know if they're locals or not. Might be some assholes, looking at taking what we got. Know what I mean?'

Drew coughed and stretched out his legs. Well, here we are. In the service of a grateful nation, about to get popped and killed, and for what? For God and country, or for a steady paycheck? Months ago, when joining up with the Defense Research Agency, he thought that it didn't mean much, that he would still be doing his job, still serving his country . . . What a piece of crock. Defense Research Agency. Whole damn thing made it easier for the DC weasels up top to pull the plug when things weren't going right. It was one thing to cut and run and abandon a group of soldiers, and another thing to do the same damn thing to a group of mercenaries. Yep, there won't be any hand-wringing editorials in the *Washington Post* about that. He coughed again, heard a rustling noise at his side. He reached for his holstered 9 mm and a croaking voice came up to him.

'Lieutenant . . . it's me, Powalski. I got through . . . Extraction in ten minutes . . . We gotta get ready . . .'

'Rudman!' he whispered as loud as he could. 'Extraction heading in! Get the gear!'

He tried to get up but shuddered at the pain in his back and fell back against the side of the truck. He took out his 9 mm and laid it across his lap. He closed his eyes then opened them at the sound of gunfire, closer. Some rounds pinged and pocked against the truck. Rudman was now next to him, his face bloody, holding a black instrument in his hand. Infrared strobe light, marking their position. He hoped the snipers out there didn't have the right NightVision gear, 'cause Rudman would be pointing their guns right at their own position.

'Here that, loo? Hear that beautiful fucking noise?'

Drew thought Rudman had gone over the side but then he heard it too. Helicopters. Lots of them. Drew said something but his voice was drowned out by the thundering noise of Cobra gunships suddenly appearing overhead, machine guns chattering, shell casings tumbling off the hood and roof of the truck. Someone was yelling, 'That's right, that's right! Hose those bastards!'

More noise. Sand and dirt stinging his face. Shouts and more gunfire. Shapes all around him, picking him up, carrying. Brought into the floor of a helicopter. Looking up at the concerned face of an Army officer, in fatigues with no insignia. The man was black, looked like the Doc. Poor Doc. The officer said, 'Hold on son. You'll be in a hospital before you know it.'

Drew yelled one word, 'Warheads!'

The helicopter shuddered and tilted up, and the officer put his mouth next to his ear. 'All accounted for, son. If it was up to me, you'd get the Medal of Honor for what you just did.'

Drew shook his head, yelled out again. 'My guys! Left behind at the air base!'

The officer patted his shoulder. 'Don't worry about that now, son. Don't worry about that now. You get some rest.'

Drew closed his eyes and tried to follow the man's orders, but couldn't. All he saw was Coughlin's face, and those words.

You'll be back, right?

I promise.

I promise.

The noise from the helicopter was quite loud.

FIFTEEN

We don't have files on every group that espouses hate in the United States. We don't deal in what people think, believe, say.
An FBI spokesman, *Boston Globe*, August 13, 1999

Sheila was in the middle of the best dream of her life and she was desperate not to wake up. For one thing she was warm, and she was dry, and she felt like she was floating in air, she was so comfortable. There was also the delicious smell of eggs cooking, a smell that made her stomach grumble with glee. Sheila shifted, heard her voice being called out. Her eyes refused to open and that was fine, and there was a hand gently stroking her cheek, and again, that voice, 'Sheila?'

She wiped at the crust around her eyes. Damn, so it was a dream after all. Damn it all to hell, couldn't she have some more peace and relaxation before waking up in that small, damp and dirty hole?

She opened her eyes. She was awake. But Sheila's dream continued.

Drew stood before her, holding a small wooden tray and on the tray was a cup of tea and a plate of scrambled eggs and what looked like sausage patties. She immediately started salivating and her stomach grumbled again, but she forced herself to look around at her surroundings. She was in a bed in a small room that had poorly hung and cheap-looking paneling pulling away from the walls. The head of a deer looked down on her with glassy eyes. Through the open door and past Drew she could make out a tiny kitchen and dining room and a table that had not a single matching chair.

'Drew . . .' she whispered, sitting up in bed. 'What is this place?'

He put the tray down next to her on a nightstand. 'When you were asleep and looked like you warmed up some I did some recon and found this place. Looks like a hunting cabin. Took a couple of trips back and forth but I got you and our gear up here.'

Sheila rubbed at her face. 'I don't remember a thing. Did I walk it?'

He fussed with a napkin for a moment before replying. 'No. You were still out. I carried you.'

'Oh, Drew . . .' No wonder the poor man looked exhausted, his unshaven face gaunt, his eyes red-rimmed. 'Couldn't you have—'

He placed a finger against her lips. 'Hush. Later. Your breakfast is getting cold.'

Breakfast! The cool and rational part of her mind wanted to know how in the world he had carried her to this place, but the part of her that hadn't eaten well in days took over. He placed the tray in her lap and she was embarrassed at how hungry she was, but the awkwardness disappeared the moment a piece of sausage patty touched her tongue. My God, did anything ever taste so fine!

When she had finished and had drunk two cups of tea, Drew sat on the edge of the bed. 'We should be safe here, at least for a day or two. It doesn't look like this place receives too many visitors. I found an old bag of chips in one of the counters that had a stale date of a month ago.'

'Then what did you just feed me?'

'Survival food. Freeze-dried stuff. There's some of it in a back closet.'

She wiped her hands on the napkin, smiling at how damn good it felt to have food in her belly. 'So there's lunch and dinner—'

'And breakfast again, yes, Sheila. There's even electricity; your lapbot's in the next room, charging up its battery.'

Sheila closed her eyes for a moment, almost giddy with all of the possibilities. Yesterday she had been a wet and scared creature, literally in a hole in the ground and starving to death. Now she had food. Now she had her lapbot. Now the both of them had power.

'Drew?'

'Yes?'

'Does this place have running water? Hot running water?'

He grinned. 'Yep. I checked. But I don't know how much hot water might be stored in the water tank. Feel like a hot shower?'

She hugged him, scraping her cheek against his stubble, feeling the greasiness of his hair and skin and not minding one bit. 'Damn it, I love you so,' she said. 'I know there's lots to do and to think about when my lapbot's up and running, but I've got to take a shower. I feel disgusting and probably look even worse.'

He squeezed her back. 'You look fine. Now get in the shower and see if you can't save some hot water for me.'

She kissed his cheek and drew back, looking at those tired eyes. 'Just one more thing. The story you were telling me, back in that hole. The last thing I remembered was when you and your other men were rescued. But I don't remember the rest of the story. What happened to the other men, the ones at the air base? Were they rescued?'

He looked at her, his gaze steady. 'No. They were all killed. Every one of them. I didn't find out until months later. They kept on fighting until their ammunition ran out, almost a day after our group was found. By the time rescue choppers got there it was too late.'

She ached at seeing the look in his face and thought, stupid girl. Why didn't you wait until later? Why bring it up now? She started, 'It wasn't—'

He touched her face. 'Yes, it was my fault. They were my men. My responsibility. And my responsibility to you right now is that hot shower. Go on, before I change my mind.'

She kissed him and rubbed against the bristles and said, 'I'll love you forever, no matter what.'

'Me, too. Now, get going.'

She got.

In the bathroom she couldn't face looking at the mirror and instead went straight to the bathtub and the shower arrangement. Typical man's place, she thought, drawing the curtain across. It was a stand-up shower, the white plastic dulled to yellow because of grime and scum. The drain was clogged with hair but she didn't care, not at all, especially when she turned on the faucet and the water coughed, gurgled, and then flew out, nice and hot. She stripped off her clothes and stepped in and just quivered at the sheer joy of it, feeling the hot water pound down on her head.

Then, remembering Drew was next, she grabbed a bar of soap and started washing, starting right at the top with her filthy hair. As she soaped and rinsed, and repeated it, again and again, she remembered what she had told Drew, about her days as a CyberGal. She felt the words in her mouth as she said the word again. CyberGal. All those long months, worrying if Drew would ever find out and what might happen if he did, all that lost time, worrying . . . Now, it was gone. CyberGal. Sally from Seattle. Something back there, in the past, never to bother her again.

Another couple of minutes, she thought, rubbing herself down with the bar of soap. Just a few minutes more. And she remembered something else from her time at Stanford, those long bull sessions at night, fueled by ice cream and coffee brandy, a bunch of giggling girls – oh, let's be real, how womanly were we at that young age – discussing careers, boys and, sometimes, philosophy. She remembered one long night's session, some philosophical crap about who had the simpler life, a peasant woman or a woman of the new century. She didn't even remember who said what. She just remembered the arguments, that the peasant had a simpler and fuller life. Why not? He or she just had to survive, that's all. When your entire livelihood and focus is on getting your next meal, or getting through the next winter, then things get pretty simple. No worries about dating or clothes or eating disorders or stress or careers or politics or the unemployment rate or anything else. Just surviving.

Okay, one more minute in the shower, she thought. Funny, isn't it, a group of safe and well-fed white girls in a benevolent college town, and they had actually stumbled into the truth. Because just yesterday she had been a peasant. She had been cold, wet, hungry, just focused on getting through the night. But now that she was warm, now that she was clean, now that she had a bellyful of food, well, now things weren't so simple any more.

Out there was her lapbot, charging back up, charging back up so she could read those words and letters again, the words on the screen that said the President was going to die very soon, the words and letters that she and Drew had learned. Which now explained all of the efforts to capture them or kill them. Case Shiloh.

Worries, we sure have worries now that we're fed. Sheila turned off the shower and looked down at the washcloth she had been using, and saw the streaks of blood, and knew that her worries were only just beginning.

Ira Woodman stood among the draperies and curtains of the stage in Ithaca, his arms folded, almost singing with joy, watching as Michaelson Lurry wound up a speech. He was alive, his wife and children were alive, and he would keep on living, at least for this day. When he had arrived here earlier by helicopter after a fretful night in a motel, he had moved slowly and automatically, convinced that Lurry was upset with the fugitive search, convinced that Lurry would cut his losses. But that hadn't happened. Nope. He had met up with Lurry this morning, just before this speech to a regional meeting of police, fire and emergency response personnel, and Lurry had just slightly tapped him on the shoulder and said, 'Looks like you've got your hands full, but I'm sure you're doing the best you can, Ira.'

'That I am, sir, that I am,' he had said, and Lurry had replied, 'We've got some people to meet, some details to wrap up, after this speech. Hang around, all right?'

Now Lurry was leaning over the podium, making the same chopping motions with his right hand that he had used during his presidential campaigns, saying, 'Now, I know what's going on in your minds. You're out here in the field, out here dealing with the real issues and problems of emergency response. You wonder how a Washington bureaucrat' – and he stretched out each syllable, getting an appreciative laugh from the audience – 'can possibly know what you face, what you need.'

He paused, as if looking at every face, and he came back sharper. 'The truth is, I do know. The truth is, I have been there. I've been serving this country, whether in the cockpit of an F-16 Falcon, or facing down some liberal do-gooder on cable TV, or reaching out to the real Americans in my columns, or meeting thousands and thousands of you in my two races for the White House.'

A shout from the audience: 'Run again, we'll vote for you.'

Lurry shot back, smiling, 'I don't think I'll run again. You know what they say. During the last election, the people spoke.' Another pause, another smile. 'The bastards.'

That brought the house down, with laughter, hoots and whistles. Ira peered out from behind the musty-smelling curtains, seeing the rows of faces out there. Mostly male, almost entirely white. All wearing uniforms of some sort, whether police or fire or civil defense. Some camouflage fatigues, so maybe a few militia units as well. There was a taped-off area to the right, filled with news media types, recording and taking pictures. Always looking for that one sound bite to twist and cut, to make a flurry of headlines, to gain a few ratings points.

Lurry raised his hand and the applause died away. 'But what I can say is that I'm still ready to join you in serving this great country. The people we serve, day in and day out, may not appreciate what we do. The people we send to Washington – on both ends of Pennsylvania Avenue – may not appreciate what we do. The people we don't elect and the people we don't choose may not accurately tell the stories of what we do.'

Some boos and shouts started, and Ira noticed how some of the news media smiled at each other, though looking a bit self-conscious. Sure, smile away, Ira thought. Just two days left. Smile away.

'But in the end . . .' and Lurry had to raise his voice over the shouts aimed at the news reporters, 'but in the end we do what we can to serve this country and its people. In times of peace, in times of war, in times of chaos. We are the thin line between the forces of barbarism and darkness. We are the thin line between a new dark age and years of chaos. We are that thin line, and together we stand as one. Thank you, and God bless.'

Lurry waved and moved off the stage as the audience stood up as one, cheering, whistling and applauding. The group of reporters surged forward, pointing, gesturing, looking for something, but Lurry grinned at them and kept on walking to the rear of the stage. A couple of his aides came forward, one with a warm towel, the other with a glass of water, and Lurry saw Ira and motioned him over.

'How did it go, do you think?' Lurry said, wiping his face and taking a long swallow of water.

'Great, sir, you did great.'

Lurry grinned, and again Ira could not believe that this man had not made it to the White House. 'That's good to hear, Ira. Honest it is. Now, come along. We've got to meet some people, wrap up some details.'

Ira fell in beside him as Lurry went through the concrete corridors and then outside, where some college students were behind some police barriers. The moment they spotted Lurry the boos started, the signs started waving. LURRY FOR DICTATOR. HATE IS NOT A FAMILY VALUE. LURRY THE HOMOPHOBE. If the signs and shouts bothered the man, he didn't show it, for he kept up the smiles and waves. Ira saw how some of the cops by the barriers snuck a glance at Lurry as he went to his armored Ford Excursion and how they were all smiling. The people, Ira thought, the real Americans are behind us.

Lurry got into the rear of the Excursion and Ira sat next to him. As it pulled away Lurry shook his head. 'College students. God love 'em. So young, so full of energy. Like great empty vessels, ready to be filled with whatever half-baked ideas and theories their professors pour into them.'

Ira said, 'Problem is, a lot of those empty vessels never get refilled with something more worthwhile. Love of God. Love of country. Love of family.'

Lurry sat back with a sigh. 'So true, so true. Tell me, where will the detention center for this college's faculty be set up?'

'I don't know, Mister Lurry, but I can find out.'

'Good.'

As the Excursion sped out of the parking lot, Ira spared a glance back at the mass of students. Just a couple more days, and you'll really have something to protest against.

But only if we let you, he thought. Only if we let you.

He knew he should feel guilty about what was going to happen later tonight but he couldn't. George Clemson felt a rising tide of excitement knowing that in less than a day he would have his partner to himself. But he tried hard to restrain himself, for Carol and the children were getting ready to leave for DC and even Carol noticed something different.

'I swear,' she said, placing a pair of slacks into her suitcase, 'you seem quite thrilled at the thought of us leaving you alone for a couple of days.'

Easy now, he thought. Don't blow this one. 'Oh, you know that's not true, baby. I'll miss you and the kids while you're gone. I just want to make sure you all have a good time at your sister's.'

She smiled up at him but he could sense a tiny edge there. 'You're not going to be lying around drunk, watching those porn movies like last time, are you?'

He acted shocked. 'Who? Me?'

Then she laughed. 'When you put that little boy pout on your face, baby, you sure do make me laugh.' She came across the side of the bed and tapped the side of his face. 'You go ahead and rent those bad movies. I don't mind. Just make sure you have something left for me when we get back.'

He hugged her, wanting to reassure her – and how come there's no guilty feeling? – and also to make sure she couldn't see the look on his face.

'Now, now, you'll be back before you know it,' he said. Then the bedroom door flew open and Clennie and Clarisse came in, both talking over each other. 'Mom, Mom, come on, we're gonna miss the bus, we've got to get going.'

Carol started laughing and he snapped the suitcase shut and they went out to the kitchen, where Clarence was waiting, standing there solemnly, his own small suitcase at his feet. Then, something lurched inside of him as he saw that boy's look. He had been proud to raise a family and keep it together, to give his boy an example of what a real man could do. A real man who'd stick with his woman and be responsible, not going around, spreading his seed, raising a bunch of illegitimate kids who'd never know what having a father would be like. Clarence. What would the boy think now if he knew what he had planned for tonight? How could he explain that? How?

He went over and touched him on the shoulder. 'You have fun in DC, Clarence. But you mind your mother and your aunt.'

Clarence seemed to sigh. 'All right, then.'

'What's wrong?'

A tiny shrug. 'I want to make sure I see some of the sights down there. Like the Capitol, and the Air and Space Museum. I don't want to be in Aunt Mary's place every day, listening to everybody gab.'

George smiled and touched the shoulder again. 'I'll call your mom later, make sure that doesn't happen.'

And in a few minutes, after the kisses and hugs and the taxi cab came up, George came back up to the empty apartment. The place seemed so still and empty, and he looked at the silent rooms and his thoughts were no longer of his family but of his partner, and that smile, and that long hair, and oh, that body.

Tonight. He wondered if he could last that long.

As he listened to the sounds of the shower on the other side of the cabin, Drew sat down at one of the mismatched chairs, their still damp gear about his feet, his fists clenched in frustration. Damn it all to fucking hell, he thought. Where could it have gone?

While Sheila was in the shower he knew it was time to do something, something he had planned to do days ago when they had innocently gone into the mountains for a few days of camping and hiking. He had intended all the time to ask

her to become his wife, and he could not believe how nervous he had been thinking about it. Considering all that had
gone on since then, asking her to marry him seemed to be
the easiest thing to do. So why not now, when they were relatively safe in this cabin, with full bellies and clean skin? It
sure would break the mood of knowing what they had to
face, what they had to decide to do about those weighty
words on her lapbot screen.

So he had gone into the pocket of his backpack, looking
for that little ring case.

Not there.

That cold knot of fear and embarrassment, all mixed in.
Fool, he had thought. Must be the other pocket.

Except it hadn't been there as well.

So while the sound of rushing water from the bathroom
seemed to echo in his ears he pulled apart all of their gear,
looking into everything, until, finally, defeated, he slowly
put everything back. Gone. At any one of a half-dozen
places, from where that poor boy got ambushed by the
Mohawks to their most recent dip in the Connecticut River,
the engagement ring he had carefully picked for the woman
he wanted as his wife was gone.

Sheila wiped herself down with a pale gray towel and then
went into her little ditty bag, going past the tweezers and
deodorant and nail clippers to a small plastic container. She
tore open the container and found three of the four tampons
inside had been soaked wet and ruined. Great, just frigging
great, she thought as she opened up the only dry package and
put the tampon to use. She had planned and always kept a
few tampons in reserve, but her period wasn't due for another
week, at least.

But let's be real. Sometimes the curse comes rolling along when you're stressed, she thought, washing her hands and looking at herself in the mirror. And we sure feel pretty safe in saying that the past few days have been stressful, right?

Right.

Damn it to hell. She went through the medicine cabinet and the little space under the sink, looking for something, anything, but she knew it would probably be fruitless. She found cans of shaving cream and men's cologne and men's deodorant, even a hair-coloring kit for some vain hunter no doubt, but nothing she could use. None of those feminine products that were advertised in that oh-so-delicate manner, and that she so desperately needed.

Typical men, she thought bitterly. Always planned for themselves. Never planned for any other possibilities, like a female guest staying up here and being in desperate need for relief.

A cramp shuddered through her and she dry-swallowed two aspirin. Oh boy, this one is going to be a doozy, and she started brushing her hair, wondering if she should even bother telling Drew, should trouble him with this problem while so many other things were going on. And things had seemed so much better just a few minutes ago, with a stomach no longer grumbling and with warm water washing away all those days of sweat and fear.

'Damn this day all to hell,' she said quietly as she continued brushing her wet hair.

Cyrus Montgomery stepped out onto his rear lawn, again walking across to the tiny stand of boulders and rocks there in the distance. The day was getting dark early, and he could see why. Out there to the west thunderheads were rising up, ready to come this way to drench everything in their path. There was the low grumble of thunder, and if he was lucky he'd make it back to the house in time to see the show. He always loved thunder and lightning, even out in the field during training or ops, when most times he got soaked. He didn't care. He just loved the flashes of light and that rumbling noise you could feel in your chest. Almost reminded him of some of his work, but the booms and light show he loved most were made by the Big Guy Himself.

He sat down on one of the boulders, crossed his arms, waited. Listened to the rumbling again, looked over the wide field, suddenly felt a spasm of despair. This was such a beautiful country, such a rich place filled with such promise. Where had it gone wrong? Where had it come to a place where her soldiers and sailors and airmen were paid poverty wages? When programs for kids and young mothers were cut year after year to feed that giant entitlement monster for the aging boomers? When politics and working for your neighbor had been replaced by polls and focus groups and spin, spin, spin? My God, imagine FDR or Martin Luther King or Colin Powell deciding what to do because of some damn focus group.

Montgomery leaned back, looked up at the clouds, wondered if the airplane would make it in such crappy weather. He hadn't expected a visit today, which meant nothing. Sometimes days would go by without a visit, and other times there'd be one right after another. Each aircraft carrying a tiny package with a message from somebody in the services or on Capitol Hill, somebody keying him into something bad that was going to happen.

Shiloh. In just a few days. He crossed his arms, wondered what it meant, and what he could do even if he did find out what the damn thing was about. I mean, let's face it, he thought. Forcibly retired and sent away, not much—

There. Another single-prop job, coming up over that ridgeline. No sound of an engine but that was to be expected. Years of being near outgoing and incoming rounds, and the growling of tank engines and trucks and jets had worn down his hearing. He stood up as the plane circled overhead, and then an object tumbled out, just like before.

Strange, he thought. Something different this time.

This object was big, and had no streamer.

He looked up as it fell towards him.

Earlier Drew had drawn the shades of the small cabin that they had taken over, and with the grumbling of storm clouds in the distance the interior was dark, with thick shadows that seemed to hide things in the corners. They were sitting on the floor, against some musty couch cushions, the glowing screen of the lapbot between them. Drew remembered earlier what he had thought as they were floundering about in the woods, escaping those helicopters. Charlie Chaplin. Cogs. Charlie Chaplin in that movie *Modern Times*, caught in the cogs and gears of the industrial machine. Drew's mind had been playing tricks on him, had been trying to show him something, and only now did he realize what it was. There had been a mention of COG in those mail messages. That's what he had remembered. COG.

Sheila looked over, her face pale, and said, 'It's gone.'

'What do you mean, it's gone? What happened?'

She played with the keyboard again, desperately tapping at the keys. 'The hard drive got damaged somewhere along the line. All this jostling around and being dumped in the water. The files got corrupted.'

'Can you do a repair?'

'Yeah, with a Norton Utilities program I could, but I don't think this cabin has that hanging around.' She looked around and said, 'And another thing. The cellphone doesn't work around here. No towers in the vicinity. But we could always send an e-mail message out to the Secret Service, no matter how nutty it might sound. Drew, we've got to do something.'

Drew rubbed at his face, feeling the smoothness of his jaw. He had shaved a while ago and his skin felt tingly and smooth. He said, 'Let's say we do get an e-mail message out. What would we warn them?'

She shook her head. 'Don't play stupid with me. You've read those words, about the President's death. They plan to assassinate him. That's what Case Shiloh is about. Presidential assassination.'

He wondered how he could choose the words without sounding like his mind had gone on vacation. There were other times when he had held similar conversations, but with guys he served with, guys he had trained with, guys you knew well. Late-night discussions over beers and mixed drinks. Talking about other missions, other assignments. They had code words in talking about these kinds of secretive missions. Going over the fence. Playing in the black backyard. Taking a ride on the mystery train.

Sometimes one heard things. About plans and procedures. There were always plans and procedures, and drills, and more plans and procedures. For one always had to practice, practice, practice. And sometimes, one got caught up in the cogs, those grinding cogs that would wear you down and spit you out when you were no longer useful.

'Sheila, in one of those e-mail messages, it talked about a

working group meeting or something. Something about COG. Am I right?'

'Yeah, I remember the acronym. What does it mean?'

'COG,' he said, the word feeling heavy on his lips, not believing but you had to believe, when the information and intel came forward, all pointing to one thing. 'It stands for Continuity of Government. It's run by something called the National Program Office. Every day it determines who's the President of the United States. That's their job.'

Her face had the look of someone who thought a loved one had quietly gone nuts. 'I'm sorry, I don't understand. Couldn't they just read the front page of the *Washington Post*?'

He tried not to show his impatience. Damn it, if she had served with him back in the DRA, she'd know, she'd know right to her bones that he was correct.

'Okay, I'm sorry, I wasn't being clear,' he said. 'Look, every day, the nation needs a president, all right? A president does many things, but first and foremost, he or she is Commander-in-Chief, the one with the authority to commit troops, send in the bombers and launch missiles. That's the job of president, being head of the National Command Authority. If the President is assassinated, then the Vice President steps in, and boom, he or she is now president. Everybody except the previous president's widow is happy. But COG does more than just saying every day, yes, everything is fine, we have a president. Each day COG also determines where the Vice President is, the Speaker of the House, the president pro tempore of the Senate, the Secretary of State, all the way down the succession list. That way, if there's a bomb or a wide assassination plot – like with Lincoln – it would only take a few minutes to get a new president sworn in, even if she's the Secretary of Treasury. But back in the late 1970s and early 1980s COG realized they had a little problem.'

'Which was what?'

He rubbed at his bare chin, trying hard to remember those long-buried details from long-ago bull sessions with guys he had worked with. 'The problem was the line of succession according to the Constitution only goes so far, down to the President's Cabinet. But COG thought – what if the Soviets decide to go for a decapitation attack?'

'Sorry, Drew, that sounds like something from the French Revolution.'

'But it's a good analogy. Biggest fear of COG was a time when everybody was in DC at once, from the President down to the Secretary of Veterans Affairs. Then the Soviets could launch a missile from a sub off Maryland. Time to impact, less than five minutes. Hardly any warning at all. Boom. The command authority of the United States has just been decapitated. Other missiles are now in-bound, aimed at our military bases. Who's the president? Everybody in the line of succession is dead. But you need a president to authorize a retaliation, to authorize any kind of military action. You might have the biggest and baddest military in the world, but without someone to issue legitimate and legal orders your military's worthless. So COG decided to do something about it in the mid-1980s, called the National Program Office. Very hush-hush, top secret. They set up alternative presidents, individuals who served in government before – like a Secretary of Defense or Secretary of State – from a previous administration. Someone who would agree to step in as acting president, so that there would be somebody in charge. Someone to issue orders. Someone to launch the missiles.'

'Drew, that can't be right. I mean, nothing in DC can remain a secret that long. Hasn't anything been in the papers or the NewsNet channels?'

Outside there was a rumble of thunder, and he had a disquieting flashback to the storm that drove them into that shelter, back in the White Mountains. 'Sure, there were a few stories. *New York Times* and CNN both did stories some years ago. But people shrugged and kept on worrying more about their mutual funds. Which brings me back to the warning, Sheila.'

Her face looked pale in the faint light. 'What do you mean?'

'I mean Case Shiloh. I don't think they intend to just kill the president. I think they want the whole thing. I think they're planning to kill the president and everyone beneath him. To kill the entire branch of the government. To put somebody they like in charge.'

'No . . .' she whispered.

'Why not?' Drew said bitterly. 'There was a plot back in the 1930s to overthrow President Roosevelt. People who didn't like the way the country was going. Wall Street types, ex-military. Country in financial trouble. Trust in government at an all-time low. Demagogues in the newspapers and on the radio. Sound familiar?'

Sheila said nothing, her face white.

'And another thing,' he said, reaching over to touch her hand. 'Care to guess who operates the National Program Office?'

She folded her arms against her chest. 'The Federal Emergency Response Agency.'

'The same. Which is run by twice presidential candidate Michaelson Lurry, backed by every loon with a grudge in this country. Jesus . . .'

The rumbling of the thunder grew louder, and Sheila rubbed at her bare arms. 'So, what do we do? Just sit here until it happens? So that creature who thinks I belong in the kitchen, barefoot and pregnant, takes over and kills—'

'No, we're not going to just sit here,' he said, interrupting her. 'In fact, I'm going to walk into Newbury, the closest town from here, and make a phone call. A call to someone I know, someone I trust, someone who lives near here and has the weight to do something about Case Shiloh before it happens.'

'And who's that?'

'Remember my story? And the officer who rescued us?'

'Yes. Some officer. You didn't say what his name was.'

'Because I didn't think you'd believe me,' he said, again remembering that reassuring smile and the strong touch as that officer brought him into the helicopter that dreadful night. 'You see, he came into Pakistan against orders from the President. He had been in Saudi Arabia, trying to keep things calm with the Persian Gulf nations when war broke out in the Crescent, and somehow his staff heard our radio calls. He had been under orders to abandon all of us, because the administration was afraid of the negative publicity. All of us were supposed to die to keep headlines out of the newspapers and NewsNet channels. Sheila, the man who rescued me and my guys in Pakistan was Cyrus Montgomery, the Chairman of the Joint Chiefs of Staff.'

SIXTEEN

A plot of Wall Street interests to overthrow President Roosevelt and establish a fascist dictatorship, backed by a private army of 500,000 ex-soldiers and others, was charged by Major General Smedley P. Butler, a retired Marine Corps officer, who appeared yesterday before the House of Representatives Committee on Un-American Activities, which began hearings on the charges.

New York Times, November 21, 1934

Ira Woodman was in a meeting room, one like so many others he had visited over the years on behalf of his man, Michaelson Lurry. There had always been a sameness and dullness to these rooms, no matter how spiffed up they had been with paintings and refreshments and comfortable furniture. There was always stuffy air, bad lighting and ugly carpeting, and here, a secure place in a small FERA retreat shelter in the Adirondacks, was no different.

Michaelson Lurry was at the head of the table as other people came in and took their place. He looked at all those faces and remembered other meetings, so many meetings over the years, and one especially, up in the mountains of Idaho. His head ached and his stomach rolled with an acidy feeling that everything inside was burning up. The past couple of years had been long ones, dealing with every group, cell or organization that had a gripe against someone else. After a while they even started blurring together, with only one thing that they had in common: they thought they were the real Americans, and that their enemies weren't, and that their enemies therefore deserved to be crushed.

He closed his eyes, remembering little snippets, like out-of-focus snapshots:

Manhattan, with a group of gay men. Their leader, an intense man with two earrings in one ear, going on and on about a city councilor who had it in for them, who was planning to be the next Mayor of New York. 'Even worse than Rudy ever was,' one of them said. A gunshot later, taken care of, and the funeral of the city councilor had been front-page news for weeks.

And – too funny, of course – two months later, back in Manhattan, with an organization that was opposed to 'special rights for obscene people,' and that same man with the two earrings dead in an apartment fire.

Denver, with animal rights activists, and a week later a doctor in the medical research facility at the University of Denver found in his office, gutted, with a sign around his neck warning other vivisectionists.

Minneapolis, with a group of hunters, and a married couple who wanted to ban hunting in the state found dead in their bedroom, shot in the back of their heads.

And on and on and on . . . He held his arms tighter. Sometimes he understood why Lurry sent him on these missions – for the most part he agreed with some of the groups that he helped – but the others? The gays? The feminists? The ones who called conservatives like himself Nazis? What possible good could it be helping them kill and destroy allies of Michaelson Lurry?

He remembered a meeting at a hunting lodge in Idaho, about a year into things, when the first plans were beginning to take shape. It had been high up in the Yellowjacket Mountains, which made the peaks back home look like bumps on a log. During the long night when discussions were held in front of a wide fireplace, a small group of men and women had come in from the mountains, wearing dark clothes, carefully mended but old, weapons slung over their shoulders. Ira had seen them and had just turned away. Another group of malcontents. Skinheads, Christian cultists, militia types. Who cared anymore?

After the session – where sites for regional detention centers in the Northwest had been established – he had lingered, asking Lurry if he could spare a moment. He could, and then Ira had just talked for long minutes, on and on about the missions he had done, the results he had achieved. What earthly good had it accomplished? If he had been targeting a specific number of groups, the ones that had worked against Lurry's presidential campaigns, then maybe that would have made sense. But this scattergun approach? What was it for?

Lurry had listened to him, nodding occasionally, and then he leaned back in his large wooden chair. They were before a picture window, showing the craggy peaks, the tall pines and, off on the horizon, a full moon rising, illuminating up the snow and ice with a cold light. Lurry stretched out his legs and said, 'In the past year, you've become my most trusted assistant, Ira.'

'Thank you sir, I appreciate it.'

'You've done dangerous work, I've forced you to spend

time away from your family, and I've forced you to put in long hours back in Boston to keep up with your normal duties. You've come to me with questions, and you deserve the answers.'

Ira folded his hands in his lap and looked at Lurry, who was wearing a Western-type plaid shirt and blue jeans. Even in the quiet light of the old ski lodge he looked like he had the energy and will to take up an F-16 and blow an Iraqi MiG out of the air, or to face down a Congressional committee, or to tell a special-interest group to go to hell. Ira was tired and questioning of what was going on, but he would still follow this man, no matter what. He answered questions. He provided solutions. And he didn't depend on spinners, pollsters and advisers to make up his mind.

'There was an election in Massachusetts, back in the 1970s. A primary in a governor's race, between a liberal Democrat and a conservative Democrat. Care to guess who won?'

'Being Massachusetts, what else? The liberal Democrat. Probably Dukakis, right?'

Lurry had smiled. 'I'm glad you know some of your history, but I'm afraid you're wrong, Ira. In this particular primary Dukakis's conservative opponent beat him and went on to become governor. Dukakis had been governor for one term and was defeated in probably the most liberal state in the country. You know how it happened?'

'No, sir, I don't.'

Lurry had turned and looked out at the landscape. 'It had been a tough election, very close, with a lot of negative ads and pressure. The conservative Democrat – and bless me, I can't remember his name right now – won when everyone thought he wouldn't. Later, after the election, a newspaper reporter asked an adviser to the conservative Democrat why he had won. His answer? "We took all of the hate groups and put 'em in a pot, and watched 'em boil." That's how they won. They went to all the groups and organizations and clubs that had a grudge, that were full of hate and anger, and they used that hate and anger and energy to get them into the governor's office.'

Now it made sense. 'We're just putting on pressure, aren't we,' Ira said. 'Pitting one group against another, raising the anger, coarsening the debate, increasing the violence. So when the time comes . . .'

Lurry completed the thought. 'So when the right time comes, the people – the poor exhausted, dispirited, cynical people – will demand a change. Will demand order. Will demand that someone take charge. Does that answer your question, Ira?'

'Yes, yes it does, sir.'

Lurry went on. 'The people will also want a rest, Ira, a place to restore themselves, a place like . . . Shiloh. An old Hebrew word, meaning a resting place. And the name of a pivotal Civil War battle. That's what we'll call our task force, Ira, and the contingency plan. Case Shiloh. How does that sound?'

'It sounds fine, sir.' He smiled at his boss, still tired after all that he had done but now feeling better about all of those trips, all of those little scraps he had helped along, all those dead bodies. 'But just one more question. This conservative Democrat, back in Massachusetts. How did he do as governor?'

Lurry laughed. 'Terrible. The news media and the liberals and everybody else hated him, and when the time came four years later Dukakis beat him in the primary and became governor again for two more terms. So that's another lesson to be learned. Once you get the power, don't lose it.'

'Yes, sir,' he had said.

Ira now rubbed the arms of his chair, looking at the people coming into the room. Once you get the power, don't lose it. A good idea. For once they got into power, they would have to keep it for a very long time, for there was so much to undo after nearly fifty years of misrule.

But still his stomach burned with pain. He opened his eyes as Lurry tapped his pencil and said, 'All right, let's get started, shall we?'

At the other end of the table a voice was raised. Mack Matherson, a retired Marine Corps general and a former radio talk show host, who served as FERA's national spokesman. 'Lurry, you still haven't answered my question from our last session. About certain people who will cause us problems after Case Shiloh is implemented. Like one former JCS chief. I'd like to get that settled before we start up again.'

Lurry smiled and toyed with the pencil. 'By now that problem should be taken care of. Understood? Taken care of. Is that all right, General?'

The General smiled. 'Perfect. God bless.'

'Right, god bless,' Lurry said. 'Let us begin.'

Cyrus Montgomery saw the falling object grow larger and then everything moved quickly as something heavy struck him from the rear. He fell among the boulders and the saplings, the branches whipping at his face and hands, a heavy weight on his back, his chin bouncing off stone and him gasping, swearing, and then an ear-bleeding *BOOM!* tore at him, even making his clothes flutter. Then, quicker than one breath to the next, chunks of wood, leaves, branches and even pieces of metal rained upon him, the metal hot and stinging, like it had been quickly heated up. There was a weight on his back and his chin hurt and his hands hurt. He tried to get up and a voice was in his ear, 'No, don't move, General. In case they come back.'

He ignored the voice and tried to shrug off the weight as a host of memories and experiences came crowding in, his body recognizing what had happened even before his mind. Anti-personnel weapon, he thought. That's what had been tossed out of the airplane. A little something for the uppity nigger who thought he could do something about . . . oh, shit, Grace, what in the world is going on here?

'General . . .'

'Shut up, will you?' and he jabbed an elbow and broke himself free. He sat up, touched his chin, felt the stickiness of blood. His hands were scraped raw and his ears still rang from the concussion. His Scribe was crouched before him, 9 mm pistol in his hands, looking cautiously over the mess of boulders and saplings. Montgomery brushed at the twigs and leaves and shrapnel that had fallen down upon them, and then his Scribe turned and Montgomery saw a thick trail of blood rolling down his cheek.

'Blakely, you're hurt,' he said, crawling over to him. 'Anyplace else you've been hit?'

Blakely touched the stream of blood and shrugged, resumed his watch. 'Not that I'm aware of, sir. I don't hear the aircraft any longer. But there might be a follow-up squad coming through to check on the attack. We should get back to the farm, activate the fence defenses and call the State Police.'

Montgomery winced as he got up and looked out over the field where he had just been standing, part of him cool and professionally observing what had just occurred. Just a few feet away was the impact point, a chewed-up crater of dirt, grass and stone. All of the brush and saplings on this side of the rock pile had been shorn of leaves and branches, like a hundred tiny metal scythes had just gone at them. Even the rocks and boulders showed signs of scarring. A dozen feet away or so there was a tiny clump of blood and feathers. Some poor bird, caught in the crossfire as one group of humans tried to kill another human. Story of this whole bloody race.

And if Blakely hadn't just come along . . .

His Scribe gently tugged at his elbow. 'General, we must get back to the farm.'

Montgomery shook his head, trying not to think of what a retired JCS chief would have looked like, crumpled out there next to the dead bird. 'Yes, you're right, we've got to get moving. But only to the farm, and only to activate the fence. No cops.'

Blakely joined him on the field as he started half-trotting to the farm. 'Why no police?'

Shiloh, Montgomery thought. Time to risk a few phone calls. Something called Shiloh was about to occur and he needed to know more. 'Because they can't do anything right now, that's why, except to bring in a convoy of press people and NewsNet types. And I'd rather face another bomb attack than to have those vultures camped out at the gate.'

Blakely said nothing, the pistol in his hands, his head moving around, his eyes constantly at work. Montgomery liked the look, liked having the man next to him, armed and ready, though the pistol looked pretty useless in his hands. He said, 'One more thing.'

'Sir?'

'How come you were out there, just now? You've never come with me on these kinds of walks before.'

Blakely kept looking around the General, not looking at him, while he answered. 'I got an urgent message from the Montpelier office of the FBI, sir, just a few minutes ago. They had intel of a possible assassination attempt against you. I was coming out to warn you when the airplane came overhead.'

Montgomery nodded, feeling himself out of breath as they reached the rear steps of the farmhouse. 'I'd like to see that message if you don't mind.'

His Scribe nodded. 'Not at all, sir. Not at all.'

Clem Badger was sitting in front of his screen at his office back in Boston, working on his fourth Undertow soda of the day, packed with twice as much caffeine as your usual Coke and Pepsi. The small countertop was littered with crumbs and scribbled notes on scraps of paper. He knew he smelled – days since he had taken a shower – and his face was scraggly with beard and his hair felt like a quart of motor oil had been dumped in it, but he didn't care. He was hunting, hunting the best way he knew how, and he was sure he was damn close to bringing something to Mr Woodman.

He wasn't sure what time it was – morning or evening – and he didn't particularly care. He also didn't particularly care that he didn't fit in with the rest of the FERA Region One folks that were part of Case Shiloh. Most of them were ex-cops or ex-military or ex-firefighters who had found God or something and wanted to do something about it. Goodie for them. He was in this for kicks and to make bonuses and to attack computer problems with the best equipment available, and he had been told that after next week the problems coming in would be fast and furious.

Fair enough. Another sip of the cola traveling down his gullet. There. The download was coming in from the Green Mountain Utility Complex, which maintained and operated the power lines, distribution centers and billing for all electrical customers in Vermont. Once he had plowed through their site – using an NSA backdoor program that he had received last year over a kiddie porn trade that would no doubt piss off Ira Woodman to a fare-thee-well if he ever found out – he had found it to be quite kludgy. Not friendly at all. Damn place had a problem differentiating between big industrial customers and little residential customers, and those residential customers were the ones he was looking for.

Ah, there it was, and he started scrolling through the addresses. Nothing fancy but something he had been thinking about, hooked into the situation reports that had been coming in from Mr Woodman and that crazy killer Harrison at his side from Vermont. The two fugitives were believed to be somewhere in the Connecticut River Valley, either in Vermont or New Hampshire. So, Clem had spent the past couple of days just cyber-tripping through the Net, not once leaving his chair except for quick visits to the bathroom or to the vending machines. He had a secret smile as he worked, thinking about all those apes up there, going door-to-door, running down leads, beating the underbrush. Hairy, stupid, apes, and while Clem knew that they belittled him and his skills, he knew better. He was the next stage of evolution. *Homo computeris*. Everything was so wired in and connected you could find anyone, anyone you wanted, from a good computer and comfortable chair. What was the point of going outside when you could do so much from your own office?

There. He leaned back in his chair, giggling. Won't Mr Woodman be surprised when he called up with this. For it was pretty simple, really. Most of the places along that stretch of the Connecticut River were summer places, cottages and fishing camps. After Labor Day, their power use dropped right off. You could chart each home in the area, look at how many kilowatt-hours they were using. Most had a perfect use curve, fairly level through the year, with a spike coming around Memorial Day, increased usage here and there all through the summer, and then, bam!, dropping off right after Labor Day.

Which meant that any place that had an increase in use during the middle of the week, where past history showed no such usage, well . . . it might show you that you've got a couple of strangers visiting, using the stove, showers, lights or whatever, strangers that don't belong.

Like this hunting camp, just outside Newbury, Vermont. Within walking distance of where the fugitives had escaped after they had been spotted by Mr Woodman and those National Guard choppers.

He giggled again, checked the time on his old-fashioned analog watch. It was eight o'clock and he wasn't sure if it was a.m. or p.m., but he was sure Mr Woodman wouldn't care. Clem picked up the phone and started dialing.

Sheila felt something heavy ooze through her as the familiar Number Hound logo popped up on her lapbot screen. Thank God her Net connectors were working. About the only thing that appeared scrambled on her hard drive had been the e-mail downloads from Ira Woodman's account. She knew she should feel better, after a good night's sleep in a real bed and a hot shower and a hot meal, but no, she didn't feel good at all. The Number Hound was there, tail wagging, and she double-clicked on the logo as the information popped up. 'Here it is,' she called out, sitting at the kitchen table with the greasy countertop. 'Private phone number of Cyrus Montgomery, Northfield, Vermont.'

'Great,' Drew said, her back to him, putting a few freeze-dried food packages into his knapsack. Sheila had felt queasy about stealing the food, but as another cramp raced through her and she could feel that her last tampon was about to surrender to the onslaught, well, she didn't care any more.

'Anything else?' Drew asked.

'Yeah,' she said, shutting down her lapbot. 'Like you suggested, I've sent a message about Case Shiloh out to about a half-dozen discussion groups on the Internet. That might slow them down a bit, trying to bluff their way out of that if any publicity buzz starts up. Plus we are now officially broke. That last request through the Number Hound wiped out my Calgary account. No more CyberGal funds left, Drew.'

He stopped suddenly and turned to her, and she wanted to be angry at him, to speak up to him on how she had been doing everything here, from chasing down information to using her hard-earned money, earned in a dangerous line of work where it had killed other CyberGals, she wanted to lash right into him. Tell him how unappreciative he had been, how she didn't like being used as the First National Bank of Sheila, how he took her and her skills and her Calgary account for granted, but he wouldn't allow it.

He came over and knelt down on the floor and held both her hands and said, 'I know what you've done, all that you've done these past few days. Trust me, it's almost over. One phone call to the General and then we pass this burden on to him. He's got connections, he still has some power left. I know he can make a difference. And when the dust settles, we'll be back home on Lake Montcalm. Just the two of us. And no more travel. No more hiking. Ever. We can just stay in the house and grow old, the two of us.'

She nodded. 'God, yes. I miss the loons, you know? I want to hear them one more time, before they head out to the Atlantic.'

'Me, too,' he said. 'The two of us, curled up on the front porch, listening to the loons say goodbye. I want that, too, more than ever.'

Sheila felt the tears start up and, without knowing why, she blurted, 'Oh, damn it, yes.'

'Yes, what?' he asked, puzzled.

She took a deep breath, knowing it was right, it would always be right. 'Yes, I'll marry you. The sooner the better.'

Drew said nothing, just drawing her hands up to his lips and kissing them.

Outside Gate 4 at Camden Yards, George Clemson paced back and forth, suddenly nervous about what the day would bring. It was a late-afternoon game between the O's and the Red Sox, and he didn't particularly give a shit who would win. All that mattered was whether or not he'd see this game alone, and he looked over at the people streaming about him, heading into the brick-lined gates. A typical mixed crowd for the O's – one of the few places in Baltimore where black, white, yellow and brown could mingle without problems – and the mood of the people going by him seemed good. He knew moods, knew how crowds could suddenly mutate into a beast determined to burn and loot everything in its path, but these people just seemed to be happy to see a game this afternoon.

'Officer, can you help me?' a soft voice said.

He turned, wondering how in hell she had snuck up on him. Nancy Thon Quong looked up at him, laughing, and he felt giddy, like he was sixteen again, unsnapping his first bra strap from a willing date. Without her uniform it seemed Nancy had shrunk, but instead of looking childlike, she just looked delicious, like she was meant to be eaten. She had on tight jeans, flat black shoes and a long-sleeved black top that was low-cut on top and bottom, revealing a tight tummy. A brief thought came to him, of Carol's heavy body after three kids, and he tried to push it away.

She tugged away some of her long black hair and said, 'Are we ready for the opening pitch?'

He smiled back at her, wondering what she thought of him being out of uniform. He had on gray slacks and a light green turtleneck, and though he was off duty, he had a back-up piece – .38 snubbie hammerless revolver – stuck in an ankle holster.

'I believe we are, rook, I believe we are,' he said, and he walked towards the gate, her by his side. After he passed over the two tickets and went into the stadium, he was thrilled when she quietly hooked her arm through his.

Baby, he thought, I certainly am ready for the first pitch, and whatever pitches come my way. Damn, there was much to do tonight. He smiled all the way to their seats.

Drew halted their hike on a small hill overlooking the equally small town of Newbury, Vermont. The walk had been reasonable, coming from the hunting camp near the banks of the Connecticut. They had followed a dirt road to a paved lane called Mill Road, and followed that for about a half-mile, packs heavy with stolen freeze-dried food weighing on their backs. All the way into town he tried to focus on what was going to happen, what he had to say in those first few minutes with General Montgomery, but all he could think about was the sentences Sheila had blurted out. Yes, she would marry him. As soon as possible. Wonderful news.

Yeah, another voice said, but who's the idiot who lost the engagement ring?

Drew swung off his backpack and helped Sheila with her own. In one hand he held a folded-over topo map, another item liberated from the camp. He pointed to the small cluster of buildings down below, mostly brick and frame structures. 'Looks to be about a ten-minute walk down there,' he said. 'You just wait here until I get back. The first payphone I get to, I'll pump in the last of our quarters and get a hold of the General.'

Sheila – hell, our soon-to-be-wife! – smiled and sat down on the ground. 'And what am I supposed to do in the meantime? Be here as the faithful woman, sitting on her ass, waiting for her man to come back?'

'That's exactly what you're going to do,' he said, hoping she wasn't in the mood for further discussion. He had many things to achieve in the next hour, including coming up with a phone message that wouldn't cause the General to hang up on him.

'Suppose you get in trouble? What then?'

Drew said, 'Then get back to that camp and stay there. That's where I'll find you.' Then he had a bleak thought. 'In a couple of days it won't matter much anyhow. Case Shiloh will have happened and we'll have more basic things to worry about. Like surviving.'

She stretched out her legs, rested against her backpack.

'Go on,' she said. 'My brave man. You go do what you have to do, and I'll be waiting here for you when you get back.'

He bent down, gave her a quick kiss. 'And then we'll let General Montgomery and his friends worry about what happens next. We will have done all that we can.'

Drew stood up and then started down the hill, almost whistling. Just one phone call, that's all. All he had to do would be to get the General's attention, just one phrase. Quicksilver, the name of that botched Pakistani operation. Then he'd listen, and would keep on listening, until he convinced him. Drew knew he could do it. Hell, there was no choice. He had to do it.

He looked back up at the hill, at Sheila, resting. He waved up at her and she waved back. He felt guilty. He had underestimated her. He thought for sure that she would demand to go to town, to at least shadow him in there. He had talked long and hard earlier, how much easier it would be for him to slide in and out as one person. All the cops and militia groups and armed citizens were looking for a male and female couple. One guy could do the job easier.

Surprise, surprise, she hadn't put up a fuss.

He gave her another wave. Idiot, he thought. You sure have underestimated her.

Sheila waited until she could no longer see Drew and then allowed another five minutes to pass and stood up. She winced as another cramp raced through her, and she hated to think what her underwear was going to look like when this day was done. Her last tampon was bravely holding back the flood – backed up by a wad of paper towel from the hunting camp – but she couldn't wait anymore.

From the rear pocket of her shorts she pulled out a folded

piece of paper, undid it and looked at it carefully. A blank check from Drew's account, kept in the rear of her wallet for emergencies, placed there at his insistence. Just in case, he had said, the SmartCard system crashed or something. It had been soaked in that dunking the other day, but it was still legible. It could still be used, if she carefully forged Drew's name, which she could with her eyes closed.

But wasn't it dangerous?

She started walking towards the town. Not as dangerous as using her SmartCard. And she was sure that with enough talking and fussing she could get out of the store with what she needed: a box of tampons, some painkillers and deodorant.

Besides, Drew said that the phone call to the general would take care of everything. Maybe not in a minute or two, but with the phone call completed they could just hunker down and stop running.

That would be such a relief, she thought, heading to the town. To stop running.

SEVENTEEN

That depends on what your definition of is is.
President William J. Clinton, August 17, 1998

Ira Woodman looked up as Michaelson Lurry gently tapped the side of his water glass. 'My dear friends, I'm afraid I've got to wrap this up. We all have jobs to do and we need to get to them as soon as we can. I'll be heading back to DC tonight but tomorrow I'll be at the Albany Regional Retreat Center for a previously scheduled drill.'

Ira looked about the room, at the collection of men and women who were about to take back this country from the liberals and extremists and feminists and homosexuals and everyone else who didn't want to follow the rules, become an American and just shut up and say the Pledge of Allegiance without asking the ACLU to sue on your behalf.

Most of the room had other FERA representatives from the other FERA regions. A few were peers of Ira – regional administrators who had been active in the two Lurry campaigns and stayed on for one last campaign – but others were officials of one sort or another in that particular FERA region. Not all of the regional administrators were trustworthy, and in the past two years Ira had read with some grim fascination of the different FERA personnel who had died by suicide, car accidents or house fires. *Erntse menchen.* Serious men. And Michaelson Lurry and his followers were serious men indeed, for taking a country back demanded absolute loyalty and absolute secrecy.

There were other people besides Mack Matherson, the retired Marine Corps general who served as a spokesman, and all were Lurry supporters, or what the media called Lurry's Legions. There was Gat Hartwell, obese and smoking a thick cigar, who was the second most popular talkshow and NewsNet commentator in the country. And in a smartly tailored suit, hair permed up to a blonde helmet, Dr Stacy Krueger, talkshow psychologist and frequent guest on those cable channel chattering skull shows. Ira thought Mack Matherson was one step removed from a caveman, Gat Hartwell was a pompous idiot and Dr Stacy was a vicious shrew, but none of that mattered. All three had tried to get Lurry elected, and all three were willing to support him even further. Especially the day after Case Shiloh, when a scared and terrified nation would need to hear reassuring voices over the radio, cable stations and NewsNet channels.

A few other key supporters were there as well, including one active-duty Air Force general, two active-duty Army generals, and an admiral as well. All were in civilian clothes. At the other end of the room a handful of congressmen were clustered around the junior senator from Louisiana who had managed to get himself elected to that office regardless of his early years in the Ku Klux Klan.

Despite the stomach pain, despite the worries, he felt a surge of pride and wonderment for what they had accomplished, especially since he had just received an important page from Clem Badger. This group and the others out there in the field, maybe a hundred or so at the most, were about to make this nation great again.

'Mr Lurry?' came a voice from the end of the table. Ira leaned forward, saw it was the Congressman from Montana. Elected because of the help of Lurry and that state's militia groups.

'Go ahead, Tom,' Lurry said.

The young man – dressed in the uniform of dark blue suit, white shirt and red necktie – looked around the room as if seeking encouragement, and then pressed on. 'It's just that . . . well, I know it's late and all that, but the trigger event for Case Shiloh . . . I'm just wondering if there's an alternative . . .'

Murmurs and disgusted looks were exchanged among the others at the table, and even Ira wondered what in hell was going through that young pup's mind. Mack Matherson slammed a hand down on the table and said, 'Look here, you Congresscritter, what in hell do you think this is? A tea party? This is a fucking revolution and in revolutions people get killed. Why, it makes me think—'

Lurry raised his hand and the murmurs stopped, as did the blustering talk from Matherson. The FERA director rubbed at his chin and said, 'Tom, I appreciate your point of view. Honest I do. And at first I was reluctant to go forth when I realized that this option was available to me. But what other choice did I have, did we have?'

Silence from the room, and Ira looked on with admiration as Lurry became more animated. A pity more people couldn't see what he was saying, how he was making sense. He said, 'Were the elite ever going to give us the respect and attention we and our followers deserve? Were they ever going to listen to our message, and to pass that message along to the rest of America without adding their own spin and twist on our words? Were we ever going to be able to compete in the marketplace of ideas when the elite control what appears in that marketplace? Was this ever going to happen, ever?'

No one replied. No one had to. Everyone knew the answer. Lurry took a breath and went on. 'Twice we went before the American media and public. Twice before our words were twisted, our true positions were ignored, and our every misstatement was highlighted and examined, while our opponent received a free ride from the media.' A slight smile. 'Even his potty habits don't get the attention they deserve.'

Some smiles, and Lurry said, 'So now we are at this point. Jobs are disappearing. Cheap oil is now expensive. Respect for the family, for the courts, for government itself has gone away. There is chaos out there, Tom, chaos that will only get worse unless we step in to do something. Step in and perform Case Shiloh. It's the only way.'

Gat Hartwell puffed on his cigar. 'For me, personally, it will be a relief to no longer say "within the Beltway". In less than two days that hateful place will be gone and I can strike it from my vocabulary.'

The Congressman seemed to squirm from the attention he was getting. 'It's just, well, the history, you know? The museums, the monuments, all that . . .'

Lurry's tone got sharper. 'So what? We lose DC, what do we lose? Some public buildings, some monuments, bureaucrats, and thousands of people who don't support us. And what do we gain? Tom, we gain a nation. A cleansed nation, ready to be led onto the right path, a path that's been ignored for more than a half-century.'

Mack Matherson said, his voice growling. 'When we're done, we'll make our own damn monuments, you see.'

Ira nodded, and then was mortified when his pager went off with a shrill beeping noise. It was supposed to be on vibration alert, but he must have accidentally switched it over to audible when he last checked Clem Badger's message about using power records to hunt down the two fugitives. Wondering if it was Glenda Sue checking up on him – she had paged him three times yesterday – he muttered, 'Excuse me,' and checked the message display.

'Well?' Dr Stacy inquired, using a sharp schoolmarm voice that sounded like steel wool on a chalkboard. 'Something you want to share with the rest of us?'

Ira felt like saying, fuck you, you overpriced and overeducated bitch, but instead he was grinning and felt the best he had in days.

'Certainly, I have a message I want to share with everyone,' he announced, reading and rereading the message display. 'It seems like one of the two fugitives my people have been hunting this past week has been captured.'

Lurry smiled right at Ira, and Ira felt as good as he did whenever Daddy praised him all those years ago. 'God bless,' Lurry said, and it seemed everyone repeated the phrase.

God bless.

Drew knew he was violating almost every bit of tradecraft he had ever learned going straight into this Vermont town, but he didn't have much choice. He should have spent two or three days on the outskirts, looking into the movement of people, to see what the police set-up was, to see if any of those damn Federal hunters were stationed here, and to note the best locations for payphones. Then he should have gone in at night to make the phone call, and then slip out again in darkness.

But there was no choice. Case Shiloh, COG and every-thing else were happening in less than two days. Drew was no fan of the President – who the hell was nowadays, after that Rose Garden pissing incident? – but that wasn't the point. It was necessary to get back at those fuckers who'd been chasing and trying to kill the two of them these past days, the same kind of fuckers who had sent him and the rest of his squad into the Crescent and advised this same befud-dled President to cut them loose.

He stopped for a moment before going out onto the road. From what he had seen up on the hill, going into town was just a matter of coming out onto the main road, walking over a small concrete bridge, and then boom, you were there. The old don't-blink-and-you'll-miss-it routine. Pretty simple, except that he and his woman were the most sought-after fugitives in all of New England. So. How to do it?

Drew shrugged and went out onto the road, and started walking into Newbury. The trick is to look like you belong. Which is why he left his gear and even his 9 mm back up on the hill with Sheila. Earlier at the camp they had done the best they could do, washing their clothes in the bathtub and using a hand-held hair dryer to dry them. He was freshly washed and clean-shaven. Drew wasn't looking for miracles – since he retired, he always found the idea of God and miracles hard to believe – but he was looking for a quiet few minutes to make his phone call and get out.

Now he was in the center of town. Pretty busy looking place. Large grass common, lots of shops and stores, every-thing from MailMart to a CompuQuickest and even a PrintShopExpress.

But all I need right now, he thought, is a phone.

The sidewalks were crowded – not bad, a good place to

mix in – and he walked casually, hands in pockets, like he didn't have a care in the world.

A couple of cars drove by, and then the white-and-blue of a Newbury Police cruiser, and he kept on walking, stopping only when he saw it, by the side of a drugstore.

A Bell Atlantic payphone.

Even though she knew Drew would be extremely pissed to know that she was shadowing him into town, she also had to stifle the giggles a few times. I mean, she thought, here's our brave man going into town, trying hard not to get noticed, and all the while he's being followed by the woman he's sleeping with.

But the urge to giggle left her when she spotted her Holy Grail, her Blue Ribbon and Gold Medal, all at once. The Newbury General Store. She could have kissed those worn wooden steps.

Instead she pranced up them, knowing that in a few minutes her increasing discomfort would at least be under control.

Drew sat on a park bench across from the town common. There was a small crowd over there, somebody on a platform trying to raise money for Canadian refugees. Yep, a beautiful day and a beautiful Bell Atlantic payphone. Just one problem. A young girl with hoop rings pierced through both eyebrows and connected by a silver nose chain was yakking away. Should he get up and start looking for another one, or just sit tight here?

At his side was a wire-mesh wastebasket, clipped to a utility pole. On top was a copy of yesterday's *USA Today*. He glanced at the headlines – *Special Prosecutor Debated For Rose*

Garden Incident, Unemployment Up Two Percent, Stock Market Takes Dive – and then raised the newspaper when the Newbury Police cruiser idled by.

Just keep cool, he thought. Just keep cool.

It only took a couple of minutes to find what she needed. Sheila wasted a second or two, just gently caressing the smooth cardboard of the box of painkillers and the tampon packages. She briefly remembered a couple of students back at Stanford, back-to-earthers who were going to school only to learn the ins and outs of the evil corporate system that oppressed everyone, blah-blah-blah. Not only did they eschew soap, deodorant and clean clothes – which is why they often had the corner of a classroom to themselves – but they also took underground drugs that counteracted the immunizations they had received for infants. Measles, diphtheria and polio were all natural. So why fight against it?

Why fight indeed?

Because there was a lot to be said about comfort and longevity. She went to the store counter, her purchases firmly in hand.

There. The young girl hung up the phone and pranced away, and Drew went up towards the phone, the newspaper firmly underneath his arm. No use in tossing it on the ground and getting charged for littering. Let's just get the job done. Make the phone call, talk to the General about Case Shiloh and COG, and then get the hell out.

Spend a couple of more days out in the woods – with the food they had taken from the camp, it would be a cinch – and then head back home. Oh, there might be the matter of a certain New Hampshire deputy sheriff to clear up, the one the FERA boys said they had murdered, but in the space of a week, ah, in just seven days, they could be back home in their safe little place on Lake Montcalm.

Never to leave again, never to camp again, just to sit there on the end of the dock and to hell with everybody else.

Drew picked up the phone, deposited a fistful of quarters, and started punching in the General's number on the keypad.

Oh, Sheila thought, this is going to be our lucky day. The store owner, a tall, skinny guy who had an angry scowl about his eyes, had to go in the rear for some inventory work, so he passed over the cash register duties to an older woman who looked like his mother. She looked to be in her seventies, plump, wearing a dark green apron that had the store's name stitched on the front in white thread. She was slow in ringing up the other customers, but she gamely went through everything.

Now it was her turn. The woman counted up the purchases and said, 'Twelve-ten, please.'

Sheila tried to be as casual as possible, writing out the check in the proper amount and passing over her driver's license for identification, explaining that the account belonged to her husband. The woman laboriously wrote down the ID information on the rear of the check, and Sheila leaned in and said, 'I have a favor to ask, and I'm embarrassed to do it.'

The woman's eyes seemed to twinkle behind her glasses. 'Oh, don't be embarrassed. It's a beautiful day out there, I'm sure it can't be that embarrassing.'

Sheila smiled, only feeling the tiniest tinge of guilt in scamming this poor woman. 'It's my husband. He's . . . well, he's rather strict about me writing checks on the account without letting him know first. That's never a problem but' – Sheila gestured to her purchases – 'I'm in a delicate situation right now. I'm seeing him tomorrow but I know he keeps an eye on his accounts almost every hour of the day. So if you process this check through right now . . .'

The woman nodded, put the check aside. 'Don't tell me any more. I know how it is, having been married to someone just like that. I swear, you think they count toilet paper sheets, they're so tight. I'll run it through tomorrow, and no one will be the wiser. Now run along and tend to your business before you make a mess of yourself.'

Before Sheila could say anything, the woman reached under the counter and came up with a key tied by a chain to a block of wood. 'We have a restroom out back, by the propane tank, for customers. I guess you're in a hurry, right?'

Sheila gave the woman her best smile. 'You guess right.'

The phone rang once, twice, and on the third ring, a voice answered, a voice that Drew recognized instantly, not just from the various television and NewsNet shows about his service to his country, his possible interest in politics, the sad tale of his wife's murder. No, not just that. Drew recognized it from the cramped quarters of a dirty and ill-maintained helicopter fighting its way back to an aircraft carrier in the Arabian Sea.

'Hello, Cyrus Montgomery here,' the man's voice said.

Terrence Carleton came out of the rear stockroom of his store, eyes knotted in anger. Goddamn inventory was off again – a case of Budweiser and a couple of cans of potato chips – and he had a good idea why. That lunkhead he had

just hired to restock on afternoons after school, Tommy
something-or-another. Ever since that football player with
the mind of a plant had started work his inventory had been
shrinking.

Well, Tommy, ol' boy, he thought grimly as he headed
back to the counter, you're going to get a wonderful life
lesson in about two hours when you come to work today. Be
thankful I won't charge you for the missing items before I fire
your ass.

'Thanks, Mom,' he said, as he sidled up next to her on the
counter. 'Why don't you take a break and I'll work through
'til noon.'

'Okay, Terry,' she said, and then she frowned. 'There was
something I was going to tell you, but darn if I can remember
it.'

Poor old Mom, he thought. She meant well and did well,
but sometimes her mind just wouldn't click in. He kissed
the top of her head. 'I'm sure it will come to you, just take it
easy.'

When she walked to the rear of the store he looked down
and frowned. An out-of-state check. He picked it up and
turned it over. Well, at least she got the ID info off the
license. But the damn thing hadn't been processed through
CheckTru. It was just for twelve bucks, but hell, Mom should
have known better. And with Tommy and his light fingers
raiding the inventory whenever he felt like it, twelve bucks
was twelve bucks.

He punched in the keypad, fed the check through the
tiny CheckTru terminal, and waited.

And waited.

Damn it, it shouldn't take that long. Overdrawn, for
twelve bucks?

Then the check came out. Little green light came on the terminal.

Approved.

Terrence smiled. Day was improving already.

One hundred forty miles away from the Newbury General Store, Clem Badger sat up in his chair and coughed out a mouthful of Undertow soda all over the keyboard. His computer terminal was chiming all sorts of alerts and alarms, and as he moved his fingers through the now-sticky keyboard he couldn't believe what just happened.

A check? A damn check written on a general store?

But it fit in with the power usage report he had just sent to Mr Woodman, and he got to work with glee, sending out alerts, pages and e-mail messages.

Man, oh, man, he thought, there is going to be one massive fist of power coming down on this little town in about sixty seconds.

Drew started in right away, saying, 'General, this is—' and then he was interrupted. 'Hold on, General, I'll take this call,' came another voice. There was a click as the other receiver hung up and the man's voice became sharper. 'This is Captain Blakely, adjutant for General Montgomery. Who's this, please? And how did you come by this number?'

He clenched the phone receiver so tight he thought he might shatter the plastic. Identify himself to this flunky? Give him the name of a fugitive accused of being a copkiller and terrorist?

'My name doesn't matter. I . . . I served once with the General, and I need to talk to him right away, just for a moment, because—'

The captain interrupted him. 'Do you know how many times we get phone calls, e-mail or snail mail from types like you, every day? Too damn many. And this is how they get treated. Every single one of them.'

Click.

Drew slammed the receiver down. Damn it, so close, so damn close! If he hadn't been so polite when the General answered, if only he had been quicker and to the point. He checked how many quarters he had, decided to try it again.

Busy signal.

Okay, stay cool, let's stay cool. That captain can't be hovering over that private line all day, and we can try later. We still have enough coinage. I head back up to the hill with Sheila and we can come back tonight.

He turned and parked not more than six feet away was a Newbury Police cruiser.

Maurice Blakely walked out of his office, leaving the phone receiver off. Let that guy try calling back as much as possible until he gave up. He touched the bandage on the side of his head and shuddered. Man, that had been fucking close. All it would have taken would be a stumble or a crossed foot and he would have been chewed up to bloody hamburger. But it had worked – maybe not in the way the people in that airplane wanted it to – but it had worked. Add that with the fake message from the FBI that the General had so quickly swallowed – like most superior officers Blakely knew, they instinctively trusted everything their Scribe showed them – and things were looking mighty fine.

Now, if only there were no more idiot phone calls. He had no idea who that guy was or what he wanted, but no interruptions, not right now. There was too much going on.

As he went downstairs, he thought about calling Bell Atlantic and having the private line changed, and he smiled to himself. In a couple of days it wouldn't matter, so why waste the time?

Sheila used a few spare quarters of her own to get a Coke from a vending machine in front of the Newbury Country Store, and damn, that cold sharp flavor felt pretty good going down her throat. What also felt good was knowing that some serious pain relief was coursing through her bloodstream, she had a fresh tampon firmly in place and enough back-ups in the paper bag in her hand to last her through the next few days.

And after that, well, twenty-eight days from now, everything should be back to as normal as possible, and she could just laze through that period from the comfort of their home back in Lake Montcalm.

My God, what a dream that seemed to be . . .

Then, the noise began. She looked up. One helicopter, and then two, appeared over a ridgeline and were heading towards the center of town.

The chant started in his mind as he walked away from the phone. Be cool, be cool, be cool. We've been in tough spots before, in Serbia and Quebec and the Crescent, and this is nothing, this is your home turf, your home territory. Be cool, be cool.

There was the sound of a car engine, close at hand. Police cruiser inching up behind us? Don't look back.

Be cool.

Doors opening. 'Hey, you! Hold up there!'

Keep on walking. Side street coming up on your left.

Duck into that hardware store, sprint through and get out through the rear.

'You! Hold up!'

Must be talking to somebody else, 'cause we've got to be cool, so cool.

He turned the corner. Another Newbury Police cruiser, and a Vermont State Police cruiser as well, blocking the way.

Houston, he thought, we have got a big fucking problem here.

A quick spin on our heels, let's get into this video store and—

Before him were two cops, service weapons drawn, aiming right down at him. Drew let himself show some shock. 'What the hell is wrong?' he said, trying to act like a common citizen, don't put your hands up automatically because then they'll know you're not common, if we're quick and good maybe we can bullshit our way out of this.

The younger cop came forward, his eyes tight, getting that focused target look that Drew knew so well, and he yelled out, 'Hands up and down on your knees, you cop killer! Right now or we'll fucking shoot you right here!'

So much for bullshit. Oh, Sheila, I screwed up, it didn't work. From the corner of his eyes he could see another cruiser roll up, lights flashing, and then the loud and depressing sounds of helicopters. People started gathering in small groups, pointing and talking among themselves. He slowly sank down on his knees, hands up, then the younger cop came around and securely cuffed him and brutally shoved an elbow into his ear.

Drew gasped in pain and rolled to his side as the cop said, 'Fucking cop killer. That's what you get.'

He tried to clear his eyes and then gasped as the other cop

came forward and kicked him twice in the head, the boot feeling as heavy as stone as it struck his cheekbones. This cop leaned down and said, 'I lost a niece in Detroit 'cause of your fucking anthrax attack, asshole, so you better say your prayers that the Feds get to you quick.'

More noise, more pain, and he thought, Sheila . . .

People started moving around her, heading towards the center of town, and along with the thrumming of the helicopters there was the whooping of sirens. She started walking, thinking, Girlie, it is now time to get the hell out of here and get back up to that hill and wait for Drew.

She went past a copier/graphic store, and heard bits of conversation as people moved quickly past her:

'. . . just right now . . .'

'. . . cop killer they've been looking for . . .'

'. . . going to the town jail . . .'

It felt like all of her insides had just melted away to a cold slush. She grabbed the arm of an older woman, hand firmly in the grasp of a girl about nine or ten.

'Excuse me,' Sheila said, trying not to let the terror break through her voice. 'What's going on? Where's everyone going to?'

The woman smiled the smile of someone in the know, someone who had a secret and was about to reveal all. 'News just came over one of the NewsNet channels. Local cops got a lucky break and just caught one of those two terrorists who have been on the loose since killing that deputy sheriff over in New Hampshire.'

She could hardly say the word. 'Really?'

The woman nodded enthusiastically. 'Really. Come on, they're bringing him to the town jail, right now.'

Sheila numbly followed in the stream of people going down the narrow street, being jostled, her feet trampled, refusing to think anymore of what must have happened, what had happened because of that little trip to the general store, that written check.

In a moment she couldn't move anymore. Dozens of townspeople were jammed in beside her, along the sides of parked cars. Cruisers and unmarked police cars were pulled up outside the small brick building with the overhanging sign that said NEWBURY POLICE DEPT. People's necks craned back and forth. More helicopters seemed to be arriving at the open grass of the town common. Her mouth was dry and her hands were shaking. Her face felt wet and she knew she had to be crying.

'There he is!' came a shout, and there were other shouts and yells. About a half-dozen police officers and State Police were lined up, nightsticks held at chest level, as the crowd surged. Two police cruisers roared up and doors popped open, and the cops dragged a man from the rear of the cruiser, hands cuffed tightly behind him, shoulders hunched forward, blood running from his hair and along the side of the face. Sheila brought both of her hands up to her face and started keening as her man was brought inside and more shouts and threats echoed out.

She moved away blindly from the crowd and started walking and then started running. Long minutes passed as she got as far away as she could, until she was back up where they started, at that hill, and she grabbed Drew's pack and held it to her chest, and she started bawling aloud, thinking of what she had just seen, what she had just caused.

Sheila held Drew's pack even tighter and rocked back and forth, crying into the stillness of the woods.

EIGHTEEN

The Republican Presidential candidate Steve Forbes said today that the Ten Commandments should be posted in schools as 'the basis of this civilization'.

'The Koran is not the basis of this civilization; the Ten Commandments are,' Mr Forbes said.

Associated Press, September 20, 1999

In the end, the O's lost to the Sox, 4 to 3, but George Clemson didn't mind one bit. Nancy had taken him up on a dinner offer and they were at Sparky's, a drinkin' and eatin' establishment near Camden Yards, drinking Anchor Steam Beer and eating local blue crabs, using hammers to smash the claws and bodies. They spent long minutes there and George wished the night could last forever. Nancy laughed with him as he told jokes and stories and gossip about the department, and she replied with some equally sharp and funny stories about growing up in Baltimore and going to college.

After a while Nancy wiped some melted butter from her chin and leaned back in her chair, her top pulling up and revealing her flat brown belly. 'Are you having fun, George?'

'More fun than you know, rook,' he said.

'Good,' and she laughed some more and came forward. 'This place is getting too crowded. How about we go back to my place for a nightcap?'

There was a roaring sound in his ears as he could not believe his luck, as all of the blood in his body seemed to race to a warm and spongy area in his groin. 'Rook, that sounds just fine.'

She nodded, smiling. 'Then let's get out of here.'

Drew was on a hard-mattressed bunk, curled up on his side, his head and ribs and hands aching. He had been tossed into the cell a few hours ago, and some sort of food tray had been slid in, but he ignored it, ignored what had been given him. He knew he should be thinking of getting out, demanding a phone call, worrying about Sheila, but all he could think about was the ache and throb of the pain in his body.

And the ache of failure. Can't forget that, now, can we?

The ache of failure.

George Clemson followed that tight swinging butt up the stairway to Nancy's apartment, not thinking of home or the job or even his wife and kids, down in DC. All he could think about was that tight denim and what kind of delights the soft flesh was hiding, just for him. Nancy giggled some as she unlocked the door and went in, and—

What the hell? He stopped, confused and embarrassed and maybe even a bit excited, for in the apartment was another woman, looking up as they came in. She was white, blonde with short hair and wearing gray sweats and a Johns Hopkins T-shirt. She was sitting on a couch with a tan blanket over the side, working on a lapbot that was balanced on a cluttered coffee table in front of her. Nancy said, 'Hey Melanie, any calls?'

'Nope, not a one,' she said. 'How was the game?'

'Red Sox won, if you can believe it. Melanie, this is my

partner at work. George Clemson. George, this is my roomie and girlfriend, Melanie Fraser.'

George realized he was slightly drunk, so he forced himself to stand still, not to rock back and forth. 'Nice to meet you.'

Melanie smiled up at him. 'The same.'

Nancy grabbed his arm. 'C'mon, George, I promised you a nightcap. Let's get into the kitchen. Poor Melanie's probably still studying, right?'

They went into the kitchen and Melanie's voice called out. 'Sure. While you're out there enjoying baseball, I get to learn the A to Zs of bloodclots. Such fun.'

George took a seat at a tiny kitchen table with three mismatched chairs, his head feeling heavy, like it was lolling around his shoulders. Nancy went to a cabinet and pulled down a bottle of cognac, and George glanced around the small kitchen and stopped looking when he spotted the refrigerator. On the door were some refrigerator magnets, other knick-knacks and photos. All of them were of Nancy and Melanie. In most, they had their arms around each other, laughing it up for the camera.

Dear me, he thought. What in hell have we gotten into?

Nancy passed over a small snifter. 'Some cognac. Got it last Christmas from Melanie's mom. Nice stuff, don't you think?'

He had never tasted cognac in his life but tonight seemed as good a night as any. He sipped and felt his throat burn and said, 'How long have you been with Melanie?'

'She's been my roommate for over a year. We've been lovers for about two.'

The cognac seemed to crawl up his throat and baste his eyeballs. 'Really?' he managed to say, hating how his voice squeaked.

Nancy's snifter was halfway up to her lips when she stopped. 'Sure. I mean, well, you knew, didn't you?'

Let's see, idiot, fool and buffoon. What else can we call ourselves? George said, 'No, I guess I missed that. Oh.' Yeah, dummy, a brief fireworks display just went off in the dim recesses of your mind. 'Back a couple of days ago, when you said you were a minority three times over.'

She nodded, took a small sip of the cognac. 'An Asian woman who also happens to be gay. Quite a combination. It took me a while to accept who I was, where I came from, and what kind of people I love. And ever since I figured that out, I've never been happier.' Then her eyes narrowed and so did her voice. 'But I'm more than just that, no matter what fools like Lurry and his followers believe, or even some of the guys on the force. I'm a cop and a good American, and I'll fight anyone who thinks otherwise.'

George was suddenly tired and humiliated. All of those fantasies, all of those naughty little thoughts that had kept him going these past weeks, even up to and including this delightful afternoon at Camden Yards, had just crumbled into dust. He blinked a couple of times and picked up his own snifter, took a long swallow. He wished he had stayed home. The guilt was now rocketing through him, and he was suddenly glad this hadn't gone any further. He felt so awful now, he couldn't imagine how he would have felt if he had got her into bed.

'Well, rook, you have a long life and career ahead of you,' he said. 'Don't get into too many fights so soon. You won't have anything left.'

'Don't worry about me,' she shot back.

'Rook, when we're out on the streets, sometimes that's all I think about.'

And a half-hour later he went back home to his empty apartment and did nothing except fall asleep.

After the flight over from New York, Ira Woodman strode across the lawn of this small town's main park, hunched over as the still-spinning helicopter blades beat at his clothes. It was now Monday and Case Shiloh was set to begin tomorrow afternoon, and he wished he was in Boston where he belonged. But yesterday's meeting with Lurry and the others took longer than anticipated, and he had to be here, in Vermont, to eliminate one nagging loose end. A call to the police chief in this small town had put Drew Connor in isolation since his arrest yesterday. So after a restless night in another bland motel room in New York state, here he was. Wrap up this matter and back to Massachusetts we'll go, he thought. He had his cellphone in his hand and was dialing his home number. He shook his head at the insanity of it all. Just hours away from his rendezvous with history, and he had to keep things quiet on the home front. He hadn't been back in days and the few e-mail messages he had received from Glenda Sue – spelling errors and messages in ALL CAPITAL LETTERS, no matter how many times he told her how irritating that was – grew more and more angry.

Cops and plain-clothes officers and other hangers-on were crowding about him, and he went into the police station and found his way into a men's room as the phone started ringing on the other end. Oh, he wished he had Henry Harrison up here with him to run interference with all these yammerers, but he was down south, getting ready for the glorious day tomorrow. The bathroom was tiny and smelled like it hadn't been cleaned in a decade, and he gingerly sat down on the sole toilet as the phone was finally answered.

'Hello?' came the tentative voice.

'Glenda Sue, it's Ira,' he said. 'What's wrong?'

He thought for a moment that the connection had failed, for he heard nothing. He shifted his position and then heard her breathing and her quiet weeping.

'Oh, Ira . . .'

Something chilled inside of him. 'The children. Are the children all right?'

'Yes, yes,' came the voice through the tiny speaker. 'The children are fine . . . it's just that . . . Ira . . .'

He shifted the phone to another ear. 'Glenda Sue,' he said sharply. 'What's wrong?'

Sniffles and a deep breath. 'It's the downstairs toilet . . . It overflowed last night and the plumber says he can't be here until tomorrow . . . I cleaned it up and it just keeps running water over the floor . . . Oh, Ira, when are you coming home?'

Someone was pounding on the restroom door. Ira leaned over, now grasping the phone in both of his hands. He said a quick prayer to try to tamp down the anger he was feeling – Case Shiloh's security held up by a leaking toilet! – and said, 'Hon, I'm doing my very best. I'll be home tonight. Honest. I've got to go.'

'Ira . . .' came the plaintive voice, and he switched off the phone and put it in his coat. He got off the toilet and went to the sink – it once was white porcelain but now was a dirty gray – and splashed some water on his face. Just a few hours more. Then that cleansing light will rise up over DC and this country will be ours again. Just hold on. Don't lose it.

He stepped outside to the tiny set of offices of this police department, brushed past a couple of more cops and said to an older man in uniform with gold stars on his collar tabs, 'Are you the chief?'

'That's right, look, can we get some assistance here, I need to—'

Ira held up his leather-enclosed badge. 'Ira Woodman, Federal Emergency Response Agency. Under the Domestic Terrorism and Tranquility Act of 2001, I'm taking control of this prisoner. I want to see him. Alone.'

The chief's face reddened but he just nodded. 'All right. Give us a minute to clear some of these people out.'

Ira put his hands in his coat, just stared at his feet, feeling the comforting touch of his pistol in there. He thought about poor Mark Quentin, killed by this same pistol just a few days ago. He wondered if his spirit would be pleased at what just happened. The man ultimately responsible for his death had just been captured. Ira kept his face down. He knew if he raised his face up these cops and hangers-on would start badgering him with questions, and he didn't have the energy to face them. A voice inside him said, you're so tired now. What makes you think you'll be any better the day after Case Shiloh?

'Mr Woodman?'

He snapped his head up. The chief was holding open a steel-gray metal door. 'Right this way.'

Ira managed a smile – no use pissing off the locals unless you had to – and he walked behind the man. The chief asked a couple of questions but Ira just grunted in the right places. The chief wanted a full debrief, a press conference, a shared task force to investigate how this fugitive and terrorist had ended up in this town, and Ira felt sorry for the man. The biggest case in this old guy's career, and Ira was going to take it away from him in just a matter of minutes.

Then he found himself in a familiar room, with the same polished steel and concrete look of dozens of prisons he had visited in the past, complete with drains set in the center of the floor. The lights were on low and there was a man in a cell, sitting on a bed, resting his bloody head in his hands. A folding metal chair was set up about six feet away from the barred door.

Ira sat down in the chair, pulled his coat about his legs. The man ignored him. Ira cleared his throat, said, 'Drew Connor?'

The man raised his head, and Ira flinched for a moment. One side of his face was bloody and bruised, and dried blood had caked about his hair and an eyebrow. His lips were puffy as well. 'I take it you're not my lawyer, are you?'

'No. My name is Ira Woodman, I'm the—'

'—the Region One administrator for the Federal Emergency Response Agency,' he said, shifting about so he could stare at Ira. 'Yes, I know a lot about you, Ira Woodman. That you've been a good boy bureaucrat for a couple of years. That before you joined FERA you were in the Kentucky State Police. And that in this brave new world of yours that you and your goons are preparing, trespassing is a crime punished by murder.'

Ira felt his throat get dry, was thankful that this man was behind bars. 'You were trespassing. You weren't suppose to be in that facility.'

By now the man was grinning. 'But we fouled up your plans some, didn't we? Case Shiloh isn't that big a secret, is it now, Mr Woodman? Tomorrow the National Program Office, they're going off the reservation and are implementing a

COG plan, right? Take out everyone from the President to the Secretary of Veterans Affairs. Do you have that many assassins lined up? Do you?'

Ira grasped his hands together, lowered his voice. 'Why did you go into the recovery facility? Why did you hack my computer system? Who are you working for, Mr Connor? The CIA? FBI? Still with the Defense Research Agency?'

Drew smiled, a rictus look that was made even more horrible by the dried blood about his face. 'A few good folks. I'm sure you've heard of them. A Mr Jefferson. A Mr Madison. A Mr Hamilton. Guys who fought against you and your kind, who still fight against you, years and years later.'

'Don't be so confident of what those men may or may not have done,' Ira shot back. 'Thomas Jefferson once said that the tree of liberty must be refreshed from time to time by the blood of tyrants.'

The man kept on smiling, damn him. 'A revolution by quotable quotes. Not bad. Is this how it's going to be in your brave new world?'

'No, it's not,' Ira said sharply. 'It's going to be a country that maintains its sovereignty. A country that doesn't get entangled in foreign affairs, that minds its own business at home. A country that protects its borders from illegals. A country where the police and courts and government are run by honest, God-fearing people again. A country where you can say a prayer in school or at a ballpark without being sued. A country where marriages are between men and women, and the rights of the unborn are protected. A country where—'

'Oh, please shut up,' the man said, rubbing at the side of his head. 'You're beginning to sound like a Lurry campaign commercial. Is this what happens when your man loses an election? Hire a bunch of assassins to kill the upper reaches of the government and take over?'

Ira felt his hands grab at the hems of his coat. 'No, this is what happens when my man can't get treated fairly in an election. When his voice is drowned out by the oh-so-smug, oh-so-educated media and NewsNet elite, where chattering heads on cable shows dissect every poll, every appearance, every haircut, trying to get better ratings. When every avenue to a fair election is blocked off by an unelected elite that is responsible to no one, then that's what happens, Mr Connor.'

The man looked away, his voice now sounding tired. 'Was it hard, hiring those assassins, getting them into place? Or is it going to be multiple car bombs this time?'

Ira smiled, feeling at last a bit triumphant at seeing this fugitive finally behind bars. 'No, nothing so complicated. Very simple, indeed. One shot. That's all. Just one shot. So. Tell me again, who are you working for? Why did you make that phone call to me? Who told you to do that?'

Quiet. Somewhere the sound of a toilet flushing, a phone ringing. Ira went on. 'We recovered the check that was written at the general store under your name. You bought some items for your woman. Where is she?'

'Far away,' he said. 'Very far away.'

'And you did this all on your own, correct? You weren't part of any group, any agency?'

'No, but the word's getting out, you know,' Drew said, trying to smile through the blood and bruises. 'We've posted messages on lots of Net discussion groups, talking about Case Shiloh and what's happening.'

Ira shrugged. 'And just as fast we'll be posting messages saying that your messages are spam, are nonsense, mean nothing and just clog bandwidth.'

'You don't think anyone will notice?'

Ira was beginning to like this man in spite of himself. 'Mr Connor, not so long ago the Chinese military were donating millions to presidential campaigns and were also practically stealing our nuclear secrets from under our noses, and nobody paid attention, for years and years. For years! That was a hostile foreign country, trying to influence our elections, stealing our most valuable nuclear secrets. No one noticed for a long time. Why would they believe you or anyone else about Case Shiloh?'

The man rubbed at his face again. 'You know, I've met your kind before, over and over again. You sit in your comfortable offices, your comfortable dining rooms. You fight over who's up, who's down. You use every tool in your arsenal to get ahead, and sometimes those tools are young men and women who have volunteered to serve this country and their neighbors. And you have no hesitation to have them wounded, killed or abandoned, if it means an uptick of two or three percentage points in the latest poll. So you're going to kill a bunch of people in DC and put a two-time loser in office. Do you really think you'll have the country behind him?'

Ira stood up, feeling that sweet glow of triumph grow even more. 'Mr Connor, by this time next week the people of this nation will be naming their first-born children after Michaelson Lurry.'

Drew listened to the clanging of the door as Ira Woodman finally left him, and he sat there, hands clasped, feeling the aching start again, but not in his head or ribs or hands. Just deep inside. So close. He had been so close in getting in contact with the General, and now?

What were the chances of the General accepting a phone call from a police station, from a man accused of being a cop-killer?

Pretty slim. About as slim as thinking Case Shiloh would be halted before tomorrow.

He rubbed his bruised and bloodstained hands together.

As Ira Woodman walked out of the cell area, it was coming together in his mind. Get a cordon of these local yokel cops together, get this Drew character handcuffed and then brought back to the lead chopper, the one he flew in from after that head session with Lurry and the others. Then, when we're up to five or six thousand feet, the side door opens up and, oops, one Drew Connor, enraged at being captured and facing trial and possibly the death penalty, attempts to escape. And during this attempt he falls out of the helicopter. Messy and maybe a few questions being asked, but in less than two days this little event will be over-shadowed by something much bigger, much more urgent than the death of a suspected cop killer and terrorist.

And his woman friend? Who cares? What could she possibly do, hiding out there in the woods by herself?

Sure, he thought. In less than fifteen minutes this problem will be a hole in the ground, and we can get back home and try to settle up with Glenda Sue before she starts drinking again.

But then he stopped. By the chief's office were a couple of men dressed in gray suits, long black overcoats hanging over their arms. One of them stepped forward, with short red hair and a lightly freckled face carrying one pissed-off expression.

'Administrator Woodman?'

'The same,' Ira said. 'And you are?'

He held up a thin leather wallet, with photo and shield. 'Gil Summers, Assistant Attorney General with the Vermont Attorney General's office.'

Ira stood quite still. 'Nice to meet you, Mr Summers. And what can I do for you?'

The lawyer made a show of pulling out a folded-over sheaf of papers and handing it over to Ira, and Ira wished he could just let the damn papers fall to the ground. 'We're taking your prisoner, Mr Woodman, and placing him in the custody of the Vermont State Police. We don't take kindly to you and your kind running through the woods, trampling over our laws and police functions.'

Though the words sounded strange in his ears – especially since what he and the others were fighting for – Ira said them anyway. 'This man's case has been Federalized under the Domestic Terrorism and Tranquility Act of 2001. He belongs in the custody of the Federal Emergency Response Agency. His crimes have been Federal crimes. The State of Vermont doesn't have jurisdiction.'

'Well, we think we do,' he said, smirking slightly.

Ira tried something else. 'Look, what is this, a game? Your governor doesn't like Washington and everything else associated with it, right? So you've made your little protest. Fine. In some ways I'm sympathetic with you, Mr Summers. You want Drew Connor? Good. Feel free to have him for an hour. Then you can go out and make a stirring press conference in front of the TV and NewsNet people, about how the State of Vermont stood fast against the tyranny of DC. Then I'll take him out a back door or something and we've both had a full day. Your Green governor gets good PR and I get to keep my prisoner. Fair enough?'

The Assistant Attorney General shook his head. 'This isn't about scoring points or spin or anything else, Mr Woodman. This is something more important. About the sovereignty of Vermont and her laws. I'm sorry, I know that's something you don't understand, that some things are more important than spin.'

My God, Ira thought, the utter and complete irony of it all, that he should be blocked by someone who could be working for the movement. 'I understand it well, Mr Summers, but I'm afraid I must insist. This prisoner belongs to my agency, and if you continue to disagree I demand a court hearing as soon as possible.'

A sly little smile from the Assistant Attorney General. 'We thought you'd say something like that. So it's already been settled. A court hearing has been scheduled for 10 a.m. tomorrow.'

'Tomorrow? Impossible! I demand a hearing now, this matter has to be settled before the day is out.'

Summers stepped closer, and Ira wished Henry Harrison were here so that he could wipe that smile off without hesitation. 'Sorry, Federal man. What you demand and what you need doesn't matter here. What matters here is what my boss and my governor want, and what they want is a nice little court hearing tomorrow, in Barre. See you then.'

Ira clenched his fists, trying to salvage something from this fuck-up. 'Then you best be sure that Mr Connor is well guarded tonight. Having him escape from Vermont custody – no matter how temporary that custody may be – would be intolerable.'

Summers put his coat on, a satisfied look on his face. 'Don't worry. We won't lose your precious prisoner. When and if you get him, he'll be well fed, showered and shaved.'

'When we get him,' Ira said. 'When, not if.'

'Whatever,' the Assistant Attorney General said.

In Wellesley, Massachusetts, Henry Harrison, formerly of the US Navy and now with the Federal Emergency Response Agency, got up from the tile bathroom floor and started wiping down the tools he had used. Mrs Woodman had come to him a little while ago in his private quarters in the carriage house, weepy and maybe a bit sauced, looking for help.

No matter, he had thought, sighing. Working for Mr Woodman had its advantages, but there had always been the little extras that hadn't come with the job description. Like picking up laundry, ferrying the two little brats to Christian day school or soccer practice, and fixing the occasional leaking toilet.

Sir, one leaky toilet found, fixed same, he thought, putting the tools away. He was careful with his tools, always had been. Your tools – whether a power drill or M-16 or Zodiac boat or even a particular GMC van – would take care of you, but only if you took care of them.

'Henry! Henry, can you hear me?' came the voice from upstairs.

He stepped out into the hallway. 'Yes, Mrs Woodman, I can. What's up?'

'I think the toilet in the upstairs bathroom is leaking now. Can you come take a look?'

'Sure, I'll be right up,' he said, and quietly adding, 'you silly bitch.'

He grabbed the toolbox and went up the stairs, thankful at least the two kids weren't here. They were at some other rich neighbor's house, spending the night, so at least he wouldn't have to fix the little girl's dolly or answer inane questions from the boy, who was getting one hell of a weird education in this rich Massachusetts town.

In the bedroom Mrs Woodman was standing near the bed, a mixed drink glass in her hand, wearing a long green dressing gown. Vodka martini, Henry thought, the drink of choice for aging ex-beauty queens from Kentucky. 'Go right in,' she said.

'Sure.'

He entered the master bath, checked the floor and the toilet. Bone dry. He left the toolbox on the floor and went back out to the bedroom. Mrs Woodman had not moved, but she was looking down a bit to her glass as she took another sip, eyeing him.

'Everything looks fine in there, Mrs Woodman,' he said.

'Well, imagine that,' she said, her voice slightly slurred.

'Yeah,' he said. 'Imagine that.'

He went up to her quickly and slapped the glass out of her hand and then grabbed an arm and pulled and twisted it around. She yelped in pain as the dressing gown flew open, revealing a shapely black teddy and nothing else. Henry threw her down on the bed, pulled the gown aside and reached down to the teddy.

'What the hell!' she screamed. 'What the hell are you doing!'

With his free hand he grabbed a fistful of hair and pushed her head into the pillow, as her cries were muffled. In another few moments, using his other hand, he tore apart her teddy and then tugged down his jeans. He entered her quickly and then went to town savagely as her screams and shouts continued to be silenced by the pillow since he kept a strong hand at the base of her neck.

He didn't last as long as he wanted – it had been a while – and a few minutes later he was in the bathroom, drinking from Mr Woodman's water glass, washing his crotch with a wet cloth. Along the way he had lost his shirt, socks and shoes. He went back out to the bedroom. Mrs Woodman was laying on her side, what was left of the teddy shrouding her belly and still impressive chest. She was smiling.

'Thanks,' she said. 'I really needed that.'

He smiled at her. 'Glad to serve.'

'You ready for another round?' she asked, winking.

'Sure,' he said. 'But you're sure Mr Woodman isn't coming back tonight?'

She rolled her eyes. 'Enough of him, already.' She patted the side of the bed. 'You just lay down here and let me do all the work this time.'

Henry stifled a yawn as he laid down on the big bed. He was scheduled for a late flight tonight from Boston, but he had enough time for one more round. 'You're the boss, Mrs Woodman.'

She reached over and bit him on the ear, hard. 'Yes,' she said. 'And don't you ever forget it.'

The crying had stopped but not the tears as Sheila remained hidden among a small collection of saplings and boulders, all of their gear here, the day after Drew's capture. She had dragged it through the dirt, even remembering to take a branch to wipe away the trail, scared of staying any longer in the cabin, but she knew it was worthless, everything was worthless. Drew had been captured and it was all her fault, all her damn fault that her man was now in jail. She rested against a moss-covered boulder, shivering, the sharp edges of the rock digging into the back of her shirt, and she didn't care. It hurt and that was fine, for everything else was hurting.

It was getting dark and a wind had come up, chilling her. Lots of things were bouncing around up in her mind, all of them chattering at her, screaming at her, chiding her. You're weak. You're so weak and fragile and because of that your man is in jail. He's hurt and bleeding and it's all your fault, all your fault. A box of tampons and some pills, is that what your man is worth? Is it? Not even twenty dollars' worth of goods, and you were ready to sacrifice him. There. Feel better now?

'No,' she whispered to the darkness. 'No, I don't.'

Then something else. A different voice. Stronger. Confident. Oh, come on now, the voice said. Let's stop this whining and start thinking, shall we? We're in trouble, deep trouble, and are we going to fix it if we sit up on this hill and freeze tonight, and cry so much our eyes bleed? Is that it, girlie? Ready to quit so soon?

'No,' came another whisper. 'No, I'm not.'

She got up and started going through the backpacks, opened hers and took out her lapbot. She also unrolled a sleeping bag – thankfully now dry – and wrapped it around her legs. She leaned back against the boulder until she found a more comfortable spot and powered up her lapbot. As it went through the booting-up process, she closed her eyes, thinking. Drew, my Drew, I've got you into trouble. And I don't know how I'm going to do it, but I'm going to get you out. Honest I am.

There. Lapbot up and running. She ran her fingers across the worn and familiar keys, and for a moment felt a deep ache of shame. She had no money. Whatever she was going to do in the next few hours would require money, lots of it.

There was no other choice, no other way of getting money save for one. Her chest ached but she went on, surprised that she was no longer weeping.

Good. There was no time for tears.

She logged on, then went through one Web server, and then to another. From there she dialed in a number that was burned into her memory, and in a few minutes of keystrokes everything was reactivated. No wonder. This site had been a nice little goldmine for wherever it was located, and even though it had been years the people who ran it probably always wondered if she would come back.

Wonder no more, she thought, typing in the letters that she had once thought for sure would cause her to break down and cry but now only caused her to look eagerly at the screen. Money, she thought, we've got to make some serious money, and soon.

The letters appeared on the screen, blood-red against black.

SALLY FROM SEATTLE IS BACK. WHO'D LIKE TO STRANGLE ME FIRST?

SIDEBAR III

Luis Raminez got home hot and sweaty from a day down on the Galveston docks. Maria glared at him as he went into the kitchen, dropped his lunch pail on the table.

'Well, what is it?' he asked.

She had her arms folded above her beautiful belly. 'How do you know something is wrong?'

He smiled as best as he could in the face of her anger. 'My little one, I may not read as well as you do, but I can read your face quite well. What is it?'

She motioned with her shoulder. 'Next door. The Anglos. Look down the side of our driveway, all the trash that they dumped there. Our new neighbors, that's how they throw their garbage out. By tossing it over the fence. In our yard. Some way to fit in our neighborhood, eh? And that's not all. I also found out that they don't even have jobs. They're on assistance. You and me, in our taxes, we're paying for them. Isn't that something?'

He rubbed at his face. Just a few days ago everything had been good. There had been the constant worries and pressures of paying the bills each month, trying to grab some extra OT from Mister Trong to sock away in the baby's fund, and those regular visits to the doctor that always filled him with a quiet terror until Maria came out all smiles.

But that was nothing to how he felt today. Their little home, their little place in the sun, had been invaded. He sighed and went over to the kitchen sink, opened up the door below and took out a couple of plastic trash bags. 'I'll take care of it. Right now.'

'Fine,' Maria said sharply. 'But what about tomorrow?'

'Tomorrow will take care of itself,' he shot back as he went out to their narrow driveway. Blessed Mary, did the woman expect him to force the Anglos to move out all by his lonesome?

He walked down the driveway, which ended in a high wall of shrubbery. A chain-link fence covered by shrubbery and brush separated their small yard from the Anglos'. There. He wondered how he had missed it, coming in just a few minutes ago.

On his hands and aching knees he picked up the tin cans, empty Lone Star beer bottles, rib bones and other crap that had been dumped. He was tired and thirsty and one pissed-off hombre that he'd have to come home from work and pick up somebody else's shit. Real neighborly, wasn't it? Frigging Anglos. He got up and cursed his aching back, then heard the music again. Accordions and strange voices. He peered through an opening in the shrubbery into the back-yard of the Anglo home. In a rear window he saw shapes.

There was a tall, gangly man with a black beard and shaved head talking with his hands to a short, dumpy woman. A couple of kids were bawling and hanging onto the woman's hips. Luis shook his head in disgust and headed back to the house. Goddamn Anglos, had to move in here and ruin his neighborhood. And he and his wife had paid for the privilege. What a wonderful country.

In Herndon, Virginia, Roscoe Gilmanton kept up his daily routine, marching to and fro in front of the small office building with the tiny windows and big parking plot. He held a sign up that said HERE IS THE GATEWAY TO HELL. In the months of his protests he had got used to the stares, the laughs, the rude comments sent his way by the people who worked in the building.

Hey, Roscoe, they would shout, how's God treating you this week? Then they would laugh and laugh as they went into their office building, the center of evil in this poor country. And he would remain out here, in wind and rain and hot and cold weather, protesting the work those people did in that small building. For in that building were rows and rows of computers lined up one atop of each other. Roscoe didn't know that much about computers but he did know about the Net and the evil that resided there. Pictures of men, women, and children performing every act of physical filth possible. Chat rooms where adultery ruled. Web pages honoring the disgusting totems of this society, from those glorifying abortionists to those in tribute to cartoonists such as those responsible for Deffy and Kate.

No, Roscoe didn't know much about computers, but he had read a few times about this building in a suburb of Virginia. For here were the computers that controlled and guided that spawn of Satan, the Internet, and Roscoe was no longer content to protest. He was now ready for action, and had been for a long time.

At his waist and underneath his coat was a pager, and when he received a certain signal tomorrow he would go into this building with a special coat, one lined with explosives and incendiary devices. Then he would set everything off, and while he would regrettably die in his death would be salvation, for he would cripple the Net. The coat was provided to him by a friend he had met while working on both

Lurry campaigns, a friend who knew him well and knew why he was out here, protesting.

A luxury sports car purred by, and another young male computer engineer looked up at him, jeering again. 'Hey, Roscoe. God treating you good today?'

He gingerly touched the pager at his side. 'Better than you know, my friend.'

On a low wall that bordered a fountain in this part of Wall Street, Phelan McBride ate his lunch, letting his feet dangle some over the sidewalk. The sun was bright but you wouldn't know it from the height of these concrete coffins blocking out most of the sunshine. About his feet were some of the few creatures that thrived in this environment, the usual rock gray pigeons, walking around, looking for handouts, looking for anything to survive.

Phelan ate his sandwich and sipped at a cup of tomato soup, which he carried in a battered blue thermos bottle. People moved in long streams up and around him on the sidewalks, most carrying briefcases and talking urgently into their little cellphones. The most advanced ones, of course, had little headsets so they could talk and look down at a handheld lapbot, see how their stocks or funds or bonds or whatever paper shit they relied on was doing.

As he ate a little tune ran through his head, anarchy, sweet anarchy, my lovely and deadly anarchy. He closed his eyes, tried to put himself back home in Oregon. Out in the high woods by Rogue River. Walking along the shores of Cape Lookout by moonlight, stripping down and swimming in the cold, cold Pacific. Climbing the high ranges of the Cascades. Sweet, sweet, anarchy. And here . . . Well, he lived over on the East Side, in what was called the meatpacking district. Narrow streets, even more narrow people. He stayed there as long as he could, day in and day out, but some nights he would have to escape. He would take an EMS sleeping bag and mattress pad and take the subway and get off at Central Park and find a place he could crawl into and spend the night in the outdoors. But it was never quite good enough. The sirens, the shouts, the ever present hum of the damn machine, humming and consuming and raping and killing all about him.

Anarchy, sweet anarchy . . .

There were a few laughs as some of the Wall Street players came by him, and Phelan allowed them their humor as he opened his eyes and finished his lunch. Some months ago he had been approached by someone with a plan, something important, something vital. Somebody he trusted in the movement, someone who hated the Machine as much as he did. And it involved this little blue thermos bottle, and getting a job in the Babylon on the Hudson, working in the belly of the beast. He had suffered during the months working here, but at his side was a pager, and by tomorrow the pager should go off on a certain code.

Tomorrow he would go to work with an identical little blue thermos bottle, except this one would have a little surprise inside. He would go into a men's room in one of the office buildings and leave it behind in the ceiling over one of the toilets, and an hour later, just as the beast and Machine were in the middle of another hectic trading day, the little surprise would go off. Phelan didn't know the ins and outs of how the new, improved thermos bottle worked, but he knew what was going to happen. A little burst of energy would spew out and magically erase every hard drive, floppy disk and storage system in the office building. And from what Phelan could figure out, there were other little thermos bottles around here as well, secured by people just like him.

Anarchy, sweet anarchy . . .

He folded his arms and hugged himself with glee. Imagine what would happen to all these suits when they realized all their paper and electronic wealth had gone poof! Just like that! Then the Machine would burp and grind to a halt, and people would flee, and then the wonderful chaos would descend. And Phelan imagined coming back in five years or ten, and sleeping out at night in Central Park and hearing nothing except the sounds of animals, reclaiming what had once been theirs.

Ah, sweet anarchy . . .

The sniper settled in for one of the last nights he would have to be out here. Things had been fairly quiet since the incident with that yellow Lab back a couple of days, and the only concern he had was when a group of men had suddenly appeared in the football field behind the school. They had talked amongst each other, had looked around and talked in handheld radios, and two of them had marched around with a long measuring tape, checking the dimensions of the field.

Later a dark green Blackhawk helicopter had gone overhead and he had remained quiet in his hidey-hole, just waiting. The helicopter made a few touch and go passes on the football field, and then had left. Later a couple of men in black jumpsuits walked around the field with German shepherds. Now, as darkness fell, it was quiet and still. There were just a few security lights on at the school, and the only sound was the low humming of traffic out on Highway 9.

The sniper took out his spotting scope, began scanning the area. This was the only entertainment he allowed himself, looking out at night. There were no radio, no books, no lapbots, nothing that would change his focus. But he didn't want to be bored, and using the nightscope was a good way to kill a few hours before getting to sleep. He had become familiar with the night sky and knew the features of the moon as well as his own living room, but there was a slight haze in the air, blocking out most of the stars.

There weren't that many homes near the school that were visible, but he did watch a young family have dinner – and together, at a dining room table, without a TV or lapbot, how delightfully old-fashioned – and for a while he saw a hot-tub bubbling away in someone's rear deck, but he turned away when an old man who looked to be about ninety shuffled out naked and slid into the waters.

He was about to call it a night when he spotted the movement, off to his left, about as far as he could see. Headlights from a car, going up another hill, on a dirt road, it looked like. The car stopped and the doors popped open. Two guys and a girl stumbled out, carrying cigarettes and glass bottles. He focused in. All were white. The guys looked about to be in their twenties, the young girl, well, he wasn't sure, but she was much younger. They were at the end of a dirt road in a little turnaround area, and then the girl started kissing one of the guys. The other guy sat on a flat rock, drinking. They were illuminated by the headlights of the car.

'Young love, how grand,' he whispered, still watching. He enjoyed being a voyeur, and always considered it training for his job. So no apologies.

Then he blinked and rubbed at his eyes at what he saw next. The guy on the rock got up and smashed his bottle on the back of the girl's head. She fell and then the two guys started talking, and the one who had been kissing her went back to the car and came back with a blanket. He spread the blanket over the rock and the two of them dragged the girl onto it, and soon both guys had their pants around their ankles as they got to work.

The sniper sighed. In a matter of moments he could get his Remington out and with his nightscope splatter both of those guys' brains – what little they had – over that poor suffering girl. It would be an easy shot. But still . . . he had been paid for a specific mission. That's all. Nothing vigilante. And if he took out these two bozos, it might upset the mission he had been hired for. And he couldn't allow that.

He went back to the spotter scope. The two guys were done, and he saw one laughing as he folded up a knife. Another visit back to the car and the blanket was rolled up over the girl's body and was securely tied, and then dumped over the side of the hill. The two guys went back into the car and the sniper sighed again. Once upon a time in Georgia he had been an Eagle Scout. Hard to believe, but he still had the medal somewhere among his belongings. Then he had joined the Army and had developed a special skill, and when he mustered out of the Army others had hired him and sent him on different jobs, jobs he had enjoyed. And with each different mission, the boy who had once been an Eagle Scout had receded far, far away, until he was practically dead. All that remained was the now.

The sniper put his spotting scope away and went to sleep in a matter of minutes.

NINETEEN

Eligible voter turnout in 1960 presidential election: 62.8 percent.
Eligible voter turnout in 1996 presidential election: 49.0 percent.

The 1999 World Almanac

Clem Badger tried to fall asleep Monday night but it wasn't working, and he knew it was more than just the caffeine from the UnderTow soda still rampaging through his blood vessels. He was back in his apartment, in his den, relaxing on his bed among the familiar sheets and blankets, but something wasn't right. Yesterday had been one of his better days, hell, even Mr Woodman had been full of praise for him – that little utility work number had gotten a lot of their assets in the right place when that general store alert had come in – and he had even promised Clem a couple of steps up in his next promotion review.

But . . . damn it, there was something missing, something not right.

Swearing, he got up and shambled into his work area, not bothering to dress. The three-room apartment, bedroom, office area and combination kitchen/dining area – and when was the last time he had turned on the stove? – was on Beacon Hill in Boston, and he would have never been able to afford it if it hadn't been for the extra funds Mr Woodman steered his way for all that Case Shiloh work. Clem knew a lot about Case Shiloh, more than Mr Woodman probably ever imagined, and that wasn't an issue as far as Clem was concerned. He didn't plan a trip to DC tomorrow, and his name wasn't on any of the arrest lists, and as long as he kept working and remained wired to the very best in access systems, he didn't care if King Charles came over from the UK to rule.

He settled down in his office chair, the cool leather feeling good against his skin. He looked at the blank screen of his computer, just waiting. Sometimes he liked to stare at the glossy darkness of the screen before powering everything up, before getting waist-deep in data. There were traffic sounds and music from a party up the street, but he continued to stare at the blank screen.

So. What was bothering him?

Let's do some narrowing down, shall we? All right. Had to be something to do with the arrest yesterday. What of it? The fact that the woman was still on the loose? So what. She'd be hunted down, soon enough. It was the Drew guy that everyone was worried about, the commando type from the DoD who got himself captured. That was the one people were hepped up about. Gotta get this Drew guy. He knows too much. He'll be able to figure out what was going on by that brief visit last week to the Northern New England Recovery Center. True. So he had been the focus. The woman had been an afterthought, a witness. No big deal.

Get the commando first, and by gum, that's just what they did.

He felt along the arms of his chair and smiled. Of course, that big bad commando did something stupid, didn't he?

Cashing a check at a general store. Not too bright. Not the kind of thing you'd expect from a commando . . .

Shit, he thought, rubbing at his forehead, but that's the kind of thing you'd expect from a woman, right? Right. Hon, gotta get some supplies, don't you worry about me. So that's what probably happened. She used one of his checks and boom, he got captured.

Another smile in the darkness. Bet you he's one pissed-off commando. Lucky for Mr Woodman and everybody else that he was in that town when he got caught, when those cops . . .

Hold on, hold on, he thought, now powering up the computer, now seeing what was bothering him. Damn it, should have caught it before.

Where had Drew been spotted?

Making a phone call.

All right, genius, one and all, who was he calling? And what was he saying?

'Oh shit, this might be good,' he thought, setting up his connections, getting everything ready, not worrying about sleep anymore. Find out who Drew was calling and Mr Woodman will be one happy boss, real fucking happy, and who knows what kind of goodies might come his way. And finding out who Drew was calling? Clem almost laughed out loud. Bell Atlantic was known as Shell Atlantic to hackers everywhere, because getting in and out of their system was a challenge only to myopic fifth-graders, if that. Just find out the phone booth that Drew had been using, narrow down the time, and boom! One more happy supervisor and lots more goodies for one Clem Badger.

But just when he was about to get to work a little rotating icon in the upper left-hand corner of the screen caught his eye. It was a dagger, blood dripping off its blade, and it was moving about in little circles, blood spray coursing out.

His mouth got dry. Could it be, after all these years? Really and truly? There had been a couple of false alarms before, but maybe, just maybe . . .

He double-clicked on the icon, went through three password-protected gates, then started murmuring in excitement, hardly believing what he saw.

SALLY FROM SEATTLE IS BACK. WHO'S FIRST TO STRANGLE ME?

BIDDING IS NOW UNDERWAY AND CLOSES IN ONE HOUR, TWENTY MINUTES, THIRTY-THREE SECONDS . . .

Clem started running through some numbers in his head, thinking about his checkbook balance, what might be available in some offshore accounts, hardly believing that she was coming back, and when he started the process that got him into the bidding – he preferred knifework over noosework, but with Sally from Seattle back he wasn't going to be picky – he thought for a moment about tracking down that phone number for Mr Woodman.

But just for a moment.

Sally from Seattle was back and it had been a very long time.

It wasn't that dark in the cell early Tuesday morning but Drew kept his eyes closed, the better to focus, the better perhaps to fall asleep. But sleep had never come during the past hours, during his second long night in jail. Too many little things rolling around in his mind, like a fistful of marbles in a tin cup. Rattle-rattle, too much noise to allow sleep, which was a bad thing. Exhaustion was as dangerous as being shot at. You get too tired, you can make mistakes, dumb ones, that end you up in a jail cell.

Like Sunday afternoon, right? Trying to get a phone call out to the good General. Should have been smarter, should have scoped out a home out in the boonies around this small town, find a place that was empty. A few minutes of magic with whatever locks were there and he could have found a phone, easy enough. But nope, we had to be legal and a law-and-order type, fighting against a group that had their own interpretation of law and order that involved internment centers.

Sorry 'bout that, he thought. Looks like things are on a big giant railroad track, heading for a wreck, and he couldn't make that one single phone call. He wondered what Sheila was doing, where she was going. He had told her to stay put, not to put herself in any jeopardy, but still . . . damn woman had come into town after him and had exposed herself by buying some groceries. What in hell had she been thinking?

He opened his eyes. There was the sound of a door opening. He wondered what time it was and his stomach grumbled. He had skipped dinner again, which hadn't taken much effort. There had been a cola drink in a cup – he had tossed it out in the metal sink and drunk tap water – and two cold cheeseburgers wrapped in paper. He had carefully looked through the burgers, saw where some helpful cook's assistance had rubbed dirt and dead ants on both patties, and had crushed them up and tossed them out onto the common area floor. Just like the day before.

Sure is nice to be hated, he thought. Nice to give people something to talk about.

'Hey,' came a voice. 'You up for breakfast?'

He turned and looked through the bars. A young cop was

there, hair cut short to a stubbly bush, face looking like it felt a razor every other week. He had a tray in his hands. His name tag said Flynn.

'Sure,' Drew said, 'I guess I am.'

'Then back away from the cell. Sit on the bunk, back up against the far wall.'

Drew did just that and the tray came under the barred door and onto the floor. There was a cup of coffee that he ignored – too easy to add some disgusting liquid – but there was a cellophane-wrapped plain doughnut that looked okay and an unopened carton of orange juice. He was opening the carton of orange juice when something flashed in his eyes, again and again.

'What the—' and he backed away as the cop lowered a small digital camera from his face. 'Sorry 'bout that,' Flynn said, smiling. 'My kid's only three but we're working on set-ting up a college fund. I figured a couple of pix of you, sent to the right tabloid or NewsNet channel, could earn us a few thousand.'

Drew said, 'Bring me a phone right now, and I'll be able to pay you whatever you want. Five thousand, ten thousand, fif-teen thousand.'

The young man's smile faltered. 'Now, you just shut up and eat your breakfast. You're getting close to bribing a police officer. That other thing, that's my own set-up. I don't cotton to getting money from a cop killer.'

'I'm not a cop killer, and I can prove it,' Drew said, think-ing frantically. 'C'mon, one phone call. You know I'm supposed to get one, and I haven't seen a phone since I've been here.'

'Sorry, that's my sergeant's call, not mine.' And the cop took one more picture for good measure, and then left.

'Shit,' Drew muttered, sitting on the thin cushion of the bunk, balancing the tray on his knees. As he drank the orange juice and ate the doughnut – stale, but he had eaten worse – he looked again at his surroundings. No window. Just the cot, sink and toilet. Barred door opened by an electronic lock somewhere else in the booking room. In movies this was where the hero managed to devise a smoke bomb or some other infernal device to blow a hole through the wall and then to freedom.

Not this hero, he said, touching the scabs on his face. Today was the day. Only thing this hero could do now was survive, and see what chances he could get. Maybe he would get a phone call, and try the general one more time. Or maybe he'd be part of a perp walk and he could yell out something about Case Shiloh, maybe get somebody's attention. Or—

The same cop's voice, 'Hey, you in there. Get ready for a visitor.'

There was the clicking sound of heels on the concrete floor and Drew looked up. A woman approached, in a dull red business suit, jacket and short skirt, black heels on. She had a black purse hanging from a shoulder and was carrying a soft leather briefcase. Her nearly white blonde hair was down to her shoulders.

She nodded to the police officer. 'I need to interview the prisoner, right away,' she said.

Flynn looked troubled. 'I don't think we can let you into the cell.'

She rolled her eyes. 'Who said anything about a cell? Don't you have an interview room available?'

'Yeah, we do, but I'll need another cop to help me escort the prisoner there.'

The woman looked at Drew, her gaze unwavering. 'Then do it, officer. Mr Woodman from FERA can't afford to waste any more time, and neither can I.'

'And who are you?' Drew asked.

'Tanya Selenekov,' she said. 'And two things, Mr Connor. I work for Mr Woodman, not for you, and I ask the questions.'

The phone rang and George Clemson rolled over, sighing, his mind still spinning from Sunday night's stupidity. The bed felt twice as large without Carol nearby, slumbering and sometimes snoring, and while he usually enjoyed the feel of a nice big empty bed he hadn't had too much sleep these past couple of days. Monday had been a day off from work, and he had hung around the apartment, too embarrassed to go outside, humiliated by what had gone on Sunday night after the baseball game. Stupid old man, letting his little head blind his big head over what was really going on with his partner Nancy. Fool. He was certain that in some odd way, his wife Carol would have found some humor in it. Of course, he thought, only after she had taken a frying pan to his head. Now, he was just a couple of hours away from seeing Nancy on the job, and he wondered how that particular shift was going to work out. Fool.

He reached over to the nightstand and brought the receiver to his head. ''Lo?'

'George, hon, how're you doin'?' came the familiar voice.

He sat up, rubbed at his chin, feeling the bristles there, tasting the foulness in his mouth. 'Hey, babe,' he said, knowing his voice sounded like a croak, 'I'm doing okay. How's your sister? How's the kids?'

'Kids are doing fine,' his wife said. 'Here, let me put 'em on.'

So for the next few minutes, while George stared up at the ceiling and that same damn stain in one corner, and while his bladder was insistently demanding to be emptied – right now, if not sooner! – he grunted at appropriate spots while his two daughters prattled on. He loved both girls dearly but within a minute or two of each of them getting on the phone he was lost as they went on and on about boys met, parties attended, and stores shopped at.

'Okay, yep, love you both,' he said, and then the phone clunked around some more as his son got on. 'Dad?'

'Yeah, boy, right here,' he said, rolling on his side, thinking that maybe that would help take some of the pressure off his bladder. 'Those girls treating you all right?'

'Sure, Dad, it's okay now,' he said, his voice sounding excited over the phone. 'You know what we did yesterday?'

'Nope, what was that?' Jesus, why did he have to drink so much before going to bed last night?

'We were at the Air and Space Museum, for the whole day, finally,' Clarence said. 'They had a special exhibit on the space shuttle, and they asked for a couple of kids to volunteer to be a pilot for the demonstration, and I got picked, Dad, I got picked! And afterwards I met this astronaut, a Colonel Powell, he shook my hand and I got my picture taken with him! An astronaut, Dad, I met a real live astronaut!'

Clarence went on, talking and talking about the astronaut he had met, the space shuttle he had flown, and maybe it was time to look at taking some extra courses at his high school on aeronautics, and on and on and on, and George started smiling. His bladder was set to explode, and he still had his family in this dumpy apartment, and their combined savings were probably less than a thousand dollars, but Clarence was back on track. No more talk of the Africa

Corps, no more talk about dropping out of school, no more talk that scared his mother so. It felt good knowing Clarence was on his way.

Then more clunking noises and Carol came back on the phone. 'Lord, I thought those three were about ready to melt the phone lines. You okay up there?'

'Sure am,' he said.

'And what were you up to Sunday night?' she asked. 'I called but there was no answer.'

'Caught the O's game with some guys from work,' he said, only feeling slightly guilty, and even more relieved. 'No big deal.'

'Well,' she said, her voice dropping down to a whisper. 'When we get back in two days, you better have a big deal waiting for me. I miss you, sleeping alone.'

His smile grew wider. 'I miss you, too, babe.'

A laugh. 'Good! Now get to work 'fore I make you late.'

Later, after a visit to the bathroom and a shower and shave, he sat alone at the kitchen table, sipping a good cup of coffee, surprised at what he felt. He felt good, waiting here for just a few minutes, knowing his loved ones would be coming home soon. Nothing major, nothing earth-shattering, nothing that would make him stand on the street corner and start preaching. He just felt good, and that was enough.

When he got out into the hallway and locked the door to their apartment, he realized that he had gone most of the morning without thinking once of his partner, Nancy Thon Quong.

And that was good, too.

Another morning, yet another anonymous motel room. After shaving and showering, Ira Woodman sat on the edge

of the unmade bed and spent a fruitless few moments, looking for a room service menu. All he found was a Gideon
Bible inside the top drawer of the small dresser. He made a
phone call to the front desk and learned there was neither
room service nor restaurant, just a place where coffee, dough-
nuts and Danishes were served. And since the place was full
up, the woman at the front desk suggested that he 'hurry up,
hon'.

'Go to hell, hon,' he said, hanging up the receiver. He
picked up the phone again and called home to Wellesley. He
let it ring twenty-three times before hanging up. He wondered where Glenda Sue was, and what she was doing. He
dialed one more number, that of the carriage house, and he
let that one ring thirty-four times. No answer there either,
but he wasn't surprised. Henry Harrison was probably well on
his way south, and my, that sounded fine.

Despite being hungry and unsettled from another night in
another strange room he felt a smile on his face. This was it,
this was the day, the day he had been working for, year after
year. By this time tomorrow, it would all be different. So
what if he had a court appearance in a few hours to decide
the fate of Drew Connor. So what. In fact, he was tempted to
skip the damn thing. Let the whole friggin' state of Vermont
keep him. What possible difference could it now make?

He got dressed and, whistling, picked up the Gideon Bible
to find a passage that would give him solace during this day,
the last day of the old United States. He opened up the flyleaf
and sat down on the bed. Inside, just under the inscription
from the Gideons, was this little charmer: *This fucking book is
full of shit, as much shit as the people who believe in it. Sammy.*

Ira gently rubbed at the page and then tore it out and
folded it in half, then quarters. He carefully placed it inside

his notebook – *I am the Grand High Executioner* – for later work, even if it meant tracking down every person who had stayed in this room the past six months.

There was no statute of limitations for blasphemy.

Cyrus Montgomery sat at the foot of the waterfall on his property thinking of what he had seen a while ago from his office. He had spent some time on-line, checking his e-mail and finding nothing there except the usual book and NewsNet offers as well as spam. He tended to delete all of his e-mail, except this time there was a mail message that had something interesting in its subject line: CASE SHILOH? WHAT DOES IT MEAN?

He had double-clicked on that icon, saw that yes, it was spam: 'Case Shiloh, Case Shiloh, sounds like a Civil War game. Right? Wrong! XXX-rated teen strippers will strip for you! Click here for more info!'

So. Just spam. And that would have been it, except he decided to dig a little deeper. Why hook up the Case Shiloh name with something like strippers? Didn't make sense.

'Unless you're looking to hide a trail,' he had whispered as he went deeper into the discussion groups and search engines and found dozens and dozens of messages:

Case Shiloh, the best beer you've ever tasted.
Case Shiloh, a Civil War set of games that are the very best.
Case Shiloh, a place where you can find peace and tranquility.

And on and on and on.

Now, well, what now? He went for a walk and ended up here, by the waterfall. His Scribe – a bandage still on his face from the previous day's attack – had been horrified at the thought of him going for a walk on his own. But Cyrus would have it no other way. Eventually he had compromised, and come out here with a 9 mm Beretta strapped to his hip – one of his many souvenirs from his JCS days – and a pager, in case Blakely saw something trying to cross over the fence.

He stretched out his legs. This stream was just a trickle when it went through the north end of his property, and by the time it reached this point it moved right along and dumped in this small pool. All about it were rocks and tall grass and some cattails, and from here the stream moved slower south. That was about the only gap in the fence, in a swampy area where the stream petered out. Still, even there he had installed surveillance equipment and little tell-tales to tell him what was going on.

So. Case Shiloh. All that spam meant something, something that was serious enough to get this kind of attention.

Serious enough to try to get him killed.

He sighed. Usually a trip to this place soothed and comforted him, but as he looked up at the rocks and the tall firs, all he saw were hiding places, spots that hid people intent on killing him.

All because of two words.

Case Shiloh.

The interview room in the police station was small, with four battered wooden chairs set around a wooden table bolted to the floor. The surface of the table was scarred with old coffee stains and burn marks from cigarettes. Off to the left wall was a mirror that was obviously one-way glass, with curtains on both sides.

Officer Flynn had escorted him in, and Drew found his waist and ankles chained to one of the chairs. His hands were also cuffed to a long chain that had been bolted underneath the table. When Officer Flynn was finished he offered to stay in the room and the woman gave him a withering look. 'I think I can handle it from here. If you'll excuse us, you can stand outside. I'll call you if I need you.'

So that's what happened. When the door had shut the woman stood up and went over to the curtains and pulled them over. She sat down and put her soft leather briefcase on the table. It had a new leather smell. 'Comfortable?' she asked.

'Not bad,' Drew said.

'Good,' she said. She opened up the briefcase and swung it around so he could peer inside. He saw a 9 mm pistol resting there on top of some legal pads.

'Think you can do something with that?' she asked.

'Yes,' he said carefully. 'But I think our best bet might be getting Officer Flynn back in here.'

'Agreed,' she said. As she stood up and went around the table, she paused for a moment as he reached into the open bag and took the familiar weight of the pistol and put it in his lap. His heart was thumping and he was no longer tired or thirsty or hungry. Just ready. He popped the clip out, saw that it was full of rounds, then popped it back into the pistol.

The door went open a bit. 'Officer Flynn, if you please,' she said. 'I've changed my mind. Would you mind coming in here for just a minute?'

Officer Flynn came in, grinning, and Drew looked up for just a moment then stared at the far wall. The FERA woman motioned to the chair next to her and they both sat down.

Drew took a deep breath. Here we go. With a fluid motion of his hand he snapped back the slide to the 9 mm and Officer Flynn's features slumped and his skin paled as he recognized the sound.

'How in—' he started.

'Here's the deal, Officer,' Drew interrupted, staring right at him. 'I've got a pistol pointed right towards your crotch. You do anything out of the ordinary, right from the start, I'm going to shoot off your manhood. You might not bleed to death, and you might survive, but you'll face the next forty or fifty years being a eunuch. Have I got your attention?'

The young officer nodded. 'Good,' Drew said. 'Now be so kind to give the lady next to you the keys to these shackles about me and we'll be on our way.'

He did as he was told, and when she came across the table with the small key in her hand she winked at him, but Drew didn't wink back. Too much could go wrong in the next few minutes.

Still, it was sure good to have a weapon in your hands and to be uncuffed. The day was looking better already.

TWENTY

Those fearing doomsday have already labeled as villains Jews, Roman Catholics, Mormons, Muslims, Freemasons, New Age devotees, peace activists, environmentalists, feminists, abortion providers, gay men, and lesbians. Members of groups ranging from the Trilateral Commission to the National Education Association are suspect – not to mention US government officials and United Nations troops.

Chip Berlet, *Boston Globe*, June 3, 1999

Drew stood up, the chains falling to the floor. Pistol in hand, he motioned the officer up and said, 'What's the floorplan like out there? And what's the easiest way to get out?'

Officer Flynn frowned and said, 'You go out this door and take a right. Corridor leads down to the locker room and weight room. There's an exit door that goes out to the parking lot.'

Drew looked over to the woman. 'Ma'am?'

She nodded. 'Exactly as he said. Except you make a left when you go out the door. You see, Officer Flynn, if you take a right you end up in the dispatch and office area. I do believe you were trying to fool Mr Connor and myself. Correct?'

The police officer's face turned red but he did not speak. Drew picked up the chains and said, 'Here's how it'll go.

The three of us will go to the locker room. I'll be in chains again but the young lady will have the key and the pistol in her purse. You'll escort me out, Officer Flynn, and the lady will be behind the two of us, with the pistol pointing at your back. Maybe you won't lose your crown jewels, but I bet she's a good shot and she'll snap your spine. We run into anybody, anybody at all, you just give 'em a big ol' grin and say I'm being transferred into the custody of FERA. No discussion, no debate. We just keep on moving. Understood?'

Another nod. Drew waggled the pistol back and forth. 'I'm sorry, I'm really going to need to hear you, Officer Flynn. Understood?'

His face remained red. 'Yes, you fuck. Understood.'

'Good.'

The chains felt oppressive again around his waist and wrists but Drew still felt jumpy, still felt good. He was moving, he was doing something, instead of sitting in the cell, brooding. He passed over the 9 mm and she put it in her purse, keeping her hand inside. He noted her knees were trembling.

'It'll be all right,' Drew said.

'Shut up and let's go,' she said.

After an hour on duty that morning, Nancy Thon Quong looked over and said, 'You're being awfully quiet this morning, George.'

He looked down the street, keeping the thought of Carol's earlier phone call in his mind. 'Nothing much to talk about, rook. It happens.'

'Well, I really enjoyed Sunday night, I really did. Thanks for a good time.'

He made a turn onto Houston Street, remembering a time when this place had been long rows of brownstones, stoops filled with kids and young moms, dads out actually working. Corner stores filled with groceries instead of crank and meth and crack. A real lively, happening place. But it all fell apart over the years, until the places had been abandoned and burned. Then the city had come through and wrecked them all, putting another gated community up in its place, 'The Baltimore Retreat. Residents and Guests Only.' More guarded and gated homes for people who just wanted to drop out and pull away from the city. Whatever happened to people who wanted to live next to each other?

'George?'

'Hmmm?'

'Are you okay? About me, that is. I mean, I think you were surprised Sunday night, when I introduced you to Melanie. That's not a problem, is it?'

Surprise, George thought. You want to talk surprises? How about an overweight married cop with an active imagination and whose small head is doing the bulk of thinking for him? How's that for surprises? Who thinks he's going to get a night full of ecstasy and instead heads home feeling like a horny thirteen-year-old turned down by his girlfriend when he tried to squeeze her boobies at the local movie theater?

George said, 'Rook, I'm all right. Honest I am. And I'm glad you had a good time last night.' He looked over, saw how she was sitting there with her arms crossed. Young, she looked so damn young. What could he have been thinking?

'And the fact I'm gay, that's not going to impact your evaluation, will it?'

He looked over again. 'Hey, rook.'

'Yes?'

'You an American? You know how to shoot? You know how to read people their Miranda warnings?'

A hint of a smile. 'Yes to all three.'

'Then it's not a problem,' he said.

Out in the hallway Drew tried to move quickly, but he could sense that Officer Flynn was taking his time, moving slow, hoping reinforcements would show up or some damn thing. The corridor was narrow, flanked on both sides by bulletin boards covered with notices and photos and even wanted posters. He wondered briefly if his own name and picture were up there along the wall. Now that would be a hell of a thing.

Each footstep seemed to last an hour as they headed towards a door at the end of the corridor with a sign that said PRIVATE. Officer Flynn was at his left and behind the two of them was the well-dressed and well-armed woman, and as pleased as he was at being out of the interview room Drew wasn't going to leave anything to chance. He wasn't sure if that woman back there could pull the trigger if things went to the shits, so he had other ideas. Any problem at all, he'd run into Officer Flynn, knock his breath out, and then wrap his handcuffed hands about his neck. Threaten to strangle him or break his neck. Not pretty but maybe it would work. At least it would give them some options.

Behind him he heard a gasp from the woman as the door at the corridor's end opened up and a cop came out dressed in gym shorts and a T-shirt that was soaked through with sweat. He was wiping at his face with a small towel and looked up, his eyes surprised, at seeing the procession coming towards him.

'Hey, Sean, what's up?' the cop said.

Flynn cleared his throat. 'Nothing, Paul. Just taking this

guy out back, avoid all the press. He's being transferred to the custody of FERA.'

'Hunh, no shit,' he said, as he passed by, close enough for Drew to smell the sweat from his body. 'Thought the AG's office was going to tie those guys in knots.'

Flynn was silent but Drew nudged him quickly with an elbow, and he said, 'Well, who knows what the hell the AG is up to most weeks?'

'Ain't that the flippin' truth,' he said, and then they came to the door and were through.

Drew saw rows of lockers, an exercise bicycle and weight machine, and a door that looked so blessed simple and wonderful he thought it would bring a tear to his eye. EXIT was lit overhead with a sign, and he moved forward and opened the door's kickbar and they were outside, in a small parking lot. Cruisers and pickup trucks and even a couple of motorcycles were parked there, and behind him the woman said, 'I've got a rental, right over there. I'll drive and I suggest the two of you sit in the rear, until we get out of the town's limits. Mr Connor, if you don't mind, I'll pass over this weapon so you can keep Officer Flynn quiet.'

'My thoughts exactly,' he said, shaking his head with amazement as they went to a dark blue Ford LTD. In a matter of moments he was in the rear with Officer Flynn, whose own hands were now handcuffed in his lap. Drew had the pistol in his lap, the end of the barrel pressed into the young cop's ribs. The car backed up in the small lot and headed to the exit, which was being watched over by another Newbury cop. Drew wondered how it would go, how they would get out of here, but the woman just held up an ID and the cop gave a half-wave and they hit a speed bump as they turned left.

Drew used both hands to hold the pistol to keep them from shaking, for now they were out on the street, moving past the camera crews and satellite trucks and State Police cruisers, a small mass of people still out in front of the police station. The engine noise grew louder as they accelerated through the town, and Drew found that breathing was beginning to get easier.

There was another noise, a softer one, and he looked around and Officer Flynn was quiet, staring out of the window, lips pursed so tight that they looked almost white, and then the noise continued. Drew realized what it was.

His driver was softly weeping.

Ira Woodman walked out of the tiny room that served as a restaurant in this shitty little hotel, a glass of orange juice in his hand. Breakfast had been two stale Danishes, about the only things that had been left in the buffet line, and a luke-warm cup of coffee. As he went into the lobby, ready to go back up to his room and prepare for that stupid court appearance, the receptionist – the one who had earlier called him 'hon' – called out. 'Oh, sir, Mr Woodman! There's a message here for you.'

He went over to the receptionist desk, picked up the pink message slip. The woman's handwriting was hard to make out, but she had carefully checked the little boxes that said URGENT and RETURN CALL IMMEDIATELY. He recognized the number before he recognized the name, and saw the scrawl was barely identifiable as Clem Badger. What could that fat weasel want so urgently? Maybe it had something to do with the other fugitive, Sheila. After all, he had done good work in narrowing down where—

'Mr Woodman?'

He turned, put the message slip in his pocket, placed the glass of orange juice down on the counter. Before him was Gil Summers, that smug little Assistant Attorney General. With him were a couple of hangers-on and two Vermont State Police officers. Ira looked at all their faces, saw the expressions, and just felt tired. That's all. Just so fucking tired.

'He's gone, isn't he?'

Summers just nodded. Ira said, 'When and how?'

'About an hour ago. By someone who said they were from your agency, complete with identification and source documents. They pulled a weapon on one of the Newbury officers and made it outside.'

'Let me guess,' Ira said. 'A woman?'

Another embarrassed nod. 'Yes, a woman.'

He closed his eyes, just for a moment, and then checked his wristwatch. Less than twelve hours to go. What could those two do in less than a half day? Answer, nothing. Summers went on, words tumbling around each other, 'We're setting up roadblocks, we have surveillance camera footage of what this woman looks like, we're going to find the both of them, Mr Woodman, they can't go far.'

Ira shrugged, smiled at the confused assistant attorney general. 'Mr Summers, right now, I could give a shit.'

Drew ran down the hill, where they had just left Officer Flynn, comfortable but chained to a tree, with a gag around his mouth that let him breathe and not do much else. The woman was next to him and he stopped, looking at her, then gently reached up and pulled off the white blonde wig. Her brown hair had been cut short, hacked really, for it looked like she had done it herself.

'Oh, Sheila,' he said, touching her face with his hands. 'How—'

'Later,' she snapped back. 'We have a car and if we're lucky we'll probably have another ten, fifteen minutes of drive time before they figure out what's going on. We must make some mileage, Drew, get some miles behind us.'

'But—'

'Jesus,' she said, tugging at his hand. 'We've got to get going.'

'Where?'

'To Northfield, you fool,' she said, pulling him down the hill to the dirt road where they had parked the car. 'To see your general friend, face to face, because we are running out of time and I'll be damned if everything I just did is going to be for nothing. All right?'

He started running with her, just nodded, and they headed to the Ford LTD.

From the second floor of the farmhouse, Maurice Blakely saw the lone form of General Montgomery trudging back home. He checked his watch. Less than twelve hours to go. In the past day he had ignored a number of phone calls, pages and and e-mails, all wanting to know what had happened here the previous day. All of them wanting to know why the General's death hadn't been reported yet to the news media and the NewsNet channels. All of them wanting to know how the weedcutter cluster bomb had worked. All of them wanting to know why he wasn't responding, why he wasn't calling back to them with the information they needed.

'Because,' Blakely said aloud. 'Because.'

Because he had plans for the next few days, and maybe

the plans involved Michaelson Lurry and maybe they didn't. For Blakely had once been at the pinnacle of something at the Pentagon, as this poor overworked man's eyes and ears and Scribe, and the past two years of exile had been awful. Blakely had stuck it through because he thought this simple little general would do something to get off his ass and back in the wheels and gears of power, so that's why he had stayed here, answering the General's mail, checking on his computer systems, and helping him write that maudlin autobiography. In any event, he was controlling the General's information, and that power was so sweet it put him to sleep every night with a smile on his face. But it only meant something back in DC. It meant hardly shit here in Vermont.

He wanted that power back, which is why the General was alive this day, walking back to his farmhouse. He just wanted to keep his options open.

And if the General didn't cooperate, well, Blakely was sure Lurry and his boys would have something available for him next week, especially if the General did turn up dead.

They were in an abandoned barn, the rental car parked in the rear, covered with a tarp and bales of soggy and decaying hay. Northfield was only a few miles away, and already they could hear the helicopters off in the distance. The chase was on again. Sheila was trembling as she undressed, tossing the new clothes to the side, washing her face of the makeup from a bucket of water, letting everything flow out as Drew sat across from her on a workbench watching, his bruised and scabbed-over face not moving as she talked. Sheila knew she was about one step away from getting hysterical and losing it all, and she didn't care. She had to spew out, let the past twelve hours out of her system, for there was no way she was going to let this stuff fester without getting it out in the open.

'It was all my fault, Drew, I'm sorry, but I didn't want to burden you with something so stupid as tampons, you know? I mean, here we are, doing what we're doing, and—'

'Don't apologize, Sheila, it's okay—'

'Jesus!' she said, standing there in bra, panties and nylons, wet cloth in her hand. 'Will you just please shut up? Just for a while? Please? I've got a lot to say, Drew, and if you interrupt and don't let me talk then I'm going to lose it, I really am. All right?'

He nodded, his arms crossed in front of him. The barn smelled musty and old and she would have loved to have just stretched out on the floor on a sleeping bag and sleep for hours, because she was down a few quarts in the sleep department, and she went back to rubbing her face, holding up a compact mirror, wanting to get that gunk off her face.

'So there I am, back up in the woods, Drew. No money and a box of tampons to my name. You were in jail. I don't know how I could get you out. But I did have my lapbot, but I had no money? All right? So I had to do what I had to do, to get some money. I promised myself I would never do this, no matter how poor I got. Before I met you I went through a winter, no heat in the house, just using wood in the fireplace, living off pancakes and syrup and government-issue cheese, though I knew by spending a day on-line in a certain place I could make enough money for steak and lobster for the rest of the year. But that's how determined I was, never to go back. So determined that even when I married Tom later in the year I never told him. Never gave him a hint about me being a CyberGal. And I wouldn't have gone back, except I had to do something. I had to try to rescue you. Which is why I went back. Do you understand?'

'Yes, I do,' he said, not taking his eyes off her.

The trembles came back, harder, as she remembered going through the checkpoints and password sites, getting into the root CyberGal system. 'It was like going back to a crime scene, or a place where somebody got seriously hurt. Except this time it's you, you know? And I got in last night and reactivated my homepages and started the bidding process.'

A deep breath, as she looked at her tired face in the mirror, the skin white and red where she had rubbed away the makeup. 'I'm a strong woman, Drew, quite a strong woman, but it sure does something to your self-esteem when you realize that for certain men you're worth more dead than alive, worth more as a cybertoy to be tortured and murdered than as the real you, the real Sheila who designs and maintains Web pages and has a home on a quiet lake.'

Drew kept quiet, just looking at her intently, and she pressed on. 'So I decided to auction myself, just like slave auctions of old, except this time I was both the auctioneer and the auction item. Ironic, hunh? And they were like wolves out there, wolves catching a bloody scent, because in an hour those men were fighting each other for the privilege of being the first to murder Sally from Seattle in years.'

He shifted some and said, 'What happened then?'

She shook her head violently, shivered and decided to keep the underwear. It was new and smelled fresh and she could use it. 'No, there's no way you're going to know any part of that, Drew. No way. I whored myself to get some money and I did it willingly, but I'm not going to share the gory details. Suffice to say that within an hour I had lots of money, plenty of money. All the money I needed, except not enough money to forget what I had just done.'

Sheila opened her knapsack and pulled out a pair of jeans and a light blue polo shirt, both of which smelled so much that they could probably stand on their own. So what. They belonged to her and weren't part of any scheme, weren't paid for by blood money. She put them on and said, 'So near midnight last night I had lots of money. Went to a couple of offshore NetBank centers, got credit all set up. Amazing what you can do with lots of money and a lapbot, even next to a small town like Newbury. Clothing stores and rental car agencies and print centers are all Webbed up so you can order stuff at any time during the night and pick it up the next morning. Even fake IDs are all right if you know how to hack into a print center's server, which is so easy you could probably even do it. Last thing I did was to steal the identity of a FERA woman, which wouldn't last long, but it did last long enough to get you out. You see, remember that day we got that newsfeed, saw those FERA people near the state cops, where the cruiser had gone into the ravine? I spotted a woman standing next to that Ira character. Found her name and bio on the FERA home-page. Figured hers was an identity I could use to spring you. Pretty funny, hunh?'

In one quick motion he came over and hugged her and held her tight, and she allowed him to do so, resting her head against his shoulder. Her jeans were still open and she didn't care. She wanted to cry but nothing came out. She just sighed against him and said, 'Drew, how long before we get to the General's house?'

'Less than an hour,' he said.

'All right, let's do it then, let's get this whole fucking

thing over with.' She pulled away and kissed his lips.
'Hon . . .'

'Yes?'

'Don't you have an engagement ring waiting for me?'

In her grasp she could feel him stiffen just a bit. 'Yes, I
do . . . How do you know?'

'Never mind that,' she said, looking up at that poor
wounded face. 'Where is it?'

He looked ashamed. 'I'm afraid to say I lost it, sometime
after that poor cigarette smuggler got killed. Don't worry, I
can get another one—'

She put a finger to his lips. 'No, don't do that. Drew . . .
when this is over, then we can talk about the ring and such.
Don't be upset, but if you gave it to me right now I'd toss it
in your face. Do you understand?'

Now his eyes were full, looked heavy. 'Yes, I do.'

She reached up and kissed him again. 'No, you don't. But
thanks for lying to me.'

Ira Woodman was walking across the small town park in
Newbury. A helicopter was waiting for him, the blades
slowly turning, the engine whining up to full speed. He had
spent the last couple of hours in his motel room, working the
phones, talking to his people. Henry Harrison had earlier
left a message from the airport in Boston, saying he was on
his way. Clem Badger hadn't been in his office, so that was
one little task that hadn't been fulfilled. And Glenda Sue
had been a joy to talk to this morning, full of energy and
cheer and love. It made him feel good that this woman was
on his side. And he had even talked briefly to Michaelson
Lurry, and that conversation had gone better than he had
expected.

'Are you all set up there?' Lurry had asked. 'You're sure that this fugitive was working on his own, that he had no other connections?'

'Positive, sir,' he had said. 'He got into the shelter area by mistake, all by himself. There's no evidence to show that he's been in contact with anyone. He and his woman tried to put out something about Case Shiloh on the Net, but we've spammed it so much that it's doubtful anyone has paid any attention.'

'Very good,' Lurry had said. 'Where are you going to be tonight?'

'In my Boston office. Where I belong.'

'Good. God bless, Ira. And when we talk tomorrow, it's going to be the real start of a new century, a true American century.'

'God bless, sir.'

And that had been that. Ira came closer to the helicopter, feeling the stirring in the air as the blades moved faster and faster. A short ride to the southeast and he'd back in Boston, in his office, watching television. He remembered some years ago, hearing about the First Gulf War, and how all the generals and admirals learned first of what was happening by tuning into CNN. Funny how that was now the way of warfare – learn all you needed to know from one of the many cable channels out there. Of course, after tomorrow there would be just one channel, one source of information, one way of telling the truth about what was out there.

The noise of the engine seemed to change, get more insistent. He looked up and then heard the sound of a horn being frantically honked. Ira turned around, saw a car speed up and over onto the green grass of the town park, and then the door flew open. A chubby man with a goatee started running out and—

'Jesus,' he said, amazed at what he saw – Clem Badger running like he had a flaming stick up his butt. He was shouting something but Ira couldn't hear him. He started walking away from the helicopter and Clem came up to him gasping, and even then Ira couldn't make out what the fat fool had been saying.

'What?' Ira said, raising his voice over the helicopter noise. 'What is it?'

'The phone call! Mr Woodman, the phone call!'

Ira shook off Clem's grasp and strode further away, looking at his watch. He did not have time for this crap, this nonsense.

'What phone call?' he demanded. 'And make it quick – I'm already hours late.'

Clem gasped for breath, his face chalky white, spittle dribbling down his chin. He nodded and spoke in quick gasps. 'The phone call. Just before he was captured. Drew Connor. He was making a phone call. From a phone stall in this town. I traced the call. When I found out, I called you. No answer, all day. Had to get up here, tell you.'

The sound of the helicopter engine seemed to rest in his bowels, churning and spinning, ready to tear everything to pieces. 'Go on. Who was he calling?'

Clem rubbed his sleeve across his face. 'One phone call, sir. To Cyrus Montgomery. General Cyrus Montgomery. Sir, his retirement home's in Northfield, a few towns over, and . . .'

The computer man was still blathering but Ira was no longer listening. General Cyrus Montgomery, who had served long, honorable years in the US Army until being forced out two years ago over some secret snafu involving the Crescent War. General Cyrus Montgomery, who had taken over the mantle of leadership and admiration that had been safely in the hands of the first African-American to hold the JCS post, Colin Powell. General Cyrus Montgomery, who with a moment's notice could hold a live news conference on each of the four major networks, dozens of cable networks and scores of NewsNet channels, and say anything he wanted.

Anything, anything at all. Especially about something called Case Shiloh.

Ira reached out and grabbed Clem's arm. 'Come on, we've got work to do,' and he started going back to the helicopter. Clem shouted, 'Are we going to Boston?'

'No, damn it,' he snapped. 'We're off to Northfield. We've got to make sure the General stays quiet.'

He remembered the meeting the other day with Lurry, where Lurry had promised that the General would be taken care of. Obviously he hadn't been. So now he would have to be convinced to keep quiet. And if he doesn't, Ira thought, then he'd have to join the long casualty list that was going to be put together later tonight. He had a moment of dismay that he was probably going to have to kill an Army general in the next few hours or so. What would his daddy have thought?

Fine, just fine, he said to himself. If killing a general meant gaining a nation, then that was a small price to pay.

A very small price, indeed.

TWENTY-ONE

Acting outside the Constitution in the early 1980s, a secret Federal agency established a line of succession to the Presidency to assure continued government in the event of a devastating nuclear attack, current and former United States officials said today.

The officials reached today refused to discuss details of the plan, the existence of which was disclosed in a television program tonight on the Cable News Network. The CNN report said that if all seventeen legal successors to the President were incapacitated, non-elected officials would assume office in extreme emergencies.

New York Times, November 18, 1991

They were sitting at the base of a willow tree, near a place in the road where a drainage pipe emptied into a swampy area where cat-tails grew and redwing blackbirds made lots of sharp noises. Across the road were a driveway and a gate, and on each side of the driveway a chain-link fence extended as far as one could see.

Drew used a pair of binoculars, scoping out the scene. They had just eaten a few minutes ago, one of the last freeze-dried packages of food they had taken from that hunter's camp. Spaghetti and meatballs, heated over their little gas stove, which finally sputtered and died when the fuel ran out. Funny thing, how one's perceptions of food would change. Back at the camp, after days of living off nuts and berries and mushrooms and not much else, that freeze-dried food had tasted like something from a New York four-star restaurant, but now the food was beginning to taste awful, like spiced chunks of soggy cardboard.

During the past few hours he and Sheila hadn't said much to each other, except during one break when she touched the scabs and bruises on his face and said, 'My fault, I'm so sorry.'

'Stop worrying about it, will you?' he had snapped back. 'Remember how I wasted time back when that poor kid got shot by the Mohawks? We both almost got captured then because of what I did. So consider us even.'

That hadn't come out right, not at all, but he was too tired and wired to do anything about it. Sheila now sat quietly near him as he scanned both sides of the fence. There were tiny insulators and wires along the fence, and at about a hundred feet in both direction from the gate closed-circuit TV cameras kept view. They were bulky and large, and Drew was certain they were there for show. There were probably many more cameras scattered around the entire perimeter, small enough to escape notice.

Sheila said quietly, 'I wonder how things are, back at home. The leaves must be almost gone by the lake. And the loons . . . I wonder if they've left yet.'

'We'll find out, soon enough, I promise,' he said. Then he put the binoculars down. Out in the distance. Helicopters, on the move. Sheila noticed as well and said, 'There was a teacher in my elementary school, Mrs Than. She was from Vietnam. Even though she was in her forties, each time a helicopter went by it made her jump. When she was a kid, back in Vietnam, the sound of a helicopter meant soldiers coming. Or rockets shooting down. Or villages being burned. That damn sound scared her so much, and now it's going to scare me forever.'

He picked up his backpack, and hers as well. 'Then let's go see someone who can ground those helicopters.'

As he helped her on with her pack, she said, 'And what if he's not home? And what if he won't see us?'

'Then I'll think of something else.'

'What's that?'

'I don't know yet. Come on.'

They went down the slight hill, jumped over a drainage ditch and then went up to the road. The wrought-iron gate was painted black and had a small brass sign in the center that said PRIVATE DRIVE. It had an electric motor and could be opened by a cardkey or probably from someone in the house, hidden up there among the trees. There was an intercom box and Drew thumbed the switch. It buzzed and then there was a click and a burst of static.

'Yes?' came the voice.

Drew looked down at the small metal box. 'I need to see General Montgomery, please.'

The voice said, 'With no appointment, I'm afraid you can't see him at all.'

'Look, tell him Lieutenant Drew Connor is here, from the Quicksilver Response Force. I've got to talk to him. It's vitally urgent.'

The speaker just hissed back at him. 'Hello? Hello?'

The speaker went dead. He thumbed the intercom switch a half-dozen more times while Sheila stood next to him, resting her back against the iron fence, her eyelids drooping. No answer. Damn it. The same squirrelly voice from when he called the other day. The General's flak catcher, the one who's out on the front lines, making sure the Man doesn't get bothered. Drew looked up at the fence. Maybe six feet, maybe seven. He took his pack off and backed up a few paces, then, with a grimace, tossed it over the fence. It landed on the driveway with a thud that made Sheila stand up and take notice.

'Drew, what the hell are you doing?'

Drew gently took her own backpack off and said, as he stepped back, 'There's an old Irish story about a young boy, walking home, trying to take a shortcut across the fields. Every time he came to a stone fence, he tossed his cap over the fence.'

He threw again, and Sheila's pack bounced to a stop next to his own. 'When he was asked why he did that, he said he wasn't sure if he could climb the wall or not. But if his cap was on the other side of the wall then he had no choice. He had to go over to retrieve it. Hon, we're going to see the General, one way or another. C'mon, let me give you a boost up and over.'

Which is exactly what he did, and he followed her, scraping his wrist on one of the metal bars. With Sheila standing next to him on the paved driveway he put his pack back on and helped her as well. It was cool, a wind coming up from the west, and she said, 'You said this place looked well guarded. How much time do we have left, do you think?'

'Maybe just a minute or two,' he said, looking at the bravery in her eyes. 'Depends how much of a security system the General has, how many people he has on staff. Only chance we've got is to see the General, if only for a few seconds. Give me a few seconds, and then we'll get a minute. Give me a minute, I'm sure I can stretch that into a half-hour.'

She smiled at him with a tinge of sadness, a look that made something inside of him ache. This past week she had changed, she had really changed from the confident, smiling woman who was certain of her skills and her place in the world. Now she was someone who didn't seem sure of anything any more.

Sheila reached out and took his hand in hers. 'Let's see if we can't get that minute or two.'

He squeezed her hand and they started walking up the driveway.

Maurice Blakely sat in his little control room, muttering curses at the changing pictures on his computer screen. The images blinking in and out in one corner of the screen showed the progression of two damn hikers as they strolled up the driveway like they owned the fucking place.

He rolled away in his chair and went to his desk, pulling out a Beretta 9 mm, which he tucked in the small of his back. He also took a small Motorola hand-held radio unit. About once or twice a month some clown would climb over the fence, intent on seeing the General. It was either an autograph seeker or a disturbed vet or someone with a grudge or an issue, or somebody who wanted the General to hurry up and run for president.

Who could give a shit. All that Blakely understood is that whether the General knew it or not, his next several hours were already accounted for, and they didn't involve talking to a couple of scruffy-looking hikers.

In the hallway outside his office, the General came to him, carrying a newspaper in his hand. Montgomery said, 'Something up, Blakely?'

'Nothing to be concerned about, sir,' he said. 'A couple of trespassers working their way up the driveway.'

Montgomery paused, looked him over. 'A problem? Anything to do with that terrorist threat you mentioned yesterday, or the Cessna attack?'

Blakely shook his head. 'Nope. Look like a couple of kids, sir, hikers. Maybe looking for an autograph or something. I'll take care of it, right away.'

The General seemed preoccupied, and he said in passing, 'All right then. Do it the usual way. Ask them politely to leave, and then call in the police. And be careful out there. If you see anything troubling, just back away and call the cops.'

'You've got it, sir.'

In a strange way Sheila felt exhilarated as she walked up the drive. The paved way had curved around so that they could make out the large farmhouse, built up on a slight rise of land. There was a wrap-around farmer's porch and a couple of outbuildings, including a large barn off to the left with a tall cupola that almost looked like a church steeple.

She knew they were trespassing, knew that they were still being chased, and knew that this probably would not end well in the next few minutes. But she didn't care. She was tired and she was with her man, and if it ended soon, well, then it would be over. No more running, no more being chased. Let Shiloh happen. She was so tired she wondered if she cared anymore.

Up on the porch a man came out in khaki pants and dark blue pullover sweater, a radio in one hand. His dark hair was cut short and his face was twisted in anger.

'Looks like somebody's coming, and it's not the General,' she said.

'That's fine,' Drew said. 'We keep on walking.'

Cyrus Montgomery was going to his office, and then thought, hell, he shouldn't have sent Blakely out there on his own. He doubled back and went into Blakely's office, looked down at the computer screen – almost as big as the TV screen he had back at his last post in Virginia – and saw the camera action as Blakely went down to confront the two hikers.

He stared at the screen, saw the tiny image of his Scribe gesturing and talking to the man and woman. Both were hikers, just as Blakely had said, and while they looked tired and dirty it seemed like Blakely had it all in control.

Montgomery left the room and headed to his office. There was a lot to do, and he decided he would have to work the phones today, no matter what breaches of security would occur as he talked over the fiber-optic cables. He had to know more of what was going on out there, as that name kept on echoing inside of him: Shiloh.

Ira Woodman couldn't believe where the meeting was taking place – in the rear area of a McDonald's restaurant – but he pressed on. With him was Clem Badger, and sitting across from them was a couple of Vermont State Police officers and Gil Summers, the Assistant Attorney General. In the background were other State Police and local police officers, here for the show, here to see a Fed get outsmarted by the local boys.

'Look here,' Ira said, trying to keep his voice calm and knowing he was failing. 'We know that Drew Connor was making a phone call before he was captured yesterday. That phone call was to the residence of General Cyrus Montgomery. Now that Connor has escaped – while in the custody of your local forces' – and my, how they all glared at him for that – 'he's most certainly on his way to General Montgomery's residence.'

'Then we'll take care of it,' Summers said stubbornly. 'We'll call the General and let him know this fugitive may be approaching. We'll even send a police cruiser or two over there to sit on the house. But we're not going to raid the General's residence. It's not going to happen! Can you imagine the publicity, of having the Vermont State Police trespassing onto the property of one our most famous citizens without even the dignity of a warrant?'

Ira imagined something else, something he wished he could tell this officious jerk. He imagined other publicity as well, the General stepping out to a mass of microphones and cameras announcing that he had information about an event related to Michaelson Lurry, an event called Case Shiloh, an event that deserved a Congressional inquiry. Jesus, what a disaster!

Ira said, 'This is a dangerous fugitive, one that—'

'And just how dangerous would it be for him to approach General Montgomery? Mr Woodman, I don't know what the hell you're trying to pull off, but it's not going to happen with the assistance of the State of Vermont. We'll take whatever heat there is for the escape of Drew Connor. But you yourself didn't seem too concerned a few hours ago, when it happened. You only became concerned when you thought you found out where he was headed. Why's that? Are you concerned more with this fugitive or with General Montgomery?'

'Damn it, you fool, you're close to capturing this fugitive, but only if you get off your bureaucratic ass and send in some people to Montgomery's farm.' His voice was now loud enough so that the clerks at the other end of the fast-food place were eyeing the small group of people. 'If Montgomery doesn't like it, then apologize and do whatever you people do here, but get some cops and troopers in there now, before you regret it.'

Summers stood up and, like they were connected to him by wires, the other police officers prepared to leave as well. 'The only thing I really regret is the misfortune of meeting you, Mr Woodman. We'll handle it from here, and we'll let you know – through channels, of course – if we apprehend Mr Connor. And we won't be doing that by stormtroopering our way onto General Montgomery's property.'

In a minute or so they were gone, leaving Ira and Clem Badger. Ira refused to look at his assistant, kept on staring at the countertop, where someone had carved in the table, 'i like little girls butts'. He sighed and wondered about the mind of someone who would deface property like this, leave a message that some young mother would have to explain to a child.

'Clem?' he asked, still looking down at the countertop.

'Sir?' came the quiet, hesitant voice.

'Your lapbot up and running?'

'Yes, sir, it is.'

'The nearest FERA mobile command post?'

'In New Hampshire, sir. About a half-hour way. Tanya Selenekov's with it, handling the media fuss over the fugitive hunt.'

'Get it heading to Northfield, now. And the nearest ECM unit that we can get our hands on?'

Ira kept on staring, listening to the chatter of the clerks out front and the clattering sound of Clem typing on his lapbot. The sound of the keys being used was almost comforting. Ira hated the sensation but there it was: he was hoping for a miracle from his computer wizard.

'Sir, there's an ECM unit in Montpelier, on maneuvers.'

'Get it to Northfield as well. And one more thing. Any and every asset we have in the area, I want it on alert, as soon as possible. I don't care if it's grandmothers, Boy Scouts or Holy Rollers. If they're on our list, I want them here, right away.'

'You've got it, sir,' Clem said.

He sighed, got up and made a note to have this table destroyed in the next couple of months, if and when he had the time after Shiloh.

'I certainly hope so,' he said.

Drew looked on as the man approached, his head shaking, then said, 'I don't know who you are and I don't care, but you're trespassing. Please leave, now.'

Drew squeezed Sheila's hand and said, 'I need to see the General. Give me thirty seconds with the General, and if he says to leave then we'll leave, no fuss, no muss.'

The man shook his head. 'Look, you're trespassing, and you're in no position to make requests. The General doesn't give autographs, doesn't do interviews, and sees people who served with him by appointment only. Understand?'

Oh yes, he understood, knew where this was going, and he stepped forward and to the right, to give Sheila some protection. 'I know that's the usual, but this isn't the usual. We have some vital information that General Montgomery has to know about, and right now. We don't have time to dick around with you.'

'Jesus,' the man said. 'Another day, another nutso case with vital information. All right, here it goes. I wanted to do it easy but you want to do it hard. It's time for the cops.'

As Drew saw him raise up the radio and considered what was about to happen, he swung off his pack and started going into the pocket, reaching for his pistol. Behind him Sheila started saying something but he ignored her, only looking at this weasel of a guy who was preventing him from getting to the General, preventing him from doing what had to be done.

And as he grabbed his pistol from his backpack, the man in front of him took a step back, dropped the radio and reached behind himself and—

Drew stood there, pistol aiming at the man, and the man was there as well, like an identical twin, pointing a pistol at him. Drew looked into those eyes, saw the same mirror image, an image that scared him, because he knew what was going on inside that mind.

The man said, 'Whatever happens, you're a trespasser. Understand? I can drop you right here and no court, no cop, is going to give me trouble. So just drop your weapon and back the fuck off. All right?'

He had a lot of things to do and say, but there was just one problem: Sheila, right behind him. Shit.

Drew started to lower his pistol when a voice rang out: 'Stop!'

Ira Woodman was driving Clem's rented Ford with one hand, holding a folded-over map with the other, as Clem Badger sat next to him, working on the lapbot, announcing progress as they grew closer to Northfield and the General's house.

'FERA command post on its way, sir.'

And a few minutes later, after passing a hay wagon on a narrow country road, nearly running the tractor into a ditch: 'Electronic Counter Measures van on its way as well, sir. Even have a county sheriff escorting. They should both be arriving at the same time, within a half-hour.'

Now he was at an intersection, braking hard. Left or right? He looked down at the map, lost his way for a moment. Behind him were some horns, a few shouts. Who gives a shit? Miles to go and you folks back there, just hold on and wait.

Right, he thought. We have to turn right.

He took the corner and sped up, and Clem said, his voice strained, 'Resources . . . Mr Woodman, I think we've lucked out. The county militia is pretty much ours.'

'Activate them,' he said, speeding up again, looking at the dashboard clock. Less than six hours to go.

'Uh . . . sir, are you sure?'

'Of course I'm sure. Why not?'

He sensed the hesitation in Clem's voice. 'Well . . . it's just that if you activate them now there's bound to be a lot of attention. We'll have camera crews and NewsNet hounds there before sunset. Won't the publicity be a problem?'

Another tractor hauling hay came to view. Jesus! Weren't the farmers in this damn state suppose to be going out of business? He slammed his foot down on the accelerator, passed while going up a hill and said, 'Activate. Activate and be damned. Set up a meeting place for both FERA vans and have the militia leadership meet me there as well. Clem, we've got just a few hours to go. I don't give a damn about publicity or the NewsNet or anything else.'

Before them a pickup truck appeared, heading down the

hill towards them. Clem said, 'Shit,' and Ira leaned on the horn, swerving and missing the front tires of the tractor by a millimeter or two. The road curved to the right and the tires screeched some as they fought to hold on. When the road straightened out, Ira said, 'Clem?'

'Sir?' he replied, voice quavery.

'Is the militia activated?'

A few clicks on the keyboard. 'Yes . . . they're activated now, sir.'

'Good. God bless.'

Clem didn't reply, but Ira didn't mind. He had more important things to think about.

Sheila saw the slim black man come down the front steps, dressed in dark gray slacks and a simple blue pullover sweater. She found herself smiling and her eyes tearing up, recognizing the face before her, one of the most famous faces in the nation. It was going to be all right, Drew would have his time with the General, it was going to be all right.

'Both of you,' he said. 'Stand down, holster your weapons. Blakely, have you called the police?'

'I was just about to sir, when this man threatened me.'

From inside the house a phone began ringing, but nobody moved. Then Drew stood straight and a tone to his voice appeared, a tone she had never heard before. 'General Montgomery,' he said, his voice firm and clipped. 'Lieutenant Drew Connor, of the Quicksilver Response Force. Sir, you rescued me and some of my men when we had been cut loose by the Defense Research Agency. Do you recall?'

The General's face changed as well, suddenly becoming more warm and open. He stepped closer, but Sheila noticed how the words betrayed the look on his face. 'Well, I'll be . . . son, what the hell do you mean, coming here and threatening my aide like that? Do you think because of what happened back there that gives you the right to come here and raise holy hell? Damn it, right now I don't care that much about Quicksilver or you or anything else. You and your lady friend here should just turn around and get going. All right?'

'Sir, if I may, just a word of explanation, and then we'll be off,' Drew said, still standing stiffly at attention.

The General folded his arms. 'Better be some damn good words.'

'Sir, my fiancée and I have information that sometime tonight an attempt is going to be made on the President's life, as well as those in the line of succession and other members of Congress. A number of people and agencies are involved with this attempt.'

'General, I know this man now,' the aide said, stepping closer, the pistol still firmly in his grasp though hanging by the side of his leg. 'He and this woman are being sought for the murder of a deputy sheriff in New Hampshire. Sir, I really think I need to call the police on this.'

'Is that true, lieutenant, that you're a fugitive?' the General asked, the look on his face getting sharp.

Damn it, Sheila thought, Drew's being too military, being too cool, and she burst out with, 'Shit! Will you both shut up and listen to us? We've been chased, shot at and practically starved out, all across two states, because we know something we're not supposed to know. Something called Case Shiloh, something that's happening tonight, and if you can't do something about it, General, then just shut up and let us be on our way. By this time tomorrow there'll be a nice, new fascist government in place, and don't be surprised at what they do. Like repealing the 1964 Civil Rights Act. Drew, come on, let's get the hell out of here.'

'Wait,' the General said, now looking more interested. 'What was that you said, about a case? What did you call it?'

'Case Shiloh,' Drew said. 'It involves members of the Federal Emergency Response Agency and—'

'Hold on,' Sheila said. 'Drew, not another word. General, I came here with Drew because he thought you could do something. General, we came a very long way here. If you want to know more, we need something in return. Like getting something to eat, someplace to wash up, and someplace I can work on my lapbot. But if you're not interested, forget it. Like I said, we'll just leave.'

The General tried to control a smile. 'Ma'am, were you ever in the military?'

'No.'

'A pity,' he said. 'We could have used you. Come on in, the both of you. Maurice, put your sidearm away and rustle up some grub for these two. I want to talk to them, soonest.'

'Yes, sir.'

Then they started going up the stairs and Drew looked at her, sharply and with a dagger gaze in his eyes, and then he just smiled. She squeezed his hand, felt good again.

Maybe, just maybe, it really was going to be all right.

TWENTY-TWO

The secret agency, the National Program Office, was
created by President Ronald Reagan in 1982 to
expand the list of successors and a network of bunkers,
aircraft and mobile command centers to insure that
the Government continued to function in a nuclear
war and afterward. Oliver L. North, then a Marine
lieutenant colonel and an aide on the National
Security Council, was a central figure in establishing
the secret program, CNN said.

New York Times, November 18, 1991

Henry Harrison stepped lively off the Boston–Baltimore
shuttle carrying a small overnight bag that didn't really contain anything vital but that helped when going through
security. Those idiots were always suspicious of someone
traveling without something in his hand, and he didn't have
time to screw around.

At the gate entrance a man was waiting for him, holding
up a sign: McVEIGH. Henry smiled. Good joke. Compared
to what they were about to do, Timothy McVeigh was a fag.
He went up to the guy, said, 'I'm McVeigh. You set?'

'As set as it can be,' he said. 'The name is Toland.'

'Then let's get rolling.'

'All right,' Toland said. 'God bless.'

'Sure, whatever.'

As he went with Toland through the crowded terminal, Henry looked about at all the people, all the faces, all the clothes. Black and brown and yellow people. Scurrying around like mud people from some great Asiatic or African village, dumped into his country. He wished there was some way he could give them all a one-way ticket to DC in the next few hours, for that would be a great way to start the cleansing process.

Oh, how beautiful it was going to be.

Montgomery was idly chit-chatting with the lieutenant and his woman – Sandy? Sheila? Damn, he had already forgotten her name – but he was also trying to restrain his excitement about what these two knew about Case Shiloh and how they came to know about it. Information, sweet information, the mother's milk of decision-making, had finally arrived in his lap and he was going to make the most of it. They had all gone into the kitchen, and while Blakely made sandwiches for the two, the lieutenant had started a debrief – and God, how seeing that face and hearing that voice brought back some killer memories about flying nearly blind over the Bay of Bengal, trying to pick up the pieces of stupid decision-making.

He had sat with them and watched the man's face as he talked, listening to what he had to say, not wanting to hear any more but forcing himself to listen, to take mental notes. The story was incredible, ranging from the way they got into a retreat bunker, the first indication of Case Shiloh, and then the great chase across two states, all the while the woman – Stacy? Casey? – hacked her way into getting some information. As Drew faltered in his story-telling – when he started chewing on a roast beef sandwich – his woman swung the screen of her lapbot around to show him what she had found.

'I'm sorry, but this is all that I've been able to recover,' she said. 'The rest of the files are scrambled, but you can see here clearly that something is being discussed, something to do with what Drew called Continuity of Government. COG. Part of the National Program Office.'

Cyrus folded his hands. Black work indeed, and he was surprised that these two had been able to get into it. He said, 'You say there's more of these files, talking about Case Shiloh?'

'Yes, sir, there is,' Drew said, wiping his face with a napkin. 'But as Sheila said, the hard drive got a bit scrambled. But I do remember what I read, sir. There was a speech all set to go, about the death of the President. There was plenty of contingency planning in cities, setting up detention centers, traffic control checkpoints, and the such. I'm afraid I just skimmed it, sir, because I know there are other details in there as well, details about Case Shiloh and implementation. And from the date we saw in the retreat bunker, today's the day.'

He nodded. 'And the President is due to speak to Congress tonight.' He had heard enough. Time for decisions, time to get some more information. 'Blakely?'

'Sir?' he stepped away from the sink.

'You know computers better than anybody I know,' he said. 'Would you be so kind to take Sheila' – okay, let's not forget her name, now, will we – 'and see if you can recover more of that information.'

Blakely nodded, wiped his hands on a towel. 'At once, sir.'

Blakely led the woman upstairs, she carrying her lapbot, and he decided to kill her in his office. Once she had been taken care of then he would have to move fast. What then? Maybe take the direct approach. Just come back downstairs with pistol in hand and walk up behind this Drew character and put two in the hat. Bam, bam, and then he'd have some quick talking to do with the General. He'd have to let the General in on what was going on, and how certain decisions had to be made. So sorry about the blood on the kitchen table, sir, but there are only a few hours left.

'This way, please,' he said, looking her over. She seemed tired and her hair looked like it had been trimmed by a hedge clipper. Not particularly bad looking but she wasn't really his type. She nodded and went ahead of him, saying, 'What I really need is something to make repairs to my lapbot's hard drive. Do you have the latest Norton Utilities recovery software?'

He smiled at her as he led her into his small office. Might as well keep her at ease. 'Sure I do,' he said. 'I've got Norton Rapid Recovery Four.'

'Four?' she asked. 'But that's not supposed to be released until this winter.'

Another smile on his part. This was going to be fun. 'Sometimes the military gets advance releases. Let me get you set up.'

Which only took a few minutes, and after running a USB cable from her lapbot to his system and checking the compatibility she started tapping away, looking intently at the screen.

He took a step back, looked around his office, and then saw a length of telephone cord on the spare desk. Perfect. He quietly picked up the cord and wrapped both ends around his fists, then approached her from the rear.

*

Henry Harrison stepped into the passenger's side of the GMC van, set in one of the airport's parking garages. It was painted white and had no windows along the side or the rear. Just the windshield and side door windows, and that was it. No need for prying eyes. Toland climbed into the driver's side and said, 'Want to take a look in the back?'

Henry grinned. 'Sure.'

Toland said, 'Barrier back there just slides away. Give it a quick peek, I'll make sure nobody's around.'

He turned in his seat and saw a handle on the left, and he tugged the folding metal screen to the right, and sighed at the beauty of it all. The warhead was nesting in a cradle of foam and lumber, and running off the rear of the warhead were cables, running into a lapbot, secured to the side. A long way from home, he thought. Smuggled into Baltimore Harbor after a slow boat from Russia some months ago. Remembering the briefings, knowing that the lapbot system worked to bypass the old Soviet PALs – Permissive Action Links – which supposedly prevented anyone from using this twenty-kiloton piece of work. Well, the Soviet Union wasn't supposed to collapse either, so that's what happens when you make assumptions.

'Looks good, don't it?' Toland said.

'It certainly does,' Henry said, wishing he had the time to go into the rear of the van and just inspect the whole set-up. What a piece of work.

'Sorry to interrupt, sir, but we need to get going.'

Henry drew the curtain back, looked over at Toland. 'Absolutely. We need to meet the schedule, don't we?'

'That we do, sir, even if we do have plenty of time.'

Henry nodded, smiled and watched as Toland maneuvered the van out of the parking garage. The driver was ex-military, seemed to be bright and on the ball.

Too bad when this evening was over, Henry was going to have to kill him.

Drew said to the General, 'I'm sorry, sir, I can't remember everything that we saw on those computer files. There were a lot of them. All I can say for sure is that they're planning to kill the President and other Cabinet officers, and that it's going to happen before the day is out.'

Montgomery nodded. 'If there's anything on those files, then Blakely will help your woman find them. He knows how to make computers sit up and beg.'

Drew felt finer than he had in days. 'If that's the case, then Sheila knows how to make them run and fetch, sir. She's very good at what she does. Sir, what do you have in mind?'

The General held a coffee cup in both of his large hands. 'I could get on the phone right now, start making calls, beginning with the Secretary of the Treasury. But what do we tell them? That something bad is going to happen tonight? We need to know more, and so do they. There's going to be a presidential address tonight, when the President is going to dispel those rumors about his capacity, either mental or physical. This administration isn't going to cancel that speech because of a phone call from a retired warhorse like me, unless I have more.'

Drew saw the General's face again before him, in that helicopter back then. 'You'd think by now they'd know enough to listen to you, sir. Especially after the Crescent.'

'Yeah, that was one rank screw-up, wasn't it?' Montgomery shook his head. 'We had an opportunity, a few years back, to defuse that war before it started. A line of countries with years of hate and mistrust among them, not to mention some of them with a nuclear capability. No one should have been surprised at what happened, but this administration and the ones before sure were surprised. And even when they tried to put out the fires, they sent you poor bastards in, a contract force. To give them deniability in case something went wrong. Of course, you start planning for deniability, it becomes a self-fulfilling prophecy.'

Drew said quietly, trying to keep the memories and emotions in check, 'A lot of good men died over there, trying to do their best in the worse circumstances. They weren't serving for money, or for deniability.'

'No, they weren't,' Montgomery said. 'And I wasn't going to cut them off and leave them there. And I'm not about to turn this country over to whoever's behind Case Shiloh.'

'Michaelson Lurry, for one,' Drew said. 'And one Ira Woodman, his Region One administrator. And there's more, sir, and I wish I remembered better from those damn e-mails we intercepted. But what I do remember is scary enough. Arrest lists. Detention centers. Traffic checkpoints. There's some scary shit in there.'

Montgomery backed away from the kitchen table. 'Then let's go see what progress they've made.'

Oh, how sweet it was to wrap that cord around that slender neck and to pull quickly and tightly before she responded. To do it snap-quick, like a snake striking. To feel the cord sink into her throat and sense the vibrations, the sweet thrumming in the cord as her air was cut off. To dance with her as she struggled, as she fought against you, fell back, gurgled and choked and spasmed.

Blakely remembered some dark times in Colombia, working with the government's hunter/killer groups, advising with his lapbot, helping the groups encrypt their communications, hack into the narco guerrilla networks. They would laugh at him, tease him about being just a toy soldier, a geek with a lapbot. One night they had captured a squad of guerrillas, a mixed bag of young men and women. The officer in charge of the government H/K squad had asked Blakely if he had the stones to do what had to be done. Exhausted and grimy and tired of being teased, Blakely had taken out his 9 mm service pistol and had popped off two of the guerrillas, young, dark-skinned men who had stoically knelt down and not moved when Blakely had placed the muzzle end of the pistol against the base of their necks.

He had moved on to one of the woman guerrillas when the H/K officer – Lopez? – had tossed him a length of para-chute cord. Go ahead, he had teased, do it nice and close. Get your hands dirty. Which is just what he had done, and he surprised himself at how much he enjoyed it.

'Blakely,' came the voice.

He turned, letting the phone cord drop from one of his hands. 'Sir?'

The General and Drew were standing in the doorway of his office. Blakely nodded at them, tried not to let the dis-appointment show in his face.

The General said, 'How goes it?'

The woman's voice, from behind him. 'Damn! This is one great application. I'm getting data recovery in just one more minute.'

'Good job, Sheila,' the man said.

Yes, Blakely thought, good job. And most likely your last.

At a dirt turnaround near the General's home, Ira Woodman sat in the rear of the FERA command post, with Clem Badger next to him, joined by one Gary Leeson, who was in charge of the other FERA mobile unit, the ECM unit. Ira didn't like the look of Gary from the moment he met him – was a Generation Z kind of guy, thin with short hair and a beard – but he and Clem hit it off right from the start. In a matter of a few minutes Ira no longer knew what the two were talking about. Their language was sprinkled with phrases such as timed pulse, overrides, electromagnetic interference, interlocks and blockage, and Ira eventually stopped them with a sharp phrase, 'Look, I don't give a shit how you two do it, can it be done?'

'Sure, Mr Woodman,' Clem said. 'It can be done. Only problem will be leakage to other homes and residences around here once we start using the jamming gear. After a while they'll notice and we'll be getting lots of attention.'

'I don't care about the attention,' he said. 'I just care about getting it done.'

'Just one thing,' Gary said. 'The ECM van is still in shakedown mode. I'll need to get her into a line-of-sight to work more efficiently. I noticed a nice hill less than a mile away to the south. Cleared with picnic tables and everything. Should work well.'

There was a knock at the door and Tanya Selenekov looked in. 'Mr Woodman, the militia commander is still waiting to see you.'

'I'll be right there,' Ira said, stepping away from the small conference table. 'Clem, you ride along with Gary. You know what we need. Just get up to that hill and start your work the moment you're ready.'

Clem and Gary started going into their techno-babble and Ira tuned them out, stepping away onto the dirt road, his pistol in his coat pocket thumping against his leg. It was a comforting feeling. The ECM van was parked under an oak tree, and Tanya was standing next to a burly man wearing blue jeans and a camo jacket. Patches and badges were on the front and shoulders of the jacket. His black and gray beard extended halfway down his chest, and one of his work-boots had been repaired by grimy duct tape.

Tanya said, a smile faintly going over her face, 'Sir, this is Carl Slocum. He's the . . . uh, he's the colonel-in-chief of the Washington County Militia.'

Ira shook the man's hand, which was rough-hewn and greasy. 'Colonel, we don't have much time. My name is Jericho. You are Gideon Twelve. Activation code is Ezekiel. Do you accept the authorization?'

He grinned, revealing brown and stained teeth. 'By God, I do. Sir, it's an honor to finally meet you, and—'

'Colonel, please, we don't have time. There's a situation that's developing near here. I need you and your militia group. How many troops do you have ready to put in the field, and how long before you can muster them?'

Slocum reached into a shirt pocket and pulled out a stained, looseleaf notebook. He started thumbing through and said, 'Let's see, Jerry can't come during the day, he's got that new job, and Hank's still in county lock-up for hammering on his bitch wife, and . . .'

As Slocum murmured to himself Ira shook his head. He remembered Daddy telling him about the different troops he had served with, both in Europe and the islands. From every-where across America, Los Angeles to Detroit to Brooklyn, all wearing the Army green, all calling themselves Americans. All looking out for each other, all dedicated to doing their duty. 'They sure as hell didn't look like much,' Daddy had said, 'but we conquered tyranny with 'em, by Jesus.'

And now? Could Ira defeat this tyranny with what this . . . this creature could pull together? Holy God, if Ira had run into this overweight fool while in the State Police he would have pulled him over and done an NCIC check just on his appearance alone.

Slocum put the notebook back into his pocket. 'Sir, I can get you twelve, maybe thirteen troops within the hour. Some of them are well armed indeed, if you know what I mean.'

So few? They'd have to do, and quickly. 'Very good. Here's the situation. Are you familiar with the farmhouse belonging to General Cyrus Montgomery?'

Slocum spat on the ground. 'Christ, everyone around here does. Fool nigger fenced some of the best snowmobiling fields around. What's going on there?'

Ira said, 'There are fugitives at the farmhouse, conspiring with General Montgomery. A man and a woman. They were involved with the anthrax attack in Detroit last year. Their goal was to set up additional terrorist attacks and blame it on the freemen, to set up gun courts and repeal the Second Amendment. Local police and the State Police won't handle it. Which is why we need your help.'

'Are these two Jews? Going against a general, even a coon like that, might cause some problems with my boys. But if there were Jews involved . . .'

Ira took the hint. 'Yes. In fact, we think they were sent here by the loyalist faction in Israel. Working for the Mossad.'

'Those bastards,' Slocum said. 'Sir, you've got us. What do you need? Go in and seize 'em?'

Ira looked at his watch. No more time for games. It was time for action.

'No,' Ira said. 'I want you and your militia to go in there and kill every person you find.'

Another spit on the ground. 'Sir, it'd be an honor.'

*

Montgomery crowded in behind Sheila, who was typing on her computer screen, the text scrolling up. Drew was standing next to him, a hand on Sheila's shoulder, encouraging her along, saying, 'That's right, hon, that's good, yeah, right there, General. See that?'

Oh, yes, the General did see that, and with every line of text that came up he could feel his head ache more and more. How in God's name had this gone on, for years at least? How was it done, how was it achieved, how in the holy hell were they able to put this together?

Easy, he thought. Quite easy. In this time of spin doctors and pollsters and nothing getting done without thinking of who would be up and who would be down, all it would take is someone with a goal as dark and grim as this to do something. Someone serious, someone who didn't give a shit about the polls, someone who just cared about power.

That's all. Power. Someone like Michaelson Lurry. And did people just expect him to go away after two failed elections? With a war chest and a campaign contributor list of every group and person with a grudge, an agenda, someone to hate?

Just like Drew had said, the evidence was there in all of its sickening glory: arrest lists, traffic checkpoints, and detention centers. Fascism 101 in one computer screen.

'There,' Drew said. 'See that, General? There's the reference to the death of a president. And more information on the National Program Office, how they're planning to implement Case Shiloh. It only tells you that. There's no details. I'm thinking perhaps an attack on the Capitol, nerve gas or something similar during the President's speech tonight. But the evidence isn't there.'

Then, a word slipped by on the computer screen, a word that struck him with almost physical force to the gut.

SW/MAGOG. 'Christ almighty, they're going to do that,' he whispered, holding his hands together and clenching his fists. 'The bastards. The black-hearted, despicable, evil bastards.'

Sheila sat back as if what was on the screen was about to attack her. 'What is it, what did you see?'

'Scroll back up a few lines. There. That phrase. SW/MAGOG, in that section on Baltimore resources. Lieutenant, you said the evidence wasn't there. Oh yes it is, right there. The bastards, the evil, evil bastards. See there? MAGOG. An old code phrase, identifying an attack on the Capitol, used in wargames and contingency planning. No place else. The Capitol. And SW? Special Weapon. A fancy phrase for a nuclear warhead. That's what they're doing tonight, during the President's address. They'll explode a nuclear weapon, take out the President, the Vice President, Congress and the Cabinet. Plus a few hundred thousand civilians while they're at it.'

Drew said, his voice hoarse, 'Decapitation attack. That's what they're planning. Jesus Christ.'

Sheila spoke up. 'But isn't there always one Cabinet officer who doesn't attend, just in case something like this occurs, a terrorist attack?'

'Don't worry,' Montgomery said, 'I'm sure they'll have that planned as well. Evil . . .' Words failed him. It all fell together, all made dark sense. From running against your opponent to demonizing your opponent was just another step away from killing your opponent. And if a few hundred thousand people got slaughtered in the process, well, so what? Most were crackheads or welfare moms or government bureaucrats. Right? God fucking bless America.

Then, another thought that pounded at him. His oldest

son Raymond, working on the SecDef staff at the Pentagon. No, not after Grace, not to lose his oldest son . . .

'Now it's time to make those phone calls,' Montgomery said, options and choices popping up in his mind, trying desperately to push the thought of his threatened son out of his mind. 'First one is to the Secretary of Treasury, the second will be to NEST, and the third will be to the Chief of Staff at the White House. In ten minutes they'll have the President out of the city. And then the rest will fall together.'

'What's NEST?' Sheila asked.

'Nuclear Emergency Search Team,' Drew explained, nodding at Montgomery's words. 'They're tasked to search for nuclear weapons in American cities, weapons placed there by terrorists. Either foreign or domestic, it doesn't matter.'

'No, but what do matter are those phone calls,' Montgomery said. 'Time to get to a phone.'

Then, as he reached over to the nearest desk, a voice: 'Sorry, sir, I can't allow that.'

Montgomery turned, stunned at who was before him. Maurice Blakely, with a 9 mm pointed in his direction. Jesus, what kind of day this had become.

'Captain,' he said, using his best OCS voice. 'What the hell are you doing? Put the weapon away. Now.'

Blakely shook his head. 'I'm afraid I can't do that, sir. You see, events are taking place, events that you can't control. The best you can do is to watch them and survive, and afterwards you'll be in an enviable position.'

'Position?' Montgomery snapped. 'What in hell are you talking about? Blakely, put the weapon away. Now. That's a direct order.'

'The position I'm talking about is something you've wanted for a long while, General,' Blakely went on, his voice still calm. 'You and I know it, the media knows it, everybody knows it. And after Case Shiloh commences tonight, you'll be there, ready to step in, without the indignity of raising millions of dollars and shaking hands with fat housewives from Iowa and drunks from New Hampshire. When it's over the country will need a leader, sir, one like you. Will the country follow Michaelson Lurry as an acting president? Perhaps. But they will certainly follow General Cyrus Montgomery. You and I both know that, sir. So, please step away from the telephone.'

Montgomery knew that other people were in the room as well, but he couldn't keep his eyes off his aide, standing there so calmly and rationally, ready to do his part at the start of this new century, to pull everything down about him. 'Blakely, listen to me, and listen to me well. Back in the 1930s, another general named Smedley Butler turned down a group of people who wanted to overthrow Roosevelt. And about fifty years before that, another general with more sense than you said something that if nominated he would not run, if elected he would not serve. Blakely, I'm not going to lead this country over the corpses of tens of thousands of people, I'm not going to do it.'

Damn it, the man looked disappointed, didn't he? Of course he would. What was worth more, being Scribe to a retired general, or Scribe to a president?

His aide shook his head. 'Then I'm afraid you leave me no choice, sir.'

And he pulled the trigger on his pistol.

TWENTY-THREE

Excerpted from the Congressional hearings into the Iran–Contra scandal. Remarks are from Sen. Daniel K. Inouye (D-Hawaii) and Rep. Jack Brooks (D-Fla). Testifying was Colonel Oliver North, with his counsel, Attorney Brendan Sullivan:

Rep. Brooks: Colonel North, in your work at the NSC [National Security Council], were you not assigned, at one time, to work on plans for the continuity of government in the event of a major disaster?

Brendan Sullivan: Mr Chairman?

Sen. Inouye: I believe that question touches upon a highly sensitive and classified area so may I request that you not touch on that.

Rep. Brooks: I was particularly concerned, Mr Chairman, because I read in Miami papers, and several others, that there had been a plan developed by that same agency, a contingency plan in the event of emergency, that would suspend the American Constitution. And I was deeply concerned about it and wondered if that was the area in which he had worked. I believe that it was and I wanted to get his confirmation.

Sen. Inouye: May I most respectfully request that that matter not be touched upon at this stage. If we wish to get into this, I'm certain arrangements can be made for an executive session.

Just outside of Baltimore proper, on Interstate 95, traffic moved down to a crawl as Toland maneuvered the van in and around the lanes of traffic inching their way south. Henry Harrison folded his arms and stared out at the skyline of Baltimore, receding too slowly for his taste.

Toland said, 'Don't worry, we've still got plenty of time. We've driven this route a dozen times, in all kinds of weather and conditions. We've got the intel work down pat. We'll be in DC with no problem and we'll get this sucker in the Mall underground parking garage, ready to rock.'

He stared out, saw what was causing the tie-up. Fender-bender in the far right lane, tow truck and cruiser, the whole mess. Jesus. How could anybody live like this, driving on concrete day in and day out, going to your little cubicle job and computer keyboard? Thank Christ he had done something different with his life, had hooked up the SEALs and then Ira Woodman.

That made him smile, thinking of his boss. Toland glanced over and said, 'What's so funny?'

'Oh, thinking of intel work, that's what. You do intel work and you find out the funniest things. Like my boss, for instance. When I started working for him, I did a background check, just to see what he was about and where he was coming from. Boring enough stuff, lots of years in service with the Kentucky State Police. Two little brats, a chubby wife who likes some close attention, if you know what I mean.'

'Unh-hunh,' Toland said, and Henry knew he probably shouldn't be saying anything to this guy about Woodman, but so what. The guy wasn't going to make it through the night – the fewer the witnesses the better, the unofficial motto of black work – and Henry loved the expression on the guy's face.

'So anyway, one thing I found out was this guy had a real hard-on about his daddy,' Henry said. 'His old man was this hero in the Second World War, served in Europe and the Pacific, got a bunch of medals, all that happy crap. A number of years ago he got capped working in a little grocery store in Kentucky by some troubled youth. Ever since then the old man and how he served and died has been pushing Woodman to do what he does. Woodman always compares himself and what he does against his father. And the funny thing?'

Toland moved into another lane. 'The old man's war record was exaggerated?'

Henry laughed. 'Exaggerated? Hell, the goddamn thing was made up from start to finish. Oh hell yes, he was in the Army, but he served stateside and was a cook. That's all. Was almost court-martialed a few times for stealing and whoring. Closest he ever got to combat was being punched out at some whorehouse. That's my boss's daddy, the war hero. Jesus, I laughed for days when I found that out.'

Toland just nodded. 'Secrets. Everybody's got 'em.'

'You said it,' Henry said, folding his arms again and staring out at the lanes of traffic. Secrets. He thought for a moment about his own. Oh, he had plenty of them, and most he didn't share with anyone at all. But at least his record was fairly intact, not like Ira Woodman's daddy's. He had served in the SEALs, had gone to some shit-ass and dirty places for this country, and he had been slowly eased out when some white-hat officers found out that he was a bit too enthusiastic about his job. And his job had been killing, and by God he had loved it. Jesus, what did they expect? They train and train and train you to kill on demand, to kill anyone and everyone who got in the way, and Jesus, so what if you began to enjoy it? If you began to look forward to it? If you derived your sole pleasure from feeling someone rattle and choke under your grasp? And if you took souvenirs, from pictures to clothing to well . . . so what?

He shifted in his seat, remembered the last bang job with Woodman's wife. Man, that had been a good one, especially since he had been thinking of this day the whole while. All those people, all those men and women and children, all living and breathing this day in DC, all going to die. Thanks to him. All because of him. Jesus, the excitement from that thought had almost caused his head to explode when he finally came.

And before he left his place in Wellesley he had rented a couple of additional television sets and VCRs and set them to record during the next twenty-four hours on all of the cable and regular network channels. My God, he would look and relook at those tapes for the rest of his life, reliving and relishing every second . . .

'Damn,' he said, 'won't this goddamn traffic hurry up and move?'

Blakely felt some regret, not much, as he pulled the trigger. He had given the General a chance, and that's all he deserved. This way, at least, he was finally fulfilling his orders from the Shiloh Task Force. Too bad he couldn't work for the General as he took over a shattered and frightened country, but he was sure he could use his skills for the new government. After all, he was certainly proving his worth here this afternoon.

Pop. The noise sounded unnaturally quiet. Montgomery flinched, as did the woman, but the other guy, Drew, stared at him with such hatred that Blakely thought, okay, cartridge misfire, let's wrap this up.

He worked the pistol's action with a practiced move, and fired again. And again.

Pop. Pop.

Everyone was still standing. The General shook his head, took a step forward. 'Blakely . . . do you think after I lost Grace that I would allow anyone in my home, even you, with a functioning weapon? Do you? Every bit of ammo in here that's not under my control has been disabled. All of it. Blakely, give it up.'

He hated himself so for doing it, but he burst into tears, tossed the pistol at the General and started running down the hallway.

He made about a half-dozen steps before he was tackled.

Drew hated to admit it but it felt good, tackling and whaling on the General's snooty aide. He knew from the start that this guy was the one on the phone back in Newbury, the one who had blown him off. And a while ago he had pulled a gun on he and Sheila. Now he was on the carpeted hallway, tears streaming down his face, not putting up much of a fight as Drew twisted both arms behind the man's back. The General was right behind him and when he saw that Drew had things under control he went into an adjoining room, came out with a handful of neckties.

'Not ropes but it'll do,' the General said. 'Give you a hand?'

'Sure,' he said, and Blakely started in, 'General, it's not too late, you can make it happen!'

'Son,' Montgomery said, his voice dripping with scorn, 'the only thing I'm going to make happen is tying up your sorry ass and then seeing you in jail.'

The room was small, spartan, with a desk and computer and bed, and Drew half dragged, half carried Blakely to the bed. He tried one more time, saying, 'Lieutenant, look, work with the General, tell him I'm right, tell him—'

Drew took out a handkerchief, wadded it up and pushed it into the man's mouth. With the General handing over the neckties Drew made quick work and secured him to the bed, tying one of the neckties around the mouth gag. When he was done, breathing hard, Drew leaned over and gently tapped Blakely on the forehead. 'No offense, Captain, but go fuck yourself. General?'

'Yes?' he said, and Drew suddenly felt a burst of sorrow for the man, standing there calmly next to the bed with his Judas of an aide. Working all his life to rise up in the ranks, to become the highest-ranking general in the US Army, and then forced out by a president known for his spinning and pollsters, then hounded by those who wanted him to be the next one in the Oval Office, and then widowed by those who hated him almost as fiercely as those who loved him. Now, betrayed again, by his closest aide.

'General, you said something about a phone call,' Drew said, standing up. 'If you don't mind me saying, I suggest you get your ass in gear and start burning up the phone lines.'

Montgomery managed a smile. 'I'd usually mind having a lieutenant telling me to move my ass, but this time I'll make an exception. Let's get back to the office.'

He followed Montgomery in where Sheila was still working on her lapbot and she looked up. 'You guys got everything handled?'

'Yeah, we do, so far,' Drew said. 'The General's about to start making some phone calls, get this thing sidetracked.'

The General went to a phone set, picked up the receiver. He frowned, and Drew noted the look, felt his hands get heavy. Jesus, so close and already?

'Phone's dead,' Montgomery said. He went over to another desk, picked it up as well. 'So's this one.'

Then a high-pitched beeping noise started to come from one of the computer terminals. Sheila put her lapbot aside and went over to the computer keyboard and said, 'Oh, shit, Drew, General, take a look at this. You've got some visitors, and I think they just nailed your phone system.'

Drew clustered in behind Sheila, saw surveillance camera input on the large computer screen. Three screens-within-screens showed camo-geared men clambering over the fence, carrying shotguns and hunting rifles. Behind him the General said, 'Damn it to hell . . . Miss, somewhere on this screen is a file called Response. Get in there and double-click on Level One.'

Sheila nodded and her fingers flew across the keyboard, and on the screen Drew noticed puffs of smoke arising from near the fences. Some of the men dropped to the ground.

'A defense system?' Drew asked.

'Yeah, but it's just noisemakers and smoke. I sure as hell didn't want to frag some kid coming over the fence to steal some apples. There's also an automated dial-in to the local cops and state police, but I'm pretty sure that's been cut out as well. The design was to slow down any intruders while the cops came. Damn it all to hell.'

Then the computer screen flickered, faded to black, and an image popped up. Yellow letters on a black screen. UNDER THE 2001 DOMESTIC TERRORISM AND TRANQUILITY ACT, THE OCCUPANTS OF THIS PROPERTY ARE UNDER ARREST. PROCEED TO THE FRONT PORCH WITH YOUR HANDS UP.

Sheila whistled. 'Those fuckers are good. They must have an electronic counter-measure unit out there. Not only did they just fry your phone system, General, they've just taken over Net access and everything else. That means no e-mail, nothing.'

The General ran both hands across his hair and said, 'Lieutenant, we've lost about every option we have except one. In my office I've got a secure uplink phone system. It might take some time for them to cut that off as well. That means one phone call, if we're lucky.'

'Then do it, sir. Like you said before, someone at the Treasury or the White House or—'

'No,' Sheila interrupted. 'It has to better than that. What happens if you get some flunky who puts you on hold? I've read about those ECM systems, Drew. They're mobile and in a van, probably parked near here. They're awfully good. If they detect an outgoing call – and I don't care how hi-tech and secret it is – they'll fry it. You've got to make this phone call count. Call somebody in the Army, somebody in the military who'll pick up the phone at the first ring, someone who can do something.'

'Like what?' Drew asked, getting steamed at Sheila's interruptions. 'Someone who can find the bomb and stop it? Hell, we don't even know where it is!'

Sheila smiled, pointed to her lapbot screen. 'I think we do.'

Tom Conway was a driver for UPS and a member of the local fire department, but the title he was most proud of was Captain of the Washington County Militia. He had joined the militia a number of years ago, had risen up in the ranks, grew to enjoy being with the guys every other weekend for drills and stuff. Joining the militia had seemed to be the thing to do just before Y2K, but after those predictions of doom and gloom had fizzled out he had considered dropping out. After you planned to help control things when a computer-driven apocalypse was approaching, shooting at tin cans when it didn't happen seemed to be a waste of time.

But then the militia started getting involved in other things over the years, and he stayed on board. Like controlling the borders up north, when the Canadian refugees started coming south after Quebec went independent. Like picketing stores that sold mostly out-of-country goods. Like doing what had to be done to protect their guns and independence.

Which is why he was grinning as he and his buddies went across the field in a skirmishing line, heading up to the farmhouse. This was going to be fun, to be actually doing something that they had been trained for. Heading over the fence had been scary at first, with those loud bangs and smoke clouds, but Porter, an ex-Army guy who had a lot of experience, had just said it was noisemakers. Nothing to worry about.

Conway kept on smiling as he approached the farmhouse. He had never met a Jew before. Too bad he'd have to kill the first one he saw.

Sheila talked fast, pointing out the text on the screen, feeling proud of herself that while these two guys were out doing guy stuff – i.e., beating up on somebody else – she had kept her eye on the ball.

'Look,' she said. 'Look here. All of these cities listed have the same sort of resource list attached. Right? Kitchens, first aid facilities, National Guard units. But in Baltimore there's a GMC van. Adapted for delivery purposes. That's all. But what kind of delivery? Flowers? Food? And how else do you transport a nuclear warhead?'

Drew looked over to the General, who was slowly nodding. 'A truck bomb. Of course. The biggest damn truck bomb in history.'

'And maybe I'm wrong, General, but I don't think you'd want something like that parked somewhere out in the open. I think you'd wait until the last minute before driving it to where your target is. The van's in the Baltimore area. It's probably heading to Washington right now. If you've got one phone call, I'd reach someone in the Pentagon.'

Then, damn the General, he shook his head. 'No. Not the Pentagon. Colorado. That's where I'm going to call.'

Drew followed the General and Sheila into his office, knowing that he should be mentioning something very urgent, urgent indeed, but he couldn't afford to joggle the General's elbow, not at this moment. Still, he looked out the windows as they crowded into the office. There were a number of bad men with weapons out there, coming here, and he had to do something about it.

Montgomery looked at the faces of the young man and woman before him, seeing the expectation in their expressions, the knowledge that this old general was about to make everything right. He should have been angry but he couldn't blame them. What other hope did they have?

He went behind his desk, looked down at the papers that marked the progress of his autobiography, and in a fit of anger swept them off. Pure bullshit, from one end to the next. By the telephone on his desk was another phone unit, dark gray and military-looking, with no keypad, just a single punch switch. He took a deep breath, rehearsed what was going to happen. He raised up the receiver, punched in the switch.

A female voice answered after one ring. 'CentComm.' Central Communications, an office in the bowels of some Army base in Virginia, able to connect you with any military base in the world.

'SpaceCom Duty Officer.'

'Hold one, please.'

Drew and Sheila stared at him. The hiss of the phone line was reassuring.

'SpaceCom, Colonel Higgins,' came another female voice.

'This is General Cyrus Montgomery,' he said. 'I need to speak to General Coombs. Authorization Delta One, repeat, Delta One.'

'Say again, who is this?' the skeptical voice asked.

'General Cyrus Montgomery. And this is a Delta One communication. Connect me with General Coombs.'

The voice remained skeptical. 'Hold one.'

Montgomery cleared his throat. His mouth had suddenly gone quite dry.

Ira Woodman was watching the progress of the militia troops on a computer screen set in one wall of the ECM, the video feed coming in from a surveillance drone about the size of a lawnmower that was orbiting the General's farmhouse. The assault line was ragged but at least the idiots were taking advantage of the cover as they moved up, ducking and halting behind some shrubbery and saplings on the side of the hill.

'Uh-oh,' said Gary Leeson, the ECM control officer. 'I've got phone traffic heading out of the farmhouse.'

Ira kept on looking at the screen. 'Stop it, then. You said you could cut off all communications.'

'This one's a bit tougher,' Leeson complained. 'Latest military. Pretty secure.'

Ira turned to him. Clem was sitting next to the Gen Z-er as well. Ira said, 'Does that mean you can't stop it?'

Leeson grinned. 'Shit, Mr Woodman, I didn't say that.'

Another click on the line. Montgomery squeezed the receiver. 'General Coombs, here.'

'Leslie, it's Cyrus.'

'Cyrus! What in God's name do you mean by phoning in with a Delta One authorization? My duty officer practically pissed herself when she passed that along to me. This had—'

'General Coombs, that was a Delta One phone call for a reason. I have information on Shiloh. It involves a special weapon, contained in a white GMC van bearing Maryland license plate' – he leaned over to look at Sheila's lapbot and read her the registration number – 'believed to be heading south to Washington. Detonation of special weapon to occur any time from now to 7 p.m. tonight.'

'Special . . . Cyrus, what in hell do you want me to do?'

'I trust you, Leslie, I've always trusted you. I don't know who else to trust at the Pentagon or anywhere else.' Including my own fucking home, he thought. He went on. 'You've got an asset, orbiting now, that could take care of this van before it gets to DC. Correct?'

'*Excalibur* . . . but we've only had that one test shot, Cyrus. This is a hell of a thing!'

'Leslie, I don't have much time. My home here is under assault. I'm going to lose this phone line once they figure out how to cut it. *Excalibur* is the best I could come up with.'

He listened to her breathing, knew what was going on out there in Colorado Springs, at the SpaceCom headquarters hundreds of feet below Cheyenne Mountain. 'Hold on, General. Let's see if we can find this van.'

Drew and Sheila were still looking at him, expectation in their faces. 'I've called Space Command,' he said. 'They're going to try to locate the van.'

Sheila said, 'But one van, in all that traffic . . .'

Montgomery slowly nodded. 'A challenge, but the assets we have up there in orbit . . . Miss, we can find anything from up there if we want to, and believe me, they will want to.'

'Cyrus?' the voice came back, quicker than expected.

'Yes? Do you have it?'

Her voice seemed strained. 'We do. It's heading south, just like you said. On I-95. It'll be in DC in less than an hour. But Cyrus . . .'

'Yes? What's wrong?'

'The orbit, that's what's wrong. *Excalibur* is clear on the other side of the globe. By the time she's in position, in about an hour, that van could be parked right next to the Capitol.'

'Shit, look, maybe—'

He yelled in pain as the phone started screeching and he dropped the receiver, which bounced off the top of his desk. Drew and Sheila looked on in shock as he gingerly picked up the phone, and then he shook his head and said, 'Dead.'

He didn't bother returning the receiver to the phone unit.

'Yee-hah,' Leeson said. 'Deader than last year's software. Man, if that phone was up to somebody's ear, I bet you they've lost their hearing.'

Ira nodded in satisfaction, then thought of something. 'Do you know who they were calling?'

'Hold on, hold on,' Leeson said, and then Clem joined in as they started tapping the computer keys. 'Got it,' Leeson announced. 'An Army outfit in Virginia called CentComm. Stands for Central Communications.'

'Gary, you're an idiot,' Clem announced, still tapping away. 'That's where the call went into. You've got to dig a bit deeper. Here it is, Mr Woodman. Call was transferred from CentComm to the Duty Officer at Cheyenne Mountain. Headquarters of US Space Command.'

For a moment Ira wondered what the phone call might have meant, and then gave up. So what. Time to make sure the damage was limited. He looked at his watch. My God, less than two hours to go.

'Can you isolate the base?'

Leeson and Badger both looked at him with the same, stupid expressions. Jaws slack, like they had just seen their first naked woman. Clem spoke up first, his voice filled with disbelief. 'Mr Woodman . . . SpaceCom's designed for the worse the Soviets could throw at them. They have hardened and encrypted information links, stuff that I could hardly imagine . . . It'd be a stretch even to attempt it. We'd need the heavy guns to make it happen.'

'What kind of heavy guns?' Ira demanded.

Badger looked to Leeson, like he was seeking reassurance, and then he shrugged. 'Mr Lurry might be able to do something, if only for a while. If we can get a hold of him.'

Ira said, 'He's in the Albany Regional Retreat Center. Get a hold of him and get it done. Whatever was said to Cheyenne Mountain, I want it to stay in there. Get moving.'

And then he went back to the computer screen, eager to see the assault begin.

*

Drew struggled to find his voice as General Montgomery slowly sat down in his chair and said, 'General, we've got something more immediate to worry about. We've got an armed gang out there and I don't think they're here to deliver birthday cards. Do you have anything high-powered around here I can use?'

Montgomery seemed lost in thought but he reached into his pants pocket and pulled out a small bunch of keys. He tossed it and Drew caught it with one snap. The General said, 'Round brass key, right on the end. Go down the hallway, last door there. My bedroom. Go in the rear closet, there's a metal safe. Take what you need.'

Drew nodded, thought of something else. He bent down to his backpack, pulled out his 9 mm and two spare clips, which he placed on the General's desk. 'Here. Something for you as well.'

Sheila spoke up, 'Hey, come on. Those guys come knocking at the house, we'll just leave them alone. If they break in, fine, we'll just go with them quietly. What's the problem? We've made the call. Who cares if we're going to be arrested or not?'

Drew looked at the General, who gazed back at him and then nodded, just a bit. Drew cleared his throat and said, 'General, keep an eye on my woman, will you? She's all that I've got.'

From outside he could hear some shouts, and Montgomery nodded again. 'You can count on it. And you better get going. On the first floor, by the kitchen. There's a mud room and breezeway that leads to the barn. From the cupola you'll have a pretty good field of fire.'

He went to Sheila, touched her poor, miscut hair and gave her a quick kiss. 'You stick close to him, hon. You do exactly what he says. All right? Exactly. And I love you. Honest to God, I do.'

Then he moved out of the office as quickly as he could.

Sheila looked on as Drew ran out, and then looked over to the General. He had picked up the pistol and examined it, and she said, 'Look, what the hell was that all about? Tell me.'

The General seemed to refuse to look at her. 'What it means, miss, is that we don't have much time. There are a number of people who have planned and plotted for years for this moment, and who have tried to kill me and the two of you as well. The seconds and minutes are ticking away, and the men out on my grounds, and the men who sent them there, are not in the mood to arrest us.'

Her stomach seemed to settle right down about her feet and do a slow flip-flop. 'Then what's Drew doing out there all alone?'

Now Montgomery raised his face, looked at her with a calm expression. 'He's trying to delay the inevitable, that's what.'

'And you sent him out there alone?!'

Montgomery worked the action of the pistol, eased the hammer back down. 'That's what he wanted, miss. And my job now is to protect you as well.'

'But . . . but . . . the general you talked to in Colorado. What is she doing?'

'There's a space-based weapon, called *Excalibur*. It fires a rod of titanium with a depleted uranium tip. It's called a kinetic energy weapon. Once they located the van, it seemed clear to me that the best way to stop it would be using *Excalibur*. You could destroy the van and the warhead, with minimal contamination and exposure. You won't have a nuclear event. But *Excalibur*'s on the other side of the globe. By the time its orbit reaches the correct position, they will have made it to Washington.'

'But won't she get the word out, what you just told her?'

Montgomery got up and pulled the shade down on the window. He said, 'Let's get to the corner over here, it's probably safest. General Coombs? Perhaps. But the Shiloh conspiracy . . . none of us know how far it reaches. Maybe she can contact someone, maybe not. But as every minute goes by, miss, that warhead gets closer to Washington.'

She looked down at her lapbot, saw that damn message flickering across again. UNDER THE 2001 DOMESTIC TERRORISM AND TRANQUILITY ACT, THE OCCU-PANTS OF THIS PROPERTY ARE UNDER ARREST. PROCEED TO THE FRONT PORCH WITH YOUR HANDS UP. And Drew, poor Drew, going out there . . . no wonder his eyes seemed to fill up when he bent over to kiss her.

The sound of a gunshot startled her, and Montgomery reached over and pulled at her hand.

'Wait!' she said. 'There's something else.'

'What's that?'

'The police.'

'Excuse me? The police? Miss, the local cops—'

'No, no, no, not the local cops. The police in Baltimore. If we can get word to them what's in the van, maybe they can stop it for questioning. Hell, I don't think these con-spirators have every cop in the country working for them, do they? And you can bet even the dumbest cop in Baltimore might ask a question or two of a van that's hauling a god-damn nuclear warhead in its back.'

Montgomery said, 'You said it yourself. The ECM van has cut us off from communications.'

'Yeah, but I didn't say I was giving up. Did you?'

The look on his face suddenly scared her, and she saw the flash of steel in his eyes that made him a general. 'No, miss, I sure as hell ain't giving up.'

TWENTY-FOUR

The Lynchburg, Va.-based evangelist Rev. Jerry Falwell told a group of pastors in Kingsport, Tenn., that the Antichrist – a New Testament figure who will spread untold evil at the end of time – 'will be a full-grown counterfeit of Christ. Of course, he'll be Jewish.'

Washington Post, January 23, 1999

Drew went into the barn, breathing hard, a Colt .45 in his hands, looking about. Bouncing on his back from a sling was a .308 Browning with a fifteen-round clip and a 4× telescopic sight that seemed rugged enough. He carried an ammo belt stuffed with additional clips in his other hand, and then he slung the belt around his neck. The barn had empty horse stalls and smelled of hay. An old wooden sleigh was in one corner, the paint having faded away. Before him was a wooden ladder, which he started climbing, after putting the Colt in his rear waistband. He was terribly thirsty and he felt an odd sense of pride as he climbed up into the barn.

Other battles he had fought, other places he had been, he had gone there under orders, under direction to accomplish a mission he had no say in. Not a problem – that's what he had been trained to do.

But today . . . this was for Sheila, and this was for the General. There was a sense of responsibility that almost made him shudder with fear, but overcoming that was the pride. He was going to do what he had to do to protect Sheila and the General. He remembered some late-night talks, in barracks and around flickering campfires, when the words came out about pulling a John Wayne. You never pulled a John Wayne for a piece of medal or ribbon. You pulled a John Wayne for those you loved. That's all.

Up on the second level of the barn was another short ladder. Dust and cobwebs caked his hands and face as he went up to the cupola. Wood creaked about him as he laid out his weapons. Some of the slats in the cupola had fallen away. He inserted a clip into the Browning, worked the action. He looked at the way the sun was shining in on the floor, remembered seeing the armed men come over on the east side of the property. East it was.

Drew went up to an opening and gingerly placed the end of the rifle barrel on one of the wooden slats. It held. He took a few deep breaths, looked through the scope. Before him and away were two men, waving and talking at each other, maybe fifty yards out by a clump of shrubbery. Both wore camouflage clothes and both had weapons in their hands.

He took another deep breath, squeezed the trigger. 'Howdy, pilgrim,' he whispered.

Maurice Blakely tugged again and felt the silk begin to slip about his right wrist. How about that, he thought. How about that. Looks like we can make some progress here, so fuck you, Drew Connor. He forced himself to relax, knowing that if he got too tensed up his muscles would expand and his bounds would get tighter.

Another deep breath, and then another. He closed his eyes and tried to focus away from the tightness about his arms and his legs and the horrid taste of the handkerchief forced into his mouth. He thought about getting out of this room, and then what he would do. Kill Drew first, and then the General, and then the woman. And the woman he would kill last and do it nice and slow, to make up for this humiliation from her man.

He took another deep breath through his nose, then moved his right hand again.

The knot slipped some more.

In her office two thousand and five hundred feet under Cheyenne Mountain, General Leslie Coombs looked out at the glass wall, which overlooked the main control center for what was once called NORAD, the North American Air Defense Command, and was now the center of the US Space Command. Beyond were the large display screens and rows of computer monitors and the cool fluorescent lights that illuminated the Air Force and Navy personnel working here, in the 'Cave'.

In years past this center received all of the early-warning information about the activities of the Great Beast, the old Soviet Union. From orbiting satellites to ground stations around the periphery of that empire to the Distant Early-Warning system up in northern Canada, this was the place that looked outward for the signs of an enemy on the move.

Now, however, she thought, as she stood up and looked out over her people, now the enemy was within. A hell of a thing, a hell of a thing. She had sworn an oath to the Constitution and to her service to follow the legitimate orders of her civilian and military leadership. And now? She had done something on her own, based on the words of a friend who was now a civilian, outside of the chain of command. She crossed her arms, looked again at the screens and displays. Before the day was out she was probably going to be a civilian as well, with a very good chance of going to prison when this mess was over.

'General?'

She turned. Her operations officer, Colonel Ray Taylor, was standing through the side door. Even in the dull lights he looked more pale than usual, his eyes blinking behind his thick glasses. Having a near-blind Air Force officer on her staff made for some good jokes, but Colonel Taylor knew computers, knew satellites, and knew enough about everything under Cheyenne Mountain to be indispensable.

'Go ahead, Colonel,' she said, looking out to her people, wondering who was loyal and who was Case Shiloh. My God, is this what we've come to? Are we back to loyalty oaths? 'What is it?'

'Ma'am, we've managed to scan that GMC van with a CYGNUS Four that was in the area. Neutron to gamma ratio confirms, right on track. Either it's carrying weapons-grade plutonium or the real thing, ma'am.'

'I see.'

'And another thing, General. We've been silenced.'

She turned suddenly to him. 'We've been what?'

He nodded, shifted his weight, clenched the papers in his hands even tighter. 'We've been silenced, ma'am. Cable transmission, SatCom, Net access, voice and data uplinks. Even our old NORAD links. We're also getting some electromagnetic jamming to most of our antenna systems. It's like somebody's pulled the plug on the outside, somebody with a lot of pull. We've got people working on it but I don't know how long we'll be kept quiet.'

General Coombs clenched her fists. 'I'll tell you how long we'll be kept quiet. Until it doesn't matter anymore.' She rubbed at her forehead and let out a sigh. Nothing else to do.

'Ray . . .'

'Ma'am?' If he seemed surprised at being called by his first name, he didn't show it.

'Ray, do we still have contact with *Excalibur*?'

'That we do, ma'am. But I don't know for how long.'

'Then I want an attack profile worked up on that van and uplinked, as soon as possible.'

'Ma'am . . .'

She turned again at the hesitation, thinking, not Ray, please, I can't lose Ray. 'Go ahead, Colonel,' she said sharply.

He stood at attention. 'General, an attack profile for the van was uplinked ten minutes ago. All *Excalibur* needs is the go order.'

She tried to hide the relief in her voice. 'And what made you do that, Colonel?'

'Intuition on my part, ma'am. I had the feeling that you wanted *Excalibur* prepped.'

'Intuition? That's all?'

Now the Colonel seemed slightly ashamed. 'No, ma'am. That's not all. My dad . . . well, my dad works on Capitol Hill. On their police force. I . . . I know I shouldn't be thinking of him, but I was thinking if there was an attack tonight . . .'

Coombs nodded, and then walked around and sat down at her desk. 'You did good, Ray. Don't worry. You did good. Give the go order, now. And then I want you to write up a report. Nothing fancy. I want you to put down that you uplinked the attack profile and the go order upon my direction. That you opposed my doing so, but that I overruled your protests.'

'General . . .'

'Shut up, Colonel. You're wasting time. Go to it.'

'Yes, ma'am.'

When he had walked out of her office she rubbed at her face and was shocked at feeling the tears about her eyes. What had she been weeping for? Her doomed career? That her own Air Force was about to mount an attack on her own people? That there were people out there who were doing their best to destroy her country?

No answers. Just the damn tears. She rubbed at her eyes until they were gone. There was no time for tears.

Maybe there had been a moment of doubt, of firing on these men without giving them warning, but to hell with it. They were on the General's property, they were coming to kill them all, and Drew wasn't in the mood for quarter.

He snapped off two shots at the guys near the shrubbery, catching one in the shoulder, the other in the thigh. Then he moved quickly to the other side of the cupola, saw a small skirmish line hit the ground by an old stone wall, and sent five shots in their direction as well. And as angry and as intense and focused as he was, he couldn't bring himself to kill the poor bastards. They were under orders, misguided and wrong, but they had been sent here.

The least he could do was to wound them, and not kill them outright.

He fired twice more at movement out there in the fields, then packed up and started down the ladder, moving quickly, splinters digging into the palms of his hands. From the quick look he had gotten through the rifle's scope, he could tell that these weren't Reserve or National Guard troops. Nope, they were probably the local militia, a bunch of guys who thought playing in woods and fields with guns was a bunch of fun. He felt good for a moment, seeing who he was up against. Let's see how much fun being shot at turns out to be.

Still, no reason to underestimate your opponent, and he ducked as he got down about three feet on the ladder and incoming fire started chewing up ragged holes in the cupola. The sudden noise of the rounds slamming through the wood startled him, and he fell the last few feet to the second level of the barn, yelping as he landed badly on his left foot.

Sheila was on the carpeted floor of the General's office. He had been busy the past few minutes, dragging furniture in front of the door. As he worked Montgomery kept on muttering under his breath, curses and exclamations and other phrases that Sheila couldn't catch. And right now she didn't particularly give a shit what the General was saying. She had been busy under his desk, looking for something and almost yelling with glee at what she found. Flush against the wall a cable TV connection, from when the office had probably previously been a bedroom. She unsnapped the door to her equipment port at the rear of her lapbot and pulled out a length of modem cable. Might work, just might work. She started screwing in the adapter and then the General was next to her under the desk, breathing hard. 'What do you have?'

'What I have is an old cable connection, General. I'm trying to get my lapbot hooked up, see if I can't get at T1 or high-line access. If I do, then it's a quick e-mail blast to the Baltimore Police Department. Ah, here we go.'

She started tapping on the keys, setting up the Internet access program, and heard the comfortable high-pitched whining noise as her computer started talking down the cable line.

'C'mon, c'mon, c'mon,' she whispered, and then she froze as the high-pitched sound shifted in tone. 'General, I think we're getting hooked up here, it looks – shit!'

On her screen, the familiar message: UNDER THE 2001 DOMESTIC TERRORISM AND TRANQUILITY ACT, THE OCCUPANTS OF THIS PROPERTY ARE UNDER ARREST. PROCEED TO THE FRONT PORCH WITH YOUR HANDS UP.

Montgomery awkwardly patted her on the shoulder. 'You did your best, Sheila.'

'Yeah, well, I'm not finished yet.' The sound of gunshots were closer, and she felt a quiver of terror, thinking of Drew out there, alone, facing all those armed bastards. She started to squirm her way out from under the desk, and then sat up. With a vicious tug she undid her modem line to the cable TV connection.

'General, don't be pissed at me or anything, but I'm afraid you're gonna have to move all that furniture. We've got someplace else to go right now.'

Behind a stone wall Neil Porter of the Washington County Militia tried to get in a relaxed position but a damn rock was digging into his hip. So what. He was covered and that's what counted. Some yards away Tom Conway, that UPS driver and second-in-command of these clowns, was screaming as someone tried to bandage up his shoulder. Neil shrugged. That's what you get when you play with the big boys. Sometimes they play back, quite rough.

More gunfire from the farmhouse coming his way, and Neil didn't budge. He had served a couple of tours with the 10th Mountain Infantry Division and had done well until his wife dumped him, forcing him to pay for her and child support and everything else. Money got tight and the military couldn't do squat – each year was the promise for more pay and more pay, and each year the promise never came true – so he had reluctantly mustered out. When he ended up in Vermont he had done okay, working for a security firm that had some contracts for some of the hi-tech industries setting up shop along the Connecticut River.

But he had missed something, missed a connection, which is why he joined the militia. It was good, being out with guys again, doing maneuvers, and he even enjoyed passing along some training tips of his own. He saw a need for the militia – it was a proven fact that criminals stayed out of counties that had active militias – but he didn't go for the crazy stuff, like hunting down Canadian refugees, spouting off about the Jews and blacks, and preparing for the day when UN peacekeeper troops set up shop in downtown Montpelier.

So he had gone along, knowing that if anything got too crazy he would duck out.

Like today. Jesus, to think they were going to attack the home of one of the best friends a grunt ever had, General Cyrus Montgomery. He thought that was a shit-ass idea from the get-go, but Carl Slocum, the C-in-C for the militia, had said he had received important information, information that terrorists were inside that farmhouse, plotting and planning to do harm.

Yeah. Sure. General Montgomery, plotting the destruction of the United States from his farmhouse.

So when Neil went across the fence and through the noisemakers, that was okay, but after the gunfire started he decided it was time to tender his resignation with the Washington County Militia. If he ran into Carl Slocum later today, he would do it face to face.

In the meantime . . . He shifted his weight, grabbed a pack of Winstons from his fatigue coat, and lit one up. He had no idea how long this particular cluster-fuck was going to last, but he knew this was the place to wait it out. He exhaled a cloud of smoke, and tried to relax. The sound of gunfire didn't bother him, but he wished in hell that Conway would just shut the fuck up and take being wounded like a man.

Drew stood up, winced. Damn ankle was bung up. Probably not broken but definitely a sprain. He could move on it but it would sure slow him down. He looked around. The second floor of the barn was open in the center in a huge square, looking down on the ground floor and the old horse stalls and the wooden sleigh. At both ends were small doors, probably used to bring in hay or feed or whatever it was that farmers dragged in. More gunfire was being poured into the cupola, where he had just been, and he shrugged off the thought of what it might have been like up there if he had stayed behind. He hadn't stayed, so it was time to move on.

He went to the nearest set of doors, gritting his teeth every time he put his left foot down, then did an awkward belly flop. The doors opened inwards and he slowly pulled one towards him, peering out. He had a good view of the open land moving down to the east and the wire fence where the militia men had come over. He saw movement by a stone wall, and off to the south, where a thick tangle of brush and saplings provided cover. More gunfire, streaming overhead, and it seemed like it was coming from the brush. Drew shook his head as he unlimbered his rifle, one of the first lessons you learned in field work.

'Cover ain't necessarily protection, fellas,' he whispered, lowering his head down to the scope.

He fired a full clip into the brush and saplings, working from one end to the next, and was satisfied at hearing the screams and yells. He pulled back and then got up. Time to see what was going on at the other end of the barn.

Toland spoke up. 'It looks like the traffic's starting to move, up on ahead.'

'About time,' Henry said. He sat back and worked the radio dial in the van, trying to find a good talk show host, speaking about the parasites in government, or the public pisser in the White House, or the welfare cheats, or the abortionists, or the UN troops in Mexico and Canada, but all he got was that coon kid music. Speaking in words he couldn't understand, talking about banging dis and banging dat, and bitches and hos and bang dis city.

Jesus, he thought, finally shutting the radio off. Worse thing this country ever did was give these mud people the right to vote back in '64. Citizenship should be earned, not awarded because you turned eighteen and breathed on your own.

He folded his arms, saw the line of traffic ahead of them. Toland was an optimist, and that's what got this country into trouble. Optimists. It was time for a heavy dose of realism, that plus the heavy dose of a thermal blast and fallout that was going to make everything all right.

There, Maurice Blakely thought, one hand free and let's get this damn . . .

'Ah!' he said, spitting out the handkerchief. He rubbed his face with his free hand, then worked on his other wrist. Just a few more minutes and he'd be out of here. Maybe that old man had disabled his ammo but there was no way he could disable a sharp blade, and Maurice knew how to work a knife as well as anyone.

He bent down, started working on his feet. For the past few minutes he had listened to the opening rounds of gunfire, knew that his Case Shiloh companions were finally moving in. If luck was with him he could take care of the General, Drew and that bitch by the time they got into the farmhouse. From there, well, the sky was the limit.

His left foot was freed. Time for the right one.

Inside the EMC van Ira leaned over the backs of the two computer operators, Clem Badger and the Gen Z-er, trying to keep up with them as they flicked through displays on their respective computer screens. It was hard to keep up with them as the two spoke to each other in tech babble. Sometimes on the screens he saw a video feed from the surveillance drone, sometimes there were columns of numbers and graphs, and other times just programming code. His head ached, trying to make sense of it.

Behind him, at a table, Tanya Selenekov was murmuring to herself as she worked on a press release about what was going on today here at the General's compound. He wondered what kind of creative lies she was coming up with. He checked his watch. Just over an hour to go.

'What's happening?' he asked. 'What's going on?'

'Good news and bad news, Mr Woodman,' Clem said. 'Bad news first. The militia's getting close to the farmhouse, but they're getting pretty chewed up. From our thermal imagery it looks like there's three people on the third floor, two in one office and a third in another room. The third person's been stationary the past half hour. We also have a guy in the barn. We think he's the gunman. We've been transmitting his location to the militia head the past few minutes, but he hasn't acknowledged yet.'

Ira felt like gripping the necks of both of these youngsters and strangling them, and he knew why: for the crime of being smarter than he was. 'Go on. What's the good news?'

'The good news is that we're still keeping a lid on communications from the house. Jamming is working across all frequencies, and they tried accessing the cable modem system a few minutes ago. No joy for them. Just our little message to surrender.'

Gary Leeson spoke up, 'Okay, we got two people on the second floor, on the move. Looks like they're going downstairs.'

Ira said, 'Pass that along to the militia. And tell them to hurry up!'

A phone at the rear of the van rang and Tanya picked it up. Ira heard her talking but kept his eyes on the display screens, trying to see what was going on.

'Mr Woodman! Please, Mr Woodman!'

He turned away from the display screens. 'Yes? What is it?'

'It's Mr Lurry, sir. He needs to talk to you. He wants to know . . . he wants to know what the hell is going on over here.'

So this was it. Ira said, 'Of course.' He strode over to Tanya – damn it, this woman has got to stop wearing her skirts so short – and he took the receiver from her hand.

Then he slammed the receiver down and ripped the phone wire from the side of the van. All three were now staring at him, wide-eyed, and he said, 'Back to your jobs, all of you. Now.'

And he was pleased to see that they did just that.

Cyrus Montgomery led the woman down to the first floor, going out front, the borrowed 9 mm firm in his hands. Sheila was right behind him, her lapbot held close to her like it was a lifevest or some damn thing. Outside was the noise of yells and gunfire, and he tried to keep it all in as he led her to the cellar door. He allowed himself a brief moment of fearful humor, thinking that just a couple of years ago he was in the command of tens of thousands of troops, armored divisions, air wings and every other bit of nasty ordnance that can be imagined. For the medals and pension and all the awards he had been given in that long, tiring climb to the top, he would have gladly traded it all in for one Bradley fighting vehicle parked on the front lawn and the crew to go with it. Hell, if pressed, he would just take the Bradley. He was sure he and Drew could figure it out fast enough to work it and cause some damage.

Now his command had shrunk to himself, one tired vet out there who was doing his best to make the attackers pay, and one young woman with wide eyes who was trying to do a job through tears in her eyes and shaking hands. He led her quickly across the living room, staying close to the walls and away from the windows.

'This way,' he said, opening up the cellar door, taking her down the musty wooden stairs. He closed the door behind them and tried to block the doorknob with a length of broomstick. Should slow them down at least a few minutes, give him enough warning so that . . . well, so that he could go out fighting. Not a bad obituary, if you thought about it.

'Hurry up, will you?' came the woman's voice from the darkness of the cellar, and he followed her down.

Drew was on his belly again, opening up from the other second-floor door on the barn. This view showed the roof of the farmhouse and a stream further off to the north. No movement and he was about to go back in, head down to the ground floor, when the buzzing sound of an insect caught his attention.

Hold on, he thought. Too loud for an insect. He peered out again and looked up to the sky, and there it was. A battlefield surveillance drone, about the size of an old-fashioned snow shovel, wide lifting body and propeller up front, narrow tail at the rear, and stuffed full of cameras, sensors, thermal detectors and everything else. The Browning came up in his hands and, after three well-placed shots, the drone tumbled down behind the roof.

Shit, big mistake. Fire erupted from the streambed, rounds going in and around him, and as he pulled back Drew gasped as something struck his left shoulder.

Inside the ECM van Gary Leeson murmured, 'Oh, I don't like this, not at all,' as his fingers flew across the keyboard. Ira wiped at his eyes, refused to look at his watch to see how many minutes were oozing around as these incompetents out in the field tried to do their job. Leeson said, 'Sorry, sir, we've lost the surveillance drone. Either it took a hit or we lost power to it.'

Clem offered, 'Those drones don't have much of a lifespan out in the field, sir, they—'

'Shut up,' Ira said, and Clem shut up. He leaned in and said, 'What was the last info we had?'

'Well, before the drone went dead, sir, we had some of the militiamen by a streambed, to the north of the farmhouse. It looks like they were moving up, to hit the house from the rear.'

'Good.'

Clem spoke up, voice hurt, like a little boy who had just been scolded. 'Mr Woodman, there's an urgent e-mail here from Mr Lurry, at the—'

'Don't answer,' Ira said, blinking his eyes again, rubbing at his face. 'No answer, not at all. We keep at it. Understand?'

Neither of them replied, which was just fine as they continued working their keyboards. Ira took a deep breath. Close, we are so close . . .

Sheila started swearing again as she tugged the phone line from the phone junction box in the basement, next to a dusty metal shelf that looked like it had a hundred years' worth of old paint and oil cans piled up. As a kid she had spent a summer interning at a local Bell Atlantic office, and she knew a bit about phone lines and such. She was hoping for another line coming in through the junction box, or a way to get access through the technician's check switch, but dead air. Nothing.

The General looked on, his face hard to make out in the dim light. The cellar was old and huge, with vaulted brick arches going off into the blackness. A few light bulbs struggled against the darkness. 'No luck, eh?'

'Shit, General, no luck at all,' she said, wiping her forehead. It was clammy and hot in the cellar, and the gunshots were getting louder. Oh Drew, my Drew . . .

'Well, you did your best, no reason to . . .'

She was no longer listening. She was looking up at the beams and planks up over her head, saw an old-style copper phone line. Sheila looked down at the Bell Atlantic junction box. The old phone line didn't go into the junction box. It bypassed it and went up and out. Holy shit.

'General, I haven't shown you my best yet,' she said, reaching up to touch the copper line. 'Help me trace this back.'

As she went deeper into the cellar she just stopped once, at the sound of feet overhead.

Drew sat back against one of the old beams and grimaced in pain as he touched his shoulder. Sticky with blood. Well, sir, do you mind the sight of blood? Only if it's my own, only if it belongs to me. He gingerly touched the edges of the wound, felt a sharp bite in his fingers. A piece of wood. A goddam piece of wood, splintered from the shooting. Well, ain't that fucking nice.

He tried to pick up the Browning, gasped in pain and dropped it. Too heavy and bulky. He reached in his waistband, drew out the Colt .45. Time for some close action work. He wondered if anybody on the outside was hearing this fracas. You'd think somebody would've called the cops by now.

He took a deep breath and stood up, wavering, and looked down at the wooden ladder. It seemed a hundred feet long and six inches wide. 'C'mon,' he whispered. 'Gotta do it. For Sheila, if nobody else.'

Drew stuck the .45 back into his waistband and started the long struggle down to the ground.

There! Maurice Blakely got off his bed, swung his feet over and stood up, feeling woozy at first then better as he walked across the floor. He went to his closet and reached in, past some old Army gear piled there in the bottom, until he found what he was looking for. Ah . . . yes, old reliable.

He pulled his hand out. A nice Mark II issue folding combat knife, and he shivered with pleasure for a moment, remembering the first time this cold steel touched flesh, down in Colombia.

Blakely pulled the knife free and went out to the hallway. From the words they spoke as they went by, he knew the General and the woman were heading to the cellar, and it was time to join them.

By God he was now seriously pissed off, and Carl Slocum felt his heart thumping against his chest as he raced the last few feet of open space to the rear door of the farmhouse. He had his shotgun at port arms as he reached it, and he looked behind to see if any of his crew were following him. Andy Tompkins was back there, and that kid, Timmy Picard, but their faces were pale and their eyes were wide and they were holding back. Fuck 'em, he would go in and do it himself.

He turned the doorknob and almost chortled. Hell, god-damn thing was unlocked. He went into a kitchen and then into a wide and open living room, holding the shotgun out, remembering what his boss had said those long minutes ago. Not a person to remain living in here, not one, and he wasn't going to let his boss down, no sir. He had waited and planned for this day for years, to do something great for his country, and today was the day. Carl could hardly wait to tell every-one tomorrow about what he was about to do in this house.

When the creaking noise came he reacted instantly, swinging his shotgun to the left as a man with a knife came running down the stairway. 'Eat this,' he yelled, pulling the trigger and working the pump action again and shooting again as the man fell back against the stairs, the booming sound of the shotgun causing pictures on the walls to shake.

Carl moved forward slowly, seeing if the guy was going to move or not, but nope, he had caught the two sets of double-ought pellets right into the chest. Man, that fucker was dead, but he kicked away the knife as he got closer. Gotta be careful but still . . . he bent over to look at the face, which was relatively unmarked. Funny, the guy sure didn't look Jewish.

Somebody coughed behind him and he turned, expecting to see Andy or Timmy, not a limping guy with blood trickling down his shoulder aiming a .45 in his direction, a big fucking pistol that was the last thing Carl Slocum ever saw.

Cyrus jerked his head again as he heard the gunfire over his head. Armed men were now in his house. He pulled some old dressers and cardboard boxes of records around them as Sheila continued to work, murmuring to herself, undoing the tangled mess of old copper lines near the oil furnace and storage tank. It was like she was oblivious of everything about her, the darkness, the gunshots, the shouts from overhead. She said, 'General, this looks like a set-up that was popular back in the sixties and seventies. A phone line led from an oil tank, set on an automatic read. If the oil level went below a certain level, a phone call would go to the oil company . . . Man, this is one hell of a mess . . .'

He said nothing, just kept the pistol pointed in the direction of the stairways. He remembered being here in this same spot with Blakely, almost an eternity ago, when the biggest worry of the day had been a leaking pipe. A lot of things had changed in those few days, a lot of fucking things. There was a bulkhead leading outdoors as well, but that had a half-dozen locks to it and he had piled some furniture in front of it. Here, he thought, Montgomery's last stand. He wondered if anyone would ever know what they had done here, or if the news tomorrow would be full of something else. Like a nuclear attack on DC, blamed on terrorists. Sure, why not? Followed by an announcement by Acting President Michaelson Lurry, invoking martial law, and here's a list of emergency actions to respond to this deadly terrorist attack.

Damn, it was hot in here. Sweat was going into his eyes, and then Sheila said something he couldn't quite hear her. He answered sharply, 'What? What is it?'

'General, I've got a dial tone.'

He was going to say something else but then he heard another sound from up top, the sound of an approaching helicopter.

Drew heard the helicopter as he dragged furniture around and tried to ignore it. The guy he just nailed wasn't moving or breathing, which was a plus, but on the minus side, his foot still throbbed, his left shoulder really hurt, and even his ears ached at the sound of gunfire in an enclosed room. He put a couch in front of the main door, and, still keeping down, pushed an easy chair into the kitchen, groaning at how his shoulder felt. The chair went up against the door just fine and as he tried to move away shots came in, shattering the glass.

He didn't bother to aim, didn't even think his arm could stay still long enough. He raised up the .45 and fired off three shots in reply, just to let them know he was alive.

Jesus, he hurt.

Clem looked up from the screen. 'Um, Mr Woodman, a FERA helicopter just dropped off Mr Lurry and he's on his way up here.'

He felt like his insides were slowly turning to bloody cold water and draining away. 'How long before he gets here?'

Then that Gen Z-er spoke. 'Hell, I see him, right over there. And he looks pissed!'

Ira bent over, looked out the side window of the van. Sure enough, there was Michaelson Lurry coming up the hill, accompanied by an aide Ira didn't recognize. 'I'll take care of this,' he said. 'You boys keep control of what's going on over there at the farmhouse. Tanya, come with me.'

Tanya joined him as he went out the rear door, down the short set of metal steps. 'Mr Woodman . . . it does not look good, does it?'

'No, it doesn't.'

In a few seconds Michaelson Lurry was there, face twisted and mottled red with anger, and he started shouting, 'Woodman! What the fuck is going on over here?'

'Sir, we're making progress—'

He pointed a finger. 'What the fuck you're doing is raising hell and screwing everything up! I pulled the plug on Cheyenne Mountain and people in DC and the Pentagon are screaming at me, and you're here, attacking a fucking famous general in his home. Woodman, you fool, you've screwed it up! You get a hold of your man Harrison and tell him to abort!'

'A . . . abort, sir? Abort what?'

The aide stood by Lurry, his face impassive, taking it all in. Ira noticed how bulky he looked, especially around the left shoulder. Lurry shouted, 'The Shiloh mission, that's what! Tell him to stand down! It's falling apart, there's too many questions, too much news media and NewsNet interest. We'll never keep the lid on until tonight. We'll have to reschedule, pull back, maybe try again in a year or two . . .'

A year . . . a year or two? Ira looked around the small hillside, at the parked ECM van. He noted the faces of

Clem Badger and Gary Leeson looking at him through the thick glass. Tanya was next to him, her face shocked, shaking her head just a bit, back and forth, back and forth. Lurry was still shouting, screaming about the proper code to abort, how to reach Henry Harrison, how they had to pull back. The aide was still staring at Ira, staring with hunter's eyes.

A year? Or two? My God, what were they thinking of, how could he explain what he had been doing all this time, leading up to this moment, all the work and sacrifice and bodies that had been piled up . . . To wait?

'No, Mr Lurry,' he said, finally finding his voice. 'I'm afraid I can't do that.'

He put his right hand into his coat pocket and then turned a bit, finding his pistol, pulling the trigger. The first shot caught the aide in the upper left leg and he fell to the ground, yelling. Ira pulled the pistol out and then shot the aide in the head, and blood and brain matter flew out onto the leaf-covered ground.

Lurry was backing up, still talking, hands raising up, and Ira fired twice more, catching Lurry both times in the chest. Lurry fell back against an oak tree, a surprised look on his face, and then his head slumped forward.

Ira turned. Tanya was running back to the ECM van. He shot her in the back, saw her tumble, her long legs flying up.

Inside the ECM van something was sounding from the computer console but Clem shouted, 'Jesus! Did you see that? Did you see that? Woodman just fragged them all!'

Leeson pushed by him, tumbled into the front seat of the ECM and turned the engine key. 'Get back there and lock the door, damn it, and keep down!'

Clem ran back, hitting his hip against the small conference table, and started toggling the locks with his fingers,
realizing with horror that he had just wet himself. 'Go!' he
screamed at Leeson. 'Get us the fuck out of here!'

Ira felt himself tremble as the pistol suddenly became heavy.
I am the Grand High Executioner . . . There was a roar of an
engine and then the ECM van suddenly started up and was
backing down the dirt road, tree branches whipping at its
side, the young Gen Z-er driving. Ira thought about sending
a couple of rounds his way, but why waste the ammo?

He checked his watch. Abort. Jesus. Henry should be
closing in on the outskirts of DC by now. How could Lurry
be thinking of giving up when they were just minutes away
from taking their country back?

Tanya wasn't moving, nor was Lurry's aide. He felt
through the coat of the aide, took out the man's pistol. A
9 mm. Good. He took the extra clips and went over to Lurry.
Michaelson Lurry, head of the Federal Emergency Response
Agency and twice a candidate for President of the United
States, stayed slumped against the tree. A horsefly buzzed
around the top of his head.

'Sorry, Mr Lurry,' Ira said. 'The battle's just begun, and I'm
not going to allow us to be defeated.'

Ira turned and started running down the hill, heading to
the farmhouse. He knew he should be heading somewhere
else, to get hold of a phone, start making calls to take control
of the FERA bureaucracy, itself about an hour away from
taking command of the nation.

But in that farmhouse were the people who had forced
him to this point, and he was going to kill them all first.

TWENTY-FIVE

We cannot quit. We can no more walk away from the culture war than we could walk away from the Cold War. For the culture war is at its heart a religious war about whether God or man shall be exalted, whose moral beliefs shall be enshrined in law, and what children shall be taught to value or abhor. With those stakes, to walk away is to abandon your post in wartime.

Patrick Buchanan, February 20, 1999

By the time George Clemson got everything cleared away from the accident on I-95 – and he remembered fondly the days early in his career when the State Police kept their eyes on the interstate and the city cops left it all alone – Nancy Thon Quong said, 'Hey, you feel like dinner?'

'Sure, I'm getting hungry,' he said, wondering why in hell traffic was still backed up. Stupid civilians.

'I think I might—'

George never heard the rest of what his partner wanted for dinner, because the underslung police radio started chiming at them, and a female dispatcher broke in: 'All units, all units, go to TAC Four. Repeat, TAC Four.'

Nancy reached over, turned a switch on the radio. 'TAC Four? I don't think I've ever gotten a message on TAC Four.'

George felt something tickle along the back of his hands.

He didn't like the feeling. 'TAC Four is a special encryption channel. Dispatch uses it rarely, 'cause the more often you use it, the better the chance for hackers to clue in and figure out – hold on.'

Another sharp set of tones and the dispatcher came on again, a voice so strained and shaky that it made George look away from the road and stare at the radio in disbelief. 'All units . . . all units . . . be on the lookout for a white GMC van, bearing Maryland registration Tango Alpha Alpha four six seven . . . occupants are armed and dangerous . . . Van is believed heading to Washington area with a Ten-Nine-Six-Six . . . repeat . . . van contains a Ten-Nine-Six-Six . . . All channels, signal one thousand, except traffic regarding this van . . . repeat . . . van heading south, bearing Maryland registration Tango Alpha Alpha four six seven . . . van contains a Ten-Nine-Six-Six . . .'

'George,' Nancy said, her voice sounding almost as concerned as the dispatcher.

'Yeah.'

'George, I thought I saw a white van a couple of minutes ago, just as we were wrapping up that MV accident.'

His chest was tightening up, as if someone had a leather belt around it and was slowly constricting it, forcing his heart to race, his lungs to labor to get a clear breath. 'George . . . what's a Ten-Nine-Six-Six?'

A Ten-Nine-Six-Six. George had a pretty good idea of what that meant but said, 'Look it up, rook. Glovebox has the codes for TAC Four traffic.' He reached over and flipped the switches activating the lights and siren. It quickly became noisy inside the cruiser and before him traffic was slowly easing to one side and another as he headed south along the interstate.

South. To DC. Where his Carol and girls and his boy were, right at this moment. Clarence, Clarisse and Clennie. Everyone he had ever loved, in DC.

'George . . . here it is . . . George, it says, a WMD. What in hell is a WMD?'

His hands were getting moist as he continued squeezing the steering wheel. 'WMD, rook,' he said, forcing each word out. 'Stands for something special. Something they'll write about, for years to come. Rook, WMD means Weapon of Mass Destruction. Don't know if it's bio, chemical or nuclear. All I do know is I see a white van, up ahead. Get ready to call it in.'

The traffic was easing out even more, and as he got closer he saw the registration.

It was a match.

Henry Harrison turned in his seat at the sound of the siren. 'What the . . . fuck, Toland, we've got a Baltimore Police cruiser coming right up our ass!'

'Screw 'em,' Toland said, looking in the rearview mirror, clenching his jaw. 'This van's armored up, from the sides to the windshields. They can't do a thing to us.'

'The fuck they can't,' Henry said, looking at the sideview mirror of the cruiser coming closer. 'You think we can run our way quietly into DC with a police escort? Jesus! What do you have for weapons on board?'

Toland spared another glance to his sideview mirror. 'Black duffel bag behind my seat. A couple of old HK-90s, about a thousand rounds of ammo.'

Henry shook his head, started running options through his mind. He got up on his knees and reached behind Toland's seat, dragged the bag free. 'A thousand rounds? Really?'

Toland said, 'I hate to think of running out.'

The duffel bag was on his lap and he unzipped the top. 'Me, too,' Henry said.

The dial tone flickered and then died away. Sheila felt exhausted and sat down against the brick wall of the cellar, the dampness seeping through her shirt, her now useless lapbot on the concrete floor next to her. 'There, General,' she said. 'We've done what we can.'

'You did good,' he said, not looking at her, just keeping his eyes forward, to the stairs.

'I don't know if it's enough.'

Still, he didn't turn, as he said, 'I guess we'll find out in a couple of hours.'

Up above them more sounds of gunfire, coming closer.

Over the sound of the cruiser's siren Nancy said urgently, 'George, if that van has a chemical or bio weapon inside, we have gas masks and field suits in the trunk, don't we?'

They were less than fifty feet away from the van and it was speeding up, but George knew he could get right up to its ass in just a manner of seconds. 'We're this close, I sure as hell ain't stopping for anything. Besides, you can't do shit wearing a gas mask. You'll pass out in a minute or two.'

'Back-up, shouldn't we wait for back-up, George, they should be here in a—'

'Damn it, rook, will you please shut the fuck up and get ready to work?' he said, snapping a furious glance at her. 'That van up ahead is going to DC and that's where my wife and kids are right this very moment, and if you want I can slow down some and you can bail out on me and tumble along the side of the highway, but this cruiser and this cop is going after them. Understood?'

Her voice was quiet. 'Understood. I'm staying.'

'Good. Look, you better with a shotgun or your pistol?'

'Pistol.'

'Okay, we're gonna pull up to the rear and you start aiming for the rear tires. This is no time for a courteous traffic stop. All right?'

She just nodded and withdrew her pistol from her holster, placed it in her lap, held tight with her tiny light brown hands. George had a guilty memory of how he had once thought those hands would look sexy running down his body, and it was like a memory of high school, a childish thought he pushed away. They were close to the van. 'Okay, get your window down and get ready.'

He punched the accelerator some more and they were right close up to the van, the windows tinted, he was thinking of what he was going to do if those rear doors flew open, then there was movement on the passenger's side and a man suddenly propelled himself out the window, stubby machine gun in his hands. Nancy started firing and the stuttering roar of the machine gun was loud as George braked and moved left and Nancy cursed, falling back into her seat.

'Fuck!' she said, her voice high-pitched. 'Asshole's got a machine gun!'

'Call it in, call it in,' George said, now trying to keep the cruiser out at an angle, making sure the guy in the passenger seat didn't have a clear shot again. Nancy picked up the radio and started shouting, 'Signal one thousand, signal one thousand, this is Unit Able Twelve. We are in pursuit of suspect van, southbound on I-95, near Exit Four. Shots fired, repeat, shots fired.'

The radio crackled some more and Nancy yelled over, 'They said back-up is on the way, George.'

'Sure it is,' he said, thinking of Carol and Clarence and Clarisse and Clennie, all in DC laughing and having fun with family, and those men in that van up ahead, ready and eager to kill them all.

'Rook.'

'Yeah?'

'Make sure your seatbelt's fastened, real fucking tight,' he said, accelerating again. 'Things are about to get real interesting.'

Henry leaned out the window again, enjoying by God the feeling of the HK-90 in his hands, ready to take out those two cops with just a few seconds' pull on the trigger. All it would take is a hose-down of the cruiser and then he'd have Toland pull off at another exit. He was sure they could move the weapon to another vehicle – another van or even a 4×4 – and then they'd poke along to DC. They might be a bit late but that was a hell of a lot better than never showing up at all.

But where in hell was the cruiser?

'Toland,' he yelled. 'Where are they?'

'On my side, coming up – shit, they're coming up real fast!'

Henry ducked back inside and was going to have Toland lean forward over the steering wheel so he could squeeze behind him and rip off a half dozen rounds or so, but as he was clambering his way to the other side of the van, a mighty *BANG!* caused the van to shake and start to skid. He fell back against the dashboard, hitting his head on the windshield, the HK-90 falling from his hands.

*

George roared right up to the rear of the van, remembering his old training in executing an eccentric curve. There had been lots of talk about inertia and centers of gravity and relative speeds and such shit, and all it boiled down to was ramming the left rear of a vehicle with the right front end of your cruiser during a high-speed pursuit, and nine times out of ten it'd cause the vehicle to spin out.

Which is surely what happened, but he didn't expect the cruiser to spin as well, and part of the van clipped it as it sped by and George practically stood on the brakes as it screeched to a halt, spinning in a half-curve.

'Bail out, bail out!' he yelled, and he climbed over the gear in the center of the seat as he followed Nancy out her door. He grabbed her arm and said, 'Here, right here, behind the engine,' and he drew his own weapon, sparing a glance. The van was about twenty feet away, crumpled into the tail end of a bright red Honda 4X4. Other cars and trucks were stopped and people were stepping out onto the highway. George swore and reached in and switched the radio to PA.

'People, get away from here,' his voice boomed out. 'We've got bad guys with guns. Take cover, get away!'

The van's tires started smoking as the driver tried to reverse, but it wasn't moving, the far-side fender being jammed into the red Honda. George flinched at the sound of sudden gunfire, but realized it was Nancy emptying her clip into the tires of the van, and he joined in, trying to shoot out the tires.

Toland tried rocking back and forth, swearing and pumping the gas, and Henry said, 'Fuck it, stop it! We've got to get ourselves freed from that fucking Honda. C'mon, you give me some suppressing fire, I'll try to get us loose.'

Henry opened the door and got out onto the highway, HK-90 in his hands. A man in a suit and tie came up, bleeding from his forehead, screaming, 'You idiot! Look what you did to my car? Where in hell did you—'

With a short burst Henry knocked him down, blood splattering the front of the suit. He went around to the side of the Honda, tugged open the passenger door. A woman in a business suit was crouched on the driver's side, screaming into a cellphone, and Henry shot her as well. He reached under the passenger's seat, felt around and pulled out a tire iron. Short but it could do the job.

More gunfire was joining the chorus, as Toland was at the rear of the van, pouring it on to those two asshole cops, a coon and a broad who were trying to screw this up. Well, fuck 'em, he'd show them both the kind of mistake they made this afternoon, trying to stop him and his mission. He stood up for a moment, chewed up the near side of the cruiser with a couple of good bursts, then got down on his knees and to work, trying to pry apart the van's fender from the Honda.

George sat up against the cruiser, putting a fresh magazine into his service pistol. Just two spares left. When that was over it'd be time to get the shotgun, but he wasn't looking forward to crawling back into the front seat and trying to unlock the shotgun with all this fucking lead zipping over their heads.

'George?' Nancy said, on her knees beside him.

'Yeah?'

'Your first shoot-out?'

'Yep.'

'Oh. When do you think back-up will get here?'

George looked around him, at the mass of cars and trucks to the north and south, the nearest ones having been abandoned, making one pretty traffic jam.

'Not for a while, rook, not for a while.' He rolled up and around on his knees. 'C'mon, at the tires, let's get those tires.'

Henry pushed against the metal with all his might, feeling the metal finally begin to strain away. Toland yelled out, 'It looks like they're moving around to the right, heading towards you!'

He dropped the tire iron and picked up his HK-90. The smell was of burned cordite and the ground was slippery with spent brass. He raised up his hands and let loose with a long hose, right to left, left to right, and was glad when heard a scream. Damn, looks like we got one of 'em. It might have been the broad – the yell sure was high-pitched enough – but Henry had been around long enough to know that guys sometimes screamed just as high as girls when they were shot.

Henry bent down and resumed his work with the fender.

The sudden onrush of fear surprised George, and he knew it was seeing Nancy wounded that had caused its roar through his mind. He had been going on by pretending in some way that this was some sort of elaborate training exercise, but hearing her yell and seeing her wounded had changed all of that. This was way too fucking real. She came back against the cruiser, her left arm bleeding, her lovely features twisted in pain, and she said, 'Oh fuck, George, I've been hit.'

'It's okay,' he said, lying to her. 'Back-up will be here soon. I can hear the sirens.'

She shook her head. 'George, you're a bad liar. Honest to Christ you are. Shit, those goddamn tires must be bullet-proof or something, George, we can't do shit to them.'

'I know, I know,' he said, thinking, Carol, if you love me, if you truly love me, you'll feel something is wrong – I don't know how! – and you'll take the kids out to Alexandria or something, someplace far away from here or DC. 'You stay here and I'll keep at it.'

Nancy said, 'The hell you will. I've still got one good arm left. Let me keep firing from here.'

George checked his ammo. Last clip was in the pistol. Time to retrieve the shotgun in a few minutes. 'All right, rook. That's all right.'

She wiped at a strand of hair and said, 'Thanks, George.'

'For what?'

'For being a good training officer, that's what. You're a good man. I know you had some thoughts towards me. I'm not that stupid. Thanks for not pressing it, thanks for being who you are. I just wanted you to know.'

He was going to say something back, like hey, rook, it's okay, you're the best rookie cop I've ever trained, male or female, straight or gay, but the gunfire started up again. He fired back, no longer looking at his partner bleeding at his side.

There, just one more piece of metal moved and we'll be off, Henry thought. Toland yelled over, 'Hey, give me some covering fire, I'm going to wrap this up.'

'You got it,' he yelled back, tired of being shot at by these two asshole cops. He replaced a clip in his HK-90, got up and moved around the Honda, stepping over the dead driver on the ground, noticing motion inside the car, where the woman was probably still alive. Oh well, no day was perfect.

He reached the front of the Honda and opened fire.

'George!' came the shout, and he dragged himself out of the front seat, where he had just unlocked the shotgun from its dashboard mount. Nancy was on her stomach and she raised her head and yelled, 'I'm out of ammo! And there's some-body behind that—'

A burst of gunfire tore into her and she rolled over, coughing and choking. He moved over to her, as quickly as possible, knees on the pavement, thinking, She's got her vest on, she's got her vest on, she can still make it, there's no reason she can't make it. He dropped the shotgun and grabbed her feet, dragged her closer to him, and she looked up and smiled through the blood about her face and then she died.

'Nancy!' he yelled, and a hammer blow struck him at the base of the neck.

After nailing the woman cop – and after tonight was over Henry was sure that there wouldn't be a broad cop on duty in the land by the end of the year – he moved quickly across the pavement, keeping his head low, knowing that if things held together they could get moving in a matter of minutes. There was an exit ramp some yards down the way, and if they could get the van down there things would be looking good indeed. Dump the van, get something else, and keep on truckin'.

Henry rounded the front end of the shot-up police cruiser, weapon out in front.

*

George slowly rolled over, feeling the pain in his back, knowing his vest had just stopped some incoming fire, but that was then and what was now was the guy in front of him standing at the rear of the cruiser. He slowly brought up the shotgun, thankful that he had pumped in a round before taking it out of the cruiser. The guy who had shot him was cursing as he tried to clear a jammed round or something in his machine gun, and George wanted to say something special as he pulled the trigger but he couldn't think of a damn thing.

Then there was a loud noise, and he thought he heard Nancy's voice.

Henry saw the coon cop raising up his shotgun to Toland and he fired off another burst, chewing up the cop's head in a burst of bone, blood and brains. Toland flinched and then looked over sheepishly. 'Fucking gun jammed, Jesus.'

Henry was thirsty and pumped up and excited, knowing they were going to make it, they were going to finish business. Just a little bump in the road, that's all. 'All right, let's get the fuck out of here before the whole Baltimore PD shows up. Something tells me they'll be rightly pissed.'

Toland laughed and slapped Henry on the arm, and Henry had a thought, Hey, this guy did well, why not let him live tonight.

He was still thinking that as they ran back to the van, until it became quite bright and Henry looked up at the sky and his world ended.

TWENTY-SIX

Fanaticism is described as redoubling your effort when
you have forgotten your aim.

George Santayana

Ira moved quickly across the farmland – hell, it was a battlefield, now wasn't it? – and he didn't like what he saw. The
amount of gunfire had dribbled away in the long minutes it
had taken to come down the hill, through a set of woods,
and head to General Montgomery's home. All along the
way, dodging the lines of brush and trees, trying not to trip
over rocks and loose patches of gravel, he refused to think
about what had happened there, back up on the hill. All he
cared was that he had done it. It had made sense. He
reflected on the memory of his daddy, and thought about
Glenda Sue and the kids and how they all depended on him,
and he wasn't going to let them down. He was going to take
care of business in this farmhouse and then he'd get a phone
hook-up to FERA and take care of things later tonight.

They were about to take their country back. How could
anyone think of stopping now, when they were so close?

He climbed over the fence and fell to the ground, breathing
heavily. He took out his pistol, kept on moving, but not as
quickly as before. A few more gunshots, but nothing like an
hour or so ago, when the assault had started. He came across a

militia man lying on the ground, dead. His shoulder was a mess and it looked as if he had bled out. He began to move around to the north, where there was more cover. Voices, up ahead.

'Washington County Militia,' Ira called out. 'Is that you?'

'Yep, over here, by the evergreens.'

He went down a slight embankment, saw two guys on the ground sharing a cigarette, their hands shaking, their weapons at their feet. Another guy was lying on his side as two others worked on him with field dressings at his rear. The wounded guy on his side had a thick moustache and was clenching his teeth, his Army surplus pants down around his ankles.

Ira said, 'Who's in charge here?'

One of the two working on the wounded man looked up with thin, wire-rim glasses. 'Well, I guess that would be Colonel Slocum, our glorious commander-in-chief and service station owner.'

'Where is he?'

The man with the cigarette in his hand said, 'And who the fuck are you, mister?'

'Ira Woodman, FERA. Colonel Slocum has been operating under my direction. Does anybody know where he is?'

'Okay, Brian, give me that tape, we'll keep it in place . . . Colonel Slocum? Heard that he personally led an assault into that farmhouse. That was a half-hour ago. He hasn't been back since. Ah, right, good job, Brian . . .'

'Then who's in command?' Ira demanded.

The man with the glasses looked surprised. 'Beats the hell out of me. You see, Mr Woodman, all about you are the former members of the Washington County Militia. We do certain things well, like organizing food drives for the elderly and providing support for our members. We don't take getting shot up for no good reason that well. Ain't that right, Jerry?'

The wounded man with the moustache whispered, 'You got that fucking right, pal.'

Ira remembered his daddy talking about deserters, shirkers, men who would run away from their responsibilities. Like this collection of white trash before him, wetting their pants because things got a little tough. He thought about trying to rally them around, to get them going, but he could see the hostility in their eyes. The wrong word and he might be on the ground, blood and brains oozing out of the back of his head.

'Are there any other militia members around?'

'That's right, give me the scissors . . . Oh, I think there's a bunch over on the west side, by a streambed. They were putting up a fight, last we heard. I guess there are true believers everywhere, right?'

Ira started to move away. 'Yes, I guess there are.'

For the past several minutes the shooting had died away, and Drew took a moment in the kitchen to sit up against the counter and extract the wood splinter that was in his left shoulder. The splinter tugged and burned as it came out, and he yelped and then got a bunch of paper towels from a roll on the counter. He shoved them under his coat and sat still for a moment, breathing, just breathing.

He checked his pockets. Ammo okay, one clip left. Pistol looking good. Person holding pistol not doing as well. And the opponents? He wasn't sure. Could be they were regrouping, trying to decide how best to continue. Maybe there were reinforcements on the way. Maybe.

And what was going on down south, with the ultimate truck bomb tooling its way to the Capitol? One bright flash of light and then everything would be turned upside down, and after the arrests and detention centers and book burnings and censorship and reeducation camps, well, maybe only a few isolated villages in this land, years later, would ever know how things had once been different.

Drew stood up, weaved a bit and then started moving. Down south was someone else's problem. His problem right now was this house and the people inside it. Time to go upstairs, see if Sheila and the General were there, then do a quick look-see from the second floor windows, determine if the militia were on the move again.

He went into the living room, past the dead militia man, and then saw the body of Maurice Blakely on the stairs.

'Hey, Captain,' he murmured as he stepped over him. 'Sorry 'bout that.'

Ira found two more militia men along the way to the streambed, and he wished he had bullets to spare to cut them down, for they were crying and ready to surrender to him. By the stream and a waterfall, he found another militia man, dead, with half his head torn away. He was lying behind a boulder, his hands outstretched, and on his back was a leather carrying case with three long tubular objects inside. Ira moved forward, knelt down, listened to the tinkling of the water flowing by him.

After running his hands up and down the objects, at long last he smiled. 'Your colonel certainly wasn't lying,' Ira said to the dead man. 'You are a well-armed militia, one of the best I've ever seen. Now, where's your weapon?'

He put his own gun down and undid the straps from the carrying case, then rolled the dead man over. A pistol-like weapon was strapped to his chest. Ira undid these straps as well, and started praying. God, you certainly have led me through some dark valleys, but I know now that you were just setting me up for the promised land. I will not fail. I will not disappoint You. I will succeed, for my wife and my children and this poor, misguided nation.

With both cases in hand he went up a slight rise to the right of the streambed, where he had a view of the farmhouse and attached barn. There had been no gunshots for the last several minutes. Ira looked down at his haul. An old Soviet-made RPG-7 and three rockets to go along with it. A rocket-propelled grenade launcher. He started giggling, remembering the start of the Second Amendment to the Constitution. 'A well-armed militia . . .'

He picked up the RPG-7 and grabbed one of the rockets. Back in Kentucky, during a seminar weekend about terrorist threats, he and other State Police officials had test-fired an RPG-7 to see what it was like. What it was like was to fire the thing into an old armored car in a gravel pit and to see that thing jump.

Ira made sure everything was set and then aimed at the farmhouse. He wasn't sure what it would do to the farmhouse, but Ira was betting that wood and glass would do much worse than steel and iron.

Drew went through the upstairs rooms at a fairly good clip. No general, no Sheila. In the cellar. They must be down in the cellar. Though he wouldn't think being in the cellar was the best option, he could see why the General took her down there. Probably just one entrance in and out. Easy to defend, but a real bitch if the bad guys decided to burn the place down around your ears.

He was in the hallway, limping and feeling his shoulder ache and the sogginess of the blood seeping into the paper towel and his coat, when he remembered. Ammo. There was more ammo in the closet safe in the General's bedroom. Better load up in case there's another visit.

He took a right into the last door, went past the carefully made bed with a photo of the General's wife on the nightstand. The closet door was still open, but the safe door was shut. Drew remembered closing it when he had left. No use letting the bad guys have access to your weapons.

As he went to the closet door, a loud noise slammed at his ears and the floor seemed to rise up and knock him down.

Ira coughed and choked and his ears rang. Man, that was one loud noise! And he remembered back in Kentucky, wearing ear protection and safety glasses, and now he knew why. He blinked as crap in his eyes made them water, and he coughed again. The blast from the rocket had caused a big cloud of dust and smoke, and it was hard to see. There! Something burning. He looked eagerly through the slowly moving cloud, and saw that he had struck . . .

The barn. Damn it, goddamn thing had pulled to the right and he had put one into the roof of the barn. It was now burning merrily along but that wasn't going to work, not at all. People in that house would be getting ready to get the hell out. Time for another round.

Ira turned, coughed some more, and didn't see the other two rocket rounds. They were missing.

Sheila noticed that for the past several minutes there had been no sounds of shooting. She thought she could have made out someone walking overhead, but her mind might have been playing tricks with her. General Montgomery was still next to her, looking out to the stairway leading up to the living room.

'Sure seems quiet,' she said.

'Yeah, it does,' he said. 'Wonder how things are up top.'

Drew. She thought of Drew, out there alone, trying to defend them both against all those men . . . She shook her head against the thoughts, tried desperately to think of something else. 'What's it like?' she asked. 'I mean, what's it like, being a general?'

In the dim light of the cellar she made out his wide smile. 'Mostly, miss, it means a lot of eyes looking at you every day. Looking to see how you talk, how you act, even how you walk. Being part of a team like the Army was the best, but one does get tired of being looked at all the time.'

She rubbed the top of her lapbot. 'Do you wonder . . . I mean, do you think if you had run for president last time around this whole mess would have happened?'

The general seemed to take a long, deep breath, and she wondered what he might be thinking. She hadn't followed politics that much – one adulterous or drug-using crook seemed pretty much like any other – but she remembered those few months when it seemed like everyone was waiting for the General to say something, to make an announce-ment, to make a difference in the sour politics everyone was used to. Everyone waited in anticipation, all the way up to that day in Buffalo when his wife had been killed.

'Truth be told . . .' the General started, and then there was a hollow-sounding *boom!* as the cellar shook and tools and cans of old paint rattled and fell off the shelves. He turned and said matter-of-factly, 'What the fuck?'

He stood up and Sheila stood as well, her lapbot under her arm. 'What was that, General? It sounded like an explosion.'

'It sure did, and I don't like being down here while people are tossing high explosives our way. Let's get going.'

'Through there?' she asked, pointing to the bulkhead door.

'No, that's been locked and bolted since we moved in here,' he said, heading over to the stairway. 'I don't even have the keys to it. Nope, let's get up to the stairs, real quiet, and then get the hell out.'

She followed him and stopped, now breathing hard. It was dark and musty on the stairs and she realized she had to use a bathroom. The General was tugging and twisting at the door knob. She shifted from one leg to the next, then sniffed the air. 'General, something's burning.'

'Damn it,' he said, stepping back and almost knocking her over. 'Sorry, Sheila. The door's stuck. That explosion back there must have shifted something, caused the door to jam. We're going to have to think of something else.'

She slowly went back downstairs, where the scent of smoke was stronger.

Drew got up, shook his head. That was incoming, sir, no doubt about it. He looked out the far window, saw smoke billowing up. Something just took out part of the barn, and then, through the other window, he saw a smaller plume of smoke drift away from a slight rise of the land.

Rocket launcher, of some sort. He went to the closet safe, trying to think if the General had anything in there that could even up the score, and then he stopped. The keys. Where in hell were the keys? He checked his pockets, winced as his shoulder started screaming at him. Goddamn keys, must have been lost back in the barn. Shit!

He went over to the window, saw where the incoming rocket round had been launched. That's where the bad guys were. Right there. And somewhere in this farmhouse Sheila was still hiding. What to do? Maybe the General had a spare key. Maybe he could find Sheila and the General and get them out. And maybe while he was doing all of this another, better-aimed rocket round would scream right in here and turn this place into a pile of burning wood. He turned and started out the bedroom, moving as fast as he could, knowing what had to be done.

The bad guys were out there, probably readying another shot, and there was no longer any more time to think. The pistol was in his hands as he went through the hallway and down the stairs. Time. There was so little time left.

Ira scrambled down the side of the hill and felt a weight lift when he saw what had happened. The blowback from the rocket launching had thrown the spare rockets down the hill. That's all. We'll be more careful, this time, he thought, putting both rockets underneath his arm. And this time, we'll aim better as well. Two more chances here, two more chances to do his duty.

By the time the ECM van was on the paved road and heading away Clem Badger saw a line of police cruisers screaming their way towards the farm. He sat down next to Gary, who was driving, and said, 'That was a hell of a fuck-up back there, wasn't it?'

'Jesus, you got that right,' Leeson said. 'What do we do now?'

Now? Clem folded his arms and looked out the windshield as they made tracks away from the farmhouse. 'Well, I've shut everything down. I figure if Mr Woodman gets arrested or something, we can always say we were just following orders. That's all.'

'Sounds good to me. You got anything else going?'

Clem thought for a moment and said, 'Yeah. Let's get

some munchies at the next store you see. I've got something
to show you.'

'Really? What's that?'

Clem managed a smile. 'You ever hear of Sally from Seattle?'

'Shit, who hasn't?'

Clem looked over at Leeson and said, 'Well, you're not
going to believe what I downloaded the other day.'

The smell of smoke was getting stronger, making
Montgomery's eyes water. He looked around the cellar, trying
not to think of the wood overhead catching fire, the beams
charring and falling, crushing them both under the flames.
During his time in the Second Gulf War he remembered
seeing shattered tanks and the charred bodies of the soldiers
trying desperately to get out of an inferno.

Water. There must be water in here somewhere. Maybe
an old hose, maybe a way to wet things down. He looked
around and Sheila was missing.

'Sheila?' he said, raising his voice. 'Sheila? Where are you?'

'Over here, General,' she said, her voice cutting through
the smoke. He made his way over to where she was crouched
down on the concrete, her lapbot open.

'Look, I think there might be some water in here, and—'

For the second time that day, she thrilled him with the
same words: 'General, I've got a dial tone.'

Any other time, from when he was a track star back in
Arapahoe through Basic Training or any other place, Drew
could have gone the distance between the farmhouse and the
slight rise of land in a matter of seconds. But this was no ordinary time. His foot was throbbing with each step and
movement, and blood was now oozing down his back and chest

from his shoulder. He didn't bother with trying to maintain a lot of cover, he just wanted to get there as quick as he could.

He spared a glance back at the farmhouse. A good part of the barn's roof was now in flames, smoke billowing up into the Vermont sky. He tried not to think where Sheila and the General might be at this moment, and a spasm of guilt raced through him, something he had not felt since the Crescent. Was he really doing what had to be done here, or had he run away, like he had back at that air force base? The mission, the mission, all hail the mission. But what dark voices did he really follow when he left that day in the Crescent, and when he ran out of the farmhouse? Duty to the mission, or duty to his own skin?

Drew looked back to the rise of land, saw movement, and raised up his pistol and fired off three rounds.

Ira looked through the optics of the rocket launcher, moved her a bit to the left to compensate, and just as he tugged the firing trigger there was somebody coming up on his left, firing just as the rocket whooshed away. He closed his eyes and reached down with his free hand for the last spare.

Drew fell to the ground and yelled as the rocket roared over-head, the yell coming from the pain in his shoulder and the knowledge that he had failed. He rolled quickly over and looked back to the farmhouse as the smoke trail hung there, like a faint gray arch.

Missed! Goddamn rocket went right over the top of the roof! He got up and looked at his pistol. The slide was locked back in an open position. He was out of ammunition.

Drew started running.

*

Ira wiped at his eyes, found the last rocket between his legs and loaded up, not wanting even to think of what had just happened, how the cursed Russian-made piece of shit had arced over the house like some cheap firework. This time he would move right up to the house and fire it through a window, just as soon as he took care of—

The shock of being struck by the weight caused him to fall backwards, losing his balance and his grip on the RPG-7. Someone was yelling at him, flailing at him with his fists, and Ira tumbled down the hill. He tried to get up and was pushed back again as a man fought with him, punched at him, screamed at him, as the sound of running water grew louder.

Ira punched back and caught a look of the man's eyes, felt the flash of recognition, knew who his enemy was. 'You!' Ira yelled. 'You son of a bitch, I should have killed you back in your jail cell!'

Ira saw the blood on Drew's shoulder and punched him there as hard as he could, and he was pleased to hear the scream coming from the man's face. Drew fell to the ground and Ira was stepping back to grab his pistol and finish it once and for all when the ground fell away from him.

Drew saw Ira stand back, reach into his coat and the small part of his consciousness that wasn't screaming from the pain in his shoulder caused his feet to kick out. He nailed the bastard across his shins, and Ira stumbled back a few inches, teetered on the edge of the stream's waterfall, and fell in.

Drew got up, wiped the spit and blood from his face, and jumped in after him. The cold water caused him to scream again and he raised himself up in the water. He was in a small pool, not much bigger than a usual backyard pool, and there was Ira, huddled up on a rock, desperately searching through his coat.

Drew slogged across and slugged him in the shoulder, knocking him over, yelling, 'You're right, you asshole, you should have killed me back then. That's the only time you've been right in your entire fucking life!'

Ira fell into the water, the spray and the movement making Drew lose sight for a second before he howled as his groin exploded in pain.

When Ira fell into the water he finally had his pistol in hand, and with his other hand he felt a brush of fabric from Drew's pant leg and punched up with the pistol, feeling it connect solidly into the son of a bitch's crotch. Ira stood up, water in his eyes and nose and mouth, but he didn't care, Drew was there, almost hunched over, looking bloody and beaten-up and raw.

He stepped back, to give himself room, and he said, 'You lose, Drew Connor. You all lose. Every single godless one of you lose. Understand? It's our time, and we're going to win today and tomorrow and forever. Because God is on our side, that's why.'

Ira coughed and raised up his pistol.

Drew listened to the man's ravings and then saw the hand come up, and he did the only thing open to him. He punched the water, sending up a splashing plume, and for a moment Ira flinched. Only for a moment.

Drew pushed himself off the bottom and struck the out-stretched hand as the pistol fired, deafening him. He kept on pushing Ira until the man fell against an outcropping of rock. Ira grunted as he fell and Drew grabbed his head, and pounded him against the rock, again and again. Blood started to come out of his mouth. Drew pulled him away and then thrust him under the water. He held Ira for what seemed to be a long time as the man struggled against him.

Darkness and cold and the water, and the memories of his daddy and Glenda Sue and the kids, and a small, tentative voice, saying, Rest, now, you've done all that you can. Rest.

His hands were cramping and freezing and his groin ached as much as his shoulder, but Drew kept the pressure, kept the pressure and force on the man until he became limp and stopped struggling. Drew coughed and then let go. There was a slight movement in the swirling water as the man's back slowly bobbed to the surface and then the body started moving downstream. Drew watched the movement, saw how it bumped against one rock and then another until it was out of view.

Drew spat some blood and mucous into the water. 'Guess God was busy today, hunh, Ira?'

He slowly got out of the pool, shivering from the cold and the exertion, and sat down on a bit of grass by the side of the stream. He leaned over and coughed for a long time, then just rested his head in his hands. Time to move, old man, time to move.

Drew got up, swayed as his head started to spin, then slowly climbed up the slight rise, coughing again. He kicked at the old Russian-made rocket launcher and the single remaining rocket, and when he got to the top of the rise he stood there, watching, as flames consumed General Cyrus Montgomery's farmhouse, the crackling roar of the collapsing roof even reaching him at this distance.

TWENTY-SEVEN

Extremism in the defense of liberty is no vice. And . . .
moderation in the pursuit of justice is no virtue.
Senator Barry Goldwater,
1964 Republican National Convention

As members of the Northfield Volunteer Fire Department
tried to contain the fire from the front lawn of the house,
Sheila sat with the General on the lawn as the local police
and state police tried to keep the news media and NewsNet
correspondents down at the other end of the driveway. The
last dial tone had worked well, contacting the police and fire
departments, even letting them know that the two of them
had been trapped in the cellar. The General looked suddenly old and Sheila reached over and rubbed at his back.

'Sorry about the house, General,' she said. 'Maybe they'll
be able to save some of it.'

'Oh, it's not the house that concerns me,' he said, his
voice low and soft. 'It's what's inside that counts. My papers.
My records. Everything that once belonged to Grace . . .'

The General bent forward and wiped at his eyes, and
Sheila felt angry at everything that had happened to this son
of Detroit, this son of America, who had devoted his life to
the service of his country. And for what? To be forced from
his job by a man whose pissing habits were the focus of world

attention, to see his wife shot down at his side, and to see his home and sanctuary destroyed by those who just hated so much. That's all. Those who hated so much.

'Still,' the General said, 'I managed to grab something as we were getting out.'

He held up a tiny radio and switched it on, scanning the dials until a signal popped up. Sheila leaned in, listening as the announcer said, 'And as Baltimore and Maryland officials continue their investigation into a deadly explosion on a section of I-95 that apparently caused the deaths of two terrorists and two Baltimore police officers, we now go live to Capitol Hill . . .'

As the voices droned on and the announcement came up – 'Ladies and gentlemen, the President of the United States' – Sheila knew that she should feel some sort of triumph, some sort of accomplishment, but she didn't feel good. Not at all. She knew she should be out there looking for Drew, knew she should move, but she dreaded the thought of finding him out there, dead, like that poor bloody boy who had been shot by the cigarette smugglers.

She was so happy when the General switched off the radio that she almost kissed him, but then someone behind her said, 'Room for one more?'

She looked up at her Drew, wet and bleeding and bruised, and she reached over and hugged his legs as hard as she could. 'Oh, yes, love, always room for one more. Always and always.'

The next day Montgomery saw them again, in Room 114 of the Snuggle Gap Inn in Northfield. All three of them had spent the night in the small motel, as police lines outside kept vigil, ensuring they weren't disturbed. A young

Assistant Attorney General and graduate of Norwich College had promised them all at least a full day of privacy, but Cyrus knew many people had many questions for him.

During the night he had slept poorly. The regular channels on television kept up with most of their programming, but the news cable channels – full of polls, pundits and politicians – had chattered on through the night about the President and his speech. Was he up? Was he down? Did the speech do its job? Other channels had gone on about how the regional administrator of FERA had gone crazy, shot his boss – the failed presidential candidate Michaelson Lurry – and had led a vendetta against famed retired General Cyrus Montgomery. Still fewer channels had gone on about the terrorist incident outside Baltimore, when a van carrying radioactive material had blown up after a long and bloody firefight with two of Baltimore's finest, and how decontamination activities were still proceeding.

Montgomery had made one phone call to Colorado, and told General Coombs, 'Leslie, the nation owes you and your folks a debt of gratitude that can never be repaid.'

Her laugh was harsh. 'Well, that's a good one, Cyrus. We did what we could but the true heroes were those two Baltimore cops, whoever they were, who slowed down that van long enough for *Excalibur* to do its job. As for me, well, I think I'm going to be out here shortly. The Joint Chiefs tend to frown on the US Space Command firing an offensive weapon without proper authorization. They need a bloody head to put on a pike, and I guess it's going to be mine.'

Cyrus had said, 'Retirement isn't so bad, once you get used to it.'

'Well, I'm going to have enough time shortly to take you up on it. Gotta run.'

Another phone call had made its way through the switchboard, and he had sat up in bed in surprise. It had been the senior senator from Ohio, and his comment had been to the point: 'I can still get that $20 million in time for the New Hampshire primary. You just give me the word, General.'

'Sorry, sir,' he had said. 'The word tonight is rest. I'll talk to you later.'

'No,' the Senator had said, laughing, 'I'll talk to you later. Get a good night's sleep.'

Now he looked at the two of them, sitting on an unmade bed, holding hands. Drew's face was bruised and puffy, and there was a bulge under his shoulder where EMTs the day before had bandaged him. Sheila looked like she hadn't slept well in a week, and she held Drew's hand quite tight, as if afraid of ever letting him go again.

Cyrus pulled up a chair and said, 'Eventually you're going to have to talk to some people. Officials from Vermont and New Hampshire, I'm sure, plus the FBI when they get around to it. I have a feeling this is going to get very public, very quickly. But for now I think you should probably head home and keep your heads down.'

Drew said, 'Thanks, General, but the problem is there are still a lot of people out there who are hunting for the both of us. They think we killed that deputy sheriff last week.'

'Not a problem,' Cyrus said. 'The Vermont AG has talked to his counterpart in New Hampshire and they've both put the word out that the two of you had nothing to do with that sheriff's death or with the Church of the Final Apocalypse. Right now people are more interested in what happened to Michaelson Lurry and Ira Woodman. I think you two can ease on back without too much fuss. Just stay away from reporters and the NewsNet.'

Sheila cleared her throat. 'It seems like forever since we've last been home. But I don't know how we can get there.'

'Taken care of. There's a rental car out to the rear of the motel. Use it to go home. Use it as long as you want. That'll be a small price to pay for what the both of you have done.'

Drew looked over at Sheila, who nodded at him. Drew said, 'General, we wanted to tell you something. We've talked about it all last night. It's uh, well, it was an honor, serving with you yesterday. If and when you decide to run, it'll be an honor to come back and work with you. The nation has always needed you, General, especially after yesterday. We were lucky yesterday. We may not be so lucky the next time.'

Cyrus rubbed his hands together, looked at the two faces staring at him, like so many other faces from the past, from audiences large and small. All these people staring at him, looking for the answer, looking for the way. All looking towards him.

'The nation doesn't need me,' he said, and he held up his hand as both Drew and Sheila started to say something. 'What the nation needs are more people like you, people who didn't give up, no matter the odds. People like those two Baltimore cops down south who did their job, protecting the public. More people like the Air Force personnel in Colorado who did their duty even though they knew it meant sacrificing their careers and quite possibly their lives. I'm not sure the nation needs another politician. It already has too many of those.'

'A lot of people will follow you,' Drew said. 'All they need is a word.'

Cyrus smiled and reached over to tap him on the knee. 'Then they'll have to wait. There's still a lot of people out there who don't care about me, they don't care about politics, they don't care about government. When they decide to leave their gated communities, log off the Net and get involved again, then I'll be waiting for them. Maybe it'll happen in time for the New Hampshire primary. Maybe not. But I will tell you this.' He paused, struggling to choose the right words, and finally said, 'Despite yesterday and what happened to Grace and my career and everything else, this country has been good to me. It allowed a poor kid from a bad part of Detroit to dream anything he wanted, and allowed him to do what I have done. I still owe a debt to this land, and I intend to repay it somehow.'

Sheila leaned forward and kissed him. 'I think you discharged the debt yesterday, General.'

He was surprised at how quickly his eyes had teared up. 'I think I'll be the judge of that, Sheila.'

SIDEBAR IV

The day after he had expected the pager to click on, Phelan McBride left work early and went home on the subway, bummed at what hadn't occurred. The pager was supposed to go off. He had a heads-up the previous day, saying the next day – the nineteenth – he would expect the go message. He had brought in the different thermos bottle, and had gone through the whole day practically trembling in anticipation, but nothing had happened. Not a damn thing.

Inside the subway it was hot and noisy and he looked around at all the drones of the Machine, whiling away their lives doing what? Processing paper? Processing electrons? Processing each other? Man, they should learn how to live, learn to get out of this death heap and survive in the wilds, like they were designed to do.

When he got off the subway and reached his street he decided he wouldn't wait anymore. He'd go into work tomorrow with the special thermos and screw whoever was out there, pulling the strings. He'd set off that little package and do his own bit for anarchy, to bring this world back to where it belonged, and he'd have a hell of a story to tell his buds back in Oregon, sitting around smoldering campfires in the old growth forest.

Then he stopped, and turned around, trying to lose himself in the crowds. He had spotted them, right away. Parked along the side of the street in front of his apartment building.

Cops. Sure. Maybe they were doing their usual rousting work against the local drug dealers, but Phelan doubted it. There were a lot of them, and those boys looked tough.

He frowned at thinking what he had left behind up there, but smiled when he realized it was over. His gig here was up. He'd make his way to Central Park and spend the night there, and maybe liberate some gear from a couple of sporting goods stores. Then, when he got off the island, a few days working somewhere at something would give him the cash to catch a bus back to the coast.

He was going home. Back to sweet anarchy.

Roscoe Gilmanton arrived at the computer building, hands trembling, fearing for his immortal soul. The day before he had expected the pager to go off, to give him the word that he was to go into this den of Satan and perform his duty. But nothing had happened. The special coat with the explosives and incendiary devices had rested heavy on him, all day long, and he had gone home in tears, to read his Bible.

This morning he was filled with resolve. He would do it now. God had put him in a place to make this change, and he was going to perform God's will. If the signal hadn't come in, then so what. He would do it on his own.

As he strode across the parking lot he remembered his briefing, when he had received the coat. He would go in, past the receptionist, and to a doorway. At the doorway would be keypad. Punch in 6-6-4-3 and go down a hallway. When you reach a place where another hallway intersects – at a cross, how appropriate – do your duty then and commend your soul to God. Easy enough to do.

When he got to the steps of the building, men came out, men wearing black clothes and heavy boots, carrying guns, all pointing at him. They were screaming at him to stop, screaming at him to put his hands up, just screaming at him. He looked at all their faces, wondered why God had put them here to block him.

His right hand was in the coat pocket, holding firmly onto the trigger switch. The men continued screaming. He smiled at them and said, 'God bless,' and decided to see if the switch would work in triggering the coat's explosives.

It did.

Luis Raminez parked his truck and paused, just resting. It had been one hot day, and the air-conditioning at the marina store had gone in and out, leaving them either too cold or too hot. Plus Maria had been snapping at him this morning – perhaps it was the hormones, perhaps not – but she wanted to start an association. A neighborhood association, and Luis knew what the first item on the agenda would be: to do something to get rid of the Anglos who had moved in next door. Blessed Mother, he thought, opening the door. Why must it always be like that, angry words, neighbor against neighbor?

After he shut the door he stopped and listened. He thought he heard the dim roar of a crowd, a group of people yelling. It was coming from next door. He went around the truck and peered over the fence. The Anglo was sitting on a lawn chair, working on something in his hand. At his side was a little round table and a radio was playing. Luis recognized the noise right away. It was that afternoon's double header, between the Rangers and the Mariners. And if he got in the house right away, he could—

The man looked up, spotted him. 'Hi,' he said.

Luis shifted his feet, embarrassed at being spotted. 'Hi there.'

The man had on cutoff jeans and a stained white T-shirt, and the top of his head was shiny where it had been shaved. His beard was black and thick. He motioned to the radio and said, 'First game is in the fourth inning.'

'What's the score?'

'Four nothing, Rangers,' he said, and Luis detected an accent, one he couldn't recognize. The man got up and wiped his hands on his shorts, and walked over, sticking a hand out. 'Jacques Pelletier. In the middle of trying to repair a gas grill.'

He shook his hand. 'Luis Raminez,' he said, and then he said, 'Your accent. I'm sorry, but where are you from?'

Jacques gave a mournful smile. 'Ah, Quebec City, and such a more beautiful city you have never seen. My family had lived there for years until . . . Well, you see, last year my employer found out that I had once given money to the opponents of the Partis Quebecois. Ah, and that was it. No job, no chance of another job, harassment at home, rocks through the windows. It was time to leave. My wife and I, we were lucky enough to get a sponsor, and we were tired of the winters. So we asked to be sent somewhere south. So here we are. In Texas.'

Luis nodded. 'Did they line up a job for you?'

'Ah, some interviews. To come next week. And I think I have a good chance, for I am bilingual in a special way. Not English-Spanish, but English-French. Perhaps I will fill a spot in Galveston that no one else can fill.'

Luis found himself smiling at his neighbor. 'Well, good luck to you.'

He nodded. 'Thank you. And my apologies for not coming to meet you sooner, but we have been busy, settling in. And cleaning up. Did you hear the noises, a few nights back?'

'No,' Luis said. 'What noises?'

'Ah, it was probably nothing. Just children having fun. But they were dumping bags of trash here and there. My lawn and a few others. I think maybe they tossed a bag in your yard as well.'

He said nothing, shifted his feet. From the radio the noise grew louder, and Jacques turned and said, 'Hey, it sounds like a run has been scored.'

'It sure has,' Luis said, and looking at the man thought of something. Maria might not like it but . . .

'Jacques?'

'Yes?'

Luis said, 'Would you like to come inside, watch the game for a while? Have a beer?'

Jacques grinned. 'That would be wonderful. We cannot afford a television quite yet, and I'd love to see the game. I'll be over in a minute or two.' He stuck out his hand again. 'Nice to meet you, neighbor.'

Luis squeezed the hand. 'The same, neighbor, the same.'

TWENTY-EIGHT

Leaving the hall in which the deliberations over the
Constitution were being secretly conducted,
Benjamin Franklin was accosted by a woman who
asked him: 'What have you given us, Dr Franklin?'
To which he replied, 'A republic, if you can keep it.'
The Wall Street Journal, September 10, 1999

A day after being seen off in Vermont by General Montgomery,
Drew came to the end of the dirt road and parked their rented
Lexus under a birch tree. Before them was their home, the
cedar wood of the small two-story house looking dark in the
setting sun. Out beyond the house was a small lawn that
sloped down to the dark waters of Lake Montcalm, and near
that was a boat dock that extended out to the lake. It was
quiet. No lights were on in the house. Beside him Sheila
sighed and said, 'My God, we're really here. We truly are.'

He slipped his arm around her and said, 'Did you ever
have any doubts?'

'God, plenty,' she said. 'I had nightmares that Woodman
and his goons had burned the place down just to get back at
us.'

Drew opened up the car door and Sheila slid across to be
next to him. 'Don't be surprised if the inside is trashed,' he
warned. 'I'm sure it's been searched from top to bottom.'

'Hon, it's still standing. That's all that counts. Look, let's get down to the dock. I want to get a good look at the lake before we go inside.'

He smiled. 'That's a deal.'

Drew took his time walking around. His shoulder was stiff and his ankle still ached, but he felt good, almost refreshed. Their home was still here. The two of them were still here. And that's all that counted.

At the end of the dock he put his arm around her. It being well past Labor Day, there were few lights from other homes and cottages on the shoreline. No boats were grumbling out on the waters, and Drew whispered, 'Listen,' as the far-off wail of a loon came echoing across the lake.

Sheila snuggled in next to him. 'Hear that? They must be getting ready to leave, Drew. They leave and spend the entire winter out on the Atlantic before coming back to this lake. I'm so glad we made it back in time.' She looked up at him. 'Promise me we won't leave. All right? No more trips, not for a long while. I can't stand the thought of leaving. I want us to be safe here. No more hacking, no more guns, no more anything. Just the two of us. That's all.'

He kissed the top of her head. 'I promise.'

'Good,' she whispered back. Drew stood there, content with his woman at his side, and she murmured, 'Give me the keys, will you? I need to use the bathroom.'

'Do you want me to go inside with you?'

'No, I'll be fine. I just need to go pee and I'll be right back.'

He kissed her again. 'Don't be gone long.'

'I won't.'

He watched her go to the end of the dock and up to the house, and when a light was switched on he turned back to look at the lake. He remembered the first time he had spent a night with her here, when a bad nightmare had sent him outdoors, covered with a blanket. She had come out and gently rubbed his shoulders, saying, 'Stay here, as long as you want. Lake water is special. It soothes. It heals.'

I certainly hope so, he thought. The two of us are going to need the whole lake to heal us this fall and winter.

He listened to the sound of feet on the dock and turned, saying, 'That didn't take so long.'

Then Drew was quiet. Coming down the dock, pistol in his hand, was Ira Woodman.

Oh, my Lord, how wonderful it was to see the expression on that evil man's face, the man responsible for derailing everything, for throwing everything in such disarray, and who had made him kill those people, from Tanya Selenekov to Michaelson Lurry and everybody else. Ira coughed as he limped down the dock, keeping the pistol out, even though his grip was wavering. It had been a long haul from that cold stream in Vermont to make his way to this place, stealing two cars along the way, but it had to be done, and he had done it.

He coughed again, and choked out the words. 'You think you've won, don't you? Well, guess again, you heathen.' Another cough. 'This is just a temporary defeat, a setback, nothing else. We win, no matter how long it takes. You know why? Because God wills it, that's why. God will not stand for this nation to trod the path of evil, to kill the unborn, to give special rights to those God hates. He will not allow it, and nor will we.'

Drew slowly raised up his hands. 'This is a place of good people, not fanatics. You should know that by now.'

Another cough, and sweet Lord, how heavy this pistol was as he lifted it up. 'What I know is this. The battle will go on, until we win, no matter the length of time.'

'Then get ready to wait for a long while.'

'I don't think so,' Ira said, steadying his pistol with both hands.

When the pistol shot roared out Drew winced and ducked. Before him Ira Woodman stumbled, looked surprised, then slowly collapsed to his knees. Drew went up and kicked the man's pistol over the side, into the lake water. Ira looked up at him, puzzled, and whispered, 'Daddy,' as he fell over.

Sheila was there, lowering one of Drew's pistols, her hands and arms trembling. 'Is he . . . did I . . .'

Drew went up to her and took the pistol from her shaking hands and said, 'It's all right, you did the right thing, it's all right,' and he gently led her into the house, as she started weeping with long, racking sobs.

That night they slept out on the front porch. Drew had been gone for a while and had come back, his hands blistered and dirty from digging. Sheila had waited for him, the now familiar pistol in her lap. Sheila had insisted on going through the entire house to make sure they were now alone – and Drew's prediction had been right, the place had been trashed, but that was easy enough to fix – but now she was on her side, with her man gently holding her.

'Drew?' she asked.

'Hmmm?'

'Will he be found? Ever?'

'No,' he said, gently scratching her lower back. 'I took him deep into the woods, on the south end of the lake, where the nature preserve is. Nobody will ever dig there, ever. He won't be found.'

She nodded, glad that the man was not on their property, would never be on their property, ever again. 'Drew?'

'Yes?'

'You know what I hated, most of all?'

'What's that?'

She looked out into the darkness of the lake, seeing just a handful of stars in the night sky. 'I hated how easy it was to shoot at him. I've always hated the times you took me shooting. It seemed obscene to hold something so small in your hands, and to know that it had so much power of death contained inside. Men and your guns. But when I saw him out there on the dock, that's how I reacted. I got one of your guns, remembered how to load it and work the action, and I was out there in a flash. To defend the both of us. To hurt that man as much as he hurt us. And it was easy, so easy. I didn't want to warn him, I didn't want to have him arrested. I wanted to kill him, and it was so damn easy. And I hate that, God, how I hate that.'

Sheila felt him lean into her and kiss the back of her neck. 'Good. I'm glad you hated it. I always want you to hate it, Sheila. Always.'

She reached over and patted his hip, and said, 'One more question, then sleep time. All right?'

'Sure.'

'Will we ever feel safe again, ever? From what we learned and what we did and what we went through, will we ever feel safe?'

It seemed to take a long time for him to answer, and she was going to repeat the question when he said, 'I don't rightly know, Sheila. I wish I could lie to you and say yes, but

I don't rightly know. But I will tell you this. I'm going to do my best to make it happen. That's the only answer I can give.'

In the darkness she smiled and patted his hip again. 'Then that's a good answer. And Drew?'

She sensed his smile. 'Another question? I thought you were finished.'

'No, not a question,' she said, realizing finally how good it was, to be back home and in his arms. 'Just a statement. Sometime in the next few days, if you want to find a justice of the peace and marry this old broad, I would love to.'

He kissed her, again and again, and he said, 'I'm so glad I allowed you that last statement.'

There was no more talking for a long time that first night back home, and Sheila finally slumbered in the arms of her man, listening to the sounds of the loons, the loons full of promise, to return and to come back home, no matter what.

EPILOGUE

A day later the sniper carefully put everything away, rolling up his overhead tarpaulin, packing up his gear, ensuring that no visible evidence remained of his ever being here. The day before had been a good one right up to a certain moment. The air had been clear and crisp, his sighting had gone in well, and when the two helicopters had landed he had his Remington right up to his shoulder, ready to squeeze that trigger. His target had stepped out of one of the helicopters and met a group of men and women in the school, and crowds of children had been lined up on either side, waving and clapping.

The shot had been an easy one, and he had the crosshairs on the target's head all the time as she was walking into the school. At the rear steps of the school she had stopped and turned away, waving, and the crosshairs were set right on her forehead. One squeeze and she would have been dead. And God, how he loved that power, loved that potential of knowing one movement of his finger would cause that woman's death, hundreds of feet away.

But the pager at his side had been silent. The go command had never arrived. So when the target went into the school and later came out, two hours later, the sniper had let her live.

He stood up and looked around his little hidey-hole. Not as bad as hidey-holes went, but he was still glad to leave. It would be good to get home.

As he climbed up the hill, heading to the parking lot where his rental car was parked, the sniper thought of two things. The first was just a question, really, of who might have hired him, and who might have wanted the Secretary of Education killed. It didn't make any difference to him. He was just curious.

And the second thought was one that made him comfortable, knowing his career was set. For whatever had happened – or hadn't happened – yesterday, he knew he would always have work.

For this was America, and in America somebody always wanted somebody else killed.